PENGUIN BOOKS

THE PENGUIN BEST
AUSTRALIAN SHORT STORIES

Mary Lord was born in Hobart, and has
worked as a lecturer in English and Australian literature
at Monash University, as a freelance journalist and arts
consultant in Sydney, and as the Executive Director of
the National Book Council. A theatre and book
reviewer, she has written many articles and features for
newspapers, magazines, and radio.

Her other books include *Modern Australian Short Stories,
Hal Porter: Man of Many Parts, The Portable Hal Porter*, and
the *Directory of Australian Authors*. She has also edited
several volumes of Australian plays.

Mary Lord now lives in Melbourne with her grandson.

THE PENGUIN BEST AUSTRALIAN SHORT STORIES

Edited by Mary Lord

PENGUIN BOOKS

Penguin Books Australia Ltd
487 Maroondah Highway, PO Box 257
Ringwood, Victoria 3134, Australia
Penguin Books Ltd
Harmondsworth, Middlesex, England
Penguin Putnam Inc.
375 Hudson Street, New York, New York 10014, USA
Penguin Books Canada Limited
10 Alcorn Avenue, Toronto, Ontario, Canada M4V IE4
Penguin Books (N.Z.) Ltd
Cnr Rosedale and Airborne Roads, Albany, Auckland, New Zealand
Penguin Books (South Africa) (Pty) Ltd
4 Pallinghurst Road, Parktown 2193, South Africa

First published by Penguin Books Australia Ltd 1991
This edition published by Penguin Books Australia Ltd 1998

10 9 8 7 6 5 4 3

Typeset in Australia by Midland Typesetters, Maryborough, Victoria
Made and printed in Australia by Australian Print Group, Maryborough, Victoria

National Library of Australia
Cataloguing-in-Publication data:

The Penguin best Australian short stories.

ISBN 0 14 027333 6.

1. Short stories, Australian. I. Lord, Mary, 1929- .
II. Title: Best Australian short stories.

A823.30108

CONTENTS

ACKNOWLEDGEMENTS

With the exception of Delia Falconer's *Acqua Alta*, which has not yet appeared in a collection but was initially published in *The Age* newspaper, the versions of the stories published here have been taken from the following editions:

William Astley ('Price Warung'), 'Parson Ford's Confessional' from *Tales of the Convict System*, ed. B. G. Andrews, UQP, 1975

John Arthur Barry, 'Far Inland Football' from *Steve Brown's Bunyip and Other Stories*, Sydney, 1893

Marjorie Barnard, 'The Lottery' from *The Persimmon Tree and other Stories*, Virago, 1985

Barbara Baynton, 'Billy Skywonkie' from *The Portable Barbara Baynton*, ed. Krimmer and Lawson, UQP, 1980

Peter Carey, 'The Last Days of a Famous Mime' from *War Crimes*, UQP, 1979

Marcus Clarke, 'Pretty Dick' from *The Portable Marcus Clarke*, ed. Michael Wilding, UQP, 1976

Jessie Couvreur ('Tasma'), 'Monsieur Caloche' from *Eclipsed: two centuries of Australian women's fiction*, eds. Burns and McNamara, Collins, 1988

Arthur H. Davis ('Steele Rudd'), 'Dad and the Donovans' from *On Our Selection*, Sydney, 1914

Edward Dyson, 'The Golden Shanty' from *The Golden Shanty*, Sydney, 1929

Beverley Farmer, 'Caffe Veneto' from *Home Time*, McPhee Gribble/Penguin, 1985

Mary Fortune ('Waif Wanderer') 'The Dead Witness' from *The Australian Journal*, January 1866, pp.329–31

Helen Garner, 'The Dark, the Light' from *Postcards from Surfers*, McPhee Gribble/Penguin, 1985

Marion Halligan, 'Belladonna Gardens' from *The Hanged Man in the Garden*, Penguin, 1989

Janette Turner Hospital, 'After Long Absence' from *Dislocations*, UQP, 1986

Elizabeth Jolley, 'A Gentleman's Agreement' from *Five Acre Virgin*, FAC Press, 1976

John Lang, 'The Ghost upon the Rail' from *Botany Bay, or True Stories of the Early Days of Australia*, London, 1859

Henry Lawson, 'Brighten's Sister-in-law' from *Joe Wilson and his mates*, Blackwood, 1901

Morris Lurie, 'Pride and Joy' from *Running Nicely*, Nelson, 1979

Olga Masters, 'On the Train', from *The Home Girls*, UQP, 1982

Frank Moorhouse, 'Francois and the Fishbone Incident' from *Room Service*, Penguin, 1987

John Morrison, 'The Children' from *Stories of the Waterfront*, Penguin, 1985

Hal Porter, 'Party Forty-two and Mrs Brewer' from *The Cats of Venice*, A&R, 1965

Katharine Susannah Prichard, 'The Curse' from *Kiss Me on the Lips*, A&R, 1932

Ethel Robertson ('Henry Handel Richardson'), 'Conversation in a Pantry' from *The End of a Childhood and other Stories*, 1934

Christina Stead, 'Street Idyll' from *Festival and other Stories*, eds. Buckley and Hamilton, Wren, 1974

Patrick White, 'Miss Slattery and Her Demon Lover' from *The Burnt Ones*, Penguin, 1968

Michael Wilding, 'The Words She Types' from *The West Midland Underground*, UQP, 1975

Tim Winton, 'Neighbours' from *Scission*, McPhee Gribble/ Penguin, 1985

INTRODUCTION

This anthology offers its readers a fresh view of the development of the short story in Australia from colonial to modern times. The stories have been chosen either to represent periods, styles and popular themes, or because of their outstanding quality, or because they invite a reappraisal of commonly held beliefs about the Australian short story.

Many of the stories included here meet all of these criteria. An overriding consideration has been that, wherever possible, these stories will not be found in other anthologies: this is not another arrangement of regularly anthologised evergreens, but a collection which introduces readers to less well-known but still first-rate stories by outstanding writers, and to the work of some others not so well-known whose writing has been overlooked or neglected.

The stories have been arranged chronologically in order of publication in book form, except in the case of Mary Fortune's 'The Dead Witness', which was originally published in *The Australian Journal* in 1866. Publication date is indicated in brackets in the Table of Contents after each title.

The first great flowering in our literature can be dated from the 1890s when major writers of verse and fiction emerged. At the same time the movement towards nationalism was growing in strength.

The most popular outlet for writers of the time was the *Bulletin*, which encouraged good writers who shared its anti-imperialist and republican sentiments and who were writing

1

realistic and sympathetic accounts of aspects of Australian life for Australian readers.

The neglect of some short story writers of the earlier part of the nineteenth century has been to some extent due to a kind of cultural chauvinism, so that stories published in English journals or in book form by English publishers have tended to be disregarded. It has also been assumed that stories written before the 1890s, whether published in Australia or overseas, were not able to stand comparison with the best stories written in other English-speaking countries.

There seems little reason in these more confident, post-bicentennial days to subject these early stories to this kind of value judgement. Any story deserving of our attention should be a good tale, well told. The earliest stories in this collection can safely claim that distinction and more. As well as their intrinsic merit, their value lies in what, as social records, they have to tell us about our past, what they reveal about the ways colonial Australians preferred to see themselves, and what they suggest about the tastes of the general reading public of their times.

It is perhaps worth remembering too that in the days before radio and television, reading was one of the major forms of entertainment, providing escape from the long hours of toil and the inescapable drudgery of pioneer life.

From the beginning writers were concerned to establish the veracity of their tales as faithful representations of real life. John Lang's 'The Ghost upon the Rail' concerns the true story of Australia's most famous apparition, Fisher's Ghost, which inspired a number of writers and exists in a variety of versions including factual articles, a verse narrative, a film and a play. The facts are that Frederick Fisher, a ticket-of-leave convict and farmer, disappeared on June 16, 1826, after visiting a neighbour, George Worrall. Months later a John Farley reported sighting Fisher's Ghost upon the rail of a bridge and pointing to the creek below, where the body was subsequently found. Worrall was hanged for Fisher's murder on February 5, 1827. Since that time the creek has been known as Fisher's Ghost Creek.

Lang elaborates on these basic facts to create a credible

story which includes a plausible motive, several witnesses to the ghost, more than one sighting, a secret accomplice, and a final confession of guilt. At the same time he aims for journalistic realism in his detached narrative manner and for psychological realism in detailing the murderer's manipulation of his victim before witnesses. 'The Ghost upon the Rail' is as much a detective story as a ghost story, one of the earliest Australian attempts in the form.

Mary Fortune's 'The Dead Witness', which uses a fictional detective as narrator, is one from a series of stories which she published under the general title 'Memories of an Australian Police Officer'. The use of her pseudonym, 'Waif Wanderer', not only allows the writer to disguise her sex but also lends authority to the first person narrator; Constable Brooke tells the story in a relaxed, conversational tone as one relating a first-hand experience. Fortune's fictional detective solves the crime by searching for clues in a way that was to become standard practice in crime stories. With his patent enjoyment of 'the tranquillity of nature', his busy mind at odds with his body's indulgence in 'the sweetness of doing nothing', and his insomnia, this character is more than a simple stereotype. And while he is not exactly boastful, neither is he unduly modest about his detecting skills nor his deductive powers.

Fortune's lyrical description of Constable Brooke's ride through the bush is typical of her response to Australian nature. It preceded by three years Marcus Clarke's grim tale of 'Pretty Dick'. While Clarke has been regarded as the predecessor to Henry Lawson in opening up the bush for Australian readers, in his story the bush is hostile, full of nameless terrors, ultimately destructive – and very different from the tranquil, harmonious and refreshing natural world of 'The Dead Witness' where man, not nature, is vicious.

Clarke's story is the best known of the Lost Child tales, which were extremely popular in nineteenth century Australian fiction. 'Pretty Dick' relies for much of its effect on pathos, a quality often evident in the work of Charles Dickens and much enjoyed by nineteenth century readers. Modern readers sometimes have difficulty with pathos and there is a danger that the feelings of pity and sympathy Clarke arouses could offer too strong a challenge to the sensibilities of some. It is worth remembering that it was widely admired in its time particularly for its ability to arouse strong sentiments without becoming maudlin. Certainly 'Pretty Dick' has provoked extreme reactions in its readers. It has been described as 'distinguished by its refined pathos and almost reverential delicacy of treatment' on the one hand, and as deserving of 'scorn and contempt . . . for [its] artificial and calculated sentimentality' on the other (see Michael Wilding's Introduction to *Marcus Clarke*, UQP, 1976).

While sentiment predominates in 'Pretty Dick', it is controlled satire which distinguishes 'Monsieur Caloche', probably the most admired Australian story written by a woman before Barbara Baynton. This story differs from others of the period not only in its use of satire, but also because it depends for its effects much more on character than plot. In Sir Matthew Bogg, Couvreur has created the archetypal self-made man, 'in the sense that money makes the man, and that he had made the money before it could by any possibility make him'. His moral bankruptcy is firmly associated with cultural philistinism, with his detestation of all 'authors, artists, or actors who were not successful'. The poised and polished prose and the multiple ironies in the unexpected but very satisfying conclusion ensure this story of classic status.

Edward Dyson's 'The Golden Shanty' is by far the best known and funniest of Australia's gold fields short stories. While it reflects the anti-Chinese attitudes that were common in Australia at that time, it is clear that Dyson does not completely endorse them. Both the Chinese and the Irish are depicted as duplicitous and grasping. But the 'Chows' or 'Johns' are also described as 'suave and civil' as well as being capable of 'wheedling obsequiousness', while the Doyles are slovenly, stupid and easily outwitted. It is by accident and not by design that the 'heathen plot' is discovered, making Doyle accidentally rich and respectable, 'a man of some standing in Victoria'. Unlike most of the stories in this collection 'The Golden Shanty' was at one time a popular choice among anthologists. It deserves resurrection.

Exposure of the iniquities of the convict system is the driving force in the tales of William Astley ('Price Warung'). These purport to be true stories of the convict system drawn from Astley's searches of actual historical records. Modern research has shown that, while many of the stories have some basis in fact, they are imaginative reconstructions of the past – in short, fictions. Actual historical figures – Governor Davey and the Rev. Bobby Knopwood in 'Parson Ford's Confessional' for example – are used to persuade the reader that the stories are literally true. 'Parson Ford's Confessional' is more satirical than realistic in spite of its dependence on circumstantial facts like the Sunday Muster at St David's and the frequency of 'irregular connections'. The point of the satire is that the colony is entirely peopled by villains, those in authority being even greater villains than those in their charge. The corruption begins at the top with the Governor who, though not vindictive, is 'drunken, rollicking, immoral' and 'has all the qualities of a good Governor except dignity, firmness, purity, honour, sobriety, and magnanimity'. Astley targets avarice, lust, corruption and hypocrisy among the more obvious evils rampant in the ruling class in the convict era.

During the early 1890s Astley was a more prolific contributor to the *Bulletin* than his better known contemporary, Henry Lawson. His stories were popular, largely because they showed that the early convicts were often more sinned against than sinning, victims of an inhuman British system. This was very much in tune with the egalitarian, republican and anti-British sentiments cultivated by the *Bulletin* and endorsed by its readers. The 1890s was a time of severe economic depression in Australia with massive unemployment and financial hardship throughout the country. Though it seems surprising, a large number of comic stories was published during this period, testifying to the popularity of tales simply intended to entertain, and to the power of humour to relieve the drudgery of everyday life.

John Barry's 'Far Inland Football', typical of the comic stories of this period, is a straightforward, humorous yarn of life in an outback town. The characters in 'Far Inland Football' take second place to the story: they are stereotypes, not given names but individualised simply by their occupations and their attitude to football, which they see merely as a harmless game with no purpose other than 'to pass the time away'. Their rude awakening brings out unsuspected aggression and lively competitiveness among the hitherto companionable citizens of 'frightfully dull' Crupperton, between Crupperton itself and the neighbouring village of Saddlestrap, and ultimately between Crupperton and the nearest city, Cantleville. Barry makes good use of comic absurdity to expose the folly of small-town vanity and to satirise the widely held view of competitive sport as character building.

The masculine view of outback life is also presented by Steele Rudd. Even seen in its humorous aspect, this view is often dominated by competitiveness, conflicts or quarrels between neighbours, the humbling of braggarts, or the triumph of the simple farmer over the underhanded trickery of the city slicker. Action is motivated by the need to settle a score or, at least, to even it, although Dad's idea of what is right and just might not be in total accord with what the law decrees. Steele Rudd wrote many successful stories along the lines of 'Dad and the Donovans' using his archetypal farmers, Dad and Dave. Dad is wise rather than wily, smart but uneducated, anti-authoritarian except in his own domain where he is undisputed lord and master. It is a generally benign world that Dad and his family inhabit, a male-oriented and male-dominated world, but one concerned with the simple human values of what is fair and right, one where commonsense and common decency prevail.

Henry Lawson's stories celebrate qualities which he sees as distinctively and admirably Australian – independence, self-reliance, a sense of fun, a capacity to endure, support for the underdog, and a distrust of authority. He is often thought of as the apostle of mateship and the male code of bush values. Less often discussed, though, is a regularly recurring theme in his best work, the bushman's capacity for tender feelings. In 'Brighten's Sister-in-law', Lawson typically uses a bushman/narrator to tell a tale in an intimate, conversational tone in the manner of one yarning around the campfire. He relies on understatement and obliquity to give a story its full emotional weight while dodging the real danger of sentimental excess. In lesser hands 'Brighten's Sister-in-law' could easily become melodramatic and maudlin. As it is, the narrative is tightly controlled so as to convey the powerful emotions it describes and arouses without allowing them to overwhelm the tale or the reader.

Lawson wrote a number of humorous short stories which are justly celebrated and of which the best known is 'The

Loaded Dog'. The basis for the humour in Lawson's comic stories is visual and situational, much as it is in Barry's 'Far Inland Football' and Dyson's 'The Golden Shanty'. In the comic yarns human figures are stereotypes or caricatures; in Lawson's serious stories, on the other hand, characters are individualised, taking on as much human dimension as is needed to make their actions and feelings convincing even when the laconic narrator affects not to see the real point of them. Even so, Lawson's irony is always gentle and his view of the bush and the men and women of the bush has more than a tinge of idealism in it however much he writes of the suffering and hardship of outback life. Lawson's memories of the bush were drawn from his childhood in Gulgong and Eurunderee; his stories were mainly based on his own observation and on experiences of his family, rendered as realistically as possible.

The stories of Barbara Baynton flatly contradict this view of the outback as benign. Baynton grew up in the country and worked there as a governess before marrying a selector by whom she bore three children. That he left her for a cousin while her children were very young might have given her a jaundiced view of men, but this seems unlikely as she married twice more. Her view of bush life is unrelievedly bleak. She sees it as brutal and brutalising, and there is little in Baynton's stories to suggest that bushmen are capable of the emotional depth and the compassion which Lawson's Joe experiences in 'Brighten's Sister-in-law'. On the contrary, her men are, at their best, bigoted and insensitive and, at their worst, violent, sexually aggressive and bestial.

In 'Billy Skywonkie' Baynton enlists the reader's sympathy for her nameless female protagonist who is travelling on a cattle train to a remote station. She is appalled at 'the desolation of the barren shelterless plains' and 'the sufferings of the emaciated cattle' on board, half of which will die before the train reaches its destination. As the train takes the woman farther away from Sydney and civilisation she becomes increasingly isolated by her age and sex from the 'Never-Never' she travels into, where she is an object of curiosity to the predatory and grotesque males who inspect then reject her. The reader is told very little about the woman's feelings, yet the mood of sexual menace is steadily heightened by the way men treat her as though she is less than human. Because of her mixed racial inheritance, she is perceived as being socially beneath 'a w'ite gin' or a 'yaller piece'; she is ultimately a non-person, not even a sexual object, even though it is the mounting sense of sexual tension which dominates the story. Baynton has drawn a stark and terrifying picture of discrimination against race and sex in its most morbid aspect. The bush is seen as a place which brings out the malignant and barbarous nature of men, and where women are rendered helpless to resist, a view characteristic of her work.

Sex and sexual love are subjects which, until very recently, Australian male writers have avoided, not only in their short stories but also in novels, poems and plays. Typically the strongest positive emotions expressed in Australian male writing until the 1960s (with the possible exception of Lawson) have been intense loyalty to mates and warm tenderness towards women and children. Baynton's adventurousness on what was virtually the taboo topic of sexual aggression, and the horror and repugnance with which she invests it, cannot be underestimated.

Katharine Susannah Prichard's 'The Curse' is remarkable in many respects, not least for its stylistic daring. The vast majority of stories written in the early years of this century were either humorous yarns or accounts of life away from the cities. They often dealt with the effects of poverty and hardship and were overtly didactic. These stories were written in the plain, unadorned prose, favoured by the social realists, which Patrick White later described as 'dun-coloured'. While 'The Curse' favours the prevailing fashion in its subject matter, it is daringly experimental. The plot emerges only by inference, so that the reader is persuaded to engage actively and imaginatively in the narrative. The story is written in two styles: poetic litanies of visual and aural images, interspersed with dramatic dialogue which is pithy, laconic and not entirely lacking in humour. This ironic counterpointing in the structure complements the ironies implicit in the point of the story and in the title of the story itself. Does the title refer to the noxious weed, Patterson's Curse? Or to Alf's preference for reading and kangarooing rather than working? Or do the ironies extend to the bitch and her litter, cursed in effect by the consequences of Alf's theft of a harness, a rifle and a bridle?

'The Curse' is rich in imagery and in repeated refrains which suggest gossiping and conversation among the creatures of the bush. Yet it is the image of the fawn-coloured bitch snarling at the door, waiting in vain for Alf to return, that lingers in the memory. The conclusion suggests that the bitch too is cursed because it has been tamed into a false loyalty to man – untamed nature is not simply indifferent but hostile to man's intrusion: 'the wood-carter's track, cicatrice of an old wound through the bush' disappears from 'backsliding eyes' at sunset when the only sound is of 'birds flying across with jargon of wild cries.'

In 'Conversation in a Pantry' the confused feelings of a thirteen-year-old girl poised on the brink of sexual awakening provide Richardson with a theme she explores with admirable tact and tenderness. The girl is as ignorant of the biological facts of reproduction as her seventeen-year-old companion. In these days of widespread sex education it is difficult to appreciate that sex was a taboo subject in the early years of this century. Many young women married knowing nothing of the facts of life. Marriage, believed to be the proper consequence of romantic love, was an ideal state to which young women aspired but its reality might, as this story suggests, be rather less than ideal.

The notion of marrying an old man or one who snored places a brake on young Trixie's imaginings about married life, and causes the snores of her friend Alice's father to take on 'a strange and sinister significance'. At the beginning of the story Trixie sees the moon hanging 'like a round cheese in the sky' drenching everything with its light – a symbol of her romantic dream of an unblemished, golden future. But Alice, though comforting and affectionate, is no source of enlightenment beyond her endorsement of the unspeakable dangers of 'what larking leads to'. The kissing episode with Harry McGillivray was violent and aggressive, filling Trixie with anger. Her quest for understanding is frustrated by Alice's blind optimism. At the end of the story Trixie is 'confused and depressed' and the moon has 'shrunk to the size of a pippin' along with her expectations of the future.

Marjorie Barnard's 'The Lottery' deals, as her stories

generally do, with urban life, in particular with married life in the suburbs. The story has a wonderful atmosphere of tranquillity and serenity, reinforced by the evocative descriptions of the water and the shore viewed from the ferry, and by the leisurely conversation of the men travelling home from work. The dramatic and surprising reversal of Ted's expectations at the conclusion is all the more effective for its contrast with the narrative leading up to it. Underlying the story is a consideration of the economic basis of marriage for both husband and wife. What precisely draws Barnard's fire is the male assumption that a wife's money is her husband's to dispose of. All Ted's acquaintances on the ferry assume so, as does his neighbour with the hard luck story. Ted himself, when not fretting over how his wife managed to save the money to buy the lottery ticket, confidently promises the neighbour, 'I won't see you stuck, old man.'

The reader is lulled into endorsing these attitudes up to a point, even though it is clear that Ted is careful with his money and is more critical of Grace than affectionate toward her. Nevertheless Barnard, by narrating the story from Ted's point of view, encourages readers to empathise with him. The story's conclusion, while it comes as a shock, is perfectly credible. Its effect is to cause us to reassess all that has gone before, particularly to reconsider our easy acceptance of the assumptions all the men made about the money, and the discriminatory attitudes behind those assumptions. 'The Lottery' has a very serious point to make and makes it brilliantly without descending to didacticism.

Australia's first recipient of the Nobel Prize for Literature, Patrick White, has published comparatively few short stories. Accomplished as these are, it is within the capacious boundaries of the novel that the complexity of his vision and the breadth of his concerns are more impressively displayed. 'Miss Slattery and her Demon Lover', like all White's short fictions, displays something of his virtuosity in certain aspects. Here he shows his comic and satiric gifts, his shrewd observation of social and sexual mores, his fine ear for the cliché that defines personality, and, in the case of his character, Tibor, an ability to exploit with wicked accuracy the comic possibilities of mangled, accented English. White's sense of humour has been much underrated, but is as essential to an appreciation of his work as its obverse, his more frequently discussed high seriousness.

In the story reprinted here the humour predominates, though this is not typical of White's work in general. A critical appraisal of contemporary society is central to his writing, as are the contrasts he draws between Australian and European attitudes and values. What is interesting in this story is that Miss Slattery – unabashedly Australian, unable to tell lino tiles from marble, uncivilised by European standards as exemplified by Tibor – possesses a kind of naiveté uncorrupted by an inherited culture. This protects her from Tibor's depraved materialism, even when it is accompanied by offers of 'a finenshul arrangement'. Miss Slattery comes round to the view that perhaps mundane married life in the suburbs is not, after all, to be despised.

Hal Porter has sometimes been accused of excessive decoration in his prose, a charge that would be difficult to sustain in the case of 'Party Forty-two and Mrs Brewer'. This story, for all its apparent digressions and intricately woven descriptions, depends as much on its prose style for effect as it does on the actions it describes. It is a wonderfully funny story from a writer who excels at comedy of manners. The humour is as much embedded in the choice and arrangement of words as in character and event.

The author's conscious artifice extends to the use of a narrator, Hal (a version of the author in his 'visitor's guise of Simple Country Boy') who had intended to enter the party 'rather vividly with a dilly-bag of witticisms'. He becomes a minor character in the action, but uses the dilly-bag of witticisms to narrate his tale. The aim is to heighten the comic effect of a situation which is already intrinsically funny, and to mock the social pretensions of the hostess, Dot – 'a doggedly brisk secretary when normal' – her s.-p. bookmaker husband, Frank, their new house and their invited guests. The importance of the narrator as raconteur and as centre of unusual experiences is signalled by his list of the highlights of his six weeks in Sydney. These apparently irrelevant revelations make up an amusingly bizarre list, one which is intended to lend credence to what follows.

For a time Porter was regarded as Australia's most outstanding practitioner of the short story after Lawson. Unlike

Lawson, though, he did not inspire a clutch of followers. His style is inimitable, his battery of verbal resources is formidable, and his range in the short story – not to mention other literary genres – is wide. His legacy to the writers who came after him has been that he broke the editorial and readership bias towards the plainness of social realism and made stylistic experimentation and linguistic sophistication respectable, even fashionable.

In sharp contrast to Porter's vastly entertaining, if idiosyncratic, narrative method is John Morrison's 'The Children', in which a hard-working family man has been caught in a moral dilemma for which there is no right solution. As a result he and his family earn the implacable hatred of their neighbours. Death would be preferable to the life Allen now has to face: he is condemned, even though there would not be 'another bloke who would have done anything else' faced with the same dilemma, even though he reacted as any other husband and father would have done. After the event only his wife's determination prevented him from a destructive and manic gesture to assuage his feelings of responsibility: 'I got it into my head there was nothing else to do but cremate the lot, truck and everything in it.' The futility of this is lost on the distraught man who insists, 'I should be shot – I wish to God they would shoot me!' So he is left with a profound sense of guilt which he can never escape. This very bleak view of the individual as victim of circumstances and his own nature has tragic implications for the protagonist and his family, and for the community as a whole.

Morrison's theme revolves around the problem of responsibility, which is the basis of the reporter's questions and Allen's replies. It is a problem which cannot be resolved by the characters, the author, or the reader. As the story makes clear, it is only human nature to lay blame outside ourselves for disastrous events. But it is Allen's human nature, his inescapable human impulse, that is responsible for his predicament and which has ruined his life. In keeping with the seriousness of his subject, Morrison tells his tale in a direct and straightforward style from which all non-essential description and ornamentation has been pared. The plainness of his narrative method, in which no authorial intrusion or stylistic extravagance is permitted, is the more effective because it is in sharp contrast to the complexity of the ethical problem he raises.

In Christina Stead's 'Street Idyll', what seems on the surface to be simple realism masks a comparatively plotless web of interlocking themes relating to love, marriage, age, time and the transience of all things. An idyll, whether in prose or verse, is a short description of some picturesque scene or incident, usually of rustic life, but in this case it is an urban scene of everyday life. Very little happens in the story. An elderly husband and wife expect to meet each other in the street; when they do, they try to hide from passersby 'the rapturous, intimate smiles which they felt irrepressibly forming behind their cheeks right up to their ears'. The story is rich in senti-ment but not in sentimentality although the feeling behind the couple's very mundane conversation is so intense that 'there is nothing to express the emotion that brought them together'. Yet they are not exceptional, nor is this meeting any different from any other meeting they have in the street. 'This has all happened before' reports the narrator/observer, who concludes the story by describing the meeting of another elderly couple with that same 'look of gold'.

The passionate feeling that binds elderly married couples together is an unusual theme in fiction, which more fre-quently associates passion with youthfulness. It is not accid-ental, therefore, that Stead withholds the age of her characters until quite late in the story so that, when it is revealed, the reader is tempted to think of them as exceptional. Yet the idyll makes them elements of a regularly recurring scene. It is an important part of Stead's art to reveal the human dimension behind the commonplace and, at the same time, to insist that patterns of human behaviour are 'predetermined'.

In 'The Words She Types' Michael Wilding has created an extremely clever, circular puzzle revolving around the rela-tionships between fiction and reality, between writers and their work, between the writing, typing and editing of the work, and between the subject of the work and the work itself. If this sounds paradoxical, then that is what lies at the heart of the puzzle, for 'truth read as fiction will never after be available as truth, whether or not it ever was'. It is both an argument about the nature of narrative and a demonstration of the argument.

This is one of those rare fictions which invites the reader to speculate on the nature of truth, the truth of fiction, the reality of fiction, the art of fiction, et cetera *ad infinitum*. As well as the challenges it offers to the logically and/or philosophically minded, it arouses admiration for the subtlety of Wilding's crafting, especially the unobtrusive move from the realism of the opening section to surrealism and then to the paradoxical speculativeness of the ending.

Elizabeth Jolley often writes of unusual characters, like Mother in 'A Gentleman's Agreement', who is seen through the eyes of her daughter. This story has the carefully pointed ending with a sting in its tail which has been favoured by short story writers and their readers since the early years of the last century. Yet the conventional structure is used here not for plotting a series of events leading to a surprising but appropriate ending, but for a character portrait. The incidents related do not so much advance the action, as reflect in some way or another on the personality of the central character. She is a devoted mother, a woman of great warmth and generosity, who has rather odd notions about ownership and property, which she demonstrates in her exploitation of a 'gentleman's agreement' she comes to with a wealthy doctor. Mother is no 'gentleman', however broadly that word may be defined, and she is not restrained by gentlemanly notions of honour or fairness, or by what may be regarded as proper.

Mother is motivated by a wish to give pleasure to others, to make them happy. Her enormous generosity, which extends to sharing with others things which do not belong to her, is primarily directed towards her family, then beyond her children to the neighbours. Through her, they are able to 'taste the pleasures rich people took for granted in their way of living'. What is most interesting about the character of Mother is that, because she is described subjectively by her daughter, she is presented as predominantly good and lovable, lacking in malice or avarice. Yet, in the matter of the 'gentleman's agreement' her behaviour is deceitful and exploitative; even though she is within her legal rights she is ethically in the wrong. And she knows it. This is a story which, for all its apparent simplicity and its lightly humorous tone, evokes a complex response not least because of the value judgements it invites.

Peter Carey is a writer with the ability to mix reality with nightmare, the ordinary with the fantastic, the intensely serious with the wildly comic, the satiric with the tragic. All these elements are compounded in 'The Last Days of a Famous Mime' which opens itself to many readings. Not the least of these is a satirical attack on the herd-like instinct of crowds whose taste is dictated by critics. As well, Carey aims his satire at the power of the press to gull the general public, at the vulnerability of those who seek popular success and those who prey on them, and at the dangers inherent in eccentricity. The story, which becomes increasingly bizarre as it progresses, is the more compelling for its cool, matter-of-fact tone. The contrast between tone and content ultimately increases the fierceness of Carey's indictment of contemporary society.

The idea of a theatrical performer who becomes famous through his ability to mime terror may seem absurd on the face of it, but only if we ignore the popularity of the horror movie over past decades. The first step in the mime's decline is provoked by a bad review in a provincial newspaper by a critic who 'cannot see the use of invoking terror in an audience'. The cultural crassness inherent in the argument for the utilitarian value of art is a major target in much of Carey's satire. Here it begins a process which inexorably leads to the death of the mime, who changes his performances to appease his critics. The implications of this pessimistic fable are inescapable.

In Morris Lurie's 'Pride and Joy', the writer's ironic gaze is squarely directed at those for whom money and what it can buy substitute for a lack of social skills and, more fundamentally, for an inability to recognize or respond to the emotional needs of others, even those closest to them. The events in the story are disclosed through the eyes of a narrator, a somewhat reticent and introspective man. Lurie uses him as a contrast to the attention-seeking and aggressively macho Ned Matthews. Where Matthews is accustomed to giving orders and having them obeyed, the narrator is indecisive. He prefers, for example, to suffer sleepless nights rather than make a fuss and change his room. There is little of the hero in him yet his behaviour is a model of gentlemanly restraint compared to that of the loutish Matthews, and his attitudes strike a responsive chord in the reader.

Early in the story it is clear that the narrator has some sympathy with Matthews' son, who is being rushed into the version of manhood or visible masculinity favoured by his father. Ned Matthews, apart from being very rich and very unlikeable, is a phoney who bases his public performances on distant but famous models like Hemingway and Clark Gable. He, his son and the hired man seem 'like three ham actors playing at being tough'. Billy's willingness to follow his father's lead suggests at first that he is either weak or stupid, a view that becomes more credible as they compete with each other at drinking.

Billy's move from follower to competitor is part of his initiation into his father's world, but it does not quite go as planned. One night he outdrinks his father and has to help him to bed. Then on the fifth night, his father competes with him for the attention of 'the princess'. The attempt to corrupt her by an ostentatious display of wealth and by flattery, and the physical violence that follows, are deeply repugnant. They move the narrator to make a decision in favour of love and stability: 'I want my girl.' They also help Billy toward a major decision which will be his first step in the direction of manhood and independence: he rejects his father's example as that of a 'dirty pig' and, in asserting himself, acts true to his emerging maturity.

In her all too brief career as a creative writer, Olga Masters claimed as her special territory the emotional turbulence which often lies behind apparently ordinary domestic life. In her story 'On the Train', a narrative as remarkable for its tight control of mounting tension as for its brevity, the reader is told no more than is absolutely essential to the author's purpose so that the story moves inexorably towards its coldly terrifying climax, at which point it ends leaving the reader suspended. Obviously some readers will wish to resolve the story in ways that might make it more comfortable, less emotionally disturbing. But Masters is concerned here to communicate a mother's distraught state of mind and feeling, not to resolve a situation rich in dramatic possibilities. The mother's state, though, is never directly described but emerges by implication from the way her daughters react to her and by her failure to react to them or to the curious passenger.

Up to a point, 'On the Train' may be regarded as an open-ended story, though this is to diminish the powerful effects it produces. It is an essential part of Masters's art that she knows what may safely be left out of a story without loss, and when the traditional, neatly-rounded ending is inappropriate. Her reduction of the narrative to its absolute and necessary minimum exemplifies the way the form has evolved in the hands of many writers from the discursive to the terse, from the leisurely and circular to the pithy and linear.

Depending on how one chooses to read it, there is either no dialogue in Helen Garner's 'The Dark, the Light' or it is all dialogue. Certainly there are no single voices speaking but a chorus of what we can assume are young, female groupies all talking at once and very excitedly about their current idol, a local boy who has hit the big time in 'the sunny place, the blue and yellow place'. This very short experimental piece, with its enthusiasm and swings of mood and its rich allusiveness, is superbly evocative of the clannish feeling that pervades young girls in groups. And with its recurring and sometimes contradictory images and repeated sound patterns as well as its strict economy of expression, it approaches the concentrated richness of poetry. It is a cameo of great originality and remarkable vivacity.

There is little point in speculating whether 'The Dark, the Light' has its basis in experience shared or experience observed – its effectiveness depends on its authenticity as a literary artefact, on its ability to communicate mood and feeling in a way which persuades the reader of its imaginative truth.

In 'Caffe Veneto' Beverley Farmer unfolds her story rather as a dramatist does. There is very little narration in the usual sense; instead there are several short descriptive passages where the scenes are set and atmosphere suggested. But the bulk of the story is expressed through dialogue between father and daughter. The dramatic action is not through visible movement but in the contrast between the daughter's probing and the father's reluctance to confide in her, in the gradual revelation of the daughter's separate relationships with each of her parents, and particularly in her cool appraisal of her father's latest love affair and her logical attack on the ethics of his planned conduct. The story reveals her as being more mature and realistic than her father, and reveals him as insensitive to the feelings of others and as 'shallow and rash'.

This reversal of the roles of wise father and impetuous child gives the story an expected poignancy, which is highlighted by the plane leaf the daughter catches at the end of the story: 'brown on one side, pale with brown veins on the other, like an imploring hand'. Throughout the conversation she is the strong one, pressing him to see himself as she sees him, 'an elderly bad boy', while he is furtive, equivocating and self-deluding. The ironic twist is that while she occupies the high moral ground in the debate, she is having a love affair with a man who is married but 'separated', as her father would be if he took Sandra with him to America. A basic difference between them is that the daughter, though in love, seems to have no romantic illusions about it, while her father is guilty and embarrassed about the pattern of his infidelities. The story's resolution involves a dramatic reversal of roles at the level of emotional power games: the father becomes the child and the daughter the parent.

Frank Moorhouse is rightly regarded as the leading contemporary writer of short fiction in Australia, his work breaking fresh ground in form, style and subject, bringing new life to a literary genre many believed was near exhaustion. Moorhouse most commonly writes in an intimate, confessional tone as himself or under versions of his name such as Francois Blase, Franco Casamaggiore and so on, representing roles he invents for literary and/or social purposes. Part of the extended joke of 'Francois and the Fishbone Incident' comes from confusion about his name and its spelling, his role as Frank Moorhouse or Francois Blase, his book with a title vaguely similar to the title of a book by another writer. In whatever guise he presents himself, and with his incipient paranoia and his awareness of terrifying potential in ordinary situations, the Moorhouse figure is the focus of irony and satire: it is his consciousness or self-consciousness which is the substance of Moorhouse's narratives and the source of his black comedy.

It is not what happens in 'Francois and the Fishbone Incident' that transforms the relating of a minor incident from simple reportage into literature. Rather, the narrative is shaped by Francois' imaginings of what might happen at any point in the story, and by his almost painful self-consciousness and his extravagant reactions. Because it is a comparatively plotless story Moorhouse gives it a satisfying artistic shape by framing it. In fact, he gives it two frames – one as a cautionary tale and the other as 'a test for young journalists'. Both serve to cap the humour as well as to provide punchlines for an extended joke that rests on an unswerving pessimism about the hazards of living.

Tim Winton writes about the concrete, physical world with an optimism and a belief in goodness that is becoming increasingly rare. In 'Neighbours' he exposes the silliness of intolerance, snobbery and racial prejudice, but without any of the overt didacticism that this might suggest. He reveals a strong sense of community that is often thought to be lacking in contemporary urban Australia, and argues, implicitly, that this sense of community is one of the more valuable gifts that migrants bring to this country. He also writes with great particularity about the physical facts of childbirth, a subject rarely encountered in our fiction. In less capable hands this story could easily slide into sentimentality. But Winton avoids this danger by relating the narrative in the impersonal third person and by the simple device of not naming his characters or fleshing them out in any great detail – though they are not any the less persuasive for that.

The story is told with a cool detachment leavened with occasional flashes of dry humour: 'it took six months for the newcomers to comprehend the fact that their neighbours were not murdering each other, merely talking.' The several references to the young man's thesis 'on the development of the twentieth century novel' ironically suggest, for him at least, that there is little relationship between literature and life, since his studies on that topic have left him totally unprepared for the surge of emotion he feels at witnessing the birth of his child, or for swell of congratulatory cheering from his neighbours. Yet the story itself is a work of literature and it is not simply about life, it pulsates with vitality. Winton is surely implying, among other things, that intellectualising about literature is sterile unless it is accompanied by active emotional engagement with it.

It matters little whether Janette Turner Hospital's 'After Long Absence' is as strongly autobiographical as is suggested by the writing and what is known of the author's life – though this possibility undoubtedly adds to its charm. Stories which involve a return to the past are usually sad tales of disillusion, tales in which the paradise lost turns out not to have been a paradise at all. In 'After Long Absence' the emancipated writer/narrator, whose attitude to her parents is a confused mixture of love and anger, discovers them to be exactly as she has remembered them – when she is with them she is still on 'a seesaw of frustration and tenderness' much as she was as a child. Memories of childhood are inextricably entangled with remembrance of scenes of shame and embarrassment, caused by her parents' nonconformist religious beliefs, and the victimisation by other children that this provoked. Her first-grade teacher brands her family as 'religious fanatics' and 'morally irresponsible'. Her only defender, the rebellious and exuberant Patrick Murphy, briefly causes her to 'squirm with mortal shame' when, years later, he sees her with a group of 'Holy Rollers', including her father, in the heart of Brisbane on a crowded Friday night. ' "They got guts," said Patrick Murphy. "I always did go for guts." '

The truth of this observation is the pivot on which the story turns. The 'theologically rigid' father breaks a moral principle, for him 'a costly self-damning act', by accepting a glass of wine and taking two sips from it at lunch rather than embarrass his daughter in front of her university friends – an act which took 'guts'. The daughter, on the other hand, cannot muster the same generosity of spirit, cannot match 'the magnitude of this gesture' by observing the long-standing ritual of choosing the Bible reading at the family dinner – 'a small thing' which in anyone else's home she 'would endure . . . with docile politeness'. And for her 'there is no moral principal at stake'. Did she lack the 'guts' to make this small but generous concession? Or did it demand more 'guts' to refuse to make a gesture of appeasement to the family? 'After Long Absence' raises but does not resolve the problems that necessarily arise when children grow up and away from their parents. It considers the kinds of dependence that are created by the love between parents and children, and the validity of the real and imagined demands that families make on their members.

The penultimate story in this collection is set in the country's political capital, which is seen in this story as being in some respects a microcosm for Australia as a whole. Marion Halligan's 'Belladonna Gardens' exposes the dark underside of life in Canberra, a city widely accepted as a modern model city with a modern, model, middle-class population, 'a garden city'. The story reveals a side of life in Canberra familiar to Australians in other parts of the country too.

The 'dregs of society' have 'no luck . . . no work', and are 'too sick, too many kids, too stupid, too spaced out, too stoned to work'. They are the social outcasts, 'pensioners of the government'. In writing about this existence, Halligan aims squarely at a number of targets: the easy availability of credit which can bankrupt a family, bureaucratic invasion of privacy, police harassment, a degraded environment which demoralises and encourages anti-social behaviour, cultural apathy, and neglect of the under-privileged.

Frank, a painter and the narrator, is gay, representing another minority group. He is therefore sympathetic to Sybil's plight, unlike the bureaucracy which dismisses her and those like her with 'the crudeness, the banality, of the category' of 'deserted mother'.

The sharp contradiction between what names suggest and the realities behind them is highlighted by Frank's disappointment at Belladonna Gardens, and at the streets with 'lovely names' that 'sang themselves'. For here Frank encounters a treeless and shrubless wasteland of 'dry grass . . . rusty cars, and tricycles, and so many rubbish bins'. Frank could transform the tiny houses and the lives of those who live in them with his *trompe l'oeil* garden vistas but the tenants would be held responsible for defacing government property. Frank's paintings deceive the eye, making ugly walls appear beautiful, just as his eye was deceived by Canberra from the air and Canberra on a map.

Delia Falconer's 'Acqua Alta' assumes a shared background of European art and history rather than any specifically Australian experience in her readers. References to the Italian Renaissance, allusions to architectural and sculptural marvels, to carnival masks and colours, to the mysteries of ancient religious practices where the 'dried skin of a flayed saint' is reverenced – these give this story a remarkable density. This is in addition to the sophisticated employment of poetic devices such as visual and sensory images, intellectual paradoxes and ideas that may express profound truths or simple absurdities, e.g. 'love often takes the form of theft'.

The ordinary rules of logic give way to the strange reasoning of a narrator whose matter-of-fact tone is at odds with her bizarre tale, and the reader is invited to journey into the realm of the surreal, to a rich and colourful fantasy of considerable emotional force. The story is no more or less improbable than any of the tales of the *Arabian Nights*. Like them, it aims to entertain by enchantment, to entrance through mystery and the inexplicable coherence of dreams.

The opening of the market for short story writers resulted from the birth and continuing health of a number of literary magazines over the last three or four decades, and from the willingness of publishers to bring out collections by our best short story writers. The large numbers of short story collections published in recent years show the continuing interest of writers and readers in this lively and very modern literary form. As the short story developed beyond the factual accounts of the nineteenth century, to the social realism that characterised the work of the followers of Lawson in the first half of this century, it radiated outward in its concerns and narrative strategies. There seems no reason why this trend should not continue.

The variety of themes explored and styles invented make generalisations about the short story in Australia difficult. Doubtless, it will continue to be a vehicle for social criticism, even when leavened with humour. Our best short story writers have rarely been constrained by literary fashion and are unlikely to become so, and their willingness to experiment augurs well for the continued vitality of the form. The strength of the short story will always lie in its diversity.

JOHN LANG
The Ghost upon the Rail

CHAPTER I

It was a winter's night – an Australian winter's night – in the middle of July, when two wealthy farmers in the district of Penrith, New South Wales, sat over the fire of a public house, which was about a mile distant from their homes. The name of the one was John Fisher, and of the other Edward Smith. Both of these farmers had been transported to the colony, had served their time, bought land, cultivated it, and prospered. Fisher had the reputation of being possessed of a considerable sum in ready money; and it was well known that he was the mortgagee of several houses in the town of Sydney, besides being the owner of a farm of three hundred acres, which was very productive, and on which he lived. Smith also was in good circumstances, arising out of his own exertions on his farm; but, unlike his neighbour, he had not put by much money.

'Why don't you go home, John, and see your friends and relations?' asked Smith; 'you be now very warm in the pocket; and, mark my words, they would be very glad to see you.'

'I don't know about that, friend,' replied Fisher. 'When I got into trouble it was the breaking of the heart of my old father and mother; and none of my brothers and sisters – in all, seven of 'em – have ever answered one of my letters.'

'You did not tell 'em you were a rich man, did you?'

'No; but I don't think they would heed that much, lad; for though they are far from wealthy, as small farmers, they are well-to-do in the world, and in a very respectable position in the country. I have often thought that if I was to go back

23

they would be sorry to see me, even if I carried with me £100,000, earned by one who had been a convict.'

'Bless your innocent heart! You don't know human natur' as I do. Money does a deal – depend on't. Besides, who is to know anything about you, except your own family? And they would never go and hint that you had been unfortunate. Why, how many years ago is it?'

'Let me see. I was then eighteen, and I am now forty-six – twenty-eight years ago. When I threw that stone at that man I little thought it would hit him, much less kill him; and that I should be sent here for manslaughter. But so it was.'

'Why I recommend you, John, to go home is because you are always talking of home and your relations. As for the farm, I'd manage that for you while you are away.'

'Thank you, Ned. I'll think about it.'

Presently, the landlord entered the room, and Smith, addressing him, said, 'What think you, Mr Dean? Here is Mr Fisher going home to England, to have a look at his friends and relations.'

'Is that true, Mr Fisher?' said the landlord.

'Oh, yes,' was Fisher's reply, after finishing his glass of punch and knocking the ashes out of his pipe.

'And *when* do you think of going?' said the landlord.

'That'll depend,' replied Fisher, smiling. 'When I'm gone you will hear of it, not before; and neighbour Smith here, who is to manage the farm during my absence, will come and pay you any little score I may leave behind.'

'But I hope you will come and say goodbye,' said the landlord.

'Oh, of course,' said Fisher, laughing. 'If I don't, depend upon it you will know the reason why.'

After a brief while the two farmers took their departure. Their farms adjoined each other and they were always on the very best of terms.

About six weeks after the conversation above given, Smith called one morning at the public house, informed the landlord that Fisher had gone, and offered to pay any little sum that he owed. There was a small score against him, and while taking the money the landlord remarked that he was sorry Mr Fisher had not kept his word and come to bid him 'goodbye'. Mr Smith explained that Fisher had very good reasons for having his departure kept a secret until after he had left the colony; not that he wanted to defraud anybody – far from it, he added; and then darkly hinted that one of Mr Fisher's principal reasons for going off so stealthily was to prevent being annoyed by a woman who wanted him to marry her.

'Ah! I see,' said the landlord; 'and that's what he must have meant that night when he said, "*if* I don't, you'll hear the reason why".'

'I feel the loss of his society very much,' said Smith, 'for when we did not come here together to spend our evening he would come to my house, or I would go to his, to play cards, smoke a pipe and drink a glass of grog. Having taken charge of all his affairs under a power of attorney, I have gone to live at his place and left my overseer in charge of my own place. When he comes back in the course of a couple of years *I* am going home to England, and he will do for me what I am now doing for him. Between ourselves, Mr Dean, he has gone home to get a wife.'

'Indeed!' said the landlord. Here the conversation ended and Mr Smith went home.

Fisher's sudden departure occasioned some surprise throughout the district; but when the explanation afforded by Mr Smith was spread abroad by Mr Dean, the landlord, people ceased to think any more about the matter.

A year elapsed, and Mr Smith gave out that he had received a letter from Fisher, in which he stated that it was not his intention to return to Sydney; and that he wished the whole of his property to be sold and the proceeds remitted to him. This letter Mr Smith showed to several of Fisher's most intimate acquaintances, who regretted extremely that they would see no more of so good a neighbour and so worthy a man.

Acting on the power of attorney which he held, Mr Smith advertised the property for sale – the farm, the livestock, the farming implements, the furniture, etc., in the farmhouse; also some cottages and pieces of land in and near Sydney and Parramatta; with Fisher's mortgagors, also, he came to an agreement for the repayment, within a few months, of the sums due by them.

CHAPTER II

About a month previous to the day of sale, an old man, one David Weir, who farmed a small piece of land in the Penrith Road, and who took every week to the Sydney market, butter, eggs, fowls, and a few bushels of Indian maize, was returning to his home when he saw, seated on a rail, the well-known form of Mr Fisher. It was very dark, but the figure and the face were as plainly visible as possible. The old man, who was not drunk, though he had been drinking at Dean's public house, pulled up and called out, 'Halloa, Mr Fisher! I thought you were at home in England!' There was no reply, and the old man, who was impatient to get home, as was his horse, loosed the reins and proceeded on his journey.

'Mother,' said old Weir to his wife, while she was helping him off with his old top-coat, 'I've seen either Mr Fisher or his ghost.'

'Nonsense!' cried the old woman; 'you could not have seen Mr Fisher, for he is in Old England; and as for spirits, you never see any without drinking them; and you are full of 'em now.'

'Do you mean to say I'm drunk, Mother?'

'No, but you have your liquor on board.'

'Yes; but I can see, and hear, and understand, and know what I am about.'

'Well, then, have your supper and go to bed; and take my advice and say nothing to anybody about this ghost, or you will only get laughed at for your pains. Ghostesses, indeed! at your age to take on about such things; after swearing all your life you never believed in them.'

'But I tell you I saw him as plain as plain could be; just as we used to see him sitting sometimes when the day was warm and he had been round looking at his fences to see that they were all right.'

'Yes, very well; tell me about it tomorrow,' said the old woman. 'As I was up before daylight, and it is now nearly midnight, I feel too tired to listen to a story about a ghost. Have you sold everything well?'

'Yes, and brought back all the money safe. Here it is.' The old man handed over the bag to his partner and retired to his bed; not to rest, however, for the vision had made so great an impression upon his mind he could not help thinking of it, and lay awake till daylight, when he arose, as did his wife, to go through the ordinary avocations of the day. After he had milked the cows and brought the filled pails into the dairy, where the old woman was churning, she said to him:

'Well, David, what about the ghost?'

'I tell you I seed it,' said the old man. 'And there's no call for you to laugh at me. If Mr Fisher be not gone away – and I don't think he would have done so without coming to say goodbye to us – I'll make a talk of this. I'll go and tell Sir John, and Doctor Mackenzie, and Mr Cox, and old parson Fulton, and everybody else in the commission of the peace. I will, as I'm a living man! What should take Fisher to England? England would be no home for him after being so many years in this country. And what's more, he has told me as much many a time.'

'Well, and so he has told me, David. But then, you know, people will alter their minds, and you heard what Mr Smith said about that woman?'

'Yes. But I don't believe Smith. I never had a good opinion of that man, for he could never look me straight in the face, and he is too oily a character to please me. If, as I tell you, Mr Fisher is not alive in this country, then that was his ghost that I saw, and he has been murdered!'

'Be careful, David, what you say; and whatever you do, don't offend Mr Smith. Remember, he is a rich man and you are a poor one; and if you say a word to his discredit he may take the law of you, and make you pay for it; and that would be a pretty business for people who are striving to lay by just enough to keep them when they are no longer able to work.'

'There's been foul play, I tell you, old woman. I am certain of it.'

'But that can't be proved by your saying that you saw a ghost sitting on a rail, when you were coming home from market none the better for what you drank upon the road. And if Mr Fisher should be still alive in England – and you know that letters have been lately received from him – what a precious fool you would look!'

'Well, perhaps you are right. But when I tell you that I saw either Mr Fisher or his ghost sitting on that rail, don't laugh at me, because you will make me angry.'

'Well, I won't laugh at you, though it must have been your

fancy, old man. Whereabouts was it you saw, or thought you saw him?'

'You know the cross fence that divides Fisher's land from Smith's – near the old bridge at the bottom of Iron Gang Hill?'

'Yes.'

'Well, it was there. I'll tell you what he was dressed in. You know that old fustian coat with the brass buttons, and the corduroy waistcoat and trousers, and that red silk bandanna handkerchief that he used to tie round his neck?'

'Yes.'

'Well, that's how he was dressed. His straw hat he held in his left hand, and his right arm was resting on one of the posts. I was about ten or eleven yards from him, for the road is broad just there and the fence stands well back.'

'And you called him, you say?'

'Yes; but he did not answer. If the horse had not been so fidgety I'd have got down and gone up to him.'

'And then you would have found out that it was all smoke.'

'Say that again and you will put me into a passion.'

The old woman held her tongue, and suffered old David to talk all that day and the next about the ghost, without making any remark whatever.

CHAPTER III

On the following Wednesday – Thursday being the market day in Sydney – old David Weir loaded his cart and made his way to the Australian metropolis. True to his word with his wife, he did not mention to a soul one syllable touching the ghost. Having disposed of his butter, eggs, poultry and maize, the old man left Sydney at 4 p.m., and at half-past ten arrived at Dean's public house.

He had travelled in that space of time thirty miles, and was now about eight or nine from home. As was his wont, he here baited the horse, but declined taking any refreshment himself, though pressed to do so by several travellers who wanted to 'treat' him. During the whole day he had been remarkably abstemious.

At a quarter a twelve the old man re-harnessed his jaded horse and was about to resume his journey when two men, who were going to Penrith, asked him for 'a lift'.

'Jump up, my lads,' said old David; and off they were driven at a brisk walk. One of the men in the cart was a ticket-of-leave man in the employ of Mr Cox, and had been to Sydney to attend 'muster'. The other was a newly-appointed constable of the district. Both of these men had lived for several years in the vicinity of Penrith and knew by sight all the inhabitants, male and female, free and bond.

When they neared the spot where the old man had seen the apparition, he walked the horse as slowly as possible and again beheld the figure of Mr Fisher seated on the upper rail of the fence, and in precisely the same attitude and the same dress.

'Look there!' said old David to the two men, 'what is that?'

'It is a man!' they both replied. 'But how odd! It seems as if a light were shining through him!'

'Yes,' said old David; 'but look at him; what man is it?'

'It is Mr Fisher,' they said, simultaneously.

'Hold the reins, one of you,' said old David. 'I'll go and speak to him. They say he is at home in England, but I don't believe it.'

Descending from the cart, the old man, who was as brave as a lion, approached the spectre and stood within a few feet of it. 'Speak!' he cried. 'Don't you know me, sir? I am David Weir. How came you by that gash in your forehead? Are you alive or dead, Mr Fisher?' To these questions no answer was returned. The old man then stretched forth his hand and placed it on what appeared to be Mr Fisher's shoulder; but it was only empty air – vacant space – that the intended touch rested upon!

'There has been foul play!' said the old man, addressing the spectre, but speaking sufficiently loud to be heard by both men in the cart. 'And, by heaven it shall be brought to light! Let me mark the spot.' And with these words he broke off several boughs from a tree near the rail and placed them opposite to where the spectre remained sitting. Nay, further, he took out his clasp-knife and notched the very part on which the right hand of the spectre rested.

Even after the old man returned to the cart the apparition of Mr Fisher, exactly as he was in the flesh, was 'palpable to the sight' of all three men. They sat gazing at it for full ten minutes, and then drove on in awe and wonderment.

CHAPTER IV

When old David Weir arrived home, his wife, who was delighted to see him so calm and collected, inquired, laughingly, if he had seen the ghost again. 'Never mind about that,' said the old man. 'Here, take the money and lock it up, while I take the horse out of the cart. He is very tired, and no wonder, for the roads are nearly a foot deep in dust. This is the fifteenth month that has passed since we had the last shower of rain; but never mind! If it holds off for a fortnight or three weeks longer our maize will be worth thirty shillings a bushel. It is wrong to grumble at the ways of Providence. In my belief it is very wicked.'

'Well, I think so, too,' said the old woman. 'Thirty shillings a bushel! Why, Lord a'bless us, that ull set us up in the world, surely! What a mercy we did not sell when it rose to nine and sixpence!'

'Get me some supper ready, for as soon as I have taken it I have some business to transact.'

'Not out of the house?'

'Never you mind. Do as I tell you.'

Having eaten his supper, the old man rose from his chair, put on his hat and left his abode. In reply to his wife's question, 'Where are you going?' he said 'To Mr Cox's; I'll be home in an hour or so. I have business, as I told you, to transact.'

The old woman suggested that he could surely wait till the morning; but he took no heed of her and walked away.

Mr Cox was a gentleman of very large property in the district, and was one of the most zealous and active magistrates in the colony. At all times of the day or the night he was accessible to any person who considered they had business with him.

It was past two o'clock in the morning when David Weir arrived at Mr Cox's house and informed the watchman that he desired to see the master. It was not the first time that the old man had visited Mr Cox at such an hour. Two years previously he had been plundered by bushrangers, and as soon as they had gone he went to give the information.

Mr Cox came out, received the old man very graciously and invited him to enter the house. Old David followed the magistrate and detailed all that the reader is in possession of touching the ghost of Mr Fisher.

'And *who* were with you,' said Mr Cox, 'on the second occasion of your seeing this ghost?'

'One is a ticket-of-leave man named Williams, a man in your own employ; and the other was a man named Hamilton, who lived for several years with Sir John Jamieson. They both rode with me in my cart,' was the old man's answer.

'Has Williams returned?'

'Yes, sir.'

'It is very late, and the man may be tired and have gone to bed; but, nevertheless, I will send for him.' And Mr Cox gave the order for Williams to be summoned.

Williams, in a few minutes, came and corroborated David Weir's statement in every particular.

'It is the most extraordinary thing I ever heard in my life,' said Mr Cox. 'But go home, Weir; and you, Williams, go to your rest. Tomorrow morning I will go with you to the spot and examine it. You say that you have marked it, Weir?'

'Yes, sir.'

The old man then left Mr Cox and Williams returned to his hut. Mr Cox did not sleep again till a few minutes before the day dawned, and then, when he dropped off for a quarter of an hour he dreamt of nothing but the ghost sitting on the rail.

CHAPTER V

The next morning – or rather, on *that* morning – Mr Cox, at eight o'clock, rode over to the township of Penrith and saw Hamilton, Weir's second witness. Hamilton, as did Williams, corroborated all that Weir had stated, so far as related to the second time the spectre had been seen; and Hamilton further volunteered the assertion that no one of the party was in the slightest degree affected by drink.

There was a tribe of blacks in the vicinity, and Mr Cox sent for the chief and several others. The European name of this chief was 'Johnny Crook', and, like all his race, he was an adept in tracking. Accompanied by Weir, Hamilton, Williams and the blacks, Mr Cox proceeded to the spot. Weir had no difficulty in pointing out the exact rail. The broken boughs and the notches on the post were his unerring guides.

Johnny Crook, after examining the rail very minutely,

pointed to some stains and exclaimed, *'white man's blood!'*
Then, leaping over the fence, he examined the brushwood
and the ground adjacent. Ere long he started off, beckoning
Mr Cox and his attendants to follow. For more than three-
quarters of a mile, over forest land, the savage tracked the
footsteps of a man, and something trailed along the earth
(fortunately, so far as the ends of justice were concerned, no
rain had fallen during the period alluded to by old David,
namely, fifteen months. One heavy shower would have
obliterated all these tracks, most probably, and, curious
enough, that very night there was a frightful downfall – such
a downfall as had not been known for many a long year) until
they came to a pond, or waterhole, upon the surface of which
was a bluish scum. This scum the blacks, after an examination
of it, declared to be 'white man's fat'. The pond in question
was not on Fisher's land, or Smith's. It was on Crown land
in the rear of their properties. When full to the brink the depth
of the water was about ten feet in the centre, but at the time
referred to there was not more than three feet and a half, and,
badly as the cattle wanted water, it was very evident, from
the absence of recent hock-prints, that they would not drink
at this pond. The blacks walked into the water at the request
of Mr Cox and felt about the muddy bottom with their feet.
They were not long employed thus when they came upon
a bag of bones – or, rather, the remains of a human body, kept
together by clothing which had become so rotten it would
scarcely bear the touch. The skull was still attached to the
body, which the blacks raised to the surface and brought on
shore, together with a big stone and the remains of a large
silk handkerchief. The features were not recognisable, but the
buttons on the clothes, and the boots, were those which Mr
Fisher used to wear! And in the pocket of the trousers was
found a buckhorn-handled knife which bore the initials 'J.F.'
engraved on a small silver plate. This was also identified by
Weir, who had seen Mr Fisher use the knife scores of times.
It was one of those knives which contained a large blade, two
small ones, a corkscrew, gimlet, horse-shoe picker, tweezers,
screwdriver, etc., etc. The murderer, whoever it might be, had
either forgotten to take away this knife or had purposely left
it with the body, for all the other pockets were turned inside
out.

'Well, sir, what do you think of that?' said old Weir to Mr Cox, who looked on in a state of amazement which almost amounted to bewilderment.

'I scarcely know what to think of it,' was Mr Cox's reply. 'But it is lucky for you, David, that you are a man of such good character that you are beyond the pale of being suspected of so foul a deed.'

'I, sir?'

'Yes, you. If it were not that this dead man's property is advertised for sale, it might have gone very hard with you, old man. It would have been suggested that your conscience had something to do with the information you gave me of the ghost. But stay here, all of you, with the body until I return. I shall not be absent for more than an hour. Have you a pair of handcuffs about you, Hamilton?'

'Several pair, sir,' replied the constable.

CHAPTER VI

After leaving the dead body, Mr Cox rode to Fisher's house, in which Mr Smith was living. Mr Smith, on being informed of the approach of so exalted a person as Mr Cox, one of the proudest men in the colony, came out to receive him with all respect and honour. Mr Cox – who would not have given his hand to an 'ex-piree' (under any circumstances), no matter how wealthy he might be – answered Mr Smith's greeting with a bow, and then asked if he could speak with him for a few minutes. Mr Smith replied, 'Most certainly, sir,' and, ordering a servant to take the magistrate's horse to the stables, he conducted his visitor into the best room of the weatherboarded and comfortable tenement. The furniture was plain and homely, but serviceable, nevertheless, and remarkably clean. The pictures on the walls formed rather a motley collection, having been picked up at various times by Mr Fisher at sales by public auction of the effects of deceased officials. Amongst others were two valuable oil-paintings which had orginally belonged to Major Ovens, an eccentric officer who was buried on Garden Island, in the harbour of Port Jackson. These had been bought for less money than the frames were worth. There were also some Dutch paintings, of which neither Mr Fisher nor those who had not bid against him little knew the real value when they were knocked down for forty-two shillings the set – six in number!

'I have come to speak to you on a matter of business,' said the magistrate. 'Is the sale of this farm and the stock to be a peremptory sale? That is to say, will it be knocked down, *bona fide*, to the highest bidder?'

'Yes, sir.'

'And the terms are cash?'

'Yes, sir.'

'Sales for cash are not very common in this country. The terms are usually ten per cent deposit, and the residue at three, six, nine and twelve months, in equal payments.'

'Very true, sir, but these are Mr Fisher's instructions, by which I must be guided.'

'What do you imagine the farm will realise, including the stock and all that is upon it?'

'Well, sir, it ought to fetch £1,500, ready money.'

'I hear that *the whole* of Mr Fisher's property is to be sold, either by auction or private contract.'

'Yes, sir.'

'What will it realise, think you, in cash?'

'Not under £12,000, I should say, sir.'

'One of my brothers has an idea of bidding for this farm; what about the title?'

'As good as can be, sir. It was originally granted to Colonel Foucaux, who sold it and conveyed it to Mr Thomas Blaxsell, who sold it and conveyed it to Fisher. But as you know, sir, twenty years' undisputed possession of itself makes a good title, and Fisher has been on this farm far longer than that. All the deeds are here; you may see them, if you please, sir.'

'There is no occasion for that; as Mr Fisher's constituted attorney, you will sign the deed of conveyance on his behalf.'

'Yes, sir.'

'What is the date of the power of attorney?'

'I will tell you, sir, in one moment'; and opening a bureau which stood in one corner of the room, Mr Smith produced the deed and placed it in Mr Cox's hands.

With the signature of Fisher, Mr Cox was not acquainted; or, at all events, he could not swear to it. He had seen it – seen Fisher write his name, it is true; but then it was that sort of hand which all uneducated and out-door working men employ when they write their names – a sprawling round-hand. But as to the signatures of the attesting witnesses there could be no question whatever. They were those of two of the most eminent solicitors (partners) in Sydney – Mr Cox's own solicitors, in fact.

'And the letter of instructions authorising you to sell by auction, *for cash*; for it says in this power, "and to sell the same, or any part thereof, in accordance with such instructions as he may receive from me by letter after my arrival in England".'

'Here is the letter, sir,' said Mr Smith, producing it.

Mr Cox read the letter attentively. It ran thus:

'Dear Sir, – I got home all right, and found my friends and relations quite well and hearty, and very glad to see me again. I am so happy among 'em, I shan't go out no more to the colony. So sell all off, by public auction or by private contract, but let it be for cash, as I want the money sharp; I am gong to buy a share in a brewery with it. I reckon it ought, altogether, to fetch about £17,000. But do your best, and let me have it quick, whatever it is.

> 'Your faithful friend,
> 'JOHN FISHER.'

There was no post mark on this letter. In those days the postage on letters was very high, and nothing was more common for persons in all conditions of life to forward communications by private hand. As to the signature of the letter, it was identical with that of the power of attorney.

'All this is very satisfactory,' said Mr Cox. 'Is this letter, dated five months ago, the last you have received?'

'Yes, sir. It came by the last ship, and there has not been another in since.'

'Good morning, Mr Smith.'

'Good morning, sir.'

CHAPTER VII

Riding away from Fisher's late abode, Mr Cox was somewhat perplexed. That power of attorney, drawn up so formally, and signed by Fisher in the presence of such credible witnesses, and then the letter written, signed in the same way by the same hand, were all in favour of the presumption that Fisher had gone to England, leaving his friend and neighbour, Smith, in charge of his property, real and personal. But then, there were the remains! And that they were the remains of Fisher, Mr Cox firmly believed. When he had returned to the pond, by a circuitous route, Mr Cox ordered the blacks to strip from a blue-gum tree, with their tomahawks, a large sheet of bark. Upon this the remains were placed, carried straightway to Fisher's house (Mr Cox, upon horseback, heading the party) and placed on the verandah. While this proceeding was in progress Mr Smith came out and wore upon his countenance an expression of surprise, astonishment, wonder. But there was nothing in that. The most innocent man in the world would be surprised, astonished, and in wonderment on beholding such a spectacle.

'What is this, Mr Cox?' he said.

'The last that I have heard and seen of Mr Fisher,' was the reply.

'Of Mr Fisher, sir!'

'Yes.'

'These were his old clothes,' said Mr Smith, examining them carefully; 'most certainly this was the old suit he used to wear. But as for the body, it can't be his; for he is alive, as you have seen by his letter. These old clothes he must have given away, as he did many other old things, the day before he left this; and the man to whom he gave 'em must have been murdered.'

'Do you think he could have given away this knife?' said David Weir. 'To *my* knowledge, he had it for better than twelve years, and often have I heard him say he would not part with it for £50.'

'Give it away? Yes!' said Smith. 'Didn't he give away his old saddle and bridle? Didn't he give away his old spurs? Didn't he give away a cow and a calf!'

'He was a good man, and an honest man, and a very fair dealing man, and in his latter days a very righteous and godly man, but he was not a giving-away man by any manner of means,' returned old David.

'And if he gave away these boots,' said Hamilton, 'they were a very good fit for the man who received them.'

'This man, whoever he is, was murdered, no doubt,' said

Mr Smith, with the most imperturbable countenance and the coolest manner. 'Just look at this crack in his skull, Mr Cox.'

'Yes, I have seen that,' said the magistrate.

'And that's where poor Fisher's ghost had it,' said old David.

'Fisher's ghost!' said Mr Smith. 'What do you mean, Weir?'

'Why, the ghost that I have twice seen sitting on the rail not far from the old bridge at the bottom of the hill yonder.'

'Ghost! You have seen a ghost, have you?' returned Mr Smith, giving Mr Cox a very cunning and expressive look. 'Well, I have heard that ghosts *do* visit those who have sent them out of this world, and I dare say Mr Cox has heard the same. Now, if I had been you, I'd have held my tongue about a ghost (for ghosts are only the creatures of our consciences) for fear of being taken in charge.'

'*I* taken in charge!' said old Weir. 'No, no! *My* conscience is clear, and what I've seen and said I'll swear to. Wherever I go I'll talk about it up to my dying hour. That was the ghost of Mr Fisher that I saw, and these are the remains of his body.'

'If I were Mr Cox, a magistrate,' said Mr Smith, 'I would give you in charge.'

'I will not do that, Mr Smith,' replied Mr Cox. 'I feel that my duty compels me to give *you* in custody of this police officer.'

'For what, sir?'

'On a charge of wilful murder. Hamilton!'

'Yes, sir.'

'Manacle Mr Smith and take him to Penrith.'

Mr Smith held up his wrists with the air of an injured and pure-minded man, who was so satisfied of his innocence that he was prepared for the strictest investigation into his conduct and had no dread as to the result.

CHAPTER VIII

A coroner's inquest was held on the remains found in the pond, and a verdict of 'Wilful Murder' was returned against Edward Smith. The jury also found that the remains were those of John Fisher, albeit they were so frightfully decomposed that personal identification was out of all question.

The vessel in which Fisher was reported to have left Sydney

happened to be in the harbour. The captain and officers were interrogated, and in reply to the question, 'Did a man named John Fisher go home in your vessel?' the reply was 'Yes, and on the Custom House officers coming on board, as usual, to look at the passengers and search the ship to see that no convicts were attempting to make their escape, he produced his parchment certificate of freedom, in which there was a description of his person.'

'And did the man answer exactly to that description?'

'Yes, making allowance for his years, on looking at the date of the certificate. If he had not, he would have been detained, as many convicts have been.'

'And during the voyage did he talk himself?'

'Frequently. He said that he was a farmer near Penrith; that after he had served his time he went to work, earned some money, rented a farm, then bought it, and by industry and perseverance had made a fortune.'

'Did he ever mention a Mr Smith – a friend of his?'

'Often. He said he had left everything in Mr Smith's hands, and that he did not like to sell his property till he saw how he should like England after so long an absence. He further said that if he did not come back to the colony he would have all his property sold off, and join some trading firm in his own country.'

The solicitor who had prepared the power of attorney, and witnessed it, said that a person representing himself as John Fisher, of Ruskdale, in the district of Penrith, came to them and gave instructions for the deed; and after it was duly executed, took it away with him and requested that a copy might be made and kept in their office, which was done accordingly. In payment of the bill, twenty dollars (£5 currency), he gave a cheque on the bank of New South Wales, which was cashed on presentation; that the man who so represented himself as John Fisher was a man of about forty-six or forty-eight years of age, about five feet eight inches in height, and rather stout; had light blue eyes, sandy hair, and whiskers partially gray, a low but intelligent forehead, and a rather reddish nose.

This description answered exactly that of Mr Fisher at the time of his departure from the colony.

The cashier of the bank showed the cheque for twenty

dollars. Mr Fisher had an account there, and drew out his balance, £200 – not in person, but by a cheque – two days previous to his alleged departure. He had written several letters to the bank, and on comparing those letters with the letter Mr Smith said he had received from England, they corresponded exactly.

Opinion was very much divided in the colony with respect to Mr Smith's guilt. Numbers of persons who knew the man, and had dealings with him, thought him incapable of committing such a crime – or any heinous offence, in fact. The records were looked into, to ascertain of what offence he had been convicted originally. It was for embezzling the sum of twenty-two shillings and fourpence, which had been entrusted to him when he was an apprentice for his master, who was a market gardener, seedsman and florist. As for the story about the ghost, very, very few put any trust in it. Bulwer was then a very young gentleman, and had never dreamt of writing about Eugene Aram; nor had Thomas Hood contemplated his exquisite little poem on the same subject. Nor had the murder of the Red Barn been brought to light through the agency of a dream. The only instance of ghosts coming to give evidence of murder were those of Banquo and Hamlet's father – and Shakespeare was not considered an authority to be relied upon in such a case as that of Fisher.

Smith's house and premises, as well as those of Fisher, were searched in the hope of finding apparel, or some garment stained with blood, but in vain. Nor did the inspection of Smith's letters and papers disclose aught that strengthened the case against him. On the contrary, his accounts touching Fisher's property were kept entirely distinct from his own, and in memorandum books were found entries of the following description –

Sept. 9. – Wrote to Fisher to say P. has paid the interest on his mortgage.

Sept. 27. – Received £27/10/- from Wilson for year's rent of Fisher's house in Castlereagh Street.

Nov. 12. – Paid Baxter £3/12/- due to him by Fisher for bullock chains.

No case had ever before created, and probably never will

again create, so great a sensation. Very many were firmly impressed with the belief that Weir was the murderer of the man who wore Fisher's clothes, crediting Smith's assertion or suggestion that he had given them away. Many others were of opinion that the remains were those of Fisher, and the man who murdered him had robbed him of his certificate of freedom, as well as of the cash and papers he had about him, and then, representing Fisher, had got out of the colony and made Smith a dupe.

CHAPTER IX

The anxiously looked-for day of trial came. The court was crowded with persons in every grade of society, from the highest to the very lowest. Mr Smith stood in the dock as firmly and as composedly as though he had been arraigned for a mere libel, or a common assault – the penalty of conviction not exceeding a fine and a few months' imprisonment.

The case was opened by the Attorney-General with the greatest fairness imaginable, and when the witnesses gave their evidence (Weir, Hamilton, Williams and Mr Cox) every-one appeared to hold his breath. Smith, who defended himself, cross-examined them all with wonderful tact and ability; and, at the conclusion of the case for the prosecution, addressed the jury at considerable length and with no mean amount of eloquence.

The judge then summed up. His honour was the last man in the world to believe in supernatural appearances; but with the ability and fairness that characterised his career in the colony, he weighted the probabilities and improbabilities with the greatest nicety. To detail all the points taken by the judge would be tedious; but if his charge had any leaning one way or other it was in favour of the prisoner.

The jury in those days was not composed of the people, but of military officers belonging to the regiment quartered in the colony. These gentlemen, in ordinary cases, did not give much of their minds to the point at issue. Some of them usually threw themselves back and shut their eyes – not to think, but 'nod'. Others whispered to each other – not about the guilt or innocence of the prisoner at the bar, but about their own affairs; whilst those who had any talent for drawing exercised it by sketching the scene or taking the likeness of the prisoner, the witnesses, the counsel, the sheriff and the judge. But in this case they seemingly devoted all their energies, in order to enable them to arrive at the truth. To every word that fell from the judge during his charge, which lasted over two hours, they listened with breathless attention, and when it was concluded they requested permission to retire to consider their verdict. This was at half-past five in the afternoon of Friday, and not until a quarter to eleven did the jury return into court and retake their places in the box.

The excitement that prevailed was intense, and when the murmurs in the crowd, so common upon such occasions, had subsided, amidst awful stillness the prothonotary put that all-momentous question, 'Gentlemen of the jury, what say you? Is the prisoner at the bar guilty, or not guilty?'

With a firm, clear voice, the foreman – a captain in the army – uttered the word –

'GUILTY!'

Murmurs of applause from some, and of disapprobation from others, instantly resounded through the hall of justice. From the reluctant manner in which the judge put the black cap upon his head, it was evident that he was not altogether satisfied with the finding of the jury. He had, however, no alternative; and in the usual formal manner he sentenced the prisoner to be hanged on the following Monday morning at eight o'clock.

Smith heard the sentence without moving a single muscle or betraying any species of emotion, and left the dock with as firm a step as that which he employed when entering it. His demeanour through the trial, and after he was sentenced, brought over many who previously thought him guilty to a belief in his innocence, and a petition to the Governor to spare his life was speedily drafted and numerously signed. It was rumoured that the Chief Justice who tried the case had also made a similar recommendation, and that the Governor, in deference thereto, had ordered a reprieve to be made out, but not to be delivered to the Sheriff until seven o'clock on Monday morning. It was further stated that the Governor was of opinion that the finding of the jury was a correct one. The press of the colony did not lead, but fell into, the most popular opinion, that it would be tantamount to murder to take away the life of any human being upon such evidence as that given on the trial.

CHAPTER X

On the Monday morning, so early as half-past six, the rocks which overlooked the gaol yard in Sydney, and commanded a good view of the gallows, were crowded with persons of the lower orders; and when, at a little before seven, the hangman came out to suspend the rope to the beam and make other preparations he was hailed with loud hisses and execrations; so emphatic was the demonstration of the multitude in favour of the condemned man. By seven o'clock the mob was doubled, and when the Under-Sheriff or any other functionary was seen in the courtyard, the yells with which he was greeted were something terrific.

At five minutes to eight the culprit was led forth, and at the foot of the gallows, and near his coffin (according to the custom prevailing in the colony), was pinioned preparatory to ascending the ladder. Whilst this ceremony was being performed the shouts of the populace were deafening. 'Shame! Shame! Shame! Hang Weir! He is the guilty man! This is a murder! A horrid murder!' Such were the ejaculations that resounded from every quarter of that dense mob assembled to witness the execution; while the calm and submissive manner in which Smith listened to the reverend gentleman who attended him in his last moments, heightened rather than suppressed the popular clamour.

At one minute past eight the fatal bolt was drawn and Smith, after struggling for about half a minute, was dead! Whereupon the mob renewed their yells, execrations, hisses, and cries of 'Shame! Shame! Shame! Murder! Murder! Murder!' These noises could not recall to life Mr Smith. He had gone to his account, and after hanging an hour his body was cut down, the coffin containing it conveyed in an uncovered cart to Slaughter-House Point (the last resting-place of all great criminals) and the grave filled in with quicklime.

There was a gloom over Sydney until the evening at half-past six o'clock. Almost everyone was now disposed to think that the blood of an innocent man had been shed. The witnesses were all perjured, not excepting Mr Cox'; 'the jury were a parcel of fools'; and 'the Governor, who would not listen to the judge, a hard-hearted and cruel man'. Such were the opinions that were current from one end of Sydney to the other. But at the hour above mentioned – half-past six in the evening – the public mind was disabused of its erroneous idea. At that hour it became generally known that on the previous night Mr Smith had sent for the Rev. Mr Cooper, and to that gentleman had confessed that he deserved the fate that awaited him; that for more than two years he had contemplated the murder of John Fisher for the sake of his wealth, which was equal to £20,000; that the man who had personated Fisher and executed the power of attorney had gone to England and written thence the letter upon which he so much relied in his defence, was a convict who resembled the deceased in person, and to whom he (Smith) gave Fisher's certificate of freedom; that it was his (Smith's) intention to have left the colony as soon as the proceeds of the sale came into his possession – partly because he longed to lead the last portion of his life in England, but chiefly because, from the day on which he committed the murder, he had been haunted by that ghost which old Weir had truly sworn he saw sitting on the rail; that the deed was done by a single blow from a tomahawk, and that the deceased never spoke after it was inflicted. He protested that the man who had personated Fisher in respect to the execution of the power of attorney, and who had escaped from the colony, was ignorant of his (Smith's) intention to murder Fisher; and that the letter which had been forwarded from England was only a copy of one which he (Smith) had told him to despatch a few months after he had arrived at home. He concluded by saying that, since he struck Fisher that fatal blow his life had been a burden to him, much as he had struggled to disguise his feelings and put a bold front on the matter; and that he would much rather, since he had been convicted, suffer death than be reprieved – although he hoped that until after the breath had left his body his confession would be kept a secret.

Mary Fortune ('Waif Wanderer')
The Dead Witness; or, The Bush Waterhole

I can scarcely fancy anything more enjoyable to a mind at ease with itself than a spring ride through the Australian bush, if one is disposed to think he can do without any disturbing influence whatever from the outer world, for to a man accustomed to the sights and sounds of nature around him there is nothing distracting in the warble of the magpie or tinkle of the 'bell bird'. The little lizards that sit here and there upon logs and stumps, and look at the passer by with their heads on one side, and such a funny air of knowing stupidity in their small eyes, are such every-day affairs to an old colonist that they scarcely attract any notice from him, and even should a monstrous iguana dart across his path and trail his four feet length up a neighbouring tree, it is not a matter of much curiosity to him; and a good horseman, with an easy going nag under him, and plenty of time to journey at leisure through the park-like bush of Australia, has, to my notion, as good an opportunity of enjoying the Italians' *dolce far niente* as any fellow can have who does not regularly lie down to it.

Something like all this was coming home to me as I slowly rode through the forest of stringy bark, box, peppermint, and other trees that creep close up to the bold ranges which divide as it were into two equal portions the district of Kooama. I had passed fifteen miles of bush and plain without seeing a face or a roof, and now, having but a mile or two before making the station to which I was bound, I loosened the reins and let my horse take his own time. While, however, I thoroughly enjoyed the calm tranquillity of nature so unbroken around me, and felt the soothing influence more or less inseparable from such scenes, I cannot exactly say that my mind was enjoying the same 'sweetness of doing nothing' as my body. My brain was busily at work, full of a professional case, on the investigation of which I was proceeding; still, thoughts of this kind cannot be said to trouble the mind, being as enjoyable to us, I dare say, as the pursuit of game to the hunter, or the search for gold to the miner.

The facts of the case were shortly these: A young photographic enthusiast, in search of colonial scenery upon which to employ his art, had taken a room in a public house at the township of Kooama, in which he had arranged his photographic apparatus, and where he had perfected the views taken in trips to all the places within twenty or thirty miles that were likely to repay the trouble. The young fellow, who was a gentlemanly and exceedingly handsome youth of barely twenty years of age, became a general favourite at Kooama, his kindness to the children, especially in that out of the way township, endearing him to all the parents.

Well, one day this young artist, whose name was Edward Willis, left Kooama, and returned no more. For a day or two the landlord of the house where he had put up thought but little of his absence, as he had upon more than one occasion before spent the night away on his excursions; but day after day passed, and they began to think it singular. He had himself expressed an intention of visiting some of the ranges to which I have alluded in search of some bolder 'bits' of scenery than he had yet acquired; but otherwise they had not the slightest clue to guide them in any attempted search for the missing youth. His decision to leave Kooama, if he had made one, must have been sudden, as nothing was removed from his room. Camera, chemicals, plates, and all the paraphernalia of a photographer's handicraft, were still scattered about just as he had left them. A week passed away – a fortnight – consumed in guesses and wonders, and then came a letter from his mother in Adelaide to the landlord, inquiring the son's whereabouts, as they were getting uneasy at not hearing from so regular a correspondent. Then it was considered time to place the thing in the hands of the police, and I was sent for. As I was proceeding through the bush then, at the leisurely pace I have described, I heard the loud crack of a stock whip ring out like the sharp report of a rifle between me and the ranges to my left, and shortly after I heard the sound of rapidly advancing horse's hoof strokes, which was echoed and re-echoed from the rocks at either side of the horseman's route. The sound came nearer and nearer, and at last a young man, mounted on a half thoroughbred, and attired like a stock-driver or overseer on a station, galloped into the road which I was following a few yards behind me. Here he pulled up, and was soon by my side. The freemasonry of bush travellers in Australia would scarcely admit of one passing another without speaking, on a road where one might journey for twenty miles without meeting a soul; so there was nothing singular in my addressing the new-comer with all the freedom of an old chum.

'Aren't you afraid of breaking your neck, mate,' I inquired, 'coming down those ranges at such a pace?'

'Not a bit of it,' he replied; 'but at any rate I'm in a devil of a hurry, so had to risk it.'

'Bound for Kooama, I suppose?'

'Yes, I'm for the police station, and if I don't look sharp, it'll be pitch dark before I get back, so I must go on; goodbye! I'll meet you again, I dare say.'

'Stay!' I shouted, as the young fellow made a start; 'I might save you a journey, as I'm a policeman myself, and am just on my way to Kooama. Is there anything wrong your way?'

The young horseman looked at me rather suspiciously, as, of course, I was in plain clothes. I dare say he did not half believe me.

'Well,' he said, 'it's nothing very particular, and if you *are* going to the police station, policeman or no policeman, you can tell all I have to say as well as I can, if you will be so kind, and I shall get home before sundown yet.'

I assured him that I was really connected with the force, when he told me his errand to the camp.

'There's been the deuce of a talk at Kooama about a young picture-man who's been missing for a couple of weeks, and some think he's come to no good end. Now, I know myself that he has been on our station since he came to Kooama, for I saw him taking views over the range there, but I thought nothing of that, as it was when first he settled at Dycer's, and he has been photographing miles away since then. This afternoon, however, about ten miles from the home station, the cattle (we're mustering just now) kicked up such a devil of a row that I couldn't make it out until I concluded they had come across the scent of blood somehow. Sure enough when I came up to the mob they were bellowing and roaring like mad ones round a spot on the grass that must have been regularly soaked in blood, as it is as red and fresh looking as possible. What made it more suspicious to me was, that the place had been carefully covered up with branches, and no one would ever have noticed it, only the cattle had pawed and scraped the dead bushes quite off it. Heaven knows what might have caused it, or whether it was worth mentioning; but it's not far from where I saw the poor young chap. I thought I would run down to the camp and tell Cassel about it.'

'Have you mentioned it to anyone else?' I inquired.

'No,' he replied; 'I haven't seen a soul since.'

'Well, don't say a word, like a good fellow: it's very strange that I should have met you; I'm Brooke, the detective, and I'm on my way to Kooama about this very business. Will you meet me at sunrise tomorrow morning, and take me to the place?'

The young man readily promised, and I found that he was the son of a squatter whose station (called Minarra) was situated at the other side of the Rocky Ranges, to which I have so frequently alluded, and then we parted, and spurring my horse to a more rapid pace I soon reached the police camp, at Kooama, and got my horse stalled and my supper, as well as all the information I could from Constable Cassel before I turned in, which I did at an early hour.

There are a good many fellows – no matter in what anxiety of mind they may be – who are able to forego it all when their usual bed-time reminds them of sleep, and they seem to shake off their troubles with their shoes, and draw up the blankets as an effectual barrier between them and the world generally; it is not so with me, I usually carry my perplexities to bed with me, and roll and tumble, and tumble and roll, under their influence, unless some happy idea of having hit the right nail on the head in my planning soothes me into resignation to my fatigue. So it was on the night in question; nevertheless, the sun was only beginning to shake himself out of the horizon when I met the young squatter at the appointed place, and together we proceeded to the indicated spot on Minarra station.

Over the range we went, and three or four miles through the primeval forest beyond, and my companion, well acquainted with the land marks on his 'run', stopped before what appeared to be a few decaying branches fallen from a near gum tree. 'This is it,' he said, dismounting and removing the dead boughs, 'I covered it up again yesterday.'

Well, there was very little to see, a patch of blood stained grass – the colour was very evident still – and nothing more. I looked round to see if perchance there was a view to make it worth an artist's while to visit this spot, and soon perceived that from the very place where we stood a photographer might catch a 'bit' of truly beautiful and entirely colonial scenery. At a distance of perhaps two miles the range over which we had come fell abruptly down into the plain in a succession of sheer faces of rock, while at the foot of what might be almost termed the precipice that terminated the whole, a deep gorge or gully ran almost directly at right angles with it, up which the eye pierced through a vista of richly-foliaged and fantastically gnarled trees and huge boulders of grey granite, altogether forming a scene that could scarcely fail to attract the eye of an artist. The sun was up above the trees now, and, closely scanning the ground at my feet, I perceived at a few yards distance a something that caught his brightness and reflected it, and stooping I picked it up; it was a small, a *very* small, piece of glass, and just such glass too, as might have been used in a camera. But near the piece of glass, which was not far from the blood spot on the grass, I found too, what I had been searching for, which was the triangular marks of the camera stand, which I thought it barely possible might be visible. The holes were indented deeper into the grass than the mere weight of the instrument would account for, especially two of them, the third was not so visible. We covered all up again as carefully yet as carelessly as possible, and after having again cautioned the young squatter to be silent, I parted with him for the present, and made the best of my way to Kooama.

An hour or so later, I was very busy in the deserted room

of the young artist, of which I had taken possession, and into which to avoid disturbance I had locked myself. I was quite at home among the poor young fellow's chemicals, &c., as I happen to be a bit of an amateur photographer myself, and I have found my knowledge in that way of service to me on one or two occasions in connection with my professional duties already. The table and mantelpiece were littered with unfinished plates; they were leaning against the wall, and against every conceivable thing that would form a support for them. Naturally supposing that those last taken would be most *come-at-able*, I confined my search at first to the outside pictures, and before very long I fancied I was repaid for my trouble. My idea, it will readily be guessed, in searching the plates at all, was the one of finding a face or a view that might possibly be a clue in my hunt for the missing youth, or for the murderer, if murder had been done. Nothing would be more likely than that some chance encounter in his excursions might have resulted in a portrait, the original of which, if discovered, might be able to give some useful information. Well, I found more than I hoped for. I lighted on a plate, only parts of which had 'come out' under the after process, and which was rubbed in several places, and had evidently been thrown aside as worthless. There were two or three duplicate copies of the same view, and among the perfected and most clear pictures which the artist had laid away more carefully by themselves, was one apparently valued, as in case of danger of damage it was 'cased' properly. It was a truly beautiful bit of entirely Australian bush scenery; a steep, rocky bank for a back ground; at its foot, a still, deep waterhole reflecting every leaf of the twisted old white-stemmed gum trees that hung over it and dipped their heavy branches in its dark waters, and to the left a reach of bush level, clustered with undergrowth on the slightly undulating ground, and shaded here and there with the tufty foliage of the stringy-bark. It was an excellent picture, every leaf had come out perfectly, and the shadows were as dark and cool as shadows could be, while the tone was all that could be wished; nevertheless on comparing this with the unfinished and imperfect one on which the artist's art had failed, my eye rested on a something in the latter which made it a hundred times more valuable to me.

In the shade of a heavy bush at the opposite side of this still, deep waterhole, there was the faint outline of a crouching human figure, an outline so faint and so shrouded in the obscurity of the faulty plate, that very likely no eye but that of a detective would have observed it, and it is more than probable that the poor lad whose art had fixed it in its place, was quite unaware of its being there; but by the aid of a powerful microscope I made it out distinctly. We all know with what perfectness to every line of its object the camera fixes its light copies, even in the greatest failures as to perfect shading and tone, and there I had this crouching and malignant looking face peering from behind a shadowy bush, as recognisable as if he had been photographed in a Collins-street or George-street studio. Steadily I set to work reproducing this hiding figure, magnifying and photographing by aid of the good camera the young artist had left behind, and I succeeded at length in completing a likeness quite clear enough for my purpose; so after taking possession of the plate holding the view of the bush waterhole, I put it and my likeness into my pocket, and locking up the room, once more sought the camp.

The likeness of the missing youth himself, was given to me by the landlady of the public house: he had given it to her a few days before he took his last walk in search of subjects for his art. Poor fellow! he was very handsome and very youthful looking; a white, sickly, noble face, with large black eyes, and a profusion of curly black hair forming a frame to a high broad forehead. I felt sick at heart as I looked at it and thought of his empty home and the red pool of blood on Minarra station.

It was late in the day when I got thus far in my search, and I was rather glad that my young squatter acquaintance did not turn up at Kooama that evening, as he had intimated an intention of doing, for I was likely to require his assistance, and did not care to trust his young gossiping propensities with my secrets any longer than was absolutely necessary.

Early on the following morning, however, he rode up to the camp, and I so arranged that we should be left alone together. 'I don't know your name, my young friend,' I was commencing, when he interrupted me.

'My name is Derrick – Thomas Derrick.'

'Well, Mr Derrick, I am sure I need not tell you upon what a serious job I am engaged, nor that it is your interest, as well as that of the public at large, that no crime should go unpunished; all this you know as well as I do; but what you do not know as well as I do, my dear fellow, is how very little will interfere with a search such as mine, and give a criminal a chance of escaping with impunity. All this I tell you because I am going to ask your assistance, and to beg that while you are affording it to me you will keep as secret as the grave anything that may pass between us until I accomplish my object, or fail in the endeavour to do so.'

The young man promised faithful secrecy, and then I laid the picture of the bush waterhole before him.

'Is there any such place as that on your run?'

'To be sure there is; it's in Minarra Creek, about half a mile from where we found the flock.'

'I thought it likely, and now I am almost sure you will be able to tell me who that is,' and I handed him my copy of the hiding figure. He looked very much astonished, but replied immediately –

'It's Dick the Devil!'

'And who is Dick the Devil?'

'A crusty, cantankerous old wretch, one of our shepherds. Do you think *he's* in it!'

'Oh, of course, we are all abroad as to that yet; where does this Dick live, and what does he do?'

'He minds a flock, and lives at an out hut ten miles from the home station.'

'Alone? or has he a hutkeeper?'

'Well, he's by himself this long time; he had two or three hutkeepers, but at last we were obliged to give it up – no one would live with him.'

'Could you manage to get me in there as hutkeeper without exciting his suspicion?'

'You! of course I could, he's always growling about not having one; but you could never stand it.'

'No fear of me, it won't be for long at any rate.'

Fancy me that same afternoon metamorphosed into a seedy tired looking coon, accompanying the young squatter to Dick's hut, where he was going, or appeared to be obliged to go at any rate, with rations in a spring cart. Dick was within sight, letting his flock feed quietly foldwards, and his young employer led me to him.

'Now, you old growler, I hope you're satisfied! here's a hutkeeper for you, and I hope you'll keep your ugly temper quiet for one week at any rate.'

I should have recognised my man anywhere, sure enough; the villainous scowling face of the hider in the photograph was before me, and so determined a looking scoundrel I had not seen for a long time, familiar as I was with criminals. He was an elderly man – about fifty, perhaps – low sized, and strongly built; his years told on him in a slight stoop, and grizzled, coarse hair, that but added to his rascally appearance, and his character was but too plainly traced in his low, repulsive forehead, and heavy, dark beetling brows. I could have almost sworn he was an old hand the moment I set eyes on him.

'Thank ye for nothing, Tom,' was his impudently given reply; 'you didn't send to town for a hutkeeper for me, I'll swear.'

'Well, you're about right; I met him as I was coming over with your rations, and as the poor fellow looked tired and hard up, I thought I'd give you another trial.'

'You be d——d,' was Dick the Devil's thanks, as the young fellow turned away with a 'well, so long, mate!' to me.

'Well,' said my new mate, turning to me, 'if you'll give me a hand to round up the flock, I'll get 'em all the sooner in, and then we can have a good yarn. I'm d——d if I'm not glad to see a fellow's face again; curse such a life as this, I say!'

''Tis a slow one; I'm blessed if it ain't,' I replied, doing as he wished; 'have you no dog?'

'No, I haven't,' he snapped out at me like a pistol shot, with such a look, half of terror and half of suspicion, that I was convinced about his dog there was something more to be learned.

After the billy was slung and the tea boiled, and the mutton and damper disposed of, Dick and I sat down in the still calm twilight outside the bush hut, and while puffing out volumes of tobacco smoke from dirty, black pipes managed to mutually interest ourselves, I dare say.

'Things are looking d—— bad in the country now, mate,' rapped out Dick.

'You may say it,' I replied; 'I've tramped over many a hundred miles without the chance of a job.'

'Where did you come from last?'

'Oh! I came from everywhere between this and Beechworth! I stopped at Kooama last night; there's a devil of a talk there about some murder.'

'Murder!' said Dick, with a sort of gasp, and a short quick look at me; 'what murder?'

'Some poor devil of a painter or picter-man, or something of that sort.'

'Oh, d—— them! they don't *know* he's murdered?'

'I see you've heard about it then. Yes, I believe you're right. I think he's only missing, and they *guess* he's made away with.'

'Let them guess and be d——d to them!' said the hardened wretch, and I thought fit to drop the subject.

'Oh, my lad!' thought I to myself, 'if you only guessed who is sitting beside you, and what his object is here, wouldn't there be another pool of red blood under some tree in the Australian forest, eh?' and then I looked at my neighbour's muscular frame and determined criminal countenance, wondering in a battle for life and death between us should I be able to come off victor. Certainly, I could at any moment lay my hand upon my trusty revolver, and dexterity and self-possession might accomplish much with the handcuffs; but let a fellow be ever so little of a coward, he must feel a *little* at being so entirely isolated and so self-dependent as I was at this moment. Far out before us lay miles of almost level grass, dotted with tall-stemmed trees and patches of undergrowth. There wasn't a living soul within miles and not a sound save as night fell the scream of the distant curlew, that came, I guessed, from the vicinity of the black waterhole in the Minarra Creek, and I could not help picturing to myself the stillness of that night-gloomed water, its heavy, overhanging foliage, and the white mangled face that *perhaps* lay below it. Altogether I was not sorry that Dick showed no disposition to prolong the conversation, but soon turned in, and I followed his example, not, however, without placing my revolver under my hand, and when I *did* sleep it was, as the saying is, with one eye open.

According to a concerted arrangement between me and my young assistant, the very earliest morning brought him to the hut at full gallop. His greeting to Dick was rather abrupt.

'What the devil's the reason you're running your flock up to the rock springs every day, Dick?' Connel complains you don't leave him half enough for his sheep, and here's a waterhole close under your nose.'

'Well, the cursed flock always head up that way; they're used to it; and it's d——d hard work to turn a thirsty mob when you've got no dog! in fact, it's onpossible.'

'What the deuce have you.*done* with your dog! you had a first-rater.'

'Done with him!' replied Dick, vindictively; 'cut his throat! He was always giving me twice the work with his playin' up!'

'Well, you'll have to get another somewhere; at any rate take the flock to Minarra waterhole in future.'

'I can't myself,' was the response.

'Your mate will lend you a hand for a day or two, as the water is not far away, and the flock will soon get used to it.'

I had been watching Dick as closely as I could, without being noticed by him, during his colloquy, and could easily see that he was much dissatisfied with this arrangement, but he could make no excuse, as the want of water was beginning to be complained of on all the surrounding runs, and so we headed the flock in the direction of Minarra waterhole. There was no opportunity for conversation on the way, as Dick and I were far apart, and the sheep were feeding quietly all the way; but when we neared the water, and the flock – which, by the way, showed no anxiety whatever to go in any other direction – had mob by mob satisfied their thirst, and were scattering out over the near pasture, I approached the waterhole, and, sitting down in almost the very spot where poor young Willis must have placed his camera to take the view I had in my pocket, I took out my pipe and commenced cutting tobacco for the purpose of filling it. All the time the sheep were drinking I could see that Dick was very uneasy. He kept away entirely, but when he saw me taking it so coolly he drew up slowly.

'D—— queer place to sit down, that,' he said; 'you'll be ate up with mosquitoes.'

'No fear,' I answered; 'I'm thinking the mosquitoes have something more to their liking to eat down here.'

'Down where?'

'Oh! about the water! What a devil of a lot of ugly things must be down at the bottom there, Dick! it's very deep.'

I couldn't see the wretch, but I *fancied* his face was growing pale, and although I daren't look at him, neither durst I trust myself with my back to him, so, affecting an air of nonchalance I was far from feeling, I got up and faced him while I affected to be searching in my pocket for matches, my hand in reality clutching the revolver.

'I wonder if that picter-man ever *took* this place?' I added, ''t would look first-rate.'

Dick's face flushed up with fury, he could stand the strain no longer.

'D—— the picter-man!' he roared, 'what the —— are you always talkin' about *him* for?'

I looked at him with affected surprise, – 'You get in a blessed pelter over it, mate! Anyone but me would be suspicious that you'd done it yourself!'

'And if I did —— to you?' he said, with a face fearful in its hardened ferocity. 'And if I *did*, you couldn't prove it – you've no witnesses!'

While he was saying this, half a dozen bubbles rose to the surface of the water directly in front of us, followed by more and more; and I do not know to this day what unaccountable influence it was that as Dick ceased speaking urged me to seize him by the wrist, and, while pointing to the bubbles before him with the other hand, to whisper in reply, – 'Haven't I? – Look!' for, of course, I had no more expectation of the awful scene that followed than has my reader at this moment.

A fearful, dripping *thing* rose to the surface – a white, ghastly face followed – and then, up – up – waist high out of the water, rose the corpse of the murdered artist!

It remained for a second or two standing, as it were, before us, with glaring, wide-open eye-balls turned toward the bank on which we stood, and then, with a horrible *plump*, the body fell backward, the feet rose to the top, and there the terrible thing lay face upward, – staring up, one might fancy, to the heavens, calling for justice on the murderer!

As I saw this awful sight, my grasp on Dick's wrist relaxed, although unconsciously, I still pointed toward the white dripping terror; until it settled, as I have attempted to describe, and then Dick the Devil, with a wild cry that I shall never forget, threw both his hands up to his head and fell heavily to the ground.

To tell you how I felt in these few moments is impossible. I was horror-struck. In all my experience of fearful and impressive sights, I never felt so completely stunned and awed. But it did not last long with me; for, of course, reason soon came to assure me that it required no supernatural agency to cause a corpse to rise from the bottom to the top of a waterhole, although the accounting for the way in which it had thus arisen would not be so simple.

With but a glance at the prostrate form of the insensible wretch beside me, I fired off one barrel of my revolver as a signal to young Derrick, who had promised to hang about; and I had soon the satisfaction of hearing in reply the echoed report of that young man's well-given stock-whip, and it was not long before he came galloping down to the side of the hole.

It may be supposed that this young fellow felt even more horrified than even I, more accustomed to deaths and murders, had done, and after I had shortly explained to him how matters stood, I do not think we had two opinions about the guilt of the still insensible old miserable. Be that as it may, I was heartless and unfeeling enough to handcuff him, even while he was unconscious, not choosing to risk an attempt at escape. And then we sprinkled water over him, and used all the means within our power for the purpose of restoring him. At length he sat up, but his first glance falling again on the floating corpse, he struggled to his feet, crying –

'Oh, my God! Take me out of this! Let me out of this!'

And, one on each side of him – he partly leading – we followed him three or four hundred yards, where, under the shade of a tree, he sat down weak as a child.

'I can't go any farther,' he said, – 'You'll have to take me to the camp in a cart.'

'Where's all your bounce now, mate?' I could not help inquiring, as I handed him a drop of grog out of a flask I carried.

He put it trembling to his lips and drained it, and then, with a heavily-drawn breath, replied – 'It's in h——!'

This was awful, but he did not give us time to think, for

he immediately, and without any encouragement, added, 'I'm goin' to tell you all about that lot while I'm able, for I feel all rotten like!' – and then he added again – 'like *him*, down below.'

We did not speak, either of us, and he went on – 'One day, that chap came pictering up yonder, and my dog playin' up as usual, runnin' the sheep wrong, he got me in a pelter, and I outs with my knife and cut his b—— throat! The young picter chap sees me, and runs to try and save the dog; but he was too late, and he ups and told me I was a villain, and a cruel wretch, and all sorts, and I told him I'd cut his too if he gave me any more of his jaw, and when he went away I swore I'd be revenged on the cheeky pup. I watched him that day down at the Minarra waterhole, but couldn't get a good chance, and then he went home to Kooama. Well, about a week after, he was pictering down yonder.'

Here he pointed in the direction of the blood marks, and I nodded, saying, 'I know.'

'You know!' he said, turning to me with something of his old ferocity 'how the d—— do you know anything about it?'

'I know all about it,' I said in reply; 'I will finish your story for you – when I go wrong, you can set me right.'

He looked at me stupidly – wonderingly. 'Who are you?' he asked.

'I am Brooke, the detective.'

'Oh!' – Dick the Devil drew a hard breath.

'Well, he was taking views with his camera near that tree there, where you covered the blood up with the bushes – you know, and you stole behind him – '

'Yes,' interrupted Dick; 'When his head was under that black rag.'

'And you struck him with something that stunned him.'

'It was a waddy,' said Dick.

'And the blow struck the camera also, capsized it, and broke it to shivers.'

'Jest so!' added the wretch, a hideous glee lighting up his ferocious countenance; 'and then I took out my clasp-knife and nagged his pipe, jest as I did the dog's, and I axed him how he liked it, but he couldn't tell me!'

'Oh, you *awful* devil!' cried young Derrick, whose face I had remarked becoming paler and paler until I gave him a nobbler too, or I positively believe the poor fellow would have fainted.

'And then I carried him all the way to the hole on my back, and I got a rope and I rolled it round him in good knots, and then I tied the rope to a good sized boulder, and I rolled him and the boulder to the bottom together! But tell me now,' he added, sinking his voice to a whisper, 'how did he get up again? How *ever* did he get up again?'

Of course, this we can only surmise, the rope might have got damaged in the roll of rock and body down the bank, and remaining attached to the feet, had given below, and given until it allowed the unfastened part of the corpse to reach the surface, and then slackened more from the rock below until the feet were able to find the surface. This is the most likely solution of the difficulty, for the rope, when the corpse was removed, was still found attached to both the body and the rock.

Dick the Devil was punished for his crime, but where and when, it is unnecessary for me to state.

MARCUS CLARKE
Pretty Dick

A hot day. A very hot day on the plains. A very hot day up in the ranges, too. The Australian sun had got up suddenly with a savage swoop, as though he was angry at the still coolness of early morning, and was determined to drive the cattle, who were munching complacently in the long rich grass of the swamp, back up under the hill among the thick she-oaks. It seemed to be a settled thing on the part of the sun to get up hotter and hotter every morning. He even went down at night with a red face, as much as to say, 'Take care, I shall be hotter than ever tomorrow!'

The men on the station did not get into smoking humour until he had been gone down at least an hour, and so they sat on a bench and a barrel or two outside the 'men's hut' on the hill, they looked away across the swamp to that jagged gap in the ranges where he had sunk, and seeing the red flush in the sky, nodded at one another, and said, 'We shall have a hot day tomorrow.' And they were right. For, when they had forgotten the mosquitoes, and the heat, and the many pleasant things that live in the crevices between the slabs of the hut, and gone to sleep, up he came again, hotter than ever, without the least warning, and sent them away to work again.

On this particular morning he was very hot. Even King Peter, who was slowly driving up the working bullocks from the swamp, felt his old enemy so fierce on his back, that he got up in his stirrups and cracked his whip, until the hills rang again, and Strawberry, and Punch, and Doughboy, and Damper, and all (except that cynical, wicked, Spot, who hated the world and always lived away by himself in a private clump of she-oak) straightened their tails and shook their heads, and galloped away up to the stockyard in mortal terror. The horses feel the heat, and King Peter's brother, who was looking for them on the side of the Stony Mount, had a long ride up and down all sorts of gullies before he found them out, and then they were unusually difficult to get together. The cockatoos knew it was hot, and screamed themselves away into the bush. The kangaroos, who had come down like gigantic shadows out of the still night, had all hopped away back into the scrub under the mountains, while the mist yet hung about the trees around the creek-bed. The parrots were uneasy, and the very station dogs got under the shadow-lee of the huts, in case of a hot wind coming up. As for the sheep – when Pretty Dick's father let them out in the dawn, he said to his dog, 'We shan't have much to do today, old woman, shall we?' At which Lassie wagged her tail and grinned, as intelligent dogs do.

But who was Pretty Dick?

Pretty Dick was the seven years old son of Richard Fielding, the shepherd. Pretty Dick was a slender little man, with eyes like pools of still water when the sky is violet at sunset, and a skin as white as milk – that is, under his little blue and white shirt, for where the sun had touched it, it was a golden brown, and his hands were the colour of the ripe chestnuts his father used to gather in England years ago. Pretty Dick had hair like a patch of sunlight, and a laugh like rippling water. He was the merriest little fellow possible, and manly too! He understood all about milking, did Pretty Dick; and could drive up a refractory cow with anybody. He could chop wood too – that is, a little, you know, because he was not very strong, and the axe was heavy. He could ride, and a buck-jumper – that was his ambition – but he would take Molly (the wall-eyed mare) into the home station for his father's rations, and come out again quite safely.

He liked going into the station, because he saw Ah Yung, the Chinaman cook, who was kind to him, and gave him sugar. He had all the news to hear too. How another mob of travelling sheep were coming through the run; how the grey mare had sliped her foal; how the bay filly had bucked off Black Harry and hurt his wrist; how Old Tom had 'got the sack' for being impudent to the overseer, and had vowed to fire the run. Besides, there was the paper to borrow for his father, Mr Trelawney's horses to look at, the chat with the carpenter, and perhaps a peep at the new buggy with its silver-mounted harness (worth, 'oh, thousands of pounds!' Pretty Dick thought); perhaps, too, he might go down to the house, with its garden, and cool verandah, and bunches of grapes; might get a little cake from Mary, the cook; or even might be smiled upon by Mrs Trelawney, the owner's young wife, who seemed to Dick to be something more than a lady – to be a sweet voice that spoke kindly to him, and made him feel as he would feel sometimes when his mother would get the Big Bible, that came all the way from England, and tell him the story about the Good Man who so loved little children.

He liked to go into the station, because everyone was so kind to him. Everyone loved Pretty Dick; even Old Tom, who had been a 'lag', and was a very wicked man, hushed the foul jest and savage oath when the curly head of Pretty Dick came within hearing; and the men always felt as if they had their Sunday clothes on in his presence. But he was not to go into the station today. It was not ration-day; so he sat on the step of his father's hut door, looking out through a break in the timber-belt at the white dots on the plain, that he knew to be his father's sheep.

Pretty Dick's father lived in the Log Hut, on the edge of the plains, and had five thousand sheep to look after. He was away all day. Sometimes, when the sheep would camp near home, Pretty Dick would go down with some fresh tea in a 'billy' for his father, and would have a very merry afternoon watching his father cut curious notches on his stick, and would play with Lassie, and look about for 'possums in the trees, or, with craning neck, cautiously inspect an ant-hill. And then when evening came, and Lassie had got the sheep together – quietly without any barking, you know – when father and son jogged homewards through the warm, still air, and the trampling hoofs of the sheep sent up a fragrance from the crushed herbage round the folding ground, Pretty Dick would repeat long stories that his mother had told him, about 'Valentine and Orson', and 'Beauty and the Beast', and 'Jack the Giant Killer', for Pretty Dick's mother had been maid in the rector's family in the Kentish village at home, and was a little above Pretty Dick's father, who was only a better sort of farm labourer. But they were all three very happy now in their adopted country. They were alone there, these three – Pretty Dick, and mother and father – and no other children came to divide the love that both father and mother had for Pretty Dick. So that when Pretty Dick knelt down by his little bed at night, and put his little brown hands together, and said, 'God bless my dear father and mother, and God bless me and make me a good boy,' he prayed for the whole family, you see. So they all three loved each other very much – though they were poor people – and Pretty Dick's mother often said that she would not have any harm happen to Pretty Dick for Queen Victoria's golden crown. They had called him Pretty Dick when he was yet a baby on board the *Star of Peach*, emigrant ship, and the name had remained with him ever since. His father called him Pretty Dick, and his mother called him Pretty Dick, and the people at the home station called him Pretty Dick, and even the cockatoo that lived on the perch over Lassie's bark kennel, would call out 'Pretty Dick! Pretty Dick! Pretty Dick!' over and over again.

Now, on this particular morning, Pretty Dick sat gazing between the trunks of the gum trees into the blue distance. It was very hot. The blue sky was cloudless, and the sun seemed to be everywhere at once. There was a little shade, to be sure, among the gum-tree trunks, but that would soon pass, and there would be no shade anywhere. The little fenced-in waterhole in the front of the hut glittered in the sunlight like a piece of burnished metal, and the tin milk-pail that was turned topsy-turvy on the pole-paling, was quite dazzling to look at. Daisy, the cow, stood stupidly under the shade of a round, punchy little she-oak close by, and seemed too lazy even to lie down, it was so hot. Of course the blow-flies had begun, and their ceaseless buzz resounded above and around, making it seem hotter than ever, Pretty Dick thought.

How hot father must be! Pretty Dick knew those terrible plains well. He had been across them two or three times. Once in the early spring, when it was pleasant enough with a cool breeze blowing, and white clouds resting on the tops of the distant mountains, and the broad rolling levels of short, crisp, grass-land sweeping up from their feet to the horizon unceasingly. But he had been across there once in the summer, when the ground was dry and cracked, when the mountains seemed so close that he almost thought that he could touch them with his hand, when the heavens were like burning brass, and the air (crepitant with the ceaseless chirping of the grass-hopper) like the flame of a heated furnace. Pretty Dick felt quite a fresh accession of heat as he thought of it, and turned his face away to the right to cool himself by thinking of the Ranges. They were deep in the bush, past the creek that ran away the other side of the Sandy Rises; deep in the bush on the right hand, and many a weary stretch of sandy slope, and rough-grassed swamp, and solemn wood, and dismal, deserted scrub, was between him and them. He could see the lofty purple peak of Mount Clear, the highest in the range, grandly rising above the dense level tops of the gum-tree forest, and he thought how cool it must be in its mighty shadow. He had never been under the mountain. That there were some strange reaches of scrub, and sand, and dense thickets, and tumbled creeper-entwined rock in that swamp-guarded land, that lay all unseen under the shadow of the hills, he knew, for he had heard the men say so. Had he not heard how men had been lost in that awesome scrub, silent and impenetrable, which swallowed up its victims noiselessly? Had he not heard how shepherds had strayed or slept, and how at night the sheep had returned alone, and that search had been in vain, until perhaps some wandering horseman, all by chance, had lighted upon a rusty rag or two, a white skull, and perhaps a tin pannikin, with hopeless scratchings of name and date? Had he not been told fearful things about those ranges? How the bushrangers had made their lair in the Gap, and how the cave was yet visible where their leader had been shot dead by the troopers; how large sums of stolen money were buried there, hidden away behind slags and slabs of rock, flung into fathomless gullies, or crammed into fissures in the mountain side, hidden so well, that all the searching hands and prying eyes of the district had not yet discovered them? Did not Wallaby Dick tell him one night about the Murder that had been done down in the flat under the large Australian moon – when the two swag-men, after eating and drinking, had got up in the bright, still night, and beaten out the brains of the travelling hawker, who gave them hospitality, and how, the old man being found beside his rifled cart, with his gray hairs matted with blood, search was made for the Murderers, and they were taken in a tap-room in distant Hamilton-town bargaining with the landlord for the purchase of their plunder?

What stories had he not heard of wild cattle, of savage bulls, red-eyed, pawing, and unapproachable? What hideous tales of snakes, black, cold, and deadly, had not been associated in his mind with that Mountain Land? What a strange, dangerous fascinating, horrible, wonderful place that Mountain Land must be, and how much he would like to explore it! But he had been forbidden to go, and he dismissed, with a childish sigh, all idea of going.

He looked up at his clock – the sun. He was just over the top of the big gum-tree – that meant ten o'clock. How late! The morning was slipping away. He heard his mother inside singing. She was making the bread. It would be very hot in the hut when the loaf was put in the camp-oven to bake. He had nothing to do either. He would go down to the creek; it was cool there. So he went into the hut and got a big piece of sweet cake, and put it in the pocket of his little jumper.

'Mother,' said Pretty Dick, 'I am going down to the creek.'

'Take care you don't get lost!' said she, half in jest, half in earnest.

'Lost! No fear!' said Pretty Dick.

– And when he went out, his mother began to sing again.

It was beautifully cool down by the creek. Pretty Dick knew that it would be. The creek had come a long way, and was tired, and ran very slowly between its deep banks, luscious with foliage, and rich with grass. It had a long way to go, too. Pretty Dick knew where it went. It ran right away down to the river. It ran on into the open, desolate, barren piece of ground where the road to the station crossed it, and where its bright waters were all red and discoloured with the trampling of horses and cattle. It ran by the old stockyard, and then turned away with a sudden jerk, and lost itself in the Five Mile Swamp, from whence it re-appeared again, broader and bigger, and wound along until it met the river.

But it did not run beyond the swamp now, Dick knew, because the weather had been so hot, and the creeks were all dried up for miles round – his father said – all but this one. It took its rise in the mountains, and when the rainfall was less than usual, grew thinner and thinner, until it became what it was now, a slender stream of water, trickling heavily betwen high banks – quite unlike the dashing, brawling, black, bubbling torrent that had rushed down the gully in flood-time.

Pretty Dick took off his little boots, and paddled about in the water, and found out all kinds of curious, gnarled roots of old trees, and funny holes under the banks. It was so cool and delicious under the stems and thick leaves of the water frondage that Pretty Dick felt quite restored again, and sang remembered scraps of his mother's songs, as he dodged round intervening trees, and slipped merrily between friendly trunks and branches. At last he came out into the open. Here his friend, the creek, divided itself into all sorts of queer shapes, and ran here, and doubled back again there, and twisted and tortured itself in an extraordinary manner, just out of pure fun and frolic.

There was a herd of cattle camped at this place, for the trees were tall, and big, and spreading. The cattle did not mind Pretty Dick at all, strange to say. Perhaps that was because he was on foot. If he had been on horseback now, you would have seen how they would have stared and wheeled about, and splashed off into the scrub. But when Pretty Dick, swinging a stick that he had cut, and singing one of his mother's songs, came by, they merely moved a little farther away, and looked at his little figure with long, sleepy eyes, slowly grinding their teeth from side to side the while. Now the way began to go up-hill, and there were big dead trees to get over, and fallen spreading branches to go round; for the men had been felling timber here, and the wasted wood lay thick upon the ground. At last Pretty Dick came to the Crossing Place. The crossing place was by the edge of the big swamp, and was a notable place for miles round. There was no need for a crossing place now though, for the limpid water was not a foot deep.

Pretty Dick had come out just on the top of a little sandy rise, and he saw the big swamp right before him speckled with feeding cattle, whose backs were just level with the tall rushes. And beyond the big swamp the ranges rose up, with the sunlight gleaming here and there upon jutting crags of granite, and with deep, cool shadows in other places, where the noble waving line of the hills sank in, and made dark recesses full of shade and coolness. The sky was bluer than ever, and the air was heavy with heat; and Pretty Dick wondered how the eagle-hawk that was poised – a floating speck above the mountain top – could bear to swoop and swing all day long in that fierce glare.

He turned down again, and crossing the creek, plunged into the bush. There was a subtle perfume about him now; not a sweet, rich perfume like the flowers in the home station garden, but a strange intoxicating smell, evolved from the heat and the water, and the many-coloured heath blossoms. The way was more difficult now, and Pretty Dick left the bank of the creek and made for the open space – sandy, and hunched with coarse clumps of grass. He went on for a long time, still upwards, and at last his little feet began to tire; and, after chasing a dragon-fly or two, and running a long way after a kangaroo rat, that started out from a patch of bloom, and ran in sharp diagonal lines away to hide itself in among the roots of a she-oak, he began to think of the piece of sweet cake in his pocket. So when, after some little time, emerging from out a dense mass of scrub, that scratched and tore at him as though it would hold him back, he found himself far up in the hills, with a great gully between him and the towering ranges, he sat down and came to the conclusion that he was hungry. But when he had eaten his sweet cake, he found that he was thirsty too, and that there was no water near him. But Pretty Dick knew there was water in the ranges; so he got up again, a little wearily, and went down the gully to look for it. But it was not so easy to find, and he wandered about for a long time, among big granite boulders, and all kinds of blind creeks, choked up with thick grass and creeping plants, and began to feel very tired indeed, and a little inclined to wish that he had not left the water-course so early. But he found it at last – a little pool, half concealed by stiff, spiky rush-grass, and lay down, and drank eagerly. How nice the first draught was! But at the second, the water felt warm, and at the third, tasted quite thick and slimy. There had been some ducks paddling about when he came up, and they flew away with a great quacking and splashing, that almost startled him. As soon as they had disappeared though, the place was quite still again, and the air grew heavier than ever.

He felt quite drowsy and tired, and laid himself down on a soft patch of mossy grass, under a tree; and so, after listening a little while to the humming of the insects, and the distant crackling of mysterious branches in the forest, he put his little head on his little arm, and went fast to sleep.

How long he slept Pretty Dick did not know, but he woke up suddenly with a start, and a dim consciousness that the sun had shifted, and had been pouring its heat upon him for some time. The moment he woke he heard a great crashing and plunging, and started up just in time to see a herd of wild cattle scouring off down the side of the range. They had come up to drink while he was asleep, and his sudden waking had frightened them. How late it must be! The place seemed quite changed. There was sunlight where no sunlight had been before, and shadow where had been sunlight. Pretty Dick was quite startled at finding how late it was. He must go home, or mother would be frightened. So he began to go back again. He knew his way quite well. No fear of his losing himself. He felt a little tired though, but that would soon wear off. So he left the little pool and turned homewards. He got back again into the gully, and clambered up to the top, and went on sturdily. But the trees did not seem familiar to him, and the succession of dips in the hills seemed interminable. He would soon reach the Big Swamp again, and then he could follow up the creek. But he could not find the Swamp. He toiled along very slowly now, and at last found the open plot of ground where he had stopped in the morning. But when he looked at it a little, it was not the same plot at all, but another something like it, and the grim ranges, heavy with shadow, rose all around him.

A terrible fear came into poor little Pretty Dick's heart, and he seemed to hear his mother say, quite plainly, 'Take care you don't get lost, Pretty Dick!' Lost! But he put the feeling away bravely, and swallowed down a lump in his throat, and went on again. The cattle-track widened out, and in a little time he found himself upon a jutting peak, with the whole panorama of the Bush at his feet. A grand sight! On the right hand towered the Ranges, their roots sunk deep in scrub and dense morass, and their heads lifted into the sky, that was beginning to be streaked with purple flushes now. On the left, the bush rolled away beneath him – one level mass of tree tops, broken here and there by an open space of yellow swamp, or a thin line of darker foliage, that marked the meanderings of some dried up creek. The sun was nearly level with his face, and cast a long shadow behind him. Pretty Dick felt his heart give a great jump, and then go on beating quicker and quicker. But he would not give in. Lost! – Oh no, he should soon be home, and telling his mother all the wonders of the walk. But it *was* so late! He must make haste. What was that! – Somebody on horseback. Pretty Dick shaded his eyes with his little hand, and peered down into the valley. A man with a white puggaree on his hat, was moving along a sort of cattle-track. Joy! – It was Mr Gaunt, the overseer. Pretty Dick cooeed. No answer. He cooeed again, – and again, but still the figure went on. Presently it emerged from the scrub, and the poor little fellow could see the rays of the setting sun gleam redly for an instant on a bright spur, like a dying spark. He gave a despairing shout. The horseman stopped, looked about him, and then glancing up at the fast clouding heavens, shook his horse's bridle, and rode off in a hand gallop.

Poor Pretty Dick! He knew that his cry had been unheard – mistaken, perhaps, for the scream of a parrot, the cry of some native bear, or strange bird, but in his present strait, the departure of the presence of something human, felt like a desertion. He fairly gave way, and sat down and cried. By-and-by he got up again, with quite a strange feeling of horror, and terror, and despair; he ran down the steep side of the range in the direction in which Mr Gaunt had gone, and followed his fast fading figure, calling, and crying with choked voice. Presently he lost him altogether, and then he felt his courage utterly fail. He had no idea of where he was. He had lost all power of thought and reason, and was possessed but by one overpowering terror, and a consciousness that whatever he did, he must keep on running, and not stop a moment. But he soon could run no longer. He could only stagger along from tree to tree in the gloomy woods, and cry, 'Mother! Mother!' But there was no mother to help him. There was no human being near him, no sound but the hideous croaking of the frogs in the marshes, and the crackling of the branches under his footsteps. The sun went down suddenly behind the hills, and the air grew cool at once. Pretty Dick felt as if he had lost a friend, and his tears burst forth afresh. Utterly tired and worn out, he sat down at the foot of a tree, and sobbed with sheer fatigue. Then he got up and ran round and round, like some hunted animals, calling, 'Mother! Mother!'

But there was no reply. Nothing living was near him, saving a hideous black crow who perched himself upon the branch of a withered tree, and mocked him, seeming to the poor boy's distorted fancy to say, 'Pretty Dick! Pretty Dick! Walk! walk! walk!'

In a burst of passionate, childish despair, he flung a piece of stick at the bird, but his strength failed him, and the missile fell short. This fresh failure made him cry again, and then he got up and ran – stumbling, and falling, and crying – away from the loathsome thing. But it followed him, flapping heavily from tree to tree, and perched quite close to him at last, croaking like an Evil Presence – 'Pretty Dick! Pretty Dick! Walk! walk! walk!'

The sweet night fell, and the stars looked down into the gullies and ravines, where poor Pretty Dick, all bruised, bleeding, and despairing, was staggering from rock to rock, sick at heart, drenched with dew, hatless, shoeless, tear-stained, crying, 'Mother! Mother! I am lost! I am lost! Oh, Mother! Mother!'

The calm, pitiless stars looked down upon him, and the broad sky spread coldly over him, and the birds flew away terrified at him; and the deadly chill of Loneliness fell upon him, and the cold, cruel, silent Night seemed to swallow him up, and hide him from human sympathy.

Poor Pretty Dick! No more mother's kisses, no more father's caresses, no more songs, no more pleasures, no more flowers, no more sunshine, no more love – nothing but grim Death, waiting remorselessly in the iron solitude of the hills. In the sad-eyed presence of the speechless stars, there, among the awful mystery and majesty of Nature, alone, a terrified little human soul, with the eternal grandeur of the forests, the mountains, and the myriad voices of the night, Pretty Dick knelt trembling down, and, lifting his little, tear-stained face to the great, grave, impassable sky, sobbed, 'Oh! take me home! Take me home! please, God, take me home!'

The night wore on – with strange sounds far away in the cruel bush, with screamings of strange birds, with gloomy noises, as of the tramplings of many cattle, with movements of leaves and snapping of branches, with unknown whirrings as of wings, with ripplings and patterings as of waterfalls, with a strange heavy pulsation in the air as though the multitudinous life of the forest was breathing around him. He was dimly conscious that any moment some strange beast – some impossible monster, enormous and irresistible, might rise up out of the gloom of the gullies and fall upon him; – that the whole horror of the bush was about to take some tangible shape and appear silently from behind the awful rocks which shut out all safety and succour. His little soul was weighed down by the nameless terror of a solitude which was no solitude, – but a silence teeming with monsters. He pictured the shapeless Bunyip lifting its shining sides heavily from the bottomless blackness of some lagoon in the shadow of the hills, and dragging all its loathsome length to where he lay. He felt suffocated; the silence that held all these indistinct noises in its bosom muffled him about like a murderous cloak; the palpable shadow of the immeasurable mountains fell upon him like a gravestone, and the gorge where he lay was like the Valley of the Shadow of Death. He screamed to break the silence, and the scream rang around him in the woods, and up above him in the mountain clefts, and beneath him in the mute mystery of the glens and swamps, – his cry seemed to be re-echoed again and again by strange voices never heard before, and repeated with indistinct mutterings and moanings in the caverns of the ranges. He dared not scream a second time lest he should wake some awful sound whose thunder should deafen him.

All this time he was staggering on, – not daring to look to right or left, or anywhere but straight on – straight on always. He fell, and tore his hands, and bruised his limbs, but the bruises did not hurt him. His little forehead was cut by a sharp stone, and his bright hair was all dusty and matted with blood. His knees shook and trembled, and his tongue clove to his mouth. He fell at every yard, and his heart seemed to beat so loud that the sound filled the air around him.

His strength was leaving him; he tottered from weakness; and at last emerging upon a little open platform of rock, white under the moon, he felt his head swim, and the black trunks, and the masses of fern-tree leaves, and the open ground, and the silent expanse of bush below him, all turned round in one crimson flash; and then the crimson grew purple-streaked, and spotted with sparks, and radiations, and bursting globes of light and colour, and then the Ranges closed in and fell upon him, and he was at once in his little bed at home – oh, so-fast-asleep!

But he woke at last, very cold and numbed, and with some feeling that he was not himself, but that he had been dreaming of a happy boy named Pretty Dick, who went away for a walk one afternoon many years ago. And then he felt for the blankets to pull them up about his shoulders, and his little fingers grasped a prickly handful of heather, and he woke with a terrible start.

Moonlight still, but a peaceful, solemn, sinking moon. She was low down in the sky, hanging, like a great yellow globe, over the swamp, that rose from far beneath him, straight up, it seemed, to a level with his face. Her clear cut rim rested on the edge of the morass now. He could almost touch her, she looked so close to him; but he could not lift his little arm so high, and besides, he had turned everything upside down before he went to sleep, and the moon was down below him and the earth up above him! To be sure! and then he shut his eyes and went to sleep again.

By-and-by it dawned. The birds twittered, and the dew sparkled, and the mists came up and wreathed themselves all about the trees, and Pretty Dick was up in the pure cool sky, looking down upon a little figure that lay on an open space among the heather. Presently, slowly at first, and then more quickly, he found out that this little figure was himself, and that he was in pain, and then it all came back with one terrible shock, and he was Lost again.

He could bear to think of it now, though. His terrors, born of darkness, had fled with the uprising of the glorious golden sun. There was, after all, no reason to be afraid. Boys had been lost before, and found again. His father would have missed him last night, and the station would be speedily roused. Oh, he would soon be found! He got up, very painfully and stiffly, and went to look for water. No difficulty in that; and when he had drunken and washed his face and hands, he felt much better. Then he began to get hungry, and to comfort himself with the thought that he would soon be found. He could almost hear the joyful shout, and the welcome, and the questioning. How slowly the time went on! He tried to keep still in one place, for he knew now that his terror-driven feet had brought him to this pass, and that he should have kept still in the place where he saw Mr Gaunt the night before.

At the recollection of that bitter disappointment, and the thought of how near he had been to succour, his tears began afresh. He tried hard to keep his terrors back – poor little fellow, – and thought of all kinds of things – of the stories his mother told him – of the calf-pen that father was putting up. And then he would think of the men at the station, and the remembrance of their faces cheered him; and he thought of Mrs Trelawney, and of his mother. O – suppose he should never see his mother again! And then he cried, and slept, and woke, and forgot his fears for awhile, and would listen intently for a sound, and spring up and answer a fancied shout, and then lie in a dull, stupid despair, with burning eyes, and aching head, and a gnawing pain that he knew was Hunger. So the hot day wore out. The same heat as yesterday, the same day as yesterday, the same sights and sounds as yesterday – but oh! how different was yesterday to today, – and how far off yesterday seemed. No one came. The shadows shifted, and the heat burnt him up, and the shade fell on him, and the sun sank again, and the stars began to shine, – and no one came near Pretty Dick. He had almost forgotten, indeed, that there was such a boy as Pretty Dick. He seemed to have lived years in the bush alone. He did not know where he was, or who he was. It seemed quite natural to him that he should be there alone, and he had no wish to get away. He had lost all his terror of the Night. He scarcely knew it was night, and after sitting on the grass a little longer, smiling at the fantastic shadows that the moonlight threw upon the ground, he discovered that he was hungry, and must go into the hut for supper. The hut was down in the gully yonder; he could hear his mother singing; – so Pretty Dick got up, and crooning a little song, went down into the Shadow.

They looked for him for five days. On the sixth, his father and another came upon something lying, half-hidden, in the long grass at the bottom of a gully in the ranges. A little army of crows flew away heavily. The father sprang to earth with a white face. Pretty Dick was lying on his face, with his head on his arm.

God had taken him home.

Jessie Couvreur ('Tasma')
Monsieur Caloche

CHAPTER I

A more un-English, uncolonial appearance had never brightened the prosaic interior of Bogg & Company's big warehouse in Flinders Lane. Monsieur Caloche, waiting in the
outer office, under fire of a row of curious eyes, was a
wondrous study of 'Frenchiness' to the clerks. His vivacious
dark eyes, shining out of his sallow face, scarred and seamed
by the marks of smallpox, met their inquisitive gaze with an
expression that seemed to plead for leniency. The diabolical
disease that had scratched the freshness from his face had
apparently twisted some of the youthfulness out of it as well;
otherwise it was only a young soul that could have been made
so diffident by the consciousness that its habitation was
disfigured. Some pains had been taken to obviate the effects
of the disfigurement and to bring into prominence the smooth
flesh that had been spared. It was not chance that had left
exposed a round white throat, guiltless of the masculine
Adam's apple, or that had brushed the fine soft hair, ruddily
dark in hue like the eyes, away from a vein-streaked temple.
A youth of unmanly susceptibilities, perhaps – but inviting
sympathy rather than scorn – sitting patiently through the
dreary silent three-quarters of an hour, with his back to the
wall which separated him from the great head of the firm of
Bogg & Co.

The softer-hearted of the clerks commiserated with him.
They would have liked to show their goodwill, after their own
fashion, by inviting him to have a 'drink', but – the possibility
of shouting for a young Frenchman, waiting for an interview

with their chief! . . . Anyone knowing Bogg, of Bogg & Co., must have divined the outrageous absurdity of the notion. It was safer to suppose that the foreigner would have refused the politeness. He did not look as though whisky and water were as familiar to him as a tumbler of *eau sucrée*. The clerks had heard that it was customary in France to drink absinthe. Possibly the slender youth in his loose-fitting French paletot reaching to his knees, and sitting easily upon shoulders that would have graced a shawl, had drunk deeply of this fatal spirit. It invested him with something mysterious in the estimation of the juniors, peering for traces of dissipation in his foreign face. But they could find nothing to betray it in the soft eyes, undimmed by the enemy's hand, or the smooth lips set closely over the even row of small French teeth. Monsieur Caloche lacked the happy French confidence which has so often turned a joke at the foot of the guillotine. His lips twitched every time the door of the private office creaked. It was a ground-glass door to the left of him, and as he sat, with his turned-up hat in his hand, patiently waiting, the clerks could see a sort of suppression overspreading his disfigured cheeks whenever the noise was repeated. It appeared that he was diffident about the interview. His credentials were already in the hands of the head of the firm, but no summons had come. His letter of recommendation, sent in fully half an hour back, stated that he was capable of undertaking foreign correspondence; that he was favourably known to the house of business in Paris whose principal had given him his letter of presentation; that he had some slight knowledge of the English language; that he had already given promise of distinguishing himself as an *homme de lettres*. This final clause of the letter was responsible for the length of time Monsieur Caloche was kept waiting. *Homme de lettres!* It was a stigma that Bogg, of Bogg and Co., could not overlook. As a practical man, a self-made man, a man who had opened up new blocks of country and imported pure stock into Victoria – what could be expected of him in the way of holding out a helping hand to a scribbler – a pauper who had spent his days in making rhymes in his foreign jargon? Bogg would have put your needy professionals into irons. He forgave no authors, artists, or actors who were not successful. *Homme de lettres!* Coupled with his poverty it was more unpardonable a title than jail-bird. There was nothing to prove that the latter title would not have fitted Monsieur Caloche as well. He was probably a ruffianly Communist. The French Government could not get hold of all the rebels, and here was one in the outer office of Bogg & Co. coolly waiting for a situation.

Not so coolly, perhaps, as Bogg, in his aggrieved state of mind, was ready to conclude. For the day was a hot-wind day, and Bogg himself, in white waistcoat and dust-coat, sitting in the cool depths of his revolving chair in front of the desk in his private office, was hardly aware of the driving dust and smarting grit emptied by shovelfuls upon the unhappy people without. He perspired, it is true, in deference to the state of his big thermometer, which even here stood above 85° in the corner, but having come straight from Brighton in his private brougham, he could wipe his moist bald head without besmearing his silk handkerchief with street grime. And it was something to be sitting here, in a lofty office, smelling of yellow soap and beeswax, when outside a north wind was tormenting the world with its puffs of hot air and twirling relays of baked rubbish and dirt. It was something to be surrounded by polished mahogany, cool to the touch, and cold iron safes, and maps that conveyed in their rippling lines of snowy undulations far-away suggestions of chill heights and mountain breezes. It was something to have iced water in the decanter at hand, and a little fountain opposite, gurgling a running reminder of babbling brooks dribbling through fern-tree valleys and wattle-studded flats. Contrasting the shaded coolness of the private office with the heat and turmoil without, there was no cause to complain.

Yet Bogg clearly had a grievance, written in the sour lines of his mouth, never too amiably expanded at the best of times, and his small, contracted eyes, full of shrewd suspicion-darting light. He read the letter sent in by Monsieur Caloche with the plentiful assistance of the tip of his broad forefinger, after a way peculiar to his early days, before he had acquired riches, or knighthood, or rotundity.

For Bogg, now Sir Matthew Bogg, of Bogg and Company, was a self-made man, in the sense that money makes the man, and that he had made the money before it could by any possibility make him. Made it by dropping it into his till in those good old times when all Victorian storekeepers were so many Midases, who saw their spirits and flour turn into gold under their handling; made it by pocketing something like three thousand per cent upon every penny invested in divers' blocks of scrubby soil hereafter to be covered by those grand and gloomy bluestone buildings which make of Melbourne a city of mourning; made it by reaching out after it, and holding fast to it, whenever it was within spirit-call or finger-clutch, from his early grog-shanty days, when he detected it in the dry lips of every grimy digger on the flat, to his later station-holding days, when he sniffed it in the drought which brought his neighbours low. Add to which he was lucky – by virtue of a certain inherent faculty he possessed in common with the Vanderbilts, the Stewarts, the Rothschilds of mankind – and far-seeing. He could forestall the news in the *Mark Lane Express*. He was almost clairvoyant in the matter of rises in wool. His luck, his foresight, were only on a par with his industry, and the end of all his slaving and sagacity was to give him at sixty years of age a liver, a paunch, an income bordering on a hundred thousand pounds, and the title of Sir Matthew Bogg.

It was known that Sir Matthew had worked his way to the colonies, acting indiscriminately as pig-sticker and deck-swabber on board the *Sarah Jane*. In his liverless, paunchless, and titleless days he had tossed for coppers with the flat-footed sailors on the forecastle. Now he was bank director, railway director, and a number of other things that formed a graceful flourish after Sir Matthew, but that would have sounded less euphonious in the wake of plain 'Bogg'. Yet 'plain Bogg' Nature had turned him out, and 'plain Bogg' he would always remain while in the earthly possession of his round, overheated face and long, irregular teeth. His hair had abandoned its lawful territory on the top of his head, and planted itself in a vagrant fashion, in small tufts in his ears and nostrils. His eyebrows had run riot over his eyes, but his eyes asserted themselves through all. They were eyes that, without being stronger or larger or bolder than any average pair of eyes to be met with in walking down the street, had such a knack of 'taking your measure' that no one could look at them without discomfiture. In the darkened atmosphere of the Flinders Lane office, Sir Matthew knew how to turn

these colourless unwinking orbs to account. To the mali-
ciously inclined among the clerks in the outer office there was
nothing more amusing than the crestfallen appearance of the
applicants, as they came out by the ground-glass door,
compared with the jauntiness of their entrance. Young men
who wanted colonial experience, overseers who applied for
managerships on his stations, youths fresh from school who
had a turn for the bush, had all had specimens of Sir Matthew's
mode of dealing with his underlings. But his favourite plan,
his special hobby, was to 'drop on to them unawares'.

There is nothing in the world that gives such a zest to life
as the possession of a hobby, and the power of indulging it.
We may be pretty certain that the active old lady's white
horse at Banbury Cross was nothing more than a hobby-
horse, as soon as we find out in the sequel that she 'had rings
on her fingers and bells on her toes', and that 'she shall have
music wherever she goes'. It is the only horse an old lady
could be perpetually engaged in riding without coming to
grief – the only horse that ever makes us travel through life
to the sound of music wherever we go.

From the days when Bogg had the merest shred of
humanity to bully, in the shape of a waif from the Chinese
camp, the minutes slipped by with a symphony they had
never possessed before. As fullness of time brought him an
increase of riches and power, he yearned to extend the terror
of his sway. It was long before he tasted the full sweetness
of making strong men tremble in their boots. Now, at nearly
sixty years of age, he knew all the delights of seeing victims,
sturdier and poorer than himself, drop their eyelids before
his gaze. He was aware that the men in the yard cleared out
of his path as he walked through it; that his managers up-
country addressed him in tones of husky conciliation; that
every eye met his with an air of deprecation, as much as to
apologise for the fact of existing in his presence; and in his
innermost heart he believed that in the way of mental
sensation there could be nothing left to desire. But how
convey the impression of rainbow-tints to eyes that have
never opened upon aught save universal blackness? Sir
Matthew had never seen an eye brighten, a small foot dance,
at his approach. A glance of impotent defiance was the only
equivalent he knew for a gleam of humid affection. He was

accustomed to encounter a shifting gaze. The lowest form of self-interest was the tie which bound his people to him. He paid them as butts, in addition to paying them as servants. Where would have been his daily appetiser in the middle of the day if there had been no yard, full of regulations impossible to obey; no warehouse to echo his harsh words of fault-finding; no servile men, and slouching fast-expanding boys, to scuttle behind the big cases, or come forth as if they were being dragged by hooks, to stand with sheepish expression before him? And when he had talked himself hoarse in town, where would have been the zest of wandering over his stations, of surveying his fat bullocks and woolly merinos, if there had been no accommodating managers to listen reverentially to his loudly-given orders, and take with dejected, apologetic air his continued rating? The savour of life would have departed – not with the bodily comfort and the consequence that riches bring, but with the power they confer of asserting yourself before your fellow-men after any fashion you please. Bogg's fashion was to bully them, and he bullied them accordingly.

But, you see, Monsieur Caloche is still waiting; in the position, as the junior clerks are well aware, of the confiding calf awaiting butchery in a frolicsome mood outside the butcher's shop. Not that I would imply that Monsieur Caloche frolicked, even metaphorically speaking. He sat patiently on with a sort of sad abstracted air; unconsciously pleating and unpleating the brim of his soft Paris hat, with long lissome fingers that might have broidered the finest silk on other than male hands. The flush of colour, the slight trembling of lips, whenever there was a noise from within, were the only signs that betrayed how acutely he was listening for a summons. Despite the indentations that had marred for ever the smoothness of the face, and pitted the forehead and cheeks as if white gravel had been shot into them, the colour that came and went so suddenly was pink as rose-coloured lake. It stained even the smooth white neck and chin, upon which the faintest traces of down were not yet visible to the scrutinising eyes of the juniors.

Outside, the north wind ran riot along the pavement, upsetting all orderly arrangements for the day with dreadful noise and fussiness, battering trimly-dressed people into red-eyed wretches heaped up with dust; wrenching umbrellas from their handles, and blinding their possessors trying to run after them; filling open mouths with grit, making havoc with people's hats and tempers, and proving itself as great a blusterer in its character of a peppery emigrant as in its original *rôle* of the chilly Boreas of antiquity.

Monsieur Caloche had carefully wiped away from his white wristband the dust that it had driven into his sleeve, and now the dust on his boots – palpably large for the mere slips of feet they enclosed – seemed to give him uneasiness; but it would seem that he lacked the hardihood to stoop and flick it away. When, finally, he extended surreptitiously a timid hand, it might have been observed of his uncovered wrist that it was singularly frail and slender. This delicacy of formation was noticeable in every exterior point. His small white ear, setting close to his head, might have been wrapped up over and over again in one of the fleshy lobes that stretched away from Sir Matthew's skull. Decidedly, the two men were of a different order of species. One was a heavy mastiff of lupine tendencies – the other a delicate Italian greyhound, silky, timorous, quivering with sensibility.

And there had been time for the greyhound to shiver long with expectancy before the mastiff prepared to swallow him up.

It was a quarter to twelve by the gloomy-faced clock in the outer office, a quarter to twelve by all the clerks' watches, adjusted every morning to the patriarch clock with unquestioning faith, when Monsieur Caloche had diffidently seated himself on the chair in the vicinity of the ground-glass door. It was·half-past twelve by the gloomy-faced clock, half-past twelve by all the little watches that toadied to it, when Sir Matthew's bell rang. It was a bell that must have inherited the spirit of a fire-bell or a doctor's night-bell. It had never been shaken by Sir Matthew's fingers without causing a fluttering in the outer office. No one knew what hair-suspended sword might be about to fall on his head before the messenger returned. Monsieur Caloche heard it ring, sharply and clamorously, and raised his head. The white-faced messenger, returning from his answer to the summons, and speaking with the suspension of breath that usually afflicted him after an interview with Sir Matthew, announced

that 'Mister Caloosh' was wanted, and diving into the gloomy
recess in the outer office, relapsed into his normal occupation
of breathing on his penknife and rubbing it on his sleeve.

Monsieur Caloche meanwhile stood erect, more like the
startled greyhound than ever. To the watchful eyes of the
clerks, staring their full at his retreating figure, he seemed to
glide rather than step through the doorway. The ground-
glass door, attached by a spring from the inside, shut swiftly
upon him, as if it were catching him in a trap, and so hid him
in full from their curious scrutiny. For the rest, they could
only surmise. The lamb had given itself up to the butcher's
knife. The diminutive greyhound was in the mastiff's grip.

Would the knife descend on the instant? Would the mastiff
fall at once upon the trembling foreigner, advancing with
sleek uncovered head, and hat held in front by two quivering
hands? Sir Matthew's usual glare of reception was more
ardent than of custom as Monsieur Caloche approached. If
every 'foreign adventurer' supposed he might come and loaf
upon Bogg, of Bogg & Company, because he was backed up
by a letter from a respectable firm, Sir Matthew would soon
let him find out he was mistaken! His glare intensified as the
adventurous stripling glided with softest footfall to the very
table where he was sitting, and stood exactly opposite to him.
None so adventurous, however, but that his lips were white
and his bloodless face a pitiful set-off to the cruelly prominent
marks that disfigured it. There was a terror in Monsieur
Caloche's expression apart from the awe inspired by Sir
Matthew's glare which might have disarmed a butcher or
even a mastiff. His large, soft eyes seemed to ache with
repressed tears. They pleaded for him in a language more
convincing than words, 'I am friendless – I am a stranger – I
am – ' but no matter! They cried out for sympathy and
protection, mutely and unconsciously.

But to Sir Matthew's perceptions visible terror had only one
interpretation. It remained for him to 'find out' Monsieur
Caloche. He would 'drop on to him unawares' one of these
days. He patted his hobby on the back, seeing a gratification
for it in prospective, and entering shortly upon his customary
stock of searching questions, incited his victim to reply
cheerfully and promptly by looking him up and down with
a frown of suspicion.

'What brought you 'ere?'

'Please?' said Monsieur Caloche, anxiously.

He had studied a vocabulary opening with 'Good-day sir. What can I have the pleasure of doing for you this morning?' The rejoinder to which did not seem to fit in with Sir Matthew's special form of inquiry.

'What brought you 'ere, I say?' reiterated Sir Matthew, in a roar, as if deafness were the only impediment on the part of foreigners in general to a clear comprehension of our language.

'De sheep, Monsieur! *La Reine Dorée,*' replied Monsieur Caloche, in low-toned, guttural, musical French.

'That ain't it,' said Sir Matthew, scornfully. 'What did you come 'ere for? What are you fit for? What can you do?'

Monsieur Caloche raised his plaintive eyes. His sad desolation was welling out of their inmost depths. He had surmounted the first emotion that had driven the blood to his heart at the outset, and the returning colour, softening the seams and scars in his cheeks, gave him a boyish bloom. It deepened as he answered with humility, 'I will do what Monsieur will! I will do my possible!'

'I'll soon see how you shape,' said Sir Matthew, irritated with himself for the apparent difficulty of thoroughly bullying the defenceless stranger. 'I don't want any of your parley-vooing in my office – do you hear! I'll find you work – jolly quick, I can tell you! Can you mind sheep? Can you drive bullocks, eh? Can you put up a post and rail? You ain't worth your salt if you can't use your 'ands!'

He cast such a glance of withering contempt on the tapering white fingers with olive-shaped nails in front of him that Monsieur Caloche instinctively sheltered them in his hat. 'Go and get your traps together! I'll find you a billet, never fear!'

'*Mais, Monsieur* – '

'Go and get your traps together, I say! You can come 'ere again in an hour. I'll find you a job up-country!' His peremptory gesture made any protest on the part of Monsieur Caloche utterly unavailing. There was nothing for him to do but to bow and to back in a bewildered way from the room. If the more sharp-eared of the clerks had not been in opportune contiguity to the ground-glass door during Sir

Matthew's closing sentences, Monsieur Caloche would have gone away with the predominant impression that 'Sir Bang' was an *enragé*, who disapproved of salt with mutton and beef, and was clamorous in his demands for 'traps', which Monsieur Caloche, with a gleam of enlightenment in the midst of his heart-sickness and perplexity, was proud to remember meant 'an instrument for ensnaring animals'. It was with a doubt he was too polite to express that he accepted the explanation tendered him by the clerks, and learned that if he 'would strike while the iron is hot' he must come back in an hour's time with his portmanteau packed up. He was a lucky fellow, the juniors told him, to jump into a billet without any bother; they wished to the Lord they were in *his* shoes, and could be drafted off to the Bush at a moment's notice.

Perhaps it seemed to Monsieur Caloche that these congratulations were based on the Satanic philosophy of 'making evil his good'. But they brought with them a flavour of the human sympathy for which he was hungering. He bowed to the clerks all round before leaving, after the manner of a court-page in an opera. The hardiest of the juniors ran to the door after he was gone. Monsieur Caloche was trying to make head against the wind. The warm blast was bespattering his injured face. It seemed to revel in the pastime of filling it with grit. One small hand was spread in front of the eyes – the other was resolutely holding together the front of his long, light paletot, which the rude wind had sportively thrown open. The junior was cheated of his fun. Somehow the sight did not strike him as being quite as funny as it ought to have been.

CHAPTER II

The station hands, in their own language, 'gave Frenchy best'. No difference of nationality could account for some of his eccentricities. As an instance, with the setting in of the darkness he regularly disappeared. It was supposed that he camped up a tree with the birds. The wit of the wool-shed surmised that 'Froggy' slept with his relatives, and it would be found that he had 'croaked' with them one of these odd times. Again, there were shearers ready to swear that he had 'blubbered' on finding some sportive ticks on his neck. He was given odd jobs of wool-sorting to do, and was found to have a mania for washing the grease off his hands whenever there was an instant's respite. Another peculiarity was his aversion to blood. By some strange coincidence, he could never be found whenever there was any slaughtering on hand. The most plausible reason was always advanced for necessitating his presence in some far-distant part of the run. Equally he could never be induced to learn how to box – a favourite Sunday morning and summer evening pastime among the men. It seemed almost to hurt him when damage was done to one of the assembled noses. He would have been put down as a 'cur' if it had not been for his pluck in the saddle, and for his gentle winning ways. His pluck, indeed, seemed all concentrated in his horsemanship. Employed as a boundary-rider, there was nothing he would not mount, and the station hands remarked, as a thing 'that beat them once and for all', that the 'surliest devils' on the place hardly ever played up with him. He employed no arts. His bridle-hand was by no means strong. Yet it remained a matter of fact that the least amenable of horses generally carried him as if they liked to bear his weight. No one being sufficiently learned to advance the hypothesis of magnetism, it was concluded that he carried a charm.

This power of touch extended to human beings. It was almost worth while spraining a joint or chopping at a finger to be bandaged by Monsieur Caloche's deft fingers. His horror of blood never stood in his way when there was a wound to be doctored. His supple hands, browned and strengthened by his outdoor work, had a tenderness and a delicacy in their way of going to work that made the sufferer feel soothed and half-healed by their contact. It was the same with his manipulation of things. There was a refinement in his disposition of the rough surroundings that made them look different after he had been among them.

And not understood, jeered at, petted, pitied alternately – with no confidant of more sympathetic comprehension than the horse he bestrode – was Monsieur Caloche absolutely miserable? Granting that it were so, there was no one to find it out. His brown eyes had such an habitually wistful expression, he might have been born with it. Very trifles brought a fleeting light into them – a reminiscence, perhaps that while it crowned him with 'sorrow's crown of sorrow', was yet a reflection of some past joy. He took refuge in his ignorance of the language directly he was questioned as to his bygone life. An embarrassed little shrug, half apologetic, but powerfully conclusive, was the only answer the most curious examiner could elicit.

It was perceived that he had a strong objection to looking in the glass, and invariably lowered his eyes on passing the cracked and uncompromising fragment of mirror supported on two nails against the planking that walled the rough, attached kitchen. So decided was this aversion that it was only when Bill, the blacksmith, asked him chaffingly for a lock of his hair that he perceived with confusion how wantonly his silken curls were rioting round his neck and temples. He cut them off on the spot, displaying the transparent skin beneath. Contrasted with the clear tan that had overspread his scarred cheeks and forehead, it was white as freshly-drawn milk.

He was set down on the whole as given to moping; but, taking him all round, the general sentiment was favourable to him. Possibly it was with some pitiful prompting of the sort that the working manager sent him out of the way one still morning, when Sir Matthew's buggy, creaking under the unwelcome preponderance of Sir Matthew himself, was discerned on its slow approach to the homestead. A most peaceful morning for the initiation of Sir Matthew's blustering presence! The sparse gum-leaves hung as motionless on their branches as if they were waiting to be photographed. Their shadows on the yellowing grass seemed painted into the soil. The sky was as tranquil as the plain below. The smoke from the homestead reared itself aloft in a long, thinly-drawn column of grey. A morning of heat and repose, when even the sunlight does not frolic and all nature toasts itself, quietly content. The dogs lay blinking at full length, their tails beating the earth with lazy, measured thumps. The sheep seemed rooted to the patches of shade, apathetic as though no one wore flannel vests or ate mutton-chops. Only the mingled voices of wild birds and multitudinous insects were upraised in a blended monotony of subdued sounds. Not a morning to be devoted to toil! Rather, perchance, to a glimmering perception of a golden age, when sensation meant bliss more than pain, and to be was to enjoy.

But to the head of the firm of Bogg & Company, taking note of scattered thistles and straggling wire fencing, warmth and sunshine signified only dry weather. Dry weather clearly implied a fault somewhere, for which somebody must be called to account. Sir Matthew had the memory of a strategist. Underlying all considerations of shorthorns and merinos was the recollection of a timid foreign lad to be suspected for his shy, bewildered air – to be suspected again for his slim white hands – to be doubly suspected and utterly condemned for his graceful bearing, his appealing eyes, that even now Sir Matthew could see with their soft lashes drooping over them as he fronted them in his darkened office in Flinders Lane. A scapegoat for dry weather, for obtrusive thistles, for straggling fencing! A waif of foreign scum to be found out! Bogg had promised himself that he would 'drop on to him unawares'. Physically, Bogg was carried over the ground by a fast trotter; spiritually, he was borne along on his hobby, ambling towards its promised gratification with airy speed.

The working manager, being probably of Bacon's way of thinking, that 'dissimulation is but a faint kind of policy', did not, in his own words, entirely 'knuckle down' to Sir Matthew. His name was Blunt – he was proud to say it – and he would show you he could make his name good if you 'crossed' him. Yet Blunt could bear a good deal of 'crossing' when it came to the point. Within certain limits, he concluded that the side on which his bread was buttered was worth keeping uppermost, at the cost of some hard words from his employer.

And he kept it carefully uppermost on this especial morning, when the quietude of the balmy atmosphere was broken by Sir Matthew's growls. The head of the firm, capturing his manager at the door of the homestead, had required him to mount into the double-seated buggy with him. Blunt reckoned that these tours of inspection in the companionship of Bogg were more conducive to taking off flesh than a week's hard training. He listened with docility, nevertheless, to plaints and ratings – was it not a fact that his yearly salaries had already made a nest-egg of large proportions? – and might have listened to the end, if an evil chance had not filled him with a sudden foreboding. For, picking his way over the plain, after the manner of Spencer's knight, Monsieur Caloche, on a fleet, newly broken-in two-year-old, was riding towards them. Blunt could feel that Sir Matthew's eyes were sending out sparks of wrath. For the first time in his life he hazarded an uncalled-for opinion.

'He's a good working chap, that, sir!' – indicating by a jerk of the head that the lad now galloping across the turf was the subject of his remark.

'Ah!' said Sir Matthew.

It was all he said, but it was more than enough.

Blunt fidgeted uneasily. What power possessed the boy to make him show off his riding at this juncture? If he could have stopped him, or turned him back, or waved him off! – but his will was impotent.

Monsieur Caloche, well back in the saddle, his brown eyes shining, his disfigured face flushed and glowing, with wide felt-hat drawn closely over his smooth small head, with slender knees close pressed to the horse's flanks, came riding on, jumping small logs, bending with flexible joints under straggling branches, never pausing in his reckless course, until on a sudden he found himself almost in front of the buggy, and, reining up, was confronted in full by the savage gleam of Sir Matthew's eyes. It was with the old scared expression that he pulled off his wideawake and bared his head, black and silky as a young retriever's. Sir Matthew knew how to respond to the boy's greeting. He stood up in the buggy and shook his fist at him; his voice, hoarse from the work he had given it that morning, coming out with rasping intensity.

'What the devil do you mean by riding my 'orses' tails off, eh?'

Monsieur Caloche, in his confusion, straining to catch the full meaning of the question, looked fearfully round at the hindquarters of the two-year-old, as if some hitherto unknown phenomenon peculiar to Australian horses might in fact have suddenly left them tailless.

But the tail was doing such good service against the flies at the moment of his observations, that, reassured, he turned his wistful gaze upon Sir Matthew.

'Monsieur,' he began apologetically, 'permit that I explain it to you. I did ga-lopp.'

'You can ga-lopp to hell!' said Sir Matthew with furious mimicry. 'I'll teach you to ruin my 'orses' legs!'

Blunt saw him lift his whip and strike Monsieur Caloche on the chest. The boy turned so unnaturally white that the manager looked to see him reel in his saddle. But he only swayed forward and slipped to the ground on his feet. Sir Matthew, sitting down again in the buggy with an uncomfortable sensation of some undue excess it might have been as well to recall, saw his white face for the flesh of an instant's space, saw its desperation, its shame, its trembling lips; then he was aware that the two-year-old stood riderless in front of him, and away in the distance the figure of a lad was speeding through the timber, one hand held against his chest, his hat gone and he unheeding, palpably sobbing and crying in his loneliness and defencelessness as he stumbled blindly on.

Runaway boys, I fear, call forth very little solicitude in any heart but a mother's. A cat may be nine-lived, but a boy's life is centuple. He seems only to think it worth keeping after the best part of it is gone. Boys run away from schools, from offices, from stations, without exciting more than an ominous prognostication that they will go to the bad. According to Sir Matthew's inference, Monsieur Caloche had 'gone to the bad' long ago – *ergo*, it was well to be rid of him. This being so, what utterly inconsistent crank had laid hold of the head of the great firm of Bogg & Company, and tortured him through a lengthy afternoon and everlasting night, with the vision of two despairing eyes and a scarred white face? Even his hobby cried out against him complainingly. It was not for this that it had borne him prancing along. Not to comfort him night and day with eyes so distressful that he could see nothing else. Would it be always so? Would they shine mournfully out of the dim recesses of his gloomy office in Flinders Lane, as they shone here in the wild bush on all sides of him? – so relentlessly sad that it would have been a relief to see them change into the vindictive eyes of the Furies who gave chase to Orestes. There was clearly only one remedy against such a fate, and that was to change the nature of the expression which haunted him by calling up another in its place. But how and when!

Sir Matthew prowled around the homestead the second morning after Monsieur Caloche's flight, in a manner unaccountable to himself. That he should return 'possessed' to his elaborate warehouse, where he would be alone all day – and his house of magnificent desolation, where he would be alone all night, was fast becoming a matter of impossibility. What sums out of all proportion would he not have forfeited to have seen the white-faced foreign lad, and to be able to pay him out for the discomfort he was causing him – instead of being bothered by the sight of his 'cursed belongings' at every turn! He could not go into the stable without seeing some of his gimcracks; when he went blustering into the kitchen it was to stumble over a pair of miniature boots, and a short curl of hair, in silken rings, fell off the ledge at his very feet. There was only one thing to be done! Consulting with Blunt, clumsily enough, for nothing short of desperation would have induced Sir Matthew to approach the topic of Monsieur Caloche, he learned that nothing had been seen or heard of the lad since the moment of his running away.

'And 'twasn't in the direction of the township, neither,' added Blunt, gravely. 'I doubt the sun'll have made him stupid, and he'll have camped down some place on the run.'

Blunt's insinuation anent the sun was sheer artifice, for Blunt, in his private heart, did not endorse his own suggestion in the least degree. It was his belief that the lad had struck a shepherd's hut, and was keeping (with a show of commonsense he had not credited him with) out of the way of his savage employer. But it was worth while making use of the artifice to see Sir Matthew's ill-concealed uneasiness. Hardly the same Sir Matthew, in any sense, as the bullying growler who had driven by his side not two days ago. For *this* morning the double-seated buggy was the scene of neither plaints nor abuse. Quietly over the bush track – where last Monsieur Caloche, with hand on his breast, had run sobbing along – the two men drove, their wheels passing over a wideawake hat, lying neglected and dusty in the road. For more than an hour and a half they followed the track, the dusty soil that had been witness to the boy's flight still indicating at intervals traces of a small footprint. The oppressive calm of the atmosphere seemed to have left even the ridges of dust undisturbed. Blunt reflected that it must have been 'rough on a fellow' to run all that way in the burning sun. It perplexed him, moreover, to remember that the shepherd's hut would be now far in their rear. Perhaps it was with a newly-born sense of uneasiness on his own account that he flicked his whip and made the trotter 'go', for no comment could be expected from Sir Matthew, sitting in complete silence by his side.

To Blunt's discerning eyes the last of the footprints seemed to occur right in the middle of the track. On either side was the plain. Ostensibly, Sir Matthew had come that way to look at the sheep. There was, accordingly, every reason for turning to the right and driving towards a belt of timber some hundred yards away, and there were apparently more forcible reasons still for making for a particular tree – a straggling tree, with some pretensions to a meagre shade, the sight of which called forth an ejaculation, not entirely coherent, from Blunt.

Sir Matthew saw the cause of Blunt's ejaculation – a recumbent figure that had probably reached 'the quiet haven of us all' – it lay so still. But whether quiet or no, it would seem that to disturb its peace was a matter of life or death to Sir Matthew Bogg. Yet surely here was satiety of the fullest for his hobby! Had he not 'dropped on to the "foreign adventurer" unawares'? So unawares, in fact, that Monsieur Caloche never heeded his presence, or the presence of his working manager, but lay with a glaze on his half-closed eyes in stiff unconcern at their feet.

The clerks and juniors in the outer office of the great firm of Bogg & Co. would have been at some loss to recognise their chief in the livid man who knelt by the dead lad's side. He wanted to feel his heart, it appeared, but his trembling fingers failed him. Blunt comprehended the gesture. Whatever tenderness Monsieur Caloche had expended in his short lifetime was repaid by the gentleness with which the working manager passed his hand under the boy's rigid neck. It was with a shake of the head that seemed to Sir Matthew like the fiat of his doom that Blunt unbuttoned Monsieur Caloche's vest and discovered the fair, white throat beneath. Unbuttoning still – with tremulous fingers, and a strange apprehension creeping chillily over him – the manager saw the open vest fall loosely asunder, and then –

Yes; then it was proven that Sir Matthew's hobby had gone its extremest length. Though it could hardly have been rapture at its great triumph that filled his eyes with such a strange expression of horror as he stood looking fearfully down on the corpse at his feet. For he had, in point of fact, 'dropped on to it unawares'; but it was no longer Monsieur Caloche he had 'dropped on to', but a girl with a breast of marble, bared in its cold whiteness to the open daylight, and to his ardent gaze. Bared, without any protest from the half-closed eyes, unconcerned behind the filmy veil which glazed them. A virgin breast, spotless in hue, save for a narrow purple streak, marking it in a dark line from the collarbone downwards. Sir Matthew knew, and the working manager knew, and the child they called Monsieur Caloche had known, by whose hand the mark had been imprinted. It seemed to Sir Matthew that a similar mark, red hot like a brand, must now burn on his own forehead for ever. For what if the hungry Australian sun, and emotion, and exhaustion had been the actual cause of the girl's death? He acknowledged, in the bitterness of his heart, that the 'cause of the cause' was his own bloodstained hand.

It must have been poor satisfaction to his hobby, after this, to note that Blunt had found a tiny pocket-book on the person of the corpse, filled with minute foreign handwriting. Of which nothing could be made? For, with one exception, it was filled with French quotations, all of the same tenor – all pointing to that one conclusion – and clearly proving (if it has not been proved already) that a woman who loses her beauty loses her all. The English quotation will be known to some readers of Shakespeare. 'So beauty blemished once for ever's lost!' Affixed to it was the faintly-traced signature of Henriette Caloche.

So here was a sort of insight into the mystery. The 'foreign adventurer' might be exonerated after all. No baser designs need be laid at the door of dead 'Monsieur Caloche' than the design of hiding the loss which had deprived her of all glory in her sex. If, indeed, the loss were a *real* one! For beauty is more than skin-deep, although Monsieur Caloche had not known it. It is of the bone, and the fibre, and the nerves that thrill through the brain. It is of the form and the texture too, as anyone would have allowed who scrutinised the body prone in the dust. Even the cruel scars seemed merciful now, and relaxed their hold on the chiselled features, as though 'eloquent, just, and mightie Death' would suffer no hand but his own to dally with his possession.

It is only in Christmas stories, I am afraid, where, in deference to so rollicking a season, everything is bound to come right in the end, that people's natures are revolutionised in a night, and from narrow-minded villains they become open-hearted seraphs of charity. Still, it is on record of the first Henry that from the time of the sinking of the *White Ship* 'he never smiled again'. I cannot say that Sir Matthew was never known to smile, in his old sour way, or that he never growled or scolded, in his old bullying fashion, after the discovery of Monsieur Caloche's body. But he was nonetheless a changed man. The outside world might rightly conjecture that henceforth a slender, mournful-eyed shadow would walk by his side through life. But what can the outside world know of the refinement of mental anguish that may be endured by a mind awakened too late? In Sir Matthew's case – relatively as well as positively. For constant contemplation of a woman's pleading eyes and a dead statuesque form might give rise to imaginings that it would be maddening to dwell upon. What a wealth of caresses those still little hands had had it in their power to bestow! What a power of lighting up the solemnest office, and – be sure – the greatest, dreariest house, was latent in those dejected eyes!

Brooding is proverbially bad for the liver. Sir Matthew died of the liver complaint, and his will was cited as an instance of the eccentricity of a wealthy Australian, who, never having been in France, left the bulk of his money to the purpose of constructing and maintaining a magnificent wing to a small-pox hospital in the south of France. It was stipulated that it should be called the 'Henriette' wing, and is, I believe, greatly admired by visitors from all parts of the world.

EDWARD DYSON
The Golden Shanty

About ten years ago, not a day's tramp from Ballarat, set well
back from a dusty track that started nowhere in particular
and had no destination worth mentioning, stood the Shamrock Hotel. It was a low, rambling, disjointed structure, and
bore strong evidence of having been designed by an amateur
artist in a moment of vinous frenzy. It reached out in several
well-defined angles, and had a lean-to building stuck on here
and there; numerous outhouses were dropped down about
it promiscuously; its walls were propped up in places with
logs, and its moss-covered shingle roof, bowed down with
the weight of years and a great accumulation of stones, hoop-
iron, jam-tins, broken glassware, and dried possum-skins,
bulged threateningly, on the verge of utter collapse. The
Shamrock was built on sun-dried bricks, of an unhealthy,
bilious tint. Its dirty, shattered windows were plugged in
places with old hats and discarded female apparel, and
draped with green blinds, many of which had broken their
moorings, and hung despondently by one corner. Groups of
ungainly fowls coursed the succulent grasshopper before the
bar door; a moody, distempered goat rubbed her ribs against
a shattered trough roughly hewn from the butt of a tree, and
a matronly old sow of spare proportions wallowed complacently in the dust of the road, surrounded by her squealing
brood.

A battered sign hung out over the door of the Shamrock,
informing people that Michael Doyle was licensed to sell
fermented and spirituous liquors, and that good accommo-
dation could be afforded to both man and beast at the lowest
current rates. But that sign was most unreliable; the man who

applied to be accommodated with anything beyond ardent beverages – liquors so fiery that they 'bit all the way down' – evoked the astonishment of the proprietor. Bed and board were quite out of the province of the Shamrock. There was, in fact, only one couch professedly at the disposal of the weary wayfarer, and this, according to the statement of the few persons who had ever ventured to try it, seemed stuffed with old boots and stubble; it was located immediately beneath a hen-roost, which was the resting-place of a maternal fowl, addicted on occasion to nursing her chickens upon the tired sleeper's chest. The 'turnover' at the Shamrock was not at all extensive, for, saving an occasional agricultural labourer who came from 'beyant' – which was the versatile host's way of designating any part within a radius of five miles – to revel in an occasional 'spree', the trade was confined to the passing 'cockatoo' farmer, who invariably arrived on a bony, drooping prad, took a drink, and shuffled away amid clouds of dust.

The only other dwellings within sight of the Shamrock were a cluster of frail, ramshackle huts, compiled of slabs, scraps of matting, zinc, and gunny-bag. These were the habitations of a colony of squalid, gibbering Chinese fossickers, who herded together like hogs in a crowded pen, as if they had been restricted to the spot on pain of death, or its equivalent, a washing.

About a quarter of a mile behind the Shamrock ran, or rather crawled, the sluggish waters of the Yellow Creek. Once upon a time, when the Shamrock was first built, the creek was a beautiful limpid rivulet, running between verdant banks; but an enterprising prospector wandering that way, and liking the indications, put down a shaft, and bottomed on 'the wash' at twenty feet, getting half an ounce to the dish. A rush set in, and within twelve months the banks of the creek, for a distance of two miles, were denuded of their timber, torn up, and covered with unsightly heaps. The creek had been diverted from its natural course half a dozen times, and hundreds of diggers, like busy ants, delved into the earth and covered its surface with red, white, and yellow tips. Then the miners left almost as suddenly as they had come; the Shamrock, which had resounded with wild revelry, became as silent as a morgue, and desolation brooded on the face of the country. When Mr Michael Doyle, whose greatest ambition in life had been to become lord of a 'pub', invested in that lucrative country property, saplings were growing between the deserted holes of the diggings, and agriculture had superseded the mining industry in those parts.

Landlord Doyle was of Irish extraction; his stock was so old that everybody had forgotten where and when it originated, but Mickey was not proud – he assumed no unnecessary style, and his personal appearance would not have led you to infer that there had been a king in his family, and that his paternal progenitor had killed a landlord 'wanst'. Mickey was a small, scraggy man, with a mop of grizzled hair and a little red, humorous face, ever bristling with auburn stubble. His trousers were the most striking things about him; they were built on the premises, and always contained enough stuff to make him a full suit and a winter overcoat. Mrs Doyle manufactured those pants after plans and specifications of her own designing, and was mighty proud when Michael would yank them up into his armpits, and amble round, peering about discontentedly over the waistband. 'They wus th' great savin' in weskits,' she said.

Of late years it had taken all Mr Doyle's ingenuity to make ends meet. The tribe of dirty, unkempt urchins who swarmed about the place 'took a power of feedin'', and Mrs D. herself was 'th' big ater'. 'Ye do be atin' twenty-four hours a day,' her lord was wont to remark, 'and thin yez must get up av noights for more. Whin ye'r not atin' ye'r munchin' a schnack, bad cess t'ye.'

In order to provide the provender for his unreasonably hungry family, Mickey had been compelled to supplement his takings as a Boniface by acting alternately as fossicker, charcoal-burner, and 'wood-jamber'; but it came 'terrible hard' on the little man, who waxed thinner and thinner, and sank deeper into his trousers every year. Then, to augment his troubles, came that pestiferous heathen, the teetotal Chinee. One hot summer's day he arrived in numbers, like a plague, armed with picks, shovels, dishes, cradles, and tubs, and with a clatter of tools and a babble of grotesque gibberish, camped by the creek and refused to go away again.

The awesome solitude of the abandoned diggings was ruthlessly broken. The deserted field, with its white mounds and decaying windlass-stands fallen aslant, which had lain like a long-forgotten cemetery buried in primeval forest, was now desecrated by the hand of the Mongol, and the sound of his weird, Oriental oaths. The Chows swarmed over the spot, tearing open old sores, shovelling old tips, sluicing old tailings, digging, cradling, puddling, ferreting into every nook and cranny.

Mr Doyle observed the foreign invasion with mingled feelings of righteous anger and pained solicitude. He had found fossicking by the creek very handy to fall back upon when the wood-jambing trade was not brisk; but now that industry was ruined by Chinese competition, and Michael could only find relief in deep and earnest profanity.

With the pagan influx began the mysterious disappearance of small valuables from the premises of Michael Doyle, licensed victualler. Sedate, fluffy old hens, hitherto noted for their strict propriety and regular hours, would leave the place at dead of night, and return from their nocturnal rambles never more; stay-at-home sucking-pigs, which had erstwhile absolutely refused to be driven from the door, corrupted by the new evil, absented themselves suddenly from the precincts of the Shamrock, taking with them cooking utensils and various other articles of small value, and ever afterwards their fate became a matter for speculation. At last a favourite young porker went, whereupon its lord and master, resolved to prosecute inquiries, bounced into the Mongolian camp, and, without any unnecessary preamble, opened the debate.

'Look here, now,' he observed, shaking his fist at the group, and bristling fiercely, 'which av ye dhirty haythen furriners cum up to me house lasht noight and shtole me pig Nancy? Which av ye is it, so't I kin bate him! ye thavin' hathins?'

The placid Orientals surveyed Mr Doyle coolly, and innocently smiling, said, 'No savee'; then bandied jests at his expense in their native tongue, and laughed the little man to scorn. Incensed by the evident ridicule of the 'haythen furriners', and goaded on by the smothered squeal of a hidden pig, Michael 'went for' the nearest Asiatic, and proceeded to 'put a head on him as big as a tank', amid a storm of kicks and digs from the other Chows. Presently the battle began to go against the Irish cause; but Mrs Mickey, making a timely appearance, warded off the surplus Chinamen by chipping at their skulls with an axe-handle. The riot was soon quelled, and the two Doyles departed triumphantly, bearing away a corpulent young pig, and leaving several broken, discouraged Chinamen to be doctored at the common expense.

After this gladsome little episode the Chinamen held off for a few weeks. Then they suddenly changed their tactics, and proceeded to cultivate the friendship of Michael Doyle and his able-bodied wife. They liberally patronised the Shamrock, and beguiled the licensee with soft but cheerful conversation; they flattered Mrs Doyle in seductive pigeon-English, and endeavoured to ensnare the children's young affections with preserved ginger. Michael regarded these advances with misgiving; he suspected the Mongolians' intentions were not honourable, but he was not a man to spoil trade – to drop the substance for the shadow.

This state of affairs had continued for some time before the landlord of the Shamrock noticed that his new customers made a point of carrying off a brick every time they visited his caravansary. When leaving, the bland heathen would cast his discriminating eye around the place, seize upon one of the sun-dried bricks with which the ground was littered, and steal away with a nonchalant air – as though it had just occurred to him that the brick would be a handy thing to keep by him.

The matter puzzled Mr Doyle sorely; he ruminated over it, but he could only arrive at the conclusion that it was not advisable to lose custom for the sake of a few bricks; so the Chinese continued to walk off with his building material. When asked what they intended to do with the bricks, they assumed an expression of the most deplorably hopeless idiocy, and suddenly lost their acquaintance with the 'Inglisiman' tongue. If bricks were mentioned they became as devoid of sense as wombats, although they seemed extremely intelligent on most other points. Mickey noticed that there was no building in progress at their camp, also that there was no bricks to be seen about the domiciles of the pagans, and he tried to figure out the mystery on a slate, but, on account of his lamentable ignorance of mathematics, failed to reach the unknown quantity and elucidate the enigma. He watched the invaders march off with all the loose bricks that were scattered around, and never once complained; but when they began to abstract one end of his licensed premises, he felt himself called upon, as a husband and father, to arise and enter a protest, which he did, pointing out to the Yellow Agony, in graphic and forcible language, the gross wickedness of robbing a struggling man of his house and home, and promising faithfully to 'bate' the next lop-eared Child of the Sun whom he 'cot shiftin' a'er a brick'.

'Ye dogs! Wud yez shtale me hotel, so't whin me family go insoide they'll be out in the rain?' he queried, looking hurt and indignant.

The Chinaman said, 'No, savee.' Yet, after his warning, doubtless out of consideration for the feelings of Mr Doyle, they went to great pains and displayed much ingenuity in abstracting bricks without his cognisance. But Mickey was active; he watched them closely, and whenever he caught a Chow in the act, a brief and one-sided conflict raged, and a dismantled Chinaman crawled home with much difficulty.

This violent conduct on the part of the landlord served in time to entirely alienate the Mongolian custom from the Shamrock, and once more Mickey and the Chows spake not when they met. Once more, too, promising young pullets, and other portable valuables, began to go astray, and still the hole in the wall grew till the after-part of the Shamrock looked as if it had suffered recent bombardment. The Chinamen came while Michael slept, and filched his hotel inch by inch. They lost their natural rest, and ran the gauntlet of Mr Doyle's stick and his curse – for the sake of a few bricks. At all hours of the night they crept through the gloom, and warily stole a bat or two, getting away unnoticed perhaps, or, mayhap, only disturbing the slumbers of Mrs Doyle, who was a very light sleeper for a woman of her size. In the latter case the lady would awaken her lord by holding his nose – a very effective plan of her own – and, filled to overflowing with the rage which comes of a midnight awakening, Mickey would turn out of doors in his shirt to cope with the marauders, and course them over the paddocks. If he caught a heathen he laid himself out for five minutes' energetic entertainment, which fully repaid him for lost rest and missing hens, and left a Chinaman too heart-sick and sore to steal anything for at least a week. But the Chinaman's friends would come as usual, and the pillage went on.

Michael Doyle puzzled himself to a prostration over this insatiable and unreasonable hunger for bricks; such an infatuation on the part of men for cold and unresponsive clay had never before come within the pale of his experience. Times out of mind he threatened to 'have the law on the yalla blaggards'; but the law was a long way off, and the Celestial housebreakers continued to elope with scraps of the Shamrock, taking the proprietor's assaults humbly and as a matter of course.

'Why do ye be shtealing me house?' fiercely queried Mr Doyle of a submissive Chow, whom he had taken one night in the act of ambling off with a brick in either hand.

'Me no steal 'em, no feah – odder fellar, him steal 'e,' replied the quaking pagan.

Mickey was dumb-stricken for the moment by this awful prevarication; but that did not impair the velocity of his kick – this to his great subsequent regret, for the Chinaman had stowed a third brick away in his clothes for convenience of transit, and the landlord struck that brick; then he sat down and repeated aloud all the profanity he knew.

The Chinaman escaped, and had presence of mind enough to retain his burden of clay.

Month after month the work of devastation went on. Mr Doyle fixed ingenious mechanical contrivances about his house, and turned out at early dawn to see how many Chinamen he had 'nailed' – only to find his spring-traps stolen and his hotel yawning more desperately than ever. Then Michael could but lift up his voice and swear – nothing else afforded him any relief.

At last he hit upon a brilliant idea. He commissioned a 'cocky' who was journeying into Ballarat to buy him a dog – the largest, fiercest, ugliest, hungriest animal the town afforded; and next day a powerful, ill-tempered canine, almost as big as a pony, and quite as ugly as any nightmare, was duly installed a guardian and night-watch at the Shamrock. Right well the good dog performed his duty. On the following morning he had trophies to show in the shape of a boot, a scrap of blue dungaree trousers, half a pigtail, a yellow ear, and a large part of a partially-shaved scalp; and just then the nocturnal visits ceased. The Chows spent a week skirmishing round, endeavouring to call the dog off, but he was neither to be begged, borrowed, nor stolen; he was too old-fashioned to eat poisoned meat, and he prevented the smallest approach of familiarity on the part of a Chinaman by snapping off the most serviceable portions of his vestments, and always fetching a scrap of heathen along with them.

This, in time, sorely discouraged the patient Children of the Sun, who drew off to hold congress and give the matter weighty consideration. After deliberating for some days, the yellow settlement appointed a deputation to wait upon Mr Doyle. Mickey saw them coming, and armed himself with a log and unchained his dog. Mrs Doyle ranged up alongside, brandishing her axe-handle, but by humble gestures and a deferential bearing the Celestial deputation signified a truce. So Michael held his dog down, and rested on his arms to await developments. The Chinamen advanced, smiling blandly; they gave Mr and Mrs Doyle fraternal greeting, and squirmed with that wheedling obsequiousness peculiar to 'John' when he has something to gain by it. A pock-marked leper placed himself in the van as spokesman.

'Nicee day, Missa Doyle,' said the moon-faced gentleman, sweetly. Then, with a sudden expression of great interest, and nodding towards Mrs Doyle, 'How you sisetah?'

'Foind out! Fwhat yer wantin'?' replied the host of the Shamrock, gruffly; ''t' shtale more bricks, ye crawlin' blaggards?'

'No, no. Me not steal 'em blick – odder feller; he hide 'em' build big house byembye.'

'Ye loi, ye screw-faced nayger! I seed ye do it, and if yez don't cut and run I'll lave the dog loose to feed on yer dhirty carcasses.'

The dog tried to reach for his favourite hold, Mickey brandished his log, and Mrs Doyle took a fresh grip of her weapon. This demonstration gave the Chows a cold shiver, and brought them promptly down to business.

'We buy 'em hotel; what for you sell 'em – eh?'

'Fwhat! yez buy me hotel? D'ye mane it? Purchis th' primisis and yez can shtale ivery brick at yer laysure. But ye're joakin'. Whoop! Look ye here! I'll have th' lot av yez aten up in two minits if yez play yer Choinase thricks on Michael Doyle.'

The Chinamen eagerly protested that they were in earnest,

and Mickey gave them a judicial hearing. For two years he had been in want of a customer for the Shamrock, and he now hailed the offer of his visitors with secret delight. After haggling for an hour, during which time the ignorant Hi Yup of the contorted countenance displayed his usual business tact, a bargain was struck. The yellow men agreed to give fifty pounds cash for the Shamrock and all buildings appertaining thereto, and the following Monday was the day fixed for Michael to journey into Ballarat with a couple of representative heathens to sign the transfer papers and receive the cash.

The deputation departed smiling, and when it gave the news of its triumph to the other denizens of the camp there was a perfect babel of congratulations in the quaint dialogue of the Mongol. The Chinamen proceeded to make a night of it in their own outlandish way, indulging freely in the seductive opium, and holding high carouse over an extemporised fantan table, proceedings which made it evident that they thought they were getting to windward of Michael Doyle, licensed victualler.

Michael, too, was rejoicing with exceeding great joy, and felicitating himself on being the shrewdest little man who ever left the 'ould sod'. He had not hoped to get more than a twenty-pound note for the dilapidated old humpy, erected on Crown land, and unlikely to stand the wear and tear of another year. As for the business, it had fallen to zero, and would not have kept a Chinaman in soap. So Mr Doyle plumed himself on his bargain, and expanded till he nearly filled his capacious garments. Still, he was harassed to know what could possibly have attached the Chinese so strongly to the Shamrock. They had taken samples from every part of the establishment, and fully satisfied themselves as to the quality of the bricks, and now they wanted to buy. It was most peculiar. Michael 'had never seen anything so quare before, savin' wanst whin his grandfather was a boy'.

After the agreement arrived at between the publican and the Chinese, one or two of the latter hung about the hotel nearly all their time, in sentinel fashion. The dog was kept on the chain, and lay in the sun in a state of moody melancholy, narrowly scrutinising the Mongolians. He was a strongly anti-Chinese dog, and had been educated to regard the almond-eyed invader with mistrust and hate; it was repugnant to his principles to lie low when the heathen was around, and he evinced his resentment by growling ceaselessly.

Sunday dawned. It was a magnificent morning; but the rattle of the Chinamen's cradles and toms sounded from the creek as usual. Three or four suave and civil Asiatics, however, still lingered around the Shamrock, and kept an eye on it in the interests of all, for the purchase of the hotel was to be a joint-stock affair. These 'Johns' seemed to imagine they had already taken lawful possession; they sat in the bar most of the time, drinking little, but always affable and genial. Michael suffered them to stay, for he feared that any fractiousness on his part might upset the agreement, and that was a consummation to be avoided above all things. They had told him, with many tender smiles and much gesticulation, that they intended to live in the house when it became theirs; but Mr Doyle was not interested – his fifty pounds was all he thought of.

Michael was in high spirits that morning; he beamed complacently on all and sundry, appointed the day as a time of family rejoicing, and in the excess of his emotion actually slew for dinner a prime young sucking-pig, an extravagant luxury indulged in by the Doyles only on state occasions. On this particular Sunday the younger members of the Doyle household gathered round the festive board and waited impatiently for the lifting on the lid of the camp-oven. There were nine children in all, ranging in years from fourteen downwards – 'foine, shtrappin' childer, wid th' clear brain', said the prejudiced Michael. The round, juicy sucker was at last placed upon the table. Mrs Doyle stood prepared to administer her department – serving the vegetables to her hungry brood – and, armed with a formidable knife and fork, Michael, enveloped in savoury steam, hovered over the pig.

But there was one function yet to be performed – a function which came as regularly as Sunday's dinner itself. Never, for years, had the housefather failed to touch up a certain prodigious knife on one particular hard yellow brick in the wall by the door, preparatory to carving the Sunday's meat. Mickey examined the edge of his weapon critically, and found it unsatisfactory. The knife was nearly ground through to the backbone; another 'touch-up' and it must surely collapse, but, in view of his changed circumstances, Mr Doyle felt that he might take the risk. The brick, too, was worn an inch deep. A few sharp strokes from Mickey's vigorous right arm were all that was required; but, alas! the knife snapped, whereupon Mr Doyle swore at the brick, as if holding it immediately responsible for the mishap, and stabbed at it fiercely with the broken carver.

'Howly Moses! Fwhat's that?'

The brick fell to pieces, and there, embedded in the wall, gleaming in the sunbeam, was a nugget of yellow gold. With feverish haste Mickey tore the brick from its bedding, and smashed the gold-bearing fragment on the hearth. The nugget was a little beauty, smooth, round, and four ounces to a grain.

The sucking-pig froze and stiffened in its fat, the 'taters' and the cabbage stood neglected on the dishes. The truth had dawned upon Michael, and, whilst the sound of a spirited debate in musical Chinese echoed from the bar, his family were gathered around him, open-mouthed, and Mickey was industriously, but quietly, pounding the sun-dried brick in a digger's mortar. Two bricks, one from either end of the Shamrock, were pulverised, and Michael panned off the dirt in a tub of water which stood in the kitchen. Result: seven grains of waterworn gold. Until now Michael had worked dumbly, in a fit of nervous excitement; now he started up, bristling like a hedgehog.

'Let loose th' dog, Mary Melinda Doyle!' he howled, and, uttering a mighty whoop, he bounded into the bar to dust those Chinamen off his premises.

'Gerrout!' he screamed – 'Gerrout av me primises, ye thavin' crawlers!' And he frolicked with the astounded Mongolians like a tornado in full blast, thumping at a shaven occiput whenever one showed out of the struggling crowd. The Chinamen left, they found the dog waiting for them outside, and he encouraged them to greater haste. Like startled fawns the heathens fled, and Mr Doyle followed them howling:

'Buy the Shamrock, wud yez! Robbers! Thaves! Fitch back th' soide o' me house, or Oi'll have th' law onto yez all.'

The damaged escapees communicated the intelligence of

their overthrow to their brethen on the creek, and the news carried consternation, and deep, dark woe to the pagans, who clustered together and ruefully discussed the situation.

Mr Doyle was wildly jubilant. His joy was only tinctured with a spice of bitterness, the result of knowing that the 'haythens' had got away with a few hundreds of his precious bricks. He tried to figure out the amount of gold his hotel must contain, but again his ignorance of arithmetic tripped him up, and already in imagination Michael Doyle, licensed victualler, was a millionaire and a J.P.

The Shamrock was really a treasure-house. The dirt of which the bricks were composed had been taken from the banks of the Yellow Creek, years before the outbreak of the rush, by an eccentric German who had settled on that sylvan spot. The German died, and his grotesque structure passed into other hands. Time went on, and then came the rush. The banks of the creek were found to be charged with gold for miles, but never for a moment did it occur to anybody that the clumsy old building by the track, now converted into a hotel, was composed of the same rich dirt; never till years after, when by accident one of the Mongolian fossickers discovered grains of gold in a few bats he had taken to use as hobs. The intelligence was conveyed to his fellows; they got more bricks and more gold – hence the robbery of Mr Doyle's building material and the anxiety of the Mongolians to buy the Shamrock.

Before nightfall Michael summoned half a dozen men from 'beyant', to help him in protecting his hotel from a possible Chinese invasion. Other bricks were crushed and yielded splendid prospects. The Shamrock's small stock of liquor was drunk, and everybody became hilarious. On the Sunday night, under cover of the darkness, the Chows made a sudden sally on the Shamrock, hoping to get away with plunder. They were violently received, however; they got no bricks, and returned to their camp broken and disconsolate.

Next day the work of demolition was begun. Drays were backed up against the Shamrock, and load by load the precious bricks were carted away to a neighbouring battery. The Chinamen slouched about, watching greedily, but their now half-hearted attempts at interference met with painful reprisal. Mr Doyle sent his family and furniture to Ballarat, and in a week there was not a vestige left to mark the spot where once the Shamrock flourished. Every scrap of its walls went through the mill, and the sum of one thousand nine hundred and eighty-three pounds sterling was cleared out of the ruins of the hostelry. Mr Doyle is now a man of some standing in Victoria, and as a highly respected J.P. has often been pleased to inform a Chinaman that it was 'foive pound or a month'.

WILLIAM ASTLEY ('PRICE WARUNG')
Parson Ford's Confessional

I

It is beyond question that Parson Ford's resolve to keep up the amount of his fee for performing marriages was responsible for the annoyance which visited him on the occasion of our story.

Eight pounds sterling was his fee. Parson Knopwood would do the work for three and take payment in currency; and it was generally the easiest thing for an expert bridegroom to relieve the old man of the money as he was returning home the same evening. When Parson Bob performed the ceremony, he invariably celebrated the event at the 'Hole in the Wall', the favourite public-house, where his welcome was always warm and his chalk-score deep, and he would seldom proceed homewards to Cottage Green till the everlasting stars came out in their glory and flaunted their drunkenness in his shame-striken eyes. At least that was what the cheery old chaplain used to say as he stumbled over Macquarie Street cobble-stones. 'Wheresh O-rion? Shure I saw O-rion (*hic*) jush now! – 'sh gone! Shtrange – th' bleshed (*hic*) stars dansh about so. Tell Gov-en-or!' And then perhaps the bridegroom, who had paid him about eleven o'clock that morning £3 in paper notes or dollars, would take his arm respectfully to help the reverend gentleman along – and himself to the £3. Sometimes, indeed, the bridegroom would not wait to tender his assistance. This was when the fee had been paid in forged notes, as several times happened.

Now, Parson Ford was a steady, pure, and sober man, and was not in the least inclined, when he became Principal

111

Chaplain on Bobby Knopwood's official retirement, to view with aught but displeasure the irregularities which his predecessor had tolerated. He never got drunk; he knew the difference between forged currency notes and general currency by the 'feel' – he could tell by the touch, so he said, any one tradesman's notes from every other man's – and he went home by dusk, or if detained after dark by pastoral duty, only after he had emptied the contents of his pockets and his fob into the keeping of a trusty acquaintance or officer of the garrison. Consequently, being possessed of these defects, he was not at this time beloved by the lower, or, indeed, any orders of society. Not till later did even the official classes come to believe in him. A community in which the heads liked to be drunk by midday, where matrimonial arrangements seldom were entered into except for the purpose of securing an additional grant of land or a right to other property, and where it was unsafe for a person to be out of doors after nightfall, because of his liability to be robbed, if not by unofficial criminals, by the men of the watch, was not prepared to take to its bosom at once a strong-minded cleric, whose pockets were never worth robbing, who would not drink to excess, whose only vice was snuffing, and who was so much of a Puritan that he had even admonished his Honour the Lieutenant-Governor for having a plurality of paramours. And when Parson Ford was so ill-advised as to raise the marriage-fee to eight pounds sterling, he placed the coping-stone to the edifice of his unpopular life. One and all, high and low, Lieutenant-Governor and lumber-yard transport, who would not have married his 'jomar' if the marriage-fee had been nothing, indignantly resented the step.

Why people who disdained marriage should have been thus irritated we do not positively know. We can only suppose it was by reason of that perverse trait of humanity which prompts it to value the thing which is beyond reach. If only a few couples could get married, nearly everybody would either wish to go through the ceremony or affect the desire to do so. Perhaps some such consideration had influenced Parson Ford in raising his fee. He assessed matrimony at a pecuniary value far beyond the reach of the mass of persons, and instantly they began to denounce the

avarice and the injustice and the wickedness which prevented them from obtaining the blessing of the Church on
their very irregular alliances. They forgot they had not rushed
to the altar when the terms were only three pounds.

II

'I hear, Mr Ford,' remarked his Honour, as the parson paid
him the usual morning visit exacted from all Hobart Town
gentlemen who drew pay from the Colonial chest, 'that you
have caused it to be known that your marriage-fee is to be
eight pounds in future?'

'That is my fixture, your Honour,' replied the chaplain.

'But I do not know whether I can allow it! You know that
the Governor in Sydney has fixed the fee at four pounds?'

'Guineas, your Honour,' gently corrected the parson. 'But
that is within two described parishes. I am sure of my legal
rights on the matter.'

'But the moral effect, Mr Chaplain – the effect! Have you
sufficiently thought of that? A heavy fee is – ahem – an
impediment to marriage!'

One great virtue had Parson Ford. He looked over a lot of
things in persons of authority, but, when put on his mettle
he never winced before a Governor, whether he was only a
'Lieutenant', or whether he was the omnipotent 'General'. He
faced his Honour now, and said distinctly, with an
uncourtier-like acidity of tone: 'Would it have proved so in
your case, your Honour? If so, I'll reduce it!'

And his Honour took the unpleasant thrust pleasantly. His
wine-reddened face was not unusually flushed as he
responded: 'Well, well, if you must have it so, you must, I
s'pose, Mr Ford. But don't you think you can make it
currency, instead of sterling?'

'With all respect, sir, I do not think I can. My object is to
make the ceremony valued in the eyes of the people, and I
conceive there is no better way of doing it than to attach an
expense to its performance. You have seen, your Honour, that
Mr Knopwood's low charges did not encourage marriages.
Now, we will see what *my* method will do.'

'Very well, Mr Ford, very well, have your own way. I think
you are mistaken, but it's your lookout, and not mine. I'm

not – h'm – my brother's keeper – of his morals, at all events. That's your duty.'

And with this, his Honour bowed his reverence out, helped himself to a glass of Spanish wine from a bottle which, one of a dozen, had been presented to him by his former comrade-in-arms, John Macarthur, in Sydney – Capt'n John had bought it at a sale of certain prize booty in the year '5, and treasured it greatly – and set to work to devise a scheme by which to revenge himself upon the clergyman. Davey was not given to vindictiveness, but he dearly liked a jest, and when by the same stroke he could have both his joke and his revenge, he would have fallen below the level of his drunken, rollicking, immoral old self if he had refrained from applying it. He had all the qualities of a good Governor except dignity, firmness, purity, honour, sobriety, and magnanimity.

As the result of his reflections he outlined a plan which, in the bosom of his irregularly constituted family circle at Government House, was fairly elaborated that same night. It was necessary, you see, for him to use an intermediary in the business. He rather prided himself on his free-and-easy manners. Had he not made his *début* in the colony in his shirt-sleeves, excusing himself on the score of its being too —— hot to wear full regimentals? Had he not established the custom of drinking and smoking in court? Was it not he who had stopped the trial-gang on their way to the wharf, and treated each of the unfortunates to a drink of rum-punch and a churchwarden pipe at Half-Hanged Jack's beershop? Did he not accept kindly their thankful 'God bless yer Honour!' and wish them in return a fair trial, and, if God and the Judge pleased, an easy death? And was it not, too, his identical old blackguard self who, instead of enclosing to Sydney with the depositions of evidence against a convicted forger, the forged note for *threepence*, put the note, and therefore the evidence, into the fire, with the remark that a throat that could give out 'Tom Bowling' so well, was too good to be fitted with a throat necklace? As a matter of fact, 'free and easy' was an absurdly weak term to apply to Lieutenant-Governor Davey's relaxed manners. Nevertheless, he felt it was 'not quite the cheese' – the phrase is not ours but the Governor's – for him to place himself in direct communication with the principal in the plot he had contrived for the discomfiture of Parson Ford. 'No, Julia,' he said to the presiding madam of the week – his two 'ladies' took week about in doing the honours of his private table (his legal family living quite apart) – 'it won't be quite the cheese, my duck, for me to see the little dears at the Factory. One of you will have to do that for me.'

'Oh,' simpered madam – she was the identical pretty piece of frailty respecting whom Captain Colnett, of HMS *Glatton*, had quarrelled with Governor King, and the twelve years since the row had only matured her charms – 'anythin' to please yer, dear Gov'nor – an' really, ye know, none of us leddies like Parson Sniff an' Snuff! Bobby's my 'dea of a parson. Ain't he yours, dear Gov'nor?'

'I'm with ye, madam, in everything, as ye know,' replied the Governor – whose gallant speeches were not yet intermingled with hiccoughs. 'Ah, old Bobby never interfered between me an' ye, did he, dear? But ye'll attend to the Factory, Ju, without fail before Monday evening? Ye know, 'twould never do for his Honour, the Gov., to be known in the business.'

'Oh, lud, your Honour, how squeamish we're gettin' all at once,' tittered the sorceress of the week; 'why, ye'll be turnin' saint yourself soon an' 'll cry "Fie!" an' blush when I do this.'

And, bending forward, she pressed with her ruby lips the viceregal forehead. Madame Julia knew the ways of Government in early Van Demonian days. Also which side her bread was buttered. She was better off with Colonel Davey than with Captain Colnett, R.N. Immeasurably.

III

What the official lights-o'-love achieved the sequel will show. The Governor did, however, make a specific contribution to the plot, but he kept the knowledge of it from his Cleopatras. He chuckled mightily as he added his fragment of fuel to the flame which was to scorch Parson Ford. He penned the following –

'Private.

'*Government House*, THURSDAY.
'REVEREND SIR, – The words that passed between us on a delicate

subject have afected me, and have not failed to impress me. As one means of helping to releeve me from his reverence's sensure it is likely that a warm discourse on the subject by which you will understand I mean the iregular connections which your reverence does not approve of, on Sunday coming, would strengthen my hands, for I have come to the conclusion that my honourable position does demand from me conduct which would not remain open to your Reverence's objection.

'Your Reverence's obedient servant,

'(Sd) THOMAS DAVEY, Lieutt-Gov.

'To the REVEREND THEOPHILUS FORD,
at St Davids Parsonage.'

Like the illustrious Wellington, Colonel Davey was weak in orthography and in grammar, but the Rev. Mr Ford was too well acquainted with official eccentricities of the kind to dwell upon those features of the document. What impressed him was the possibility it held out of a reform in popular morals. And he resolved to accept the hint, 'and to give it 'em warm'.

It was on the succeeding Sunday that he rose to the occasion. It was the first Sunday in the month, consequently a muster-Sunday, and pretty well everybody in Hobart Town was crowded into the church or within its precincts. A muster-Sunday for the bond or ticket-of-leave classes was, of course, compulsory, and those who were emancipated or 'free' by 'servitude' were almost as regular in attendance, for, besides the fun of the thing, there was the gratification of witnessing the subjection of others to a procedure once so galling to themselves. Then the few people who 'came free' and the 'garrison ladies' came also to witness the spectacle. It was *so* amusing, you will understand, to note the distress of some poor 'ticket-of-leave', as, from some more or less real peccadillo, his 'ticket' was withdrawn, perhaps a little home or business sacrificed, and he himself re-consigned to the purgatory of the lumber-yard or the hell of the road-gang. In an epoch when popular entertainments were rare, the Sunday muster was highly valued by all except those who were compelled to attend it.

On this Sunday the muster was before Church. The Muster-Master, as though in anticipation of the coming storm, was righteously indignant in the cases of a couple of dissolute fellows, who, having permission to marry, had gone no nearer the altar than the broomstick. They pleaded Parson Ford's increased fee, but 'twas no use. Their tickets were withdrawn, and they were ordered to present themselves before the Police Magistrate in the morning for sentence.

This incident had so agreeably entertained the 'free' people, 'irregularly-attached' or not, that they would have been prepared to enjoy even a less thrilling sermon than that Mr Ford preached to them. Therefore, when he gave out his text from Ecclesiastes vii. and 26th –

> 'And I find more bitter than death the woman whose heart is snares and nets, and her hands as bonds; whoso pleaseth God shall escape from her; but the sinner shall be taken by her' –

they settled down with an unusual zest. They knew by instinct something interesting was coming.

Illustrating his theme by pretty well every Scriptural passage having the remotest relation to it, the preacher denounced the iniquity of 'irregular connections'. Then, by way of contrast, he painted the virtues of the typical British home, drew tears from many eyes by a description of the conjugal felicity which prevailed in the palace of the Sovereign – he was discreetly silent as to the Regent – and, having insinuated a refined advertisement of his reasons for raising the marriage-fee – 'that which costs nothing or next to nothing,' he said, 'is never valued,' – he concluded with a most touching peroration. With eyes alternately directed to the roof and upon the viceregal pew, he thanked Heaven that he had it from the best, he might say the *very best*, authority that *henceforth* the Local Representative of that pure and pious Personage whose virtues added lustre to the Crown of England, contemplated reflecting *in his person and establishment* the example of his Gracious Sovereign. With so striking an exemplar on the spot, he reminded his hearers that there would be no excuse for their permitting their irregular unions to remain unblessed by the Church and unsanctioned by the Law.

The effect was tremendous. New South Wales and Van Demonia in the early days had, of course, no opportunity of showing how a C —— could throw an aristocratic splendour over the gallows, or how a H —— could transform by grace of manner a niggardliness of expenditure into a refined economy; but yet they possessed, all things considered, as devoted a regard for the representative of the throne as we can claim today. The eye of the congregation seemed fixed upon the broad shoulders of the Lieutenant-Governor as he sat a few yards away from the pulpit. A kindly shadow from a pillar prevented, however, all save those in the immediate vicinity observing that the viceregal form shook as though with suppressed emotion. Frequent applications of a yellow handkerchief to his eyes further testified to the impression the sermon had made upon him. Was the Colonel really going to reform? Was he smitten with sorrow for the past, and moved by passionate desire for better things in the future? It seemed so, indeed, and one portly merchant – a conditional pardon man from Sydneyside – reflected ruefully that, eight pounds or no eight pounds, he'd be obliged to follow the Governor's example, if the great man really meant to abandon his harem.

But the merchant and those who noticed his Honour's emotion need not have been afraid. True, he did wipe tears from his eyes, but – it pains us to say it – they were of mirth. The Colonel of Marines was all the time wondering to himself how Jess and Ju were taking the sermon. He had never gone so far as to install them in the viceregal pew – the ladies of his family proper would have drawn the line at that – but he knew they were in church. He'd have given a day's pay in sterling money, and not in those rascally rupees which were worth no more than eighty per cent of their nominal value, to have been able to look round and wink at the sweet creatures. But that he dare not do: it would have spoilt the sport, for did he catch their eyes in return he would to a certainty burst into laughter. Accordingly, he had to wait till afternoon.

IV

The Parson dined with his Excellency, and received the latter's great compliments for the unstinted and fervid morality of the discourse. The Colonel now coincided with

Mr Ford as to the wisdom of the increased fee, and expressed a hope that not many months would elapse before it would be – er – as difficult to find an irregularly-attached couple in Hobart Town as a needle in the proverbial truss of hay! And the joy which is generated by the consciousness that a good work is meeting with the applause of the high and mighty settled upon Parson Ford's soul as he bade his Honour goodbye, and betook himself to the church for afternoon service. It was a joy undimmed by the least doubt as to the sincerity of the Governor's conversion.

After second service he was asked to tea at the table of one of the two married ladies of the garrison. The garrison was, matrimonially considered, very badly organised indeed. With the exception of two, the ladies who looked after the comfort of the officers, drawing married men's lodging and fuel allowances, however frequently they quarrelled among themselves, had one characteristic in common. They possessed no certificate of marriage – at least, they owned no certificates that sanctified their present relationships. And now, in consequence of Parson Ford's sermon, the virtuous and duly married two were more determined than ever to look down upon their unlicensed sisters of the quarters. Accordingly, as a preliminary, they mutually arranged an applausive tribute to that dear man, the clergyman, who at last had put his foot resolutely down 'on the shocking, *the really too shocking,* state of things that prevailed in the town, and *particularly* within our *brother officers'* quarters, you know, dear'. Mrs Lieutenant Bobbin had wished to do the honours, and invited Mrs Captain D'Ewes, her sister in matrimonial distinction, to take tea with her and the dear parson, but Mrs Captain D'Ewes, by virtue of her husband's rank, pressed for the privilege of first entertainment, which Mrs Bobbin at once effusively and affectionately conceded. And so at half-past five o'clock the Rev. Theophilus found himself seated at a table with Mrs D'Ewes and Captain D'Ewes, and Mrs Bobbin and her Lieutenant. It may be remarked, by the way, that the Lieutenant's experience of wedded life was rather regarded in the town as strong evidence of the advantages of single blessedness.

Mr Ford having said grace (the circumstance from its unusual nature deserves to be chronicled), and accepted some of the hospitalities of the table, his hostess lost no time in expressing her congratulations on his proper, very proper, course that day. And did he really think his Honour would alter the disgraceful, very disgraceful, condition of Government House society?

'I am, ma'am, firmly convinced in my own mind he really contemplates a change of conduct,' affirmed the Parson.

'Then – then – those women – Oh, really, Mr Ford, I blush for my sex to think such things are possible! And will his Honour *at once* dismiss them to the Factory?' Thus spoke the virtuous Bobbin dame.

'I am quite of opinion that he will do so. In fact, I may tell you – in confidence, ladies, of course – that I believe they have already been returned there!'

'No!' exclaimed both ladies in a breath.

'Indeed, I think so. As I was taking off my surplice in the vestry, the matron of the Factory came in and said that the Governor's ladies – you know, ma'am, that the way those low-class women *will* speak of these disgraces to their sex – '

'Yes, indeed!' indignantly said Mrs D'Ewes, 'this misuse of words ought to be put down! And the matron said?'

'That those sinful women had been driven out to the Factory. The matron, bringing in the rest of the Protestant women for afternoon service as usual, met them half-way. They looked in a fine fluster – to use Mrs Chubb's words – just as though the consequences of their sin had at last fallen upon them.'

'Ah!' said Mrs D'Ewes, 'there comes an end to all wrongdoing sooner or later.'

'Why,' said the Lieutenant, 'didn't the matron stop and ask them why they were going out?'

'Oh, Lieutenant, you don't know what a trouble 'tis to that poor woman to get those drabs of Factory girls to church! – she could not attend to anything else! She has to bring them in two batches – morning and afternoon – for it would take her whole staff to march the lot in together, and she must, of course, leave two or three wards-women behind to look after the sick ones.'

'We'd always tell off a corporal's guard to help her,' said Captain D'Ewes flippantly. 'Our men would not object to

guard-duty there. "Guardians of beauty, if not of virtue", and
so on, eh, Bobbin?'

Bobbin, with his spouse's eye upon him, dare not acquiesce
verbally, but in his heart he approved of his comrade's
sentiment. Of course, their respective wives were not aware
that among the Lotharios of the camp, D'Ewes and Bobbin
were included, even though they were married. Had he
wished to reply, however, he would not have found it
possible to do so, for Mrs D'Ewes sharply remonstrated with
her husband.

'I think, Captain,' she said, 'that you should keep your wit
for the low associates of the barrick-room. Remember, a
clergyman is present, if you have no respect for ladies. And
now, dear Mr Ford, I *should* like so much to know whether
those – those creatures are really at the Factory! You, I
suppose, will find out in due course?'

'Oh, tomorrow, ma'am, is my usual Factory day – Monday
succeeding Muster-Sunday, y' know!'

'Oh, yes.' broke in that ribald D'Ewes, 'tomorrow's your
confessional day, is it, Mr Ford?'

'My what – sir?' returned the astonished Parson, who was
nothing, if he was not a sturdy Evangelical.

'That, I believe, sir, is the term given in the town to
your – ah – method of interrogating those frisky young
madams at the Factory, of whom you're so fond.'

'Sir!' exclaimed the insulted Parson, rising.

'D'Ewes!' appealed his better-half.

'Captain D'Ewes!' ejaculated the horrified Mrs Bobbin,
whose husband simply chuckled to himself under cover of
the storm.

And though D'Ewes apologised, and handsomely withdrew the imputation, which he averred, was merely a jocular
nothing, the Parson's sense of injury was not appeased until
both Mrs D'Ewes and Mrs Bobbin had consented to accompany him to the Factory on the morrow. 'Then, ladies, I beg
you'll interrogate every woman for yourselves. Ask them
what questions you like as to my treatment of them, and
see if I've ever acted in a manner unbefitting my sacred
office!'

As a simple fact, Parson Ford could not have played more
nicely into his adversaries' hands than when he extended that

invitation. Davey's plan had been merely to suggest a very naughty idea to the frail fair ones in Mrs Chubb's charge, and to trust to chance for the result finding its way to the knowledge of the townspeople. But here Ford himself had provided the means for his own discomfiture.

v

On the Monday afternoon, the Rev. Theophilus, accompanied by Mesdames D'Ewes and Bobbin, was respectfully welcomed by Mrs Chubb. As the matron made her final curtsey, she said –

'Twelve new ones, your Rev'runce!'

'All – ahem – er – delicate?'

Mrs Chubb simpered and looked down. 'Yes, sir!' she said.

'Now, ladies,' and Mr Ford turned to the garrison ladies, 'of course you don't understand what Mrs Chubb means?'

'No – not exactly, Mr Ford,' said Mrs D'Ewes.

'Well, I must tell you, ma'am. You know, of course, why so many girls are sent back to the Factory from service?'

Mrs Bobbin blushed. Mrs D'Ewes didn't, but replied 'Yes.'

'Well, in the interests, first of morality, and then of the finances of the colony, I'm determined to put a stop to that sort of thing, ladies!'

'Quite right, I'm sure,' said Mrs D'Ewes.

'Quite right, sir,' echoed Mrs Bobbin.

'Now, there's only one way, and that is to punish the fathers of the children. But to reach the fathers you must know their names.'

'Of course, Mr Ford!' said both ladies together.

'That is why, then, I have what the Captain very improperly called my confessional, Mrs D'Ewes. I interrogate each girl separately as to the paternity of her child. Now, today, I will ask you ladies to pursue my inquiries for me. Have you any objection, ladies? Then you can tell the Captain the nature of my method.'

'No objection at all,' chorused the gentle beings.

'Then, as there are twelve to be examined, may I suggest you take six, Mrs D'Ewes, and you the other six, Mrs Bobbin, and I'll simply look on!'

The twelve girls – they were nearly all on the youthful side of womanhood – were ranged in a row, each standing by the foot of her pallet. Some were quivering with suppressed shame – or laughter. Others were biting their lips. But all were silent till the interrogation began.

Humming a hymn, Parson Ford walked up and down. His back was to the line of women, and consequently he did not see the startled looks which were bestowed upon him and then upon each other by the two ladies. By the time, however, he turned in his walk, each interrogator had examined her second girl, and as she obtained a reply, she glanced so strangely at the clergyman that he could not help but notice her manner. He put the singularity of the look down, however, to some surprising revelation. 'Revelations' under the like circumstances were so common, that they had long since ceased to be surprising to him.

As Mrs Bobbin interrogated her third girl, Mrs D'Ewes finished the examination of her fourth. They exchanged a look of horror – then moving simultaneously into the centre of the room, they exclaimed together –

'Oh, Mr Ford! You wretch!' called Mrs D'Ewes.

'Mr Ford, you're a hypocritical villain!' cried Mrs Bobbin, and she hysterically searched for her handkerchief.

'Ladies!' exclaimed Parson Ford, not believing his ears.

'Yes, sir, I'm glad I came today to unmask a scoundrel! Each of these four girls says *you* are the father of her child!' cried Mrs D'Ewes.

'Madam!'

'And – oh – infamous! – these three girls all say – they – owe – their – ruin to you!' gasped Mrs Bobbin, in tears.

'And I say the same!' said a girl as yet uninterrogated.

'He's the father of my child too!' said another.

'And of ours!' cried the rest in chorus.

Under this terrible avalanche of accusation Parson Ford was dumb!

Governor Davey and his 'leddies' had calculated only on surprising Parson Ford himself – by bribing the girls with a ticket-of-leave apiece to allege that he, the clergyman, was responsible for her presence in the lying-in ward of the Factory. They had not contemplated so astonishing a success for their little plot, as was achieved through Ford's invitation to the garrison ladies.

Not for many years was Ford allowed to forget this episode. Governor Arthur, fifteen years afterwards, referred, at a birthday dinner, to Parson Ford as one of the 'fathers of the colony', and was immensely surprised at the uproarious laughter his compliment elicited from all colonists present – save Ford.

JOHN ARTHUR BARRY
Far Inland Football

'Frightfully dull, isn't it?' said the Doctor.

'Dull's no name for it,' said the Clerk of Petty Sessions; 'this is the awfullest hole I ever was in.'

'Never knew it so bad,' chimed in the Chemist and the Saddler, who were on this frosty night drinking whisky hot in the snug parlour of the Shamrock Inn in the little township of Crupperton.

'I tell you what,' said the C.P.S. presently; 'I see by the paper they've started a football club at Cantleville. Why shouldn't we do the same? It'll help to pass away the time, anyhow.'

The Doctor pricked up his ears with interest. The Chemist seconded the motion enthusiastically.

'A capital idea,' said he, 'and, although I never have played, I'll go in for it. It's simple enough, I should imagine.'

'Simple!' said the C.P.S., who had once seen a match in Sydney. 'It's as easy as tea-drinking. There's no expense, except the first one of the ball. It's not like cricket, you know, where you're always putting your hands in your pockets for something or other.'

'I'll give ten shillings, Mr Brown,' said the Doctor softly.

'Same here,' said the Chemist.

'How do you play it?' asked the Saddler, and the Blacksmith, and the Constable, who had just dropped in for a warm and a yarn that chilly evening.

'Well,' explained the C.P.S., who had ideas, 'first you get your ball. Then you put up a couple of sticks with a cross one on the top of 'em. Then you measure a distance, say one hundred yards by, say, fifty, on a level bit of ground, and put up another set of sticks. Then you get your men, and pick

125

sides, and pop the ball down in the middle, and wade in. For instance,' he continued, 's'pose we're playing Saddlestrap. Well, then, d'ye see, we've got one goal – that's what they call the sticks – and they've got the other. We're to try and block 'em from kicking the ball over our cross-bar, and do our best, meantime, to send it over theirs. It's just a splendid game for this weather, and nothing could well be simpler.'

More men came in, the idea caught; a club was formed, and that very night the C.P.S. wrote to the capital for a ball 'of the best make and the latest fashion'.

But it was a very long way to the capital. So, in the interval, the C.P.S., who was an enterprising young Native, procured and erected goal-posts and cross-bars of barked pine; and very business-like they looked with a little pink flag fluttering from the summit of each.

At last the new ball arrived. But, to the secret astonishment of the C.P.S., in place of being round it was oval. However, he was not going to expose his ignorance and imperil the reputation already earned as an exponent of the game, so he only said, –

'I sent for the very best they had, and I can see we've got our money's worth. I'll take her home and blow her up ready for tomorrow.'

For a long time the ball seemed to go in any direction but the right one, kick they never so hardly; whilst, as a rule, the strongest and most terrific kickers produced the least effect.

They tried the aggravating thing in every position they could think of, and, for a considerable period, without much success.

It was a sight worth seeing to watch the Blacksmith, after scooping a little hollow in the ground and placing the ball perpendicularly therein, retire and prepare for action. Opening his shoulders and spitting on his hands, he would come heavily charging down, and putting the whole force of fifteen stone into his right foot, deliver a tremendous kick; then stand amazed to see the ball, after twirling meekly up for a few yards, drop on his head instead of soaring between the posts as it should have done.

'I'm out of practice myself – haven't played for years, in fact,' said the C.P.S. when explanation as to this erratic behaviour was demanded. 'It's simply a matter of practice, you know, like everything else.'

But all the same for a long time, deep down in his heart, there was a horrible misgiving that the thing was not a football at all – that it should have been round. At last, by dint of constant perseverance, some of the men began to kick fairly well – kick goals even from a good distance.

The first difficulty arose from a lack of side-boundaries. Hence, at times, a kicking, struggling, shouting mob might be seen half-a-mile away, at the far end of the main street, whereas it should have been in front of the post-office.

To remedy this state of affairs, the C.P.S. drove in pegs at what was voted 'a fair thing' to serve as guides. When the ball was sent beyond the pegs no one pursued, and little boys stationed there kicked it back again. Also, the cows, pigs and goats of Crupperton, who must have imagined that a lunatic asylum had taken possession of their feeding grounds, returned, and henceforth fed peacefully about the grass-grown streets and allotments at the lower end of the township. Presently, to vary the monotony, the Crupper-tonians got up a match amongst themselves for drinks – East *versus* West was the title of it. But it never went beyond the first scrimmage, if that can be called a first where all was one big scrimmage, caused by two compact bodies of men fighting for the possession of a ball. Out of this quickly emerged the Chemist with, as he averred, a fractured wrist. Anyhow, he wore a bandage, and played no more.

Then the Blacksmith accused the Saddler of kicking him on the shins, wilfully and of malice prepense. For some time past there had been bad blood between these two, and the fight that ensued was so gorgeous that the game was quite forgotten in the excitement of it.

Presently, the village of Saddlestrap, a little lower down the river, in emulation of its larger neighbour, started football also.

The Saddlestraps mostly got their living by tankmaking, were locally known as 'Thicklegs', and were a pretty rough lot. So that, when a match was arranged between the two places, fun was foretold.

The rules of the Saddlestrap club were, like those of the Crupperton one, simplicity itself, consisting, as they did, of the solitary axiom – 'Kick whatever or wherever you can, only kick.'

Therefore, as remarked, fun was expected. The C.P.S. chose his team carefully, and with an eye to weight and size. Superior fleetness, he rightly imagined, would have but little to do with the result of the day's sport.

With the exception of half-a-dozen of the townspeople, the Crupperton players consisted of young fellows from a couple of stations adjoining. Therefore, the Saddlestraps somewhat contemptuously dubbed their opponents 'Pastorialites'.

The Doctor pleaded exemption on account of his age, and was, therefore, appointed 'Referee'.

For a while the play was somewhat weak and desultory, and lacking in effect. The ball was continually being sent outside the pegs, and the urchins stationed there were kept busy. But, at length, to the delight of the spectators, consisting of the entire population of the two townships, there was a hot scrimmage. 'For all the world like a lot o' dorgs a-worryin' a 'possum!' as one excited bystander yelled, whilst the crowd surged around the mixed-up heap of humanity, the outside ring of which was frantically kicking and shoving at the prostrate inner one, serving friend and foe alike.

'A very manly and interesting game,' remarked the Doctor, placidly ringing his bell for 'Spell, oh!' whilst the Chemist ran to his shop for plaster and bandage.

Presently, the undermost man of all was dragged out, torn and gory, and spitting teeth from a broken jaw.

Him the Doctor caused to be carried to the nearest house, and, after attending to his wounds, returned hurriedly to the field, where his coadjutor was looking to the minor casualties, and both teams were refreshing themselves with rum, and boasting of their prowess.

The Doctor rang his bell, and play was resumed. It was, he explained, unhealthy to dawdle about in such weather and after severe exertion.

As the C.P.S. pointed out very eloquently that night at the banquet, football was a game in which people must learn to give and take, and that, until this had been fully understood and practised, the game would never get beyond an initial stage.

This was probably the reason that on a Saddlestrap in full

pursuit of the ball being deliberately tripped up by a 'Pastorialite', and sent headlong to mother earth, which was hard and knobby, in place of rising and going on with the game, he began to punch the tripper.

Five minutes afterwards might be seen the curious spectacle of a ball lying neglected in the centre of the ground, whilst outside raged a big fight of thirty.

For a time the trouble was strictly confined to the two teams. But when it was observed that Crupperton was getting the worst of it, partisans quickly peeled off and took sides; so that, directly, both townships were up to their eyes in fight, and the Doctor seriously contemplated sending for professional assistance to Cantleville.

For some time victory hovered in the balance. But men fight well on their own ground, and at last the Saddlestraps broke and fled for their horses and buggies. Those who stayed behind did so simply because there was no doctor in their native village.

A banquet for both teams had been prepared at the leading (and only) hotel. But there was only a remnant of one side that felt like banqueting, so the gaps were filled by residents who had been prominent in the fray.

The C.P.S., with a couple of beautifully blackened eyes, took the chair. At the other end of the table presided the Constable, whose features presented a curiously intricate study in diachylon, many of the Saddlestraps having seized a mean opportunity of wiping off old scores.

Speeches and toasts were made and drunk, and football enthusiastically voted the king of all games. As the Blacksmith – whose arm was in a sling – observed, 'It was a fair an' square game. A man know'd what he'd got to do at it. There wasn't no tiddleywinkin' in the thing.'

The Doctor had been too busy to come early; but he dropped in for a minute or so during the evening, and with great fire, and amidst much applause, made a splendid speech. In its course he quoted Gordon's well-known lines – 'A game's not worth a rap for a rational man to play', etc.; and also adapted that saying of the 'Iron Duke's' about the battle of Waterloo being won upon the British football grounds.

It was decidedly the 'speech of the evening', and was

greeted with hearty cheers as, concluding, he retired to look after his patients.

But Crupperton was very sore next morning; and for a whole week there was no more football. Then they looked about them for more victims to their prowess. But they found none at all near home.

At last, in despair, and in defiance of the advice of the C.P.S., the executive challenged Cantleville itself – agreeing to journey thither. In due course, and after the C.F.C. had recovered from its surprise, and consulted a 'Gazetteer', it accepted.

Cantleville was a very long distance away. Moreover, it was the 'City' of those inland parts, and the headquarters of the Civil Service therein. Therefore the C.P.S. and the Constable discreetly refused to accompany their fellows. One of the pair, at least, had doubts as to whether Cantleville played the Crupperton game.

So the Blacksmith was elected Captain. 'You'd better stay at home,' said the C.P.S, 'the chaps over there are regular swells, up to all the latest dodges, and they wear uniforms. Besides they may not quite understand our rules.'

'Then we'll teach 'em,' said the Blacksmith. But the question of a uniform troubled him. So he took counsel with his now fast friend the Saddler, and the result was that everyone packed a stiffly-starched white shirt and a pair of black trousers into his valise.

'How about your uniforms now?' said the Blacksmith, 'nothin' can't be neater'n that.'

So they went forth to battle, accompanied by the good wishes of the populace; but neither by Doctor nor Chemist. There were plenty of both at Cantleville. Also they were wise in their generation, and had doubts.

Communication in these days was limited. Cantleville news arrived *via* Sydney, and the newspapers were a week old when delivered. So that the team brought its own tidings home. They had not had a good time. They had also been heavily fined, and they proposed to go afield no more. The Blacksmith and the Saddler, who had 'taken it out', were the last to appear.

'I suppose you play Rugby rules?' he asked blandly the Secretary of the C.F.C., as he curiously surveyed the 'Bushies' on their arrival.

'No, we don't,' said the Blacksmith. 'We plays Crupperton,' and no more questions were asked. But when it was seen what Crupperton rules meant, backs, half-backs, forwards, and all the rest of it, struck and refused to continue. Instead, they took to chaffing the 'black and white magpies'.

Whereupon, Crupperton, putting the question of football on one side, went at its opponents *à la* Saddlestrap. Their places, however, they presently found taken by policemen. These latter every man handled to the best of his ability, and had to pay for accordingly.

'Shoo!' said the Blacksmith, as he finished. 'They're nothin' but a lot o' tiddleywinkers up there. Let's have another match with Saddlestrap.'

ARTHUR HOEY DAVIS
('STEELE RUDD')
Dad and the Donovans

A sweltering summer's afternoon. A heat that curled and withered the very weeds. The corn-blades drooping, sulking still. Mother and Sal ironing, mopping their faces with a towel and telling each other how hot it was. The dog stretched across the doorway. A child's bonnet on the floor – the child out in the sun. Two horsemen approaching the slip-rails.

Dad had gone down the gully to Farmer, who had been sick for four days. The ploughing was at a standstill in consequence, for we had only two draught-horses. Dad erected a shelter over him, made of boughs, to keep the sun off. Two or three times a day he cut green stuff for him – which the cows ate. He humped water to him which he sullenly refused to drink; and did all in his power to persuade Farmer to get up and go on with the ploughing. I don't know if Dad knew anything of mesmerism, but he used to stand for long intervals dumbly staring the old horse full in the eyes till in a commanding voice he would bid him 'Get up!' But Farmer lacked the patriotism of the back-block poets. He was obdurate, and not once did he 'awake', not to mention 'arise'.

This afternoon, as Dad approached his dumb patient, he suddenly put down the bucket of water which he was carrying and ran, shouting angrily. A flock of crows flew away from Farmer and 'cawed' from a tree close by.

Dad was excited, and when he saw that one of the animal's eyes was gone and a stream of blood trickled over its nose he sat down and hid his face in his big rough hands.

'*Caw, caw!*' came from the tree.

Dad rose and looked up.

'*Curse* you!' he hissed – 'you black wretches of hell!'

'*Caw, caw, caw!*'

He ran towards the tree as though he would hurl it to the ground, and away flew the crows.

Joe arrived.

'W-w-wuz they at him, Dad?'

Dad turned on him, trembling with rage.

'Oh, *you* son of the Devil!' he commenced. '*You* worthless pup, you! Look there! Do you see that?' (He pointed to the horse.) 'Didn't I tell you to mind him? Didn –'

'Yes,' snivelled Joe; 'but Anderson's dog had a k-k-k-angaroo bailed up.'

'*Damn* you, be off out of this!' And Dad aimed a block of wood at Joe which struck him on the back as he made away. But nothing short of two broken legs would stop Joe, who the next instant had dashed among the corn like an emu into a scrub.

Dad returned to the house, foaming and vowing to take the gun and shoot Joe down like a wallaby. But when he saw two horses hanging up he hesitated and would have gone away again had Mother not called out that he was wanted. He went in reluctantly.

Red Donovan and his son, Mick, were here. Donovan was the publican, butcher, and horse-dealer at the Overhaul. He was reputed to be well-in, though some said that if everybody had their own he wouldn't be worth much. He was a glib-tongued Irishman who knew everything – or fondly imagined he did – from the law to horse-surgery. There was money to be made out of selections, he reckoned, if selectors only knew how to make it – the majority, he proclaimed, didn't know enough to get under a tree when it rained. As a dealer, he was a hard nut, never giving more than a 'tenner' for a £20 beast, or selling a £10 one for less than £20. And few knew Donovan better than did Dad, or had been taken in by him oftener; but on this occasion Dad was in no easy or benevolent frame of mind.

He sat down, and they talked of crops and the weather,

and beat about the bush until Donovan said:

'Have you any fat steers to sell?'

Dad hadn't. 'But,' he added, 'I can sell you a horse.'

'Which one?' asked Donovan, for he knew the horses as well as Dad did – perhaps better.

'The bay – Farmer.'

'How much?'

'Seven pounds.' Now, Farmer was worth £14, if worth a shilling – that is, before he took sick – and Donovan knew it well.

'Seven,' he repeated, ponderingly. 'Give you six.'

Never before did Dad show himself such an expert in dissimulation. He shook his head knowingly, and enquired of Donovan if he would take the horse for nothing.

'Split the difference, then – make it six-ten?'

Dad rose and looked out the window.

'There he is now,' he remarked, sadly, 'in the gully there.'

'Well, what's it to be – six-ten or nothing?' renewed Donovan.

'All right, then,' Dad replied, demurely, 'take him!'

The money was paid there and then and receipts drawn up. Then, saying that Mick would come for the horse on the day following, and after offering a little gratuitous advice on seed-wheat and pig-sticking, the Donovans left.

Mick came the next day, and Dad showed him Farmer, under the bushes. He wasn't dead, because when Joe sat on him he moved. 'There he is,' said Dad, grinning.

Mick remained seated on his horse, bewildered-looking, staring first at Farmer, then at Dad.

'Well?' Dad remarked, still grinning. Then Mick spoke feelingly.

'*You swindling old crawler!*' he said, and galloped away. It was well for him he got a good start.

For long after that we turned the horses and cows into the little paddock at night, and if ever the dog barked Dad would jump up and go out in his shirt.

We put them back into the big paddock again, and the first night they were there two cows got out and went away, taking with them the chain that fastened the slip-rails. We never saw or heard of them again; but Dad treasured them in his heart. Often, when he was thoughtful, he would ponder out plans for getting even with the Donovans – we knew it was the Donovans. And Fate seemed to be of Dad's mind; for the Donovans got into 'trouble', and were reported to be 'doing time'. That pleased Dad; but the vengeance was a little vague. He would have liked a finger in the pie himself.

Four years passed. It was after supper, and we were all husking corn in the barn. Old Anderson and young Tom Anderson and Mrs Maloney were helping us. We were to assist them the following week. The barn was illuminated by fat-lamps, which made the spiders in the rafters uneasy and disturbed the slumbers of a few fowls that for months had insisted on roosting on the cross-beam.

Mrs Maloney was arguing with Anderson. She was claiming to have husked two cobs to his one, when the dogs started barking savagely. Dad crawled from beneath a heap of husks and went out. The night was dark. He bade the dogs 'Lie down.' They barked louder. '*Damn* you – lie down!' he roared. They shut up. Then a voice from the darkness said:

'Is that you, Mr Rudd?'

Dad failed to recognise it, and went to the fence where the visitor was. He remained there talking for fully half-an-hour. Then he returned, and said it was young Donovan.

'*Donovan! Mick* Donovan?' exclaimed Anderson. And Mother and Mrs Maloney and Joe echoed '*Mick* Donovan?' They *were* surprised.

'He's none too welcome,' said Anderson, thinking of his horses and cows. Mother agreed with him, while Mrs Maloney repeated over and over again that she was always under the impression that Mick Donovan was in gaol along with his bad old father. Dad was uncommunicative. There was something on his mind. He waited till the company had gone, then consulted with Dave.

They were outside, in the dark, and leant on the dray. Dad said in a low voice: 'He's come a hundred mile today, 'n' his horse is dead-beat, 'n' he wants one t' take him t' Back Creek t'morrer 'n' leave this one in his place . . . Wot d' y' think?' Dave seemed to think a great deal, for he said nothing.

'Now,' continued Dad, 'it's me opinion the horse isn't his; it's one he's shook – an' I've an idea.' Then he proceeded to instruct Dave in the idea. A while later he called Joe and drilled him in the idea.

That night, young Donovan stayed at Shingle Hut. In the morning Dad was very affable. He asked Donovan to come and show him his horse, as he must see it before thinking of exchanging. They proceeded to the paddock together. The horse was standing under a tree, tired-looking. Dad stood and looked at Donovan for fully half-a-minute without speaking.

'Why, damn it!' he exclaimed, at last, 'that's *my own* horse . . . You don't mean . . . S'help me! Old Bess's foal!' Donovan told him he was making a mistake.

'Mistake be hanged!' replied Dad, walking round the animal. 'Not much of a mistake about *him!*'

Just here Dave appeared, as was proper.

'Do you know this horse?' Dad asked him. 'Yes, of course,' he answered, surprisedly, with his eyes open wide, 'Bess's foal! – of course it is.'

'There you are!' said Dad, grinning triumphantly.

Donovan seemed uneasy.

Joe in his turn appeared. Dad put the same question to him. Of course Joe knew Bess's foal – 'the one that got stole'.

There was a silence.

'Now,' said Dad, looking very grave, 'what have y' got t' say? Who'd y' get him off, and show's y'r receipt.'

Donovan had nothing to say; he preferred to be silent.

'Then,' Dad went on, 'clear out of this as fast as you can go, an' think y'self lucky.'

He cleared, but on foot.

Dad gazed after him, and, as he left the paddock, said:

'One too many f' y' that time, Mick Donovan!' Then to Dave, who was still looking at the horse: 'He's a stolen one right enough, but he's a beauty, and we'll keep him; and if the owner ever comes for him, well – if he *is* the owner – he can have him, that's all.'

We had the horse for eighteen months and more. One day Dad rode him to town. He was no sooner there than a man came up and claimed him. Dad objected. The man went off and brought a policeman. 'Orright' – Dad said – '*take* him.' The policeman took him. He took Dad too. The lawyer got

Dad off; but it cost us five bags of potatoes. Dad didn't grudge them, for he reckoned we'd had value. Besides, he was even with the Donovans for the two cows.

HENRY LAWSON
Brighten's Sister-in-law

Jim was born in Gulgong, New South Wales. We used to say
'on' Gulgong – and old diggers still talked of being 'on th'
Gulgong' – though the goldfield there had been worked out
for years, and the place was only a dusty little pastoral town
in the scrubs. Gulgong was about the last of the great alluvial
'rushes' of the 'roaring days' – and dreary and dismal enough
it looked when I was there. The expression 'on' came from
being on the 'diggings' or goldfield – the workings or the
goldfield was all underneath, of course, so we lived (or
starved) on them – not in nor at 'em.

Mary and I had been married about two years when Jim
came – His name wasn't 'Jim', by the way, it was 'John
Henry', after an uncle godfather; but we called him Jim from
the first – (and before it) – because Jim was a popular bush
name, and most of my old mates were Jims. The bush is full
of good-hearted scamps called Jim.

We lived in an old weather-board shanty that had been a
sly-grog shop, and the Lord knows what else! in the palmy
days of Gulgong; and I did a bit of digging ('fossicking',
rather), a bit of shearing, a bit of fencing, a bit of bush-
carpentering, tank-sinking – anything, just to keep the billy
boiling.

We had a lot of trouble with Jim with his teeth. He was
bad with every one of them, and we had most of them
lanced – couldn't pull him through without. I remember we
got one lanced and the gum healed over before the tooth came
through, and we had to get it cut again. He was a plucky little
chap, and after the first time he never whimpered when the
doctor was lancing his gum: he used to say 'tar' afterwards,

139

and want to bring the lance home with him.

The first turn we got with Jim was the worst. I had had the wife and Jim camping with me in a tent at a dam I was making at Cattle Creek; I had two men working for me, and a boy to drive one of the tip-drays, and I took Mary out to cook for us. And it was lucky for us that the contract was finished and we got back to Gulgong, and within reach of a doctor, the day we did. We were just camping in the house, with our goods and chattels anyhow, for the night; and we were hardly back home an hour when Jim took convulsions for the first time.

Did you ever see a child in convulsions? You wouldn't want to see it again: it plays the devil with a man's nerves. I'd got the beds fixed up on the floor and the billies on the fire – I was going to make some tea, and put a piece of corned beef on to boil overnight – when Jim (he'd been queer all day, and his mother was trying to hush him to sleep) – Jim, he screamed out twice. He'd been crying a good deal, and I was dog-tired and worried (over some money a man owed me) or I'd have noticed at once that there was something unusual in the way the child cried out: as it was I didn't turn round till Mary screamed 'Joe! Joe!' You know how a woman cries out when her child is in danger or dying – short, and sharp, and terrible. 'Joe! Look! look! Oh, my God, our child! Get the bath, quick! quick! it's convulsions!'

Jim was bent back like a bow, stiff as a bullock-yoke, in his mother's arms, and his eyeballs were turned up and fixed – a thing I saw twice afterwards and don't want ever to see again.

I was falling over things getting the tub and the hot water, when the woman who lived next door rushed in. She called to her husband to run for the doctor, and before the doctor came she and Mary had got Jim into a hot bath and pulled him through.

The neighbour woman made me up a shake-down in another room, and stayed with Mary that night; but it was a long while before I got Jim and Mary's screams out of my head and fell asleep.

You may depend I kept the fire in, and a bucket of water hot over it for a good many nights after that; but (it always happens like this) there came a night, when the fright had worn off, when I was too tired to bother about the fire, and that night Jim took us by surprise. Our wood-heap was done, and I broke up a new chair to get a fire, and had to run a quarter of a mile for water; but this turn wasn't so bad as the first, and we pulled him through.

You never saw a child in convulsions? Well, you don't want to. It must be only a matter of seconds, but it seems long minutes; and half an hour afterwards the child might be laughing and playing with you, or stretched out dead. It shook me up a lot. I was always pretty high-strung and sensitive. After Jim took the first fit, every time he cried, or turned over, or stretched out in the night, I'd jump: I was always feeling his forehead in the dark to see if he was feverish, or feeling his limbs to see if he was 'limp' yet. Mary and I often laughed about it – afterwards. I tried sleeping in another room, but for nights after Jim's first attack I'd just be dozing off into a sound sleep, when I'd hear him scream, as plain as could be, and I'd hear Mary cry, 'Joe! – Joe!' – short, sharp, and terrible – and I'd be up and into their room like a shot, only to find them sleeping peacefully. Then I'd feel Jim's head and his breathing for signs of convulsions, see to the fire and water, and go back to bed and try to sleep. For the first few nights I was like that all night, and I'd feel relieved when daylight came. I'd be in first thing to see if they were all right; then I'd sleep till dinner-time if it was Sunday or I had no work. But then I was run down about that time: I was worried about some money for a wool-shed I put up and never got paid for; and besides, I'd been pretty wild before I met Mary.

I was fighting hard then – struggling for something better. Both Mary and I were born to better things, and that's what made the life so hard for us.

Jim got on all right for a while: we used to watch him well, and have his teeth lanced in time.

It used to hurt and worry me to see how – just as he was getting fat and rosy and like a natural happy child, and I'd feel proud to take him out – a tooth would come along, and he'd get thin and white and pale and bigger-eyed and old-fashioned. We'd say, 'He'll be safe when he gets his eye-teeth'; but he didn't get them till he was two; then. 'He'll be safe when he gets his two-year-old teeth'; they didn't come till he was going on for three.

He was a wonderful little chap – Yes, I know all about parents thinking that their child is the best in the world. If your boy is small for his age, friends will say that small children make big men; that he's a very bright, intelligent child, and that it's better to have a bright, intelligent child than a big, sleepy lump of fat. And if your boy is dull and sleepy, they say that the dullest boys make the cleverest men – and all the rest of it. I never took any notice of that sort of clatter – took it for what it was worth; but, all the same, I don't think I ever saw such a child as Jim was when he turned two. He was everybody's favourite. They spoilt him rather. I had my own ideas about bringing up a child. I reckoned Mary was too soft with Jim. She'd say, 'Put that' (whatever it was) 'out of Jim's reach, will you, Joe?' and I'd say, 'No! leave it there, and make him understand he's not to have it. Make him have his meals without any nonsense and go to bed at a regular hour,' I'd say. Mary and I had many a breeze over Jim. She'd say that I forgot he was only a baby: but I held that a baby could be trained from the first week; and I believe I was right.

But, after all, what are you to do? You'll see a boy that was brought up strict turn out a scamp; and another that was dragged up anyhow (by the hair of the head, as the saying is) turn out well. Then, again, when a child is delicate – and you might lose him any day – you don't like to spank him, though he might be turning out a little fiend, as delicate children often do. Suppose you gave a child a hammering, and the same night he took convulsions, or something, and died – how'd you feel about it? You never know what a child is going to take, any more than you can tell what some women are going to say or do.

I was very fond of Jim, and we were great chums. Sometimes I'd sit and wonder what the deuce he was thinking about, and often, the way he talked, he'd make me uneasy. When he was two he wanted a pipe above all things, and I'd get him a clean new clay and he'd sit by my side, on the edge of the veranda, or on a log of the wood-heap, in the cool of the evening, and suck away at his pipe, and try to spit when he saw me do it. He seemed to understand that a cold empty pipe wasn't quite the thing, yet to have the sense to know that he couldn't smoke tobacco yet: he made the best he could of things. And if he broke a clay pipe he wouldn't have a new one, and there'd be a row; the old one had to be mended up, somehow, with string or wire. If I got my hair cut, he'd want his cut too; and it always troubled him to see me shave – as if he thought there must be something wrong somewhere, else he ought to have to be shaved too. I lathered him one day, and pretended to shave him: he sat through it as solemn as an owl, but didn't seem to appreciate it – perhaps he had sense enough to know that it couldn't possibly be the real thing. He felt his face, looked very hard at the lather I scraped off, and whimpered, 'No blood, Daddy!'

I used to cut myself a good deal: I was always impatient over shaving.

Then he went in to interview his mother about it. She understood his lingo better than I did.

But I wasn't always at ease with him. Sometimes he'd sit looking into the fire, with his head on one side, and I'd watch him and wonder what he was thinking about (I might as well have wondered what a Chinaman was thinking about) till he seemed at least twenty years older than me: sometimes, when I moved or spoke, he'd glance round just as if to see what that old fool of a dadda of his was doing now.

I used to have a fancy that there was something Eastern, or Asiatic – something older than our civilisation or religion – about old-fashioned children. Once I started to explain my idea to a woman I thought would understand – and as it happened she had an old-fashioned child, with very slant eyes – a little tartar he was too. I suppose it was the sight of him that unconsciously reminded me of my infernal theory, and set me off on it, without warning me. Anyhow it got me mixed up in an awful row with the woman and her husband – and all their tribe. It wasn't an easy thing to explain myself out of it, and the row hasn't been fixed up yet. There were some Chinamen in the district.

I took a good-size fencing contract, the frontage of a ten-mile paddock, near Gulgong, and did well out of it. The railway had got as far as the Cudgegong River – some twenty miles from Gulgong and two hundred from the coast – and 'carrying' was good then. I had a couple of draught-horses, that I worked in the tip-drays when I was tank-sinking, and one or two others running in the bush. I bought a broken-down wagon cheap, tinkered it up myself – christened it 'The Same Old Thing' – and started carrying from the railway terminus through Gulgong and along the bush roads and tracks that branch out fanlike through the scrubs to the one-pub towns and sheep and cattle stations out there in the howling wilderness. It wasn't much of a team. There were the two heavy horses for 'shafters'; a stunted colt, that I'd bought out of the pound for thirty shillings; a light, spring-cart horse; an old grey mare, with points like a big red-and-white Australian store bullock, and with the grit of an old washer-woman to work; and a horse that had spanked along in Cobb & Co's mail-coach in his time. I had a couple there that didn't belong to me: I worked them for the feeding of them in the dry weather. And I had all sorts of harness, that I mended and fixed up myself. It was a mixed team, but I took light stuff, got through pretty quick, and freight rates were high. So I got along.

Before this, whenever I made a few pounds I'd sink a shaft somewhere, prospecting for gold; but Mary never let me rest till she had talked me out of that.

I made up my mind to take on a small selection farm – that an old mate of mine had fenced in and cleared, and afterwards chucked up – about thirty miles out west of Gulgong, at a place called Lahey's Creek. (The places were all called Lahey's Creek, or Spicer's Flat, or Murphy's Flat, or Ryan's Crossing, or some such name – round there.) I reckoned I'd have a run for the horses and be able to grow a bit of feed. I always had a dread of taking Mary and the children too far away from a doctor – or a good woman neighbour; but there were some people came to live on Lahey's Creek, and besides, there was a young brother of Mary's – a young scamp (his name was Jim, too, and we called him 'Jimmy' at first to make room for our Jim – he hated the name 'Jimmy' or James). He came to live with us – without asking – and I thought he'd find enough work at Lahey's Creek to keep him out of mischief. He wasn't to be depended on much – he thought nothing of riding off, five hundred miles or so, 'to have a look at the country' – but he was fond of Mary, and he'd stay by her till I got someone else to keep her company while I was on the road. He would be a protection against 'sundowners' or any shearers who happened to wander that way in the 'd.t.'s' after a spree. Mary had a married sister come to live at Gulgong just before we left, and nothing would suit her and her husband but we must leave little Jim with them for a month or so – till we got settled down at Lahey's Creek. They were newly married.

Mary was to have driven into Gulgong, in the spring-cart, at the end of the month, and taken Jim home; but when the time came she wasn't too well – and besides, the tyres of the cart were loose, and I hadn't time to get them cut, so we let Jim's time run on a week or so longer, till I happened to come out through Gulgong from the river with a small load of flour for Lahey's Creek way. The roads were good, the weather grand – no chance of it raining, and I had a spare tarpaulin if it did – I would only camp out one night; so I decided to take Jim home with me.

Jim was turning three then, and he was a cure. He was so old-fashioned that he used to frighten me sometimes – I'd almost think that there was something supernatural about him; though, of course, I never took any notice of that rot about some children being too old-fashioned to live. There's always the ghoulish old hag (and some not so old nor haggish either) who'll come round and shake up young parents with such croaks as, 'You'll never rear that child – he's too bright for his age.' To the devil with them! I say.

But I really thought that Jim was too intelligent for his age, and I often told Mary that he ought to be kept back, and not let talk too much to old diggers and long lanky jokers of bushmen who rode in and hung their horses outside my place on Sunday afternoons.

I don't believe in parents talking about their own children everlastingly – you get sick of hearing them; and their kids are generally little devils, and turn out larrikins as likely as not.

But, for all that, I really think that Jim, when he was three years old, was the most wonderful little chap, in every way, that I ever saw.

For the first hour or so, along the road, he was telling me all about his adventures at his auntie's.

'But they spoilt me too much, Dad,' he said, as solemn as a native bear. 'An' besides, a boy ought to stick to his parrans!'

I was taking out a cattle-pup for a drover I knew, and the

pup took up a good deal of Jim's time.

Sometimes he'd jolt me the way he talked; and other times I'd have to turn away my head and cough, or shout at the horses, to keep from laughing outright. And once, when I was taken that way, he said:

'What are you jerking your shoulders and coughing, and grunting, and going on that way for, Dad? Why don't you tell me something?'

'Tell you what, Jim?'

'Tell me some talk.'

So I told him all the talk I could think of. And I had to brighten up, I can tell you, and not draw too much on my imagination – for Jim was a terror at cross-examination when the fit took him; and he didn't think twice about telling you when he thought you were talking nonsense. Once he said:

'I'm glad you took me home with you, Dad. You'll get to know Jim.'

'What!' I said.

'You'll get to know Jim.'

'But don't I know you already?'

'No, you don't. You never has time to know Jim at home.'

And, looking back, I saw that it was cruel true. I had known in my heart all along that this was the truth; but it came to me like a blow from Jim. You see, it had been a hard struggle for the last year or so; and when I was home for a day or two I was generally too busy, or too tired and worried, or full of schemes for the future to take much notice of Jim. Mary used to speak to me about it, sometimes. 'You never take notice of the child,' she'd say. 'You could surely find a few minutes of an evening. What's the use of always worrying and brooding? Your brain will go with a snap some day, and, if you get over it, it will teach you a lesson. You'll be an old man, and Jim a young one, before you realise that you had a child once. Then it will be too late.'

This sort of talk from Mary always bored me and made me impatient with her, because I knew it all too well. I never worried for myself – only for Mary and the children. And often, as the days went by, I said to myself, 'I'll take more notice of Jim and give Mary more of my time, just as soon as I can see things clear ahead a bit.' And the hard days went on, and the weeks, and the months, and the years – Ah, well!

Mary used to say, when things would get worse, 'Why don't you talk to me, Joe? Why don't you tell me your thoughts, instead of shutting yourself up in yourself and brooding – eating your heart out? It's hard for me: I get to think you're tired of me, and selfish. I might be cross and speak sharp to you when you are in trouble. How am I to know, if you don't tell me?'

But I didn't think she'd understand.

And so, getting acquainted, and chumming and dozing, with the gums closing over our heads here and there, and the ragged patches of sunlight and shade passing up, over the horses, over us, on the front of the load, over the load, and down on to the white, dusty road again – Jim and I got along the lonely bush road and over the ridges some fifteen miles before sunset, and camped at Ryan's Crossing on Sandy Creek for the night. I got the horses out and took the harness off. Jim wanted badly to help me, but I made him stay on the load; for one of the horses – a vicious, red-eyed chestnut – was a kicker: he'd broken a man's leg. I got the feedbags stretched across the shafts, and the chaff-and-corn into them; and there stood the horses all round with their rumps north, south, west, and their heads between the shafts, munching and switching their tails. We use double shafts, you know, for horse-teams – two pairs side by side – and prop them up, and stretch bags between them, letting the bags sag to serve as feed boxes. I threw the spare tarpaulin over the wheels on one side, letting about half of it lie on the ground in case of damp, and so making a floor and a breakwind. I threw down bags and the blankets and possum rug against the wheel to make a camp for Jim and the cattle-pup, and got a gin-case we used for a tucker-box, the frying-pan and billy down, and made a good fire at a log close handy, and soon everything was comfortable. Ryan's Crossing was a grand camp. I stood with my pipe in my mouth, my hands behind my back, and my back to the fire, and took the country in.

Reedy Creek came down along a western spur of the range: the banks here were deep and green, and the water ran clear over the granite bars, boulders, and gravel. Behind us was a dreary flat covered with those gnarled, grey-barked, dry-rotted 'native apple-trees' (about as much like apple-trees as the native bear is like any other), and a nasty bit of sand-dusty road that I was always glad to get over in wet weather. To the left on our side of the creek were reedy marshes, with frogs croaking, and across the creek the dark box-scrub-covered ridges ended in steep 'sidings' coming down to the creek-bank, and to the main road that skirted them, running on west up over a 'saddle' in the ridges and on towards Dubbo. The road by Lahey's Creek to a place called Cobborah branched off, through dreary apple-tree and stringy-bark flats to the left, just beyond the crossing: all these fanlike branch tracks from the Cudgegong were inside a big horse-shoe in the Great Western Line, and so they gave small carriers a chance, now that Cobb& Co's coaches and the big teams and vans had shifted out of the main western terminus. There were tall she-oaks all along the creek and a clump of big ones over a deep waterhole just above the crossing. The creek oaks have rough barked trunks, like English elms, but are much taller and higher to the branches – and the leaves are reedy: Kendall, the Australian poet, calls them the 'she-oak harps Aeolian'. Those trees are always sigh-sigh-sighing – more of a sigh than a sough or the 'whoosh' of gum-trees in the wind. You always hear them sighing, even when you can't feel any wind. It's the same with telegraph wires: put your head against a telegraph-post on a dead, still day, and you'll hear and feel the far-away roar of the wires. But then the oaks are not connected with the distance, where there might be wind; and they don't *roar* in a gale, only sigh louder and softer according to the wind, and never seem to go above or below a certain pitch – like a big harp with all the strings the same. I used to have a theory that those creek oaks got the wind's voice telephoned to them, so to speak, through the ground.

I happened to look round and there was Jim (I thought he was on the tarpaulin playing with the pup): he was standing close beside me with his legs wide apart, his hands behind his back, and his back to the fire.

He held his head a little on one side, and there was such an old, old, wise expression in his big brown eyes – just as if he'd been a child for a hundred years or so, or as though he were listening to those oaks, and understanding them in a fatherly sort of way.

'Dad!' he said presently – 'Dad! do you think I'll ever grow up to be a man?'

'Wh – why, Jim?' I gasped.

'Because I don't want to.'

I couldn't think of anything against this. It made me uneasy. But I remember *I* used to have a childish dread of growing up to be a man.

'Jim,' I said, to break the silence, 'do you hear what the she-oaks say?'

'No, I don't. Is they talking?'

'Yes,' I said, without thinking.

'What is they saying?' he asked.

I took the bucket and went down to the creek for some water for tea. I thought Jim would follow with a little tin billy he had, but he didn't: when I got back to the fire he was again on the possum rug, comforting the pup. I fried some bacon and eggs that I'd brought out with me. Jim sang out from the wagon:

'Don't cook too much, Dad – I mightn't be hungry.'

I got the tin plates, and pint-pots and things out on a clean new flour-bag, in honour of Jim, and dished up. He was leaning back on the rug looking at the pup in a listless sort of way. I reckoned he was tired out, and pulled the gin-case up close to him for a table and put his plate on it. But he only tried a mouthful or two, and then he said:

'I ain't hungry, Dad! You'll have to eat it all.'

It made me uneasy – I never liked to see a child of mine turn from his food. They had given him some tinned salmon in Gulgong, and I was afraid that that was upsetting him. I was always against tinned muck.

'Sick, Jim?' I asked.

'No, Dad, I ain't sick; I don't know what's the matter with me.'

'Have some tea, sonny?'

'Yes, Dad.'

I gave him some tea, with some milk in it that I'd brought in a bottle from his aunt's for him. He took a sip or two and then put the pint-pot on the gin-case.

'Jim's tired, Dad,' he said.

I made him lie down while I fixed up a camp for the night. It had turned a bit chilly, so I let the big tarpaulin down all round – it was made to cover a high load, the flour in the wagon didn't come above the rail, so the tarpaulin came down well on to the ground. I fixed Jim up a comfortable bed under the tail-end of the wagon: when I went to lift him in he was lying back, looking up at the stars in a half-dreamy, half-fascinated way that I didn't like. Whenever Jim was extra old-fashioned, or affectionate, there was danger.

'How do you feel now, sonny?'

It seemed a minute before he heard me and turned from the stars.

'Jim's better, Dad.' Then he said something like, 'The stars are looking at me.' I thought he was half asleep. I took off his jacket and boots and carried him in under the wagon and made him comfortable for the night.

'Kiss me 'night-night, Daddy,' he said.

I'd rather he hadn't asked me – it was a bad sign. As I was going to the fire he called me back.

'What is it, Jim?'

'Get me my things and the cattle-pup, please, Daddy.'

I was scared now. His things were some toys and rubbish he'd brought from Gulgong, and I remembered, the last time he had convulsions, he took all his toys and a kitten to bed with him. And ''night-night' and 'daddy' were two-year-old language to Jim. I'd thought he'd forgotten those words – he seemed to be going back.

'Are you quite warm enough, Jim?'

'Yes, Dad.'

I started to walk up and down – I always did this when I was extra worried.

I was frightened now about Jim, though I tried to hide the fact from myself. Presently he called me again. 'What is it, Jim?'

'Take the blankets off me, Fahver – Jim's sick!' (They'd been teaching him to say father.)

I was scared now. I remembered a neighbour of ours had a little girl die (she swallowed a pin), and when she was going she said:

'Take the blankets off me, Muvver – I'm dying.'

And I couldn't get that out of my head.

I threw back a fold of the possum rug, and felt Jim's head – he seemed cool enough.

'Where do you feel bad, sonny?'

No answer for a while; when he said suddenly, but in a voice as if he were talking in his sleep:

'Put my boots on, please, Daddy. I want to go home to Muvver!'

I held his hand, and comforted him for a while; then he slept – in a restless, feverish sort of way.

I got the bucket I used for water for the horses and stood it over the fire; I ran to the creek with the big kerosene-tin bucket and got it full of cold water and stood it handy. I got the spade (we always carried one to dig wheels out of bogs in wet weather) and turned a corner of the tarpaulin back, dug a hole, and trod the tarpaulin down in the hole to serve for a bath, in case of the worst. I had a tin of mustard, and meant to fight a good round for Jim, if death came along.

I stooped in under the tail-board of the wagon and felt Jim. His head was burning hot, and his skin parched and dry as a bone.

Then I lost nerve and started blundering backward and forward between the wagon and the fire, and repeating what I'd heard Mary say the last time we fought for Jim: 'God! don't take my child! God! don't take my boy!' I'd never had much faith in doctors, but, my God! I wanted one then. The nearest was fifteen miles away.

I threw back my head and stared up at the branches in desperation; and – well, I don't ask you to take much stock in this, though most old bushmen will believe anything of the bush by night; and – now, it might have been that I was unstrung, or it might have been a patch of the sky outlined in the gently moving branches, or the blue smoke rising up. But I saw the figure of a woman, all white, come down, down, nearly to the limbs of the trees, point on up the main road, and then float up and up and vanish, still pointing. I thought Mary was dead! Then it flashed on me –

Four or five miles up the road, over the 'saddle', was an old shanty that had been a half-way inn before the Great Western Line got round as far as Dubbo, and took the coach traffic off those old bush roads. A man named Brighten lived there. He was a selector; did a little farming, and as much sly-grog selling as he could. He was married – but it wasn't that: I'd thought of them, but she was a childish, worn-out, spiritless woman, and both were pretty 'ratty' from hardship and loneliness – they weren't likely to be of any use to me. But it was this: I'd heard talk, among some women in Gulgong, of a sister of Brighten's wife who'd gone out to live with them lately: she'd been a hospital matron in the city, they said; and there were yarns about her. Some said she got the sack for exposing the doctors – or carrying on with them – I didn't remember which. The fact of a city woman going out to live in such a place, with such people, was enough to make talk among women in a town twenty miles away, but then there must have been something extra about her, else bushmen wouldn't have talked and carried her name so far; and I wanted a woman out of the ordinary now. I even reasoned this way, thinking like lightning, as I knelt over Jim between the big back wheels of the wagon.

I had an old racing mare that I used as a riding hack, following the team. In a minute I had her saddled and bridled; I tied the end of a half-full chaff-bag, shook the chaff into each end and dumped it on to the pommel as a cushion or buffer for Jim; I wrapped him in a blanket, and scrambled into the saddle with him.

The next minute we were stumbling down the steep bank, clattering and splashing over the crossing, and struggling up the opposite bank to the level. The mare, as I told you, was an old racer, but broken-winded – she must have run without wind after the first half-mile. She had the old racing instinct in her strong, and whenever I rode in company I'd have to pull her hard else she'd race the other horse or burst. She ran low fore and aft, and was the easiest horse I ever rode. She ran like wheels on rails, with a bit of a tremble now and then – like a railway carriage – when she settled down to it.

The chaff-bag had slipped off, in the creek I suppose, and I let the bridle-rein go and held Jim up to me like a baby the whole way. Let the strongest man, who isn't used to it, hold a baby in one position for five minutes – and Jim was fairly heavy. But I never felt the ache in my arms that night – it must have gone before I was in a fit state of mind to feel it. And at home I'd often growled about being asked to hold the baby for a few minutes. I could never brood comfortably and nurse a baby at the same time. It was a ghostly moonlight night. There's no timber in the world so ghostly as the

Australian bush in moonlight – or just about daybreak. The all-shaped patches of moonlight falling between ragged, twisted boughs; the ghostly blue-white bark of the 'white-box' trees; a dead, naked white ring-barked tree, or dead white stump starting out here and there, and the ragged patches of shade and light on the road that made anything, from the shape of a spotted bullock to a naked corpse laid out stark. Roads and tracks through the bush made by moon-light – every one seeming straighter and clearer than the real one; you have to trust to your horse then. Sometimes the naked white trunk of a red stringy-bark tree, where a sheet of bark had been taken off, would start out like a ghost from the dark bush. And dew or frost glistening on these things, according to the season. Now and again a great grey kangaroo, that had been feeding on a green patch down by the road, would start with a 'thump-thump', and away up the siding.

The bush seemed full of ghosts that night – all going my way – and being left behind by the mare. Once I stopped to look at Jim: I just sat back and the mare 'propped' – she'd been a stock-horse, and was used to 'cutting-out'. I felt Jim's hands and forehead; he was in a burning fever. I bent forward, and the old mare settled down to it again. I kept saying out loud – and Mary and me often laughed about it (afterwards): 'He's limp yet! – Jim's limp yet!' (the words seemed jerked out of me by sheer fright) – 'He's limp yet!' till the mare's feet took it up. Then, just when I thought she was doing her best and racing her hardest, she suddenly started forward, like a cable tram gliding along on its own and the grip put on suddenly. It was just what she'd do when I'd be riding alone and a strange horse drew up from behind – the old racing instinct. I *felt* the thing too! I felt as if a strange horse *was* there! And then – the words just jerked out of me by sheer funk – I started saying, 'Death is riding to-night! . . . Death is racing to-night! . . . Death is riding to-night!' till the hoofbeats took that up. And I believe the old mare felt the black horse at her side and was going to beat him or break her heart.

I was mad with anxiety and fright: I remember I kept saying, 'I'll be kinder to Mary after this! I'll take more notice of Jim!' and the rest of it.

I don't know how the old mare got up the last 'pinch'. She

must have slackened pace, but I never noticed it: I just held Jim up to me and gripped the saddle with my knees – I remember the saddle jerked from the desperate jumps of her till I thought the girth would go. We topped the gap and were going down into a gully they called Dead Man's Hollow, and there, at the back of a ghostly clearing that opened from the road where there were some black-soil springs, was a long, low, oblong weatherboard-and-shingle building, with blind, broken windows in the gable-ends, and a wide steep veranda roof slanting down almost to the level of the window-sills – there was something sinister about it, I thought – like the hat of a jail-bird slouched over his eyes. The place looked both deserted and haunted. I saw no light, but that was because of the moonlight outside. The mare turned in at the corner of the clearing to take a short cut to the shanty, and, as she struggled across some marshy ground, my heart kept jerking out the words, 'It's deserted! They've gone away! It's deserted!' The mare went round to the back and pulled up between the back door and a big bark-and-slab kitchen. Someone shouted from inside:

'Who's there?'

'It's me. Joe Wilson. I want your sister-in-law – I've got the boy – he's sick and dying!'

Brighten came out, pulling up his moleskins. 'What boy?' he asked.

'Here, take him,' I shouted, 'and let me get down.'

'What's the matter with him?' asked Brighten, and he seemed to hang back. And just as I made to get my leg over the saddle, Jim's head went back over my arm, he stiffened, and I saw his eyeballs turned up and glistening in the moonlight.

I felt cold all over then and sick in the stomach – but *clear-headed* in a way: strange, wasn't it? I don't know why I didn't get down and rush into the kitchen to get a bath ready. I only felt as if the worst had come, and I wished it were over and gone. I even thought of Mary and the funeral.

Then a woman ran out of the house – a big, hard-looking woman. She had on a wrapper of some sort, and her feet were bare. She laid her hand on Jim, looked at his face, and then snatched him from me and ran into the kitchen – and me down and after her. As great good luck would have it they had some dirty clothes on to boil in a kerosene-tin – dish-cloths or something.

Brighten's sister-in-law dragged a tub out from under the table, wrenched the bucket off the hook, and dumped in the water, dish-cloths and all, snatched a can of cold water from a corner, dashed that in, and felt the water with her hand – holding Jim up to her hip all the time – and I won't say how he looked. She stood him in the tub and started dashing water over him, tearing off his clothes between the splashes.

'Here, that tin of mustard – there on the shelf!' she shouted to me.

She knocked the lid off the tin on the edge of the tub, and went on splashing and spanking Jim.

It seemed an eternity. And I? Why, I never thought clearer in my life. I felt cold-blooded – I felt as if I'd like an excuse to go outside till it was all over. I thought of Mary and the funeral – and wished that that was past. All this in a flash, as it were. I felt that it would be a great relief, and only wished the funeral was months past. I felt – well, altogether selfish. I only thought of myself.

Brighten's sister-in-law splashed and spanked him hard – hard enough to break his back I thought, and – after about half an hour it seemed – the end came: Jim's limbs relaxed, he slipped down into the tub, and the pupils of his eyes came down. They seemed dull and expressionless, like the eyes of a new baby, but he was back for the world again.

I dropped on the stool by the table.

'It's all right,' she said. 'It's all over now. I wasn't going to let him die.' I was only thinking, 'Well it's over now, but it will come on again. I wish it was over for good. I'm tired of it.'

She called to her sister, Mrs Brighten, a washed-out, helpless little fool of a woman, who'd been running in and out and whimpering all the time:

'Here, Jessie! bring the new white blanket off my bed. And you, Brighten, take some of that wood off the fire, and stuff something in that hole there to stop the draught.'

Brighten – he was a nuggety little hairy man with no expression to be seen for whiskers – had been running in with sticks and back logs from the wood-heap. He took the wood out, stuffed up the crack, and went inside and brought out a black bottle – got a cup from the shelf, and put both down near my elbow.

Mrs Brighten started to get some supper or breakfast, or whatever it was, ready. She had a clean cloth, and set the table tidily. I noticed that all the tins were polished bright (old coffee and mustard-tins and the like, that they used instead of sugar-basins and tea-caddies and salt-cellars), and the kitchen was kept as clean as possible. She was all right at little things. I knew a haggard, worked-out bushwoman who put her whole soul – or all she'd got left – into polishing old tins till they dazzled your eyes.

I didn't feel inclined for corned beef and damper, and post-and-rail tea. So I sat and squinted, when I thought she wasn't looking, at Brighten's sister-in-law. She was a big woman, her hands and feet were big, but well-shaped and all in propor-tion – they fitted her. She was a handsome woman – about forty I should think. She had a square chin, and a straight thin-lipped mouth – straight save for a hint of a turn down at the corners, which I fancied (and I have strange fancies) had been a sign of weakness in the days before she grew hard. There was no sign of weakness now. She had hard grey eyes and blue-black hair. She hadn't spoken yet. She didn't ask me how the boy took ill or I got there, or who or what I was – at least not until the next evening at tea-time.

She sat upright with Jim wrapped in the blanket and laid across her knees, with one hand under his neck and the other laid lightly on him, and she just rocked him gently.

She sat looking hard and straight before her, just as I've seen a tired needlewoman sit with her work in her lap, and look away back into the past. And Jim might have been the work in her lap, for all she seemed to think of him. Now and then she knitted her forehead and blinked.

Suddenly she glanced round and said – in a tone as if I was her husband and she didn't think much of me:

'Why don't you eat something?'

'Beg pardon?'

'Eat something!'

I drank some tea, and sneaked another look at her. I was beginning to feel more natural, and wanted Jim again, now that the colour was coming back into his face, and he didn't

look like an unnaturally stiff and staring corpse. I felt a lump
rising, and wanted to thank her. I sneaked another look at
her.

She was staring straight before her – I never saw a woman's
face change so suddenly – I never saw a woman's eyes so
haggard and hopeless. Then her great chest heaved twice, I
heard her draw a long shuddering breath, like a knocked-out
horse, and two great tears dropped from her wide open eyes
down her cheeks like rain-drops on a face of stone. And in
the firelight they seemed tinged with blood.

I looked away quick, feeling full up myself. And presently
(I hadn't seen her look around) she said:

'Go to bed.'

'Beg pardon?' (Her face was the same as before the tears.)

'Go to bed. There's a bed made for you inside on the sofa.'

'But – the team – I must –'

'What?'

'The team. I left it at the camp. I must look to it.'

'Oh! Well, Brighten will ride down and bring it up in the
morning – or send the half-caste. Now you go to bed, and get
a good rest. The boy will be all right. I'll see to that.'

I went out – it was a relief to get out – and looked to the
mare. Brighten had got her some corn and chaff in a candle-
box, but she couldn't eat yet. She just stood or hung resting
one hind leg and then the other, with her nose over the
box – and she sobbed. I put my arms round her neck and my
face down on her ragged mane, and cried for the second time
since I was a boy.

As I started to go in I heard Brighten's sister-in-law say,
suddenly and sharply:

'Take *that* away, Jessie.'

And presently I saw Mrs Brighten go into the house with
the black bottle.

The moon had gone behind the range. I stood for a minute
between the house and the kitchen and peeped in through
the kitchen window.

She had moved away from the fire and sat near the table.
She bent over Jim and held him up close to her and rocked
herself to and fro.

I went to bed and slept till the next afternoon. I woke just
in time to hear the tail-end of a conversation between Jim and

Brighten's sister-in-law. He was asking her out to our place, and she promising to come.

'And now,' says Jim, 'I want to go home to "Muffer" in "The Same Ol' Fling".'

'What?'

Jim repeated.

'Oh! "The Same Old Thing", – the wagon.'

The rest of the afternoon I poked round the gullies with old Brighten, looking at some 'indications' (of the existence of gold) he had found. It was no use trying to 'pump' him concerning his sister-in-law; Brighten was an 'old hand', and had learned in the old bushranging and cattle-stealing days to know nothing about other people's business. And, by the way, I noticed then that the more you talk and listen to a bad character, the more you lose your dislike for him.

I never saw such a change in a woman as in Brighten's sister-in-law that evening. She was bright and jolly, and seemed at least ten years younger. She bustled round and helped her sister to get tea ready. She rooted out some old china that Mrs Brighten had stowed away somewhere, and set the table as I seldom saw it set out there. She propped Jim up with pillows, and laughed and played with him like a great girl. She described Sydney and Sydney life as I'd never heard it described before; and she knew as much about the bush and old diggings days as I did. She kept old Brighten and me listening and laughing till nearly midnight. And she seemed quick to understand everything when I talked. If she wanted to explain anything that we hadn't seen, she wouldn't say that it was 'like a – like a' – and hesitate (you know what I mean); she'd hit the right thing on the head at once. A squatter with a very round, flaming red face and a white cork hat had gone by in the afternoon: she said it was 'like a mushroom on the rising moon'. She gave me a lot of good hints about children.

But she was quiet again next morning. I harnessed up, and she dressed Jim and gave him his breakfast, and made a comfortable place for him on the load with a possum rug and a spare pillow. She got up on the wheel to do it herself. Then was the awkward time. I'd half start to speak to her, and then turn away and go fixing up round the horses, and then make another false start to say goodbye. At last she

took Jim up in her arms and kissed him, and lifted him on
the wheel; but he put his arms tight round her neck, and
kissed her – a thing Jim seldom did with anybody, except
his mother, for he wasn't what you'd call an affectionate
child – he'd never more than offer his cheek to me, in his
old-fashioned way. I'd got up the other side of the load to
take him from her.

'Here, take him,' she said.

I saw his mouth twitching as I lifted him. Jim seldom cried
nowadays – no matter how much he was hurt. I gained some
time fixing Jim comfortable.

'You'd better make a start,' she said. 'You want to get home
early with that boy.'

I got down and went round to where she stood. I held out
my hand and tried to speak, but my voice went like an
ungreased wagon-wheel, and I gave it up, and only squeezed
her hand.

'That's all right,' she said; then tears came into her eyes,
and she suddenly put her hand on my shoulder and kissed
me on the cheek. 'You be off – you're only a boy yourself.
Take care of that boy; be kind to your wife, and take care of
yourself.'

'Will you come to see us?'

'Some day,' she said.

I started the horses, and looked round once more. She was
looking up at Jim, who was waving his hand to her from the
top of the load. And I saw that haggard, hungry, hopeless look
come into her eyes in spite of the tears.

I smoothed over that story and shortened it a lot when I told
it to Mary – I didn't want to upset her. But, some time after
I brought Jim home from Gulgong, and while I was at home
with the team for a few days, nothing would suit Mary but
she must go over to Brighten's shanty and see Brighten's
sister-in-law. So James drove her over one morning in the
spring-cart: it was a long way, and they stayed at Brighten's
overnight and didn't get back till late the next afternoon. I'd
got the place in a pig-muck, as Mary said, 'doing for' myself,
and I was having a snooze on the sofa when they got back.
The first thing I remember was someone stroking my head

and kissing me, and I heard Mary saying 'My poor boy! My poor old boy!'

I sat up with a jerk. I thought that Jim had gone off again. But it seems that Mary was only referring to me. Then she started to pull grey hairs out of my head and put 'em in an empty match-box – to see how many she'd got. She used to do this when she felt a bit soft. I don't know what she said to Brighten's sister-in-law or what Brighten's sister-in-law said to her, but Mary was extra gentle for the next few days.

BARBARA BAYNTON
Billy Skywonkie

The line was unfenced, so with due regard to the possibility of the drought-dulled sheep attempting to chew it, the train crept cautiously along, stopping occasionally, without warning, to clear it from the listless starving brutes. In the carriage nearest the cattle-vans, some drovers and scrub-cutters were playing euchre, and spasmodically chorusing the shrill music from an uncertain concertina. When the train stopped, the player thrust his head from the carriage window. From one nearer the engine, a commercial traveller remonstrated with the guard, concerning the snail's pace and the many unnecessary halts.

'Take yer time, old die-ard,' yelled the drover to the guard. 'Whips er time, – don't bust yerself fer no one. Wot's orl the worl' to a man w'en his wife's a widder?' He laughed noisily and waved his hat at the seething bagman. 'Go an' 'ave a snooze. I'll wake yer up ther day after termorrer.'

He craned his neck to see into the nearest cattle-van. Four were down, he told his mates, who remarked, with blasphemous emphasis, that they would probably lose half before getting them to the scrub country.

The listening woman passenger in a carriage between the drover and the bagman, heard a thud soon after in the cattle-truck, and added another to the list of the fallen. Before dawn that day the train had stopped at a siding to truck them, and she had watched with painful interest these drought-tamed brutes being driven into the crowded vans. The tireless, greedy sun had swiftly followed the grey dawn, and in the light that even now seemed old and worn, the desolation of the barren shelterless plains, that the night had hidden,

161

appalled her. She realised the sufferings of the emaciated cattle. It was barely noon, yet she had twice emptied the water bottle, 'shogging' in the iron bracket.

The train dragged its weary length again, and she closed her eyes from the monotony of the dead plain. Suddenly the engine cleared its throat in shrill welcome to two iron tanks, hoisted twenty feet and blazing like evil eyes from a vanished face.

Beside them it squatted on its hunkers, placed a blackened thumb on its pipe, and hissed through its closed teeth like a snared wild cat, while gulping yards of water. The green slimy odour penetrated to the cattle. The lustiest of these stamped feebly, clashing their horns and bellowing a hollow request.

A long-bearded bushman was standing on the few slabs that formed a siding, with stockwhip coiled like a snake on his arm. The woman passenger asked him the name of the place.

'This is ther Never-Never, – ther lars' place Gord made,' answered one of the drovers who were crowding the windows.

'Better'n ther 'ell-'ole yous come from, any'ow,' defended the bushman. 'Breakin' ther 'earts, and dying' from suerside, 'cos they lef' it,' he added derisively, pointing to the cattle.

In patriotic anger he passed to the guard-van without answering her question, though she looked anxiously after him. At various intervals during the many halts of the train, she had heard some of the obscene jokes, and with it in motion, snatches of lewd songs from the drovers' carriage. But the language used by this bushman to the guard, as he helped to remove a ton of fencing wire topping his new saddle, made her draw back her head. Near the siding was a spring cart, and she presently saw him throw his flattened saddle into it and drive off. There was no one else in sight, and in nervous fear she asked the bagman if this was Gooriabba siding. It was nine miles further, he told her.

The engine lifted its thumb from its pipe. 'Well – well – to – be – sure; well – well – to – be – sure,' it puffed, as if in shocked remembrance of its being hours late for its appointment here.

She saw no one on the next siding, but a buggy waited near

the slip-rails. It must be for her. According to Sydney arrangements she was to be met here, and driven out twelve miles. A drover inquired as the train left her standing by her portmanteau, 'Are yer travellin' on yer lonesome, or on'y goin' somew'ere!' and another flung a twist of paper towards her, brawling unmusically, that it was 'A flowwer from me angel mother's ger-rave'.

She went towards the buggy, but as she neared it the driver got in and made to drive off. She ran and called, for when he went she would be alone with the bush all round her, and only the sound of the hoarse croaking of the frogs from the swamp near, and the raucous 'I'll - 'ave - 'is - eye - out', of the crows.

Yes, he was from Gooriabba Station, and had come to meet a young 'piece' from Sydney, who had not come.

She was ghastly with bilious sickness, – the result of an over-fed brain and an under-fed liver. Her face flushed muddily. 'Was it a housekeeper?'

He was the rouseabout, wearing his best clothes with awful unusualness. The coat was too long in the sleeve, and wrinkled across the back with his bush slouch. There was that wonderful margin of loose shirt between waistcoat and trouser, which all swagger bushies affect. Subordinate to nothing decorative was the flaring silk handkerchief, drawn into a sailor's knot round his neck.

He got out and fixed the winkers, then put his hands as far as he could reach into his pockets – from the position of his trousers he could not possibly reach bottom. It was apparently some unknown law that suspended them. He thrust forward his lower jaw, elevated his pipe, and squirted a little tobacco juice towards his foot that was tracing semi-circles in the dust. 'Damned if I know,' he said with a snort, 'but there'll be a 'ell of a row somew'ere.'

She noticed that the discoloured teeth his bush grin showed so plainly, were worn in the centre, and met at both sides with the pipe between the front. Worn stepping-stones her mind insisted.

She looked away towards the horizon where the smoke of the hidden train showed faintly against a clear sky, and as he was silent, she seemed to herself to be intently listening to the croak of the frogs and the threat of the cows. She knew that, from under the brim of the hat he wore over his eyes, he was looking at her sideways.

Suddenly he withdrew his hands and said again, 'Damned if I know. S'pose it's all right! Got any traps? Get up then 'an 'ole the Neddy while I get it.' They drove a mile or so in silence; his pipe was still in his mouth though not alight.

She spoke once only. 'What a lot of frogs seem to be in that lake!'

He laughed. 'That's ther Nine Mile Dam!' He laughed again after a little – an intelligent, complacent laugh.

'It used ter be swarmin' with teal in a good season, but Gord A'mighty knows w'en it's ever goin' ter rain any more! I dunno!' This was an important admission, for he was a great weather prophet. 'Lake!' he sniggered and looked sideways at his companion. 'Thet's wot thet there bloke, the painter doodle, called it. An' 'e goes ter dror it, an' 'e sez wot 'e 'll give me five bob if I'll run up ther horses, an' keep 'em so's 'e ken put 'em in ther picshure. An' 'e drors ther Dam an' ther trees, puts in thet there ole dead un, an' 'e puts in ther 'orses right clost against ther water w'ere the frogs is. 'E puts them in too, an' damned if 'e don't dror ther 'orses drinkin' ther water with ther frogs, an' ther frogs spit on it! Likely yarn ther 'orses ud drink ther water with ther blanky frogs' spit on it! Fat lot they know about ther bush! Blarsted nannies!'

Presently he inquired as to the place where they kept pictures in Sydney, and she told him, the Art Gallery.

'Well, some of these days I'm goin' down ter Sydney,' he continued, 'an' I'll collar thet one 'cos it's a good likerness of ther 'orses – you'd know their 'ide on a gum tree – an' that mean mongrel never paid me ther five bob.'

Between his closed teeth he hissed a bush tune for some miles, but ceased to look at the sky and remarked, 'No sign er rain! No lambin' this season; soon as they're dropt we'll 'ave ter knock 'em all on ther 'ead!' He shouted an oath of hatred at the crows following after the tottering sheep that made in a straggling line for the water. 'Look at 'em!' he said, 'scoffin' out ther eyes!' He pointed to where the crows hovered over the bogged sheep. 'They puttywell lives on eyes! "Blanky bush Chinkies!" I call 'em. No one carn't tell 'em apart!'

There was silence again, except for a remark that he could

spit all the blanky rain they had had in the last nine months.

Away to the left along a side track his eyes travelled searchingly, as they came to a gate. He stood in the buggy and looked again.

'Promised ther "Konk" t' leave 'im 'ave furst squint at yer,' he muttered, 'if 'e was 'ere t' open ther gate! But I'm not goin' t' blanky well wait orl day!' He reluctantly got out and opened the gate, and he had just taken his seat when a 'Cooee' sounded from his right, heralded by a dusty pillar. He snorted resentfully. ''Ere 'e is; jes' as I got out an' done it!'

The 'Konk' cantered to them, his horse's hoofs padded by the dust-cushioned earth. The driver drew back, so as not to impede the newcomer's view. After a moment or two, the 'Konk', preferring closer quarters, brought his horse round to the left. Unsophisticated bush wonder in the man's face met the sophisticated in the girl's.

Never had she seen anything so grotesquely monkeyish. And the nose of this little hairy horror, as he slewed his neck to look into her face, blotted the landscape and dwarfed all perspective. She experienced a strange desire to extend her hand. When surprise lessened, her mettle saved her from the impulse to cover her face with both hands, to baffle him.

At last the silence was broken by the driver drawing a match along his leg, and lighting his pipe. The hairy creature safely arranged a pair of emu eggs, slung with bush skill round his neck.

'Ain't yer goin' to part?' inquired the driver, indicating his companion as the recipient.

'Wot are yer givin' us; wot do yer take me fur?' said the 'Konk' indignantly, drawing down his knotted veil.

'Well, give 'em ter me fer 'Lizer.'

'Will yer 'ave 'em now, or wait till yer get 'em?'

'Goin' ter sit on 'em yerself?' sneered the driver.

'Yes, an' I'll give yer ther first egg ther cock lays,' laughed the 'Konk'.

He turned his horse's head back to the gate. 'I say, Billy Skywonkie! Wot price Sally Ah Too, eh?' he asked, his gorilla mouth agape.

Billy Skywonkie uncrossed his legs, took out the whip. He tilted his pipe and shook his head as he prepared to drive, to show that he understood to a fraction the price of Sally

Ah Too. The aptness of the question took the sting out of his having had to open the gate. He gave a farewell jerk.

'Goin' ter wash yer neck?' shouted the man with the nose, from the gate.

'Not if I know it.'

The 'Konk' received the intimation incredulously. 'Stinkin' Roger!' he yelled. In bush parlance this was equal to emphatic disbelief.

This was a seemingly final parting, and both started, but suddenly the 'Konk' wheeled round.

'Oh, Billy!' he shouted.

Billy stayed his horse and turned expectantly.

'W'en's it goin' ter rain?'

The driver's face darkened. 'Your blanky jealersey'll get yer down, an' worry yer yet,' he snarled, and slashing his horse he drove rapidly away.

'Mickey ther Konk,' he presently remarked to his companion, as he stroked his nose.

This explained her earlier desire to extend her hand. If the 'Konk' had been a horse she would have stroked his nose.

'Mob er sheep can camp in the shadder of it,' he said.

Boundless scope for shadows on that sun-smitten treeless plain!

'Make a good ploughshere,' he continued; 'easy plough a cultivation paddock with it!'

At the next gate he seemed in a mind and body conflict. There were two tracks; he drove along one for a few hundred yards. Then stopping he turned, and finding the 'Konk' out of sight abruptly drove across to the other. He continually drew his whip along the horse's back, and haste seemed the object of the movement, though he did not flog the beast.

After a few miles on the new track, a blob glittered dazzlingly through the glare, like a fallen star. It was the iron roof of the wine shanty – the Saturday night and Sunday resort of shearers and rouseabouts for twenty miles around. Most of its spirits was made on the premises from bush recipes, of which bluestone and tobacco were the chief ingredients. Every drop had the reputation of 'bitin' orl ther way down'.

A sapling studded with broken horse-shoes seemed to

* 'Skywonkie' signifies weather prophet

connect two lonely crow stone trees. Under their scanty shade groups of dejected fowls stood with beaks agape. Though the buggy wheels almost reached them, they were motionless but for the quivering gills. The ground both sides of the shanty was decorated with tightly pegged kangaroo skins. A dog, apathetically blind and dumb, lay on the verandah, lifeless save for eyelids blinking in antagonism to the besieging flies.

'Jerry can't be far off,' said Billy Skywonkie, recognising the dog. He stood up in the buggy. 'By cripes, there 'e is – goosed already, an' 'e on'y got 'is cheque lars' night.'

On the chimney side of the shanty a man lay in agitated sleep beside his rifle and swag. There had been a little shade on that side in the morning, and he had been sober enough to select it, and lay his head on his swag. He had emptied the bottle lying at his feet since then. His swag had been thoroughly 'gone through', and also his singlet and trouser pockets. The fumes from the shanty-grog baffled the flies. But the scorching sun was conquering; the man groaned, and his hands began to search for his burning head.

Billy Skywonkie explained to his companion that it was 'Thet fool. Jerry ther kangaroo-shooter, bluein' 'is cheque fer skins.' He took the water bag under the buggy, and poured the contents into the open mouth and over the face of the 'dosed' man, and raised him into a sitting posture. Jerry fought this friendliness vigorously, and, staggering to his feet, picked up his rifle, and took drunken aim at his rescuer, then at the terrified woman in the buggy.

The rouseabout laughed unconcernedly. ''E thinks we're blanky kangaroos,' he said to her. 'Jerry, ole cock, yer couldn't 'it a woolshed! Yer been taking ther sun!'

He took the rifle and pushed the subdued Jerry into the chimney corner.

He tilted his hat, till, bush fashion, it ''ung on one 'air', and went inside the shanty.

'Mag!' he shouted, thumping the bar (a plank supported by two casks).

The woman in the buggy saw a slatternly girl with doughy hands come from the back, wiping the flour from her face with a kitchen towel. They made some reference to her she knew, as the girl came to the door and gave her close scrutiny. Then, shaking her head till her long brass earrings swung like pendulums, she laughed loudly.

'Eh?' inquired the rouseabout.

'My oath!' 'Square dinkum!' she answered, going behind the bar.

He took the silk handkerchief from his neck, and playfully tried to flick the corner into her eye. Mag was used to such delicate attentions and well able to defend herself. With the dirty kitchen towel she succeeded in knocking off his hat, and round and round the house she ran with it, dexterously dodging the skin-pegs. He could neither overtake nor outwit her with any dodge, so he gave in, and ransomed his hat with the 'shouts' she demanded.

From the back of the shanty, a bent old woman, almost on all fours, crept towards the man, again prostrate in the corner. She paused, with her ear turned to where the girl and the rouseabout were still at horse-play. With catlike movements she stole on till within reach of Jerry's empty pockets. She turned her terrible face to the woman in the buggy, as if in expectation of sympathy. Keeping wide of the front door, she came to the further side of the buggy. With the fascination of horror the woman looked at this creature, whose mouth and eyes seemed to dishonour her draggled grey hair. She was importuning for something, but the woman in the buggy could not understand till she pointed to her toothless mouth (the mission of which seemed to be, to fill its cavernous depths with the age-loosened skin above and below). A blue bag under each eye aggressively ticked like the gills of the fowls, and the sinews of the neck strained into *bassi relievi*. Alternately she pointed to her mouth, or laid her knotted fingers on the blue bags in pretence of wiping tears. Entrenched behind the absorbed skin-terraces, a stump of purple tongue made efforts at speech. When she held out her claw, the woman understood and felt for her purse. Wolfishly the old hag snatched and put into her mouth the coin, and as the now merry driver, followed by Mag, came, she shook a warning claw at the giver, and flopped whining in the dust, her hands ostentatiously open and wiping dry eyes.

'Ello Biddy, on ther booze again!'

The bottle bulging from his coat pocket made speech with him intelligible, despite the impeding coin.

He placed the bottle in the foot of the buggy, and turning to Mag, said 'Give ther poor ole cow a dose!'

'Yes, one in a billy; anything else might make her sick!' said Mag, 'I caught 'er jus' now swiggin' away with ther tap in 'er mug!'

He asked his companion would she like a wet. She asked for water, and so great was her need, that, making a barricade of closed lips and teeth to the multitude of apparently wingless mosquitoes thriving in its green tepidity, she moistened her mouth and throat.

'Oh, I say, Billy!' called Mag as he drove off. Her tones suggested her having forgotten an important matter, and he turned eagerly. 'W'en's it goin' ter rain?' she shrieked, convulsed in merriment.

'Go an' crawl inter a' oller log!' he shouted angrily.

'No, but truly, Billy,' Billy turned again. 'Give my love to yaller 'Lizer; thet slues yer!'

They had not gone far before he looked round again. 'Gord!' he cried excitedly. 'Look at Mag goin' through 'er ole woman!'

Mag had the old woman's head between her knees, dentist-fashion, and seemed to concentrate upon her victim's mouth, whose feeble impotence was soon demonstrated by the operator releasing her, and triumphantly raising her hand.

What the finger and thumb held the woman knew and the other guessed.

'By Gord. Eh! thet's prime, ain't it? No flies on Mag; not a fly!' he said admiringly.

'See me an' 'er?' he asked, as he drove on.

His tone suggested no need to reply, and his listener did not. A giddy unreality took the sting from everything, even from her desire to beseech him to turn back to the siding, and leave her there to wait for the train to take her back to civilisation. She felt she had lost her mental balance. Little matters became distorted, and the greater shrivelled.

He was now more communicative, and the oaths and adjectives so freely used were surely coined for such circumstances. 'Damned' the wretched, starving, and starved sheep looked and were; 'bloody' the beaks of the glutted crows; 'blarsted' the whole of the plain they drove through!

Gaping cracks suggested yawning graves, and the skeleton fingers of the drooping myalls seemingly pointed to them.

'See me an' Mag?' he asked again. 'No flies on Mag; not a wink 'bout 'er!' He chuckled in tribute. 'There wus thet damned flash fool, Jimmy Fernatty,' he continued; ' – ther blanky fool; 'e never 'ad no show with Mag. An' yet 'e'd go down there! It wus two mile furder this way, yet damned if ther blanky fool wouldn't come this way every time, 'less ther boss 'e wus with 'im, 'stead er goin' ther short cut, – ther way I come this mornin'. An' every time Mag ud make 'im part 'arf a quid. I wus on'y there jus' 'bout five minits meself, an' I stuck up nea'ly 'arf a quid! An' there's four gates' (he flogged the horse and painted them crimson when he remembered them) 'this way, more'n on ther way I come this mornin'.'

Presently he gave her the reins with instructions to drive through one. It seemed to take a long time to close it, and he had to fix the back of the buggy before he opened it, and after it was closed.

After getting out several times in quick succession to fix the back of the buggy when there was no gate, he seemed to forget the extra distance. He kept his hand on hers when she gave him the reins, and bade her 'keep up 'er pecker'. 'Someone would soon buck up ter 'er if their boss wusn't on.' But the boss, it seemed, was a 'terrer for young uns. Jimmy Fernatty 'as took up with a yaller piece an' is livin' with 'er. But not me; thet's not me! I'm like ther boss, thet's me! No yaller satin for me!'

He watched for the effect of this degree of taste on her.

Though she had withdrawn her hand, he kept winking at her, and she had to move her feet to the edge of the buggy to prevent his pressing against them. He told her with sudden anger that any red black-gin was as good as a half chow any day, and it was no use gammoning, for he knew what she was.

'If Billy Skywonkie 'ad ter string onter yaller 'Lizer, more 'air on 'is chest fer doin' so' (striking his own). 'I ken get as many w'ite gins as I wanter, an' I'd as soon tackle a gin as a chow any day!'

On his next visit to the back of the buggy she heard the crash of glass breaking against a tree, then after a few snatches of song he lighted his pipe, and grew sorrowfully reminiscent.

'Yes, s'elp me, nea'ly 'arf a quid! An' thet coloured ole 'og of a cow of a mother, soon's she's off ther booze, 'll see thet she gets it!' Then he missed his silk handkerchief. 'Ghost!' he said breathing heavily, 'Mag's snavelled it! 'Lizer'll spot thet's gone soon's we get 'ithin cooee of 'er!'

Against hope he turned and looked along the road; felt every pocket, lifted his feet, and looked under the mat. His companion, in reply, said she had not seen it since his visit to the shanty.

'My Gord!' he said, 'Mag's a fair terror!' He was greatly troubled till the braggart in him gave an assertive flicker. 'Know wot I'll do ter 'Lizer soon's she begins ter start naggin' at me?' He intended this question as an insoluble conundrum, and waited for no surmises. 'Fill 'er mug with this!' and the shut fist he shook was more than a mugful. ''Twoudn't be ther firt time I done it, nor ther lars'.' But the anticipation seemed little comfort to him.

The rest of the journey was done in silence, and without even a peep at the sky. When they came to the homestead gate he said his throat felt as though a 'goanner' had crawled into it and died. He asked her for a pin and clumsily dropped it in his efforts to draw the collar up to his ears, but had better luck with a hairpin.

He appeared suddenly subdued and sober, and as he took his seat after closing the gate, he offered her his hand, and said, hurriedly: 'No 'arm done, an' no 'arm meant; an' don't let on ter my missus – thet's 'er on the verander – thet we come be ther shanty.'

It was dusk, but through it she saw that the woman was dusky too.

'Boss in, 'Lizer?' There was a contrition and propitiation in his voice.

'You've bin a nice blanky time,' said his missus, 'an' lucky fer you Billy Skywonkie 'e ain't.'

With bowed head, his shoulders making kindly efforts to hide his ears, he sat silent and listening respectfully. The woman in the buggy thought that the volubility of the angry half-caste's tongue must be the nearest thing to perpetual motion.

Under her orders both got down, and from a seat under the open window in the little room to which 'Lizer had motioned, she gave respectful attention to the still rapidly flowing tirade. The offence had been some terrible injustice to a respectable married woman, 'slavin' an' graftin' an' sweatin' from mornin' ter night, for a slungin', idlin', lazy blaggard'. In an indefinable way the woman felt that both of them were guilty, and to hide from her part of the reproof was mean and cowardly. The half-caste from time to time included her, and by degrees she understood that the wasted time of which 'Lizer complained was supposed to have been dissipated in flirtation. Neither the shanty nor Mag had mention.

From the kitchen facing the yard a Chinaman came at intervals, and with that assumption of having mastered the situation in all its bearings through his thorough knowledge of the English tongue, he shook his head in calm, shocked surprise. His sympathies were unmistakably with 'Lizer, and he many times demonstrated his grip of the grievance by saying, 'By Cli', Billy, it's a bloo'y shame!'

Maybe it was a sense of what was in his mind that made the quivering woman hide her face when virtuous Ching Too came to look at her. She was trying to eat when a dog ran into the dining-room, and despite the violent beating of her heart, she heard the rouseabout tell the boss as he unsaddled his horse, 'The on'y woman I see was a 'alf chow, an' she ses she's the one, an' she's in ther dinin'-room 'avin' a tuck in.'

She was too giddy to stand when the boss entered, but she turned her mournful eyes on him; and, supporting herself by the table, stood and faced him.

He kept on his hat, and she, watching, saw curiosity and surprise change into anger as he looked at her.

'What an infernal cheek *you* had to come! Who sent you?' he asked stormily.

She told him, and added that she had no intention of remaining.

'How old?' She made no reply. His last thrust, as in disgust he strode out, had the effect of a galvanic battery on her dying body.

Her bedroom was reeking with a green heavy scent. Empty powder boxes and rouge pots littered the dressing table, and various other aids of nature evidenced her predecessor's frailty. From a coign in its fastness a black spider eyed her malignantly, and as long as the light lasted she watched it.

The ringing of a bell slung outside in the fork of a tree awoke her before dawn. It was mustering – bush stocktaking – and all the station hands were astir. There was a noise of galloping horses being driven into the stockyard, and the clamour of the men as they caught and saddled them. Above the clatter of plates in the kitchen she could hear the affected drawl of the Chinaman talking to 'Lizer, who trod heavily along the passage, preparing the boss's breakfast. This early meal was soon over, and with the dogs snapping playfully at the horses' heels, all rode off.

Spasmodic bars of 'A Bicycle Built for Two' came from the kitchen, 'Mayly, Mayly, give me answer do!' There was neither haste nor anxiety in the singer's tones. Before the kitchen fire, oblivious to the heat, stood the Chinaman cook, inert from his morning's opium. It was only nine, but this was well on in the day for Ching, whose morning began at four.

He ceased his song as she entered. 'You come Sydiney? Ah! You mally? Ah! Sydiney welly ni' place. This placee welly dly – too muchee no lain – welly dly.'

She was watching his dog. On a block lay a flitch of bacon, and across the freshly cut side the dog drew its tongue, then snapped at the flies.

'That dog will eat the bacon,' she said.

'No!' answered the cook. ''E no eat 'em – too saw.'

It was salt; she had tried it for breakfast.

He began energetically something about, 'by-an'-bye me getty mally. By Cli', no 'alf cas' – too muchee longa jlaw.' He laughed and shook his head, reminiscent of 'las' a-night', and waited for applause. But, fascinated, she still watched the dog, who from time to time continued to take 'saw' with his flies.

'Go ou' si', Sir,' said the cook in a spirit of rivalry. The dog stood and snapped. 'Go ou' si', I say!' No notice from the dog. 'Go ou' si', I tella you!' stamping his slippered feet and taking a fire stick. The dog leisurely sat down and looked at his master with mild reproof. 'Go insi' then, any bloo'y si' you li'!' but pointing to their joint bedroom with the lighted stick. The dog went to the greasy door, saw that the hens sitting on the bed were quietly laying eggs to go with the bacon, and came back.

She asked him where was the rouseabout who had driven her in yesterday.

'Oh, Billy Skywonkie, 'e mally alri'! 'Lizer 'im missie!' He went on to hint that affection there was misplaced, but that he himself was unattached.

She saw the rouseabout rattle into the yard in a spring cart. He let down the backboard and dumped three sheep under a light gallows. Their two front feet were strapped to one behind.

He seemed breathless with haste. 'Oh, I say!' he called out to her. 'Ther boss 'e tole me this mornin' thet I wus ter tell you, you wis ter sling yer 'ook. To do a get,' he explained. 'So bundle yer duds tergether quick an' lively! 'Lizer's down at ther tank, washin'. Le's get away afore she sees us, or she'll make yer swaller yer chewers.' Lowering his voice, he continued: 'I wanter go ter ther shanty – on'y ter get me 'ankercher.'

He bent and strained back a sheep's neck, drew the knife and steel from his belt, and skilfully danced an edge on the knife.

She noticed that the sheep lay passive, with its head back, till its neck curved in a bow, and that the glitter of the knife was reflected in its eye.

KATHARINE SUSANNAH PRICHARD
The Curse

Azure, magenta, tetratheca, mauve and turquoise: the hut, a
wrecked ship in halcyon seas.

Sun steeped the valley among folding hills, dark with red
gum and jarrah. No sign or sound of life, but the life of the
trees, squirt of a bird's song, a bird's body through stirring
leaves. Chatter of leaves. Clatter and clatter of leaves, husky,
frail. Small green tongues, lisping and clicking together,
twisting over and licking each other; whispering, gossiping,
as we rode into the clearing.

'Come to see Alf!'
'Alf?'
'He's in gaol.'
'In gaol?'
'Ayeh!'
'Harness, a rifle and bridle.'

'That all?'
'All they found . . .'
'Under the floor of the hut.'
'Who?'
'The trooper . . .'
'Trooper and black tracker . . .'
'When they came for Alf.'
'In gaol . . .'
'For a rifle, harness and bridle.'

Long slope of hill-side facing the hut, with scrub of saplings,
tall, straight-stemmed, symmetrical fleece of leaves, young

175

green and gold, tight-packed as wool on a sheep's back.

'Many's the time we've seen him . . .'
'Come down this track?'
'On his brumby.'
'Rough-haired, chestnut . . .'
'Weedy and starved looking.'
'Alf?'
'No, the brumby.'
'Both of them.'
'Hat tucked under the sides.'
'Hair over his ears.'
'And his kangaroo dogs . . .'
'Two, black, snake-headed.'
'Tails curled in circles over their backs.'
'And the bitch . . .'
'Tawny, fawn-coloured.'
'Eyes like Alf's . . .'
'Light, empty eyes.'

Horses nudging, reins chinkle-chinkle over a post by the gate. Snuffing the blue, turned aside from it. Jim picked a flower. Blue and purple, the silky tissue swooning to his grip; a plushy leaf, harsh green. His hand, clutched fingers and jutty knuckles, crouched over it.

The blue cut itself into flowers about us; flowers holding themselves on stiff stalks, spires and pagodas of little umbrellas, folded and spread turquoise and azure, or fading mauve and magenta. Crowding upon us, reaching up to shin and calves, they thrust themselves against walls of the hut, lapping the doorstep; swirled under a fig tree and down through the orchard. Coarse, lush, growing stems of plants pressed so close, no weed, or bud, or blade could grow between them. Feeding, ravening on the earth, spread over ploughed land set to the mould of an old furrow, and under the fruit trees. The curse, sucking all the life blood from their soil, elixirs, manganese, phosphates, ammonia, and flaunting them in her seas – blue, sulphate of copper and magenta, as the sari of a Tamil dancing girl.

Chatter and clatter of leaves; a vague, sly gibberish running through all the hills:

'The curse!'
'Patterson's curse?'
'A noxious weed . . . ,'
'That's what it is, he says.'
'Salt and poisonous as the sea.'
'An enchanted sea.'
'Sea of dreams.'
'Dead sea.'
'Did for Alf all right.'
'Got him down?'
'Never tried to beat it!'
'No guts to let it.'
'What?'
'Beat him.'
'Alf?'
'No guts at all, he had.'
'Lost hope.'
'Starved.'
'Took to stealing.'
'Little things at first . . .'
'Bridle and tommy-axe.'

'Drowned, was he?'
'Daft?'
'Not a bit . . .'
'Touched, they said.'
'To let a place go, like this.'
'No.'
'Only done for.'
'Gutless.'
'Lazy.'
'Liked reading.'
' "Got any books?" he'd say.'
'Ride away with a bag full . . .'
'Happy as Larry.'
'On his brumby.'
'With his kangaroo dogs.'
'Didn't like work.'
'Said so.'
'Liked reading.'

'And kangarooin'.'
'Bit of kangaroo tail soup . . .'
'Goes all right.'
'Ever taste it?'

The hut, dead trees row by row to make walls, with sheet iron for roof, beaten by storms and sun to the gleam and white light of silver; empty, derelict. Rusty, the share of an old plough; a barrow of bush timber falling to pieces. Cart wheel under the fig-trees.

But prowling beside the door, she sprang at us, the fawn-coloured bitch. Fell back, snarling, too weak to stand, belly sagging, a white bag beneath her. Starved, she crouched waiting for Alf to return.

Laughter of leaves, inhuman, immortal. From time immemorial into eternity, leaves laughing; innumerable small green tongues clacking, their dry murmur falling away with the wind.

Dark in the forest, under the red gums and jarrah. The wood-carter's track, cicatrice of an old wound through the bush; but the leaves still chattering, lisping and muttering endlessly of Alf and the fawn-coloured bitch straining over her puppies down there in the sunshine. Gone from back-sliding eyes the sun-steeped valley between folding hills, and hut, dim, ghostly, in calm seas, fading tetratheca and turquoise; birds flying across with jargon of wild cries.

ETHEL ROBERTSON
('HENRY HANDEL RICHARDSON')
Conversation in a Pantry

It was no use, she simply could not sleep. She had tried lying
all sorts of ways: with the blanket pulled over her or the
blanket off; with her knees doubled up to her chin or
stretched so straight that her feet nearly touched the bottom
of the bed; on her back with her hands under her neck, or
with her face burrowed in the pillow. Nothing helped. Going
on in her she could still feel the bumps and lurches of the
coach in which she had ridden most of the day. Then the log
that had been smouldering in the brick fireplace burnt away
in the middle, and collapsed with a crash; and the two ends,
rolling together, broke into flames again. These threw shadows which ran about the ceiling, and up and down the white
walls, like strange animals.

She was spending the night with Alice, and they had had
a fire 'just for luxury', and had sat by it for nearly an hour
before going to bed. It would be her last chance of anything
like that, Alice said: in schools, you never had fires, and all
lights went out to the minute. And their talk had been
fearfully interesting. For Alice was in love – she was over
seventeen – and had told her about it just as if she was grown
up, too: looking into the fire with ever such a funny little smile,
and her blue eyes quite small behind their thick, curly lashes.

'Oh, don't you wish we could see into the future, Trix? And
what it's going to bring us?'

But though she said yes, she wasn't sure if she did, really;
she liked surprises better. Besides, all the last part of the time
Alice talked, she had been screwing up her courage to put

a question. But she hadn't managed to get it out. And that was one reason why now she couldn't sleep.

With a fresh toss, she sighed gustily. And, where her tumblings and fidgetings had failed, this sound called her companion back from the downy meadows.

'What's the matter, child? Aren't you asleep yet?'

'No, I simply can't.'

Alice sat up in bed, and shook her hair back from her face. 'You're over-excited. Try a drink of water.'

'I have. I've drunk it all up.'

'Then you must be hungry.'

'Well, yes, I am perhaps . . . a little.'

'Come on then, let's forage.' And throwing back the sheet, the elder girl slid her feet to the floor.

One tall white figure, one short, they opened the door and stepped out on the verandah.

Here it was almost as bright as day; for the moon hung like a round cheese in the sky, and drenched everything with its light. Barefoot they pattered, the joins in the verandah floor-boards, which had risen, cutting into their soles. Had they to pass open windows, dark holes in which people lay sleeping, Alice laid a finger on her lips. From one of these came the sound of snores – harsh snores of the chromatic kind, which went up the scale and down, over and over again, without a pause.

Turning a corner, they stepped off the verandah and took a few steps on hard pebbly ground. Inside the pantry, which was a large outhouse, there were sharp contrasts of bluish-white moonlight and black shadows.

Swiftly Alice skimmed the familiar shelves. 'Here's lemon-cheesecakes . . . and jam tarts . . . and gingersnaps . . . and pound cake. But I can't start you on these, or you'd be sick.' And cutting a round off a home-made loaf, she spread it thickly with dairy butter, topped by a layer of quince jelly. 'There, that's more wholesome.'

Oh, had anything ever tasted so delicious? . . . as this slice eaten at dead of night. Perched on an empty, upturned kerosene-tin, the young girl munched and munched, holding her empty hand outspread below, lest the quivering jelly glide over the crust's edge.

Alice took a cheesecake and sat down on a lidded basket.

'I say, *did* you hear Father? Oh, Trix, wouldn't it be positiviely too awful if one discovered *afterwards*, one had married a man who snored?'

The muncher made no answer: the indelicacy of the question stunned her: all in the dark as she was, she felt her face flame. And yet . . . was this not perhaps the very chance she had been waiting for? If Alice could say such a thing, out loud, without embarrassment . . . Hastily squeezing down her last titbit – she felt it travel, overlarge, the full length of her gullet – she licked her jellied fingers clean and took the plunge.

'Dallie, there's something I . . . I want to ask you something . . . something I want to know.'

'Fire away!' said Alice, and went on nibbling at the pastry-edging that trimmed her tartlet.

'Yes. But . . . well, I don't quite . . . I mean I . . .'

'Like that, is it? Wait a tick,' and rather more rapidly than she had intended, Alice bolted her luscious circle of lemon-cheese, picked up her basket and planted it beside the tin. 'Now then.'

Shut away in this outhouse, the young girl might have cried her words aloud. But leaning over till she found the shell of her friend's ear, she deposited them safely inside. Alice, who was ticklish, gave an involuntary shudder. But as the sense of the question dawned on her, she sat up very stiff and straight, and echoed perturbed: '*How?* Oh, but Kid, I'm not sure – not at all sure – whether you ought to know. At your age!' said seventeen to thirteen.

'But I must, Dallie.'

'But why, my dear?'

'Because of something Ruth said.'

'Oh, Ruth!' said Alice scornfully. 'Trust Ruth for saying the wrong thing. What was it?'

'Why, that . . . now I was growing up . . . was as good as grown up . . . I must take care, for . . . for fear . . . But, Dallie, how can I? . . . if I don't know?' This last question came out with a rush, and with a kind of click in the throat.

'Well, well! I always have felt sorry for you children, with no mother but only Ruth to bring you up – and she for ever prinking before her glass. But you know you'll be perfectly safe at school, Trix. They'll look after you, never fear!'

But there was more to come.

It was Ella, it seemed, Ella Morrison, who was two years older than her, who'd begun it. She'd said her mother said now she mustn't let the boys kiss her any more.

'And you have, eh?'

Trixie's nod was so small that it had to be guessed at. Haltingly, word by word, the story came out. It had been at Christmas, at a big party, and they were playing games. And she and some others, all boys, had gone off to hide from the rest, and they'd climbed into the hayloft, Harry MacGillivray among them; and she rather liked Harry, and he liked her, and the other boys knew it and had teased them. And then they said he wasn't game to kiss her and dared him to. And she didn't want him to, not a bit . . . or only a teeny weeny bit . . . and anyhow she wasn't going to let him, there before them all. But the other boys grabbed her, and one held her arms and another her legs and another her neck, so that he could. And he did – three times – hard. She'd been as angry as anything; she'd hit them all round. But only angry. Afterwards, though . . . when Ellie told her what her mother had said . . . and now Ruth . . .

But she got no further; for Alice had thrown back her head and was shaking with ill-repressed laughter. 'Oh, you babe . . . you blessed infant, you! Why, child, there was no more harm in that than . . . well, than in this!' And pulling the girl to her she kissed her soundly, some half-dozen times, with scant pause between. An embarrassing embrace, from which Trixie made uneasy haste to free herself; for Alice was plump, and her nightgown thin.

'No, you can make your little mind easy,' continued the elder girl on recovering her breath. 'Larking's all that was and couldn't hurt a fly. *It's what larking leads to,*' said Alice, and her voice sank, till it was hollow with mystery.

'What does it?'

'Ah!' said Alice in the same sepulchral tone. 'You asked me just now how babies came. Well, *that's how*, my dear.'

'Yes, but . . .'

'Come, you've read your Bible, haven't you? The Garden of Eden, and so on? And male and female created He them?'

'But . . .'

'Well, Trix, in *my* opinion, you ought to be content with

that . . . in the meanwhile. Time enough for more when . . . well, when you're married, my dear.' Not for the world would Alice have admitted her own lack of preciser knowledge, or have uncovered to the day her private imaginings of the great unknown.

'But suppose I . . . Not *every* lady gets married, Dallie! And then I'd never know.'

'And wouldn't need to. But I don't think there's much fear of that, Trix! You're not the stuff old maids are made of,' said Alice sturdily, welcoming the side issue.

Affectionately Trixie snuggled up to her friend. This tribute was most consoling. (How awful should nobody want you, you remain unchosen!) All the same she did not yield; a real worm for knowledge gnawed in her. 'Still, I don't quite see . . . truly I don't, Dallie . . . how you *can* "take care", if you don't know how.'

At this outlandish persistence Alice drew a heavy sigh. 'But, child, there's surely something in you . . . at least if there isn't there ought to be . . . that tells you what's skylarking and what isn't? Just you think of undressing. Suppose you began to take your clothes off in front of somebody, somebody who was a stranger to you, wouldn't something in you stop you by saying: it isn't done, it's not *nice*?'

'Gracious, yes!' cried Trixie hotly. 'I should think so indeed!' (Though she could not imagine herself *beginning*.) But here, for some reason, what Alice had said about a husband who snored came back to her, and got tangled up with the later question. 'But, Dallie, you have to . . . do that, take your clothes off . . . haven't you? . . . if you . . . sleep in the same bed with somebody,' was what she wanted to say, but the words simply would not come out.

Alice understood. 'But *only* if you're married, Trixie! And then, it's different. Then everything's allowed, my dear. If once you're married, it doesn't matter what you do.'

'Oh, doesn't it?' echoed Trixie feebly, and her cheeks turned so hot that they scorched. For at Alice's words horrid things, things she was ashamed even to think, came rushing into her mind, upsetting everthing she had been taught or told since she was a little child. But *she* wouldn't be like that, no, never, no matter how much she was married; there would always be something in *her* that would say 'don't, it's not nice'.

A silence followed, in which she could hear her own heart beating. Then, out of a kind of despair, she asked: 'Oh, *why* are men and women, Dallie? Why have they got to be?'

'Well now, really!' said Alice, startled and sincerely shocked. 'I hope to goodness you're not going to turn irreligious, and begin criticising what God has done and how He's made us?'

'Of course not! I know everything He does is right,' vowed Trixie, the more hotly because she couldn't down the naughty thought: if He's got all that power, then I don't see why He couldn't have arranged things differently, let them happen without . . . well, without all this bother . . . and so many things you weren't supposed to know . . . and what you were allowed to, so . . . so unpleasant. Yes, it *was* unpleasant, when you thought of undressing . . . and the snores . . . and – and everything.

And then quite suddenly and disconcertingly came a memory of Alice sitting looking into the fire, telling about her sweetheart. She had never known before that Alice was so pretty, with dimples round her mouth, and her eyes all shady. Oh, could it mean that . . . yes, it must: Alice simply didn't *mind*.

Almost as if this thought had passed to her, Alice said: 'Just you wait till you fall in love, Trix, and then it'll be different – as different as chalk from cheese. Then you'll be only too glad, my dear, that we're not all the same – all men or all women. Love's something that goes right through you, child, I couldn't even begin to describe it – and you wouldn't understand it if I did – but once you're in love, you can't think of anything else, and it gives you such a strange feeling here that it almost chokes you!' – and laying one hand over the other on the place where she believed her heart to be, Alice pressed hard. 'Why, only to be in the same room with him makes you happy, and if you know he's feeling the same, and that he likes to look at you and to hold your hand – oh, Trix, it's just Heaven!'

I do believe she'd even like him snoring, thought Trixie in dismay. (But perhaps it was only *old* men who snored.) Confused and depressed, she could not think of anything to reply. Alice did not speak again either, and there was a long silence, in which, though it was too dark to see her, Trixie guessed she would have the same funny little smile round her mouth and the same funny half-shut eyes, from thinking about George. Oh dear! what a muddle everything was.

'But come!' cried Alice, starting up from her dreams. 'To bed and to sleep with you, young woman, or we shall never get you up in time for the morning coach. Help yourself to a couple of cheesecakes . . . we can eat them as we go.'

Tartlets in hand, back they stole along the moon-blanched verandah; back past the row of dark windows, past the chromatic snores – to Trixie's ears these had now a strange and sinister significance – guided by a moon which, riding at the top of the sky, had shrunk to the size of a pippin.

MARJORIE BARNARD
The Lottery

The first that Ted Bilborough knew of his wife's good fortune was when one of his friends, an elderly wag, shook his hand with mock gravity and murmured a few words of manly but inappropriate sympathy. Ted didn't know what to make of it. He had just stepped from the stairway on to the upper deck of the 6.15 p.m. ferry from town. Fred Lewis seemed to have been waiting for him, and as he looked about he got the impression of newspapers and grins and a little flutter of half derisive excitement, all focused on himself. Everything seemed to bulge towards him. It must be some sort of leg pull. He felt his assurance threatened, and the corner of his mouth twitched uncomfortably in his fat cheek, as he tried to assume a hard boiled manner.

'Keep the change, laddie,' he said.

'He doesn't know, actually he doesn't know.'

'Your wife's won the lottery!'

'He won't believe you. Show him the paper. There it is as plain as my nose. Mrs Grace Bilborough, 52 Cuthbert Street.' A thick, stained forefinger pointed to the words. 'First prize £5000 Last Hope Syndicate.'

'He's taking it very hard,' said Fred Lewis, shaking his head.

They began thumping him on the back. He had travelled on that ferry every week day for the last ten years, barring a fortnight's holiday in January, and he knew nearly everyone. Even those he didn't know entered into the spirit of it. Ted filled his pipe nonchalantly but with unsteady fingers. He was keeping that odd unsteadyness, that seemed to begin somewhere deep in his chest, to himself. It was a wonder that fellows in the office hadn't got hold of this, but they had been

187

busy today in the hot loft under the chromium pipes of the
pneumatic system, sending down change and checking up
on credit accounts. Sale time. Grace might have let him know.
She could have rung up from Thompson's. Bill was always
borrowing the lawn mower and the step ladder, so it would
hardly be asking a favour in the circumstances. But that was
Grace all over.

'If I can't have it myself, you're the man I like to see get
it.'

They meant it too. Everyone liked Ted in a kind sort of way.
He was a good fellow in both senses of the word. Not namby
pamby, always ready for a joke but a good citizen too, a good
husband and father. He wasn't the sort that refused to wheel
the perambulator. He flourished the perambulator. His wife
could hold up her head, they payed their bills weekly and
he even put something away, not much but something, and
that was a triumph the way things were, the ten per cent
knocked off his salary in the depression not restored yet, and
one thing and another. And always cheerful, with a joke for
everyone. All this was vaguely present in Ted's mind. He'd
always expected in a trusting sort of way to be rewarded, but
not through Grace.

'What are you going to do with it, Ted?'

'You won't see him for a week, he's going on a jag.' This
was very funny because Ted never did, not even on Anzac
Day.

A voice with a grievance said, not for the first time 'I've
had shares in a ticket every week since it started, and I've
never won a cent.' No one was interested.

'You'll be going off for a trip somewhere?'

'They'll make you president of the Tennis Club and you'll
have to donate a silver cup.'

They were flattering him underneath the jokes.

'I expect Mrs Bilborough will want to put some of it away
for the children's future,' he said. It was almost as if he were
giving an interview to the press, and he was pleased with
himself for saying the right thing. He always referred to Grace
in public as Mrs Bilborough. He had too nice a social sense
to say 'the Missus'.

Ted let them talk, and looked out of the window. He wasn't
interested in the news in the paper tonight. The little boat

vibrated fussily, and left a long wake like moulded glass in the quiet river. The evening was drawing in. The sun was sinking into a bank of grey cloud, soft and formless as mist. The air was dusky, so that its light was closed into itself and it was easy to look at, a thick golden disc more like a moon rising through smoke than the sun. It threw a single column of orange light on the river, the ripples from the ferry fanned out into it, and their tiny shadows truncated it. The bank, rising steeply from the river and closing it in till it looked like a lake, was already bloomed with shadows. The shapes of two churches and a broken frieze of pine trees stood out against the gentle sky, not sharply, but with a soft arresting grace. The slopes, wooded and scattered with houses, were dim and sunk in idyllic peace. The river showed thinly bright against the dark land. Ted could see that the smooth water was really a pale tawny gold with patches, roughened by the turning tide, of frosty blue. It was only when you stared at it and concentrated your attention that you realised the colours. Turning to look down stream away from the sunset, the water gleamed silvery grey with dark clear scrabblings upon it. There were two worlds, one looking towards the sunset with the dark land against it dreaming and still, and the other looking down stream over the silvery river to the other bank, on which all the light concentrated. Houses with windows of orange fire, black trees, a great silver gasometer, white oil tanks with the look of clumsy mushrooms, buildings serrating the sky, even a suggestion seen or imagined of red roofs, showing up miraculously in that airy light.

'Five thousand pounds,' he thought. 'Five thousand pounds.' Five thousand pounds at five per cent, five thousand pounds stewing gently in its interest, making old age safe. He could do almost anything he could think of with five thousand pounds. It gave his mind a stretched sort of feeling, just thinking of it. It was hard to connect five thousand pounds with Grace. She might have let him know. And where had the five and threepence to buy the ticket come from? He couldn't help wondering about that. When you budgeted as carefully as they did there wasn't five and threepence over. If there had been, well, it wouldn't have been over at all, he would have put it in the bank. He hadn't noticed any difference in the housekeeping, and he prided himself he noticed everything. Surely she hadn't been running up bills to buy lottery tickets. His mind darted here and there suspiciously. There was something secretive in Grace, and he'd thought she told him everything. He'd taken it for granted, only, of course, in the ordinary run there was nothing to tell. He consciously relaxed the knot in his mind. After all, Grace had won the five thousand pounds. He remembered charitably that she had always been a good wife to him. As he thought that he had a vision of the patch on his shirt, his newly washed cream trousers laid out for tennis, the children's neatness, the tidy house. That was being a good wife. And he had been a good husband, always brought his money home and never looked at another woman. Theirs was a model home, everyone acknowledged it, but – well – somehow he found it easier to be cheerful in other people's homes than in his own. It was Grace's fault. She wasn't cheery and easy going. Something moody about her now. Woody. He'd worn better than Grace, anyone could see that, and yet it was he who had had the hard time. All she had to do was to stay at home and look after the house and the children. Nothing much in that. She always seemed to be working, but he couldn't see what there was to do that could take her so long. Just a touch of woman's perversity. It wasn't that Grace had aged. Ten years married and with two children, there was still something girlish about her – raw, hard girlishness that had never mellowed. Grace was – Grace, for better or for worse. Maybe she'd be a bit brighter now. He could not help wondering how she had managed the five and three. If she could shower five and threes about like that, he'd been giving her too much for the housekeeping. And why did she want to give it that damnfool name 'Last Hope'. That meant there had been others, didn't it? It probably didn't mean a thing, just a lucky tag.

A girl on the seat opposite was sewing lace on silkies for her trousseau, working intently in the bad light. 'Another one starting out,' Ted thought.

'What about it?' said the man beside him.

Ted hadn't been listening.

The ferry had tied up at his landing stage and Ted got off. He tried not to show in his walk that his wife had won £5000. He felt jaunty and tired at once. He walked up the hill with a bunch of other men, his neighbours. They were still teasing him about the money, they didn't know how to stop. It was a very still, warm evening. As the sun descended into the misty bank on the horizon it picked out the delicate shapes of clouds invisibly sunk in the mass, outlining them with a fine thread of gold.

One by one the men dropped out, turning into side streets or opening garden gates till Ted was alone with a single companion, a man who lived in a semi-detached cottage at the end of the street. They were suddenly very quiet and sober. Ted felt the ache round his mouth where he'd been smiling and smiling.

'I'm awfully glad you've had this bit of luck.'

'I'm sure you are, Eric,' Ted answered in a subdued voice.

'There's nobody I'd sooner see have it.'

'That's very decent of you.'

'I mean it.'

'Well, well, I wasn't looking for it.'

'We could do with a bit of luck like that in our house.'

'I bet you could.'

'There's an instalment on the house due next month, and Nellie's got to come home again. Bob can't get anything to do. Seems as if we'd hardly done paying for the wedding.'

'That's bad.'

'She's expecting, so I suppose Mum and Dad will be let in for all that too.'

'It seems only the other day Nellie was a kid getting round on a scooter.'

'They grow up,' Eric agreed. 'It's the instalment that's the rub. First of next month. They expect it on the nail too. If we hadn't that hanging over us it wouldn't matter about Nellie coming home. She's our girl, and it'll be nice to have her about the place again.'

'You'll be as proud as a cow with two tails when you're a grandpa.'

'I suppose so.'

They stood mutely by Eric's gate. An idea began to flicker in Ted's mind, and with it came a feeling of sweetness and happiness and power such as he had never expected to feel.

'I won't see you stuck, old man,' he said.

'That's awfully decent of you.'

'I mean it.'

They shook hands as they parted. Ted had only a few steps more and he took them slowly. Very warm and dry, he thought. The garden will need watering. Now he was at his gate. There was no one in sight. He stood for a moment looking about him. It was as if he saw the house he had lived in for ten years, for the first time. He saw that it had a mean, narrow-chested appearance. The roof tiles were discoloured, the woodwork needed painting, the crazy pavement that he had laid with such zeal had an unpleasant flirtatious look. The revolutionary thought formed in his mind. 'We might leave here.' Measured against the possibilities that lay before him, it looked small and mean. Even the name, 'Emoh Ruo,' seemed wrong, pokey.

Ted was reluctant to go in. It was so long since anything of the least importance had happened between him and Grace, that it made him shy. He did not know how she would take it. Would she be all in a dither and no dinner ready? He hoped so but feared not.

He went into the hall, hung up his hat and shouted in a big bluff voice 'Well, well, well, and where's my rich wife?'

Grace was in the kitchen dishing dinner.

'You're late,' she said. 'The dinner's spoiling.'

The children were quiet but restless, anxious to leave the table and go out to play. 'I got rid of the reporters,' Grace said in a flat voice. Grace had character, trust her to handle a couple of cub reporters. She didn't seem to want to talk about it to her husband either. He felt himself, his voice, his stature dwindling. He looked at her with hard eyes. 'Where did she get the money,' he wondered again, but more sharply.

Presently they were alone. There was a pause. Grace began to clear the table. Ted felt that he must do something. He took her awkwardly into his arms. 'Gracie, aren't you pleased?'

She stared at him a second then her face seemed to fall together, a sort of spasm, something worse then tears. But she twitched away from him. 'Yes,' she said, picking up a pile of crockery and making for the kitchen. He followed her.

'You're a dark horse, never telling me a word about it.'

'She's like a Red Indian,' he thought. She moved about the kitchen with quick nervous movements. After a moment she answered what was in his mind:

'I sold mother's ring and chain. A man came to the door buying old gold. I bought a ticket every week till the money was gone.'

'Oh,' he said. Grace had sold her mother's wedding ring to buy a lottery ticket.

'It was my money.'

'I didn't say it wasn't.'

'No, you didn't.'

The plates chattered in her hands. She was evidently feeling something, and feeling it strongly. But Ted didn't know what. He couldn't make her out.

She came and stood in front of him, her back to the littered table, her whole body taut. 'I suppose you're wondering what I'm going to do? I'll tell you. I'm going away. By myself. Before it is too late. I'm going tomorrow.'

He didn't seem to be taking it in.

'Beattie will come and look after you and the children. She'll be glad to. It won't cost you a penny more than it does now,' she added.

He stood staring at her, his flaccid hands hanging down, his face sagging.

'Then you meant what it said in the paper, "Last Hope"?' he said.

'Yes,' she answered.

PATRICK WHITE
Miss Slattery and her Demon Lover

He stood holding the door just so far. A chain on it too.

'This,' she said, 'is Better Sales Pty. Ltd.' Turning to a fresh page. 'Market research,' she explained. 'We want you to help us, and hope, indirectly, to help you.'

She moistened her mouth, easing a threat into an ethical compromise, technique pushed to the point where almost everyone was convinced. Only for herself the page on her pad would glare drearily blank.

Oh dear, do not be difficult, she would have said for choice to some old continental number whose afternoon sleep she had ruined.

'Faht do you vornt?' he asked.

'I want to ask you some questions,' she said.

She could be very patient when paid.

'Kvestions?'

Was he going to close the door?

'Not you. Necessarily. The housewife.'

She looked down the street, a good one, at the end of which the midday sun was waiting to deal her a blow.

'Housevife?'

At last he was slipping the chain.

'Nho! Nho! Nho!'

At least he was not going to grudge her a look.

'No lady?' she asked. 'Of any kind?'

'Nho! Nefer! Nho! I vould not keep any vooman of a permanent description.

'That is frank,' she answered. 'You don't like them.'

195

Her stilettos were hurting.

'Oh, I *lihke*! How I *lihke*! Zet is *vhy*!'

'Let us get down to business?' she said, looking at her blank pad. 'Since there is no lady, do you favour Priceless Pearl? Laundry starch. No. Kwik Kreem Breakfast Treat? Well,' she said, 'it's a kind of porridge that doesn't get lumps.'

'Faht is porritch?'

'It is something the Scotch invented. It is, well, just *porridge*, Mr Tibor.'

'Szabo.'

'It is Tibor on the bell.'

'I am Hoongahrian,' he said. 'In Hoongary ze nimes are beck to front. Szabo Tibor. You onderstend?'

He could not enlist too much of himself, as if it were necessary to explain all such matters with passionate physical emphasis.

'Yes,' she said. 'I see. Now.'

He had those short, but white teeth. He was not all that old; rather, he had reached a phase where age becomes elastic. His shoes could have cost him a whole week's pay. Altogether, all over, he was rather suède, brown suède, not above her shoulder. And hips. He had hips!

But the hall looked lovely, behind him, in black and white.

'Vinyl tiles?' Her toe pointed. 'Or lino?'

After all, she was in business.

'Faht? Hoh! Nho! Zet is all from marble.'

'Like in a bank!'

'Yehs.'

'Well, now! Where did you find all that?'

'I brought it. Oh, yehs. I bring everysing. Here zere is nossing. Nossing!'

'Oh, come, Mr Tibor – Szabo – we Australians are not all that uncivilised. Not in 1961.'

'Civilahsed! I vill learn you faht is civilahsed!'

She had never believed intensely in the advantages of knowledge, so that it was too ridiculous to find herself walking through the marble halls of Tibor Szabo Tibor. But so cool. Hearing the door click, she remembered the women they saw into pieces, and leave in railway cloak-rooms, or dispose of in back yards, or simply dump in the Harbour.

There it was, too. For Szabo Tibor had bought a View.

Though at that hour of day the water might have been cut out of zinc, or aluminium, which is sharper.

'You have got it good here,' she said.

It was the kind of situation she had thought about, but never quite found herself in, and the strangeness of it made her languid, acting out a part she had seen others play, over life-size.

'Everysing I hef *mosst* be feuhrst class,' Szabo Tibor was explaining. 'Faht is your nime, please?'

'Oh,' she said. 'Slattery. Miss Slattery.'

'Zet is too match. Faht little nime else, please?'

Miss Slattery looked sad.

'I hate to tell you,' she said. 'I was christened Dimity. But my friends,' she added, 'call me Pete.'

'Vitch is veuorse? Faht for a nime is zet? Pete!'

'It is better than going through life with Dimity attached.'

'I vill call you nossing,' Szabo Tibor announced.

Miss Slattery was walking around in someone else's room, with large, unlikely strides, but it made her feel better. The rugs were so easy, and so very white, she realized she hadn't taken her two-piece to the cleaner.

'A nime is not necessary,' Szabo Tibor was saying. 'Tike off your het, please; it is not necessary neither.'

Miss Slattery did as she was told.

'I am not the hatty type, you know. They have us wear them for business reasons.'

She shook out her hair, to which the bottle had contributed, not altogether successfully, though certain lights gave it a look of its own, she hoped: tawnier, luminous, dappled. There was the separate lock, too, which she had persuaded to hang in the way she wanted.

An Australian girl, he saw. Another Australian girl.

Oh dear, he was older perhaps than she had thought. But cuddly. By instinct she was kind. Only wanted to giggle. At some old teddy bear in suède.

Szabo Tibor said:

'Sit.'

'Funny,' she said, running her hands into the depths of the chair, a habit she always meant to get out of, 'I have never mixed business and pleasure before.'

But Szabo Tibor had brought something very small and

sweet, which ran two fiery wires out of her throat and down her nose.

'It is good. Nho?'

'I don't know about *that*' – she coughed – 'Mr Szabo. It's effective, though!'

'In Australien,' Mr Szabo said, and he was kneeling now, 'people call me Tibby.'

'Well! Have you a sense of humour!'

'Yehs! Yehs!' he said, and smiled. '*Witz!*'

When men started kneeling she wanted more than ever to giggle.

But Tibby Szabo was growing sterner.

'In Australien,' he said, 'no *Witz*. Nho! Novair!'

Shaking a forefinger at her. So that she became fascinated. It was so plump, for a finger, banana-coloured, with hackles of little black hairs.

'Do you onderstend?'

'Oh, yes, I understand all right. I am nossing.'

She liked it, too.

'Then faht is it?' asked Tibby Szabo, looking at his finger.

'I am always surprised,' she answered, 'at the part texture plays.'

'Are you intellectual girl?'

'My mind,' she said, re-crossing her legs, 'turned to fudge at puberty. Isn't that delicious?'

'Faht is futch?'

'Oh, dear,' she said, 'you're a whale for knowing. Aren't there the things you just accept?'

She made her lock hang, for this old number who wouldn't leave off kneeling by the chair. Not so very old, though. The little gaps between his white teeth left him looking sort of defenceless.

Then Tibby Szabo took her arm, as though it didn't belong to her. The whole thing was pretty peculiar, but not as peculiar as it should have been. He took her arm, as if it were, say, a cob of corn. As if he had been chewing on a cob of corn. She wanted to giggle, and did. Supposing Mum and Wendy had seen! They would have had a real good laugh.

'You have the funniest ways,' she said, 'Tib.'

As Tibby Szabo kept on going up and down her arm. When he started on the shoulder, she said:

'Stoput! What do you think I *am*?'

He heard enough to alter course.

A man's head in your lap somehow always made you feel it was trying to fool itself – it looked so detached, improbable, and ridiculous.

He turned his eyes on then, as if knowing: here is the greatest sucker for eyes. Oh God, nothing ever went deeper than eyes. She was a goner.

'Oh God!' she said, 'I am not like this!'

She was nothing like what she thought she was like. So she learned. She was the trampoline queen. She was an enormous, staggery spider. She was a rubber doll.

'You Austrahlian girls are visout *Temperament*,' Tibby Szabo complained. 'You are all gickle and talk. Passion is not to resist.'

'I just about broke every bone in my body not resisting.' Miss Slattery had to protest.

Her body that continued fluctuating overhead.

'Who ever heard of a glass ceiling!'

'Plenty glass ceiling. Zet is to see vis.'

'Tibby,' she asked, 'this wouldn't be – mink?'

'Yehs. Yehs. Meenk beds are goot for ze body.'

'I'll say!' she said.'

She was so relaxed. She was half-dead. When it was possible to lift an arm, the long silken shudders took possession of her skin, and she realised the southerly had come, off the water, in at the window, giving her the goose-flesh.

'We're gunna catch a cold,' she warned, and coughed.

'It is goot.'

'I am glad to know that something is good,' she said, sitting up, destroying the composition in the ceiling. 'This sort of thing is all very well, but are you going to let me love you?'

Rounding on him. This fat and hairy man.

'Lof? Faht execkly do you mean?'

'Oh, Tibby!' she said.

Again he was fixing his eyes on her, extinct by now, but even in their dormancy they made her want to die. Or give. Or was it possible to give and live?

'Go to sleep,' he ordered.

'Oh, Tibby!'

She fell back floppy whimpery but dozed. Once she looked sideways at his death-mask. She looked at the ceiling, too. It was not unlike those atrocity pictures she had always tried to avoid, in the papers, after the War.

It was incredible, but always had been.

By the time Miss Slattery stepped into the street, carrying her business hat, evening had drenched the good address with the mellower light of ripened pears. She trod through it, tilted, stilted, tentative. Her neck was horribly stiff.

After that there was the Providential, for she did not remain with Better Sales Pty. Ltd; she was informed that her services would no longer be required. What was it, they asked, had made her so unreliable? She said she had become distracted.

In the circumstances she was fortunate to find the position with the Providential. There, too, she made friends with Phyllis Wimble.

'A Hungarian,' Phyllis said, 'I never met a Hungarian. Sometimes I think I will work through the nationalities like a girl I knew decided to go through the religions. But gave up at the Occultists.'

'Why?'

'She simply got scared. They buried a man alive, one Saturday afternoon, over at Balmoral.'

When old Huthnance came out of his office.

'Miss Slattery,' he asked, 'where is that Dewhurst policy?'

He was rather a sweetie really.

'Oh yes,' Miss Slattery said. 'I was checking.'

'What is there to check?' Huthnance asked.

'Well,' Miss Slattery said.

And Huthnance smiled. He was still at the smiling stage.

Thursday evenings Miss Slattery kept for Tibby Szabo. She would go there Saturdays too, usually staying over till Sunday, when they would breakfast in the continental style.

There was the Saturday Miss Slattery decided to give Tibby Szabo a treat. Domesticity jacked her up on her heels; she was full of secrecy and little ways.

When Tibby asked:

'Faht is zet?'

'What is what?'

'Zet stench! Zet blue *smoke* you are mecking in my kitchenette. Faht are you prepurring?'

'That is a baked dinner,' Miss Slattery answered. 'A leg of lamb, with pumpkin and two other veg.'

'Lemb?' cried Tibby Szabo. 'Lemb! It stinks. Nefer in Budapest did lemb so much as cross ze doorways.'

And he opened the oven, and tossed the leg into the Harbour.

Miss Slattery cried then, or sat, rather, making her hand-kerchief into a ball.

Tibby Szabo prepared himself a snack. He had *Paprikawurst*, a breast of cold paprika chicken, paprikas in oil, paprika in cream cheese, and finally, she suspected, paprika.

'Eat!' he advised.

'A tiny crumb would choke me.'

'You are not crying?' he asked through some remains of paprika.

'I was thinking,' she replied.

'So! *Sink*-ing!'

Afterwards he made love to her, and because she had chosen love, she embraced it with a sad abandon, on the mink coverlet, under the glass sky.

Once, certainly, she sat up and said:

'It is all so *carnal!*'

'You use zeese intellectual veuords.'

He had the paprika chicken in his teeth.

There was the telephone, too, with which Miss Slattery had to contend.

'Igen! *Igen!* IGEN!' Tibby Szabo would shout, and bash the receiver on somebody anonymous.

'All this *iggy* stuff!' she said.

It began to get on her nerves.

'Demn idiots!' Tibby Szabo complained.

'How do you make your money, Tib?' Miss Slattery asked, picking at the mink coverlet.

'I am Hoongahrian,' he said. 'It come to me over ze telephown.'

Presently Szabo Tibor announced he was on his way to inspect several properties he owned around the city.

He had given her a key, at least, so that she might come and go.

'And you have had keys cut,' she asked, 'for all these other women, for Monday, Tuesday, Wednesday, and Friday, in all these other flats?'

How he laughed.

'At least a real *Witz*! An Australian *Witz*!' he said on going.

It seemed no time before he returned.

'Faht,' he said, 'you are still here?'

'I am the passive type,' she replied.

Indeed, she was so passive she had practically set in her own flesh beneath that glass conscience of a ceiling. Although a mild evening was ready to soothe, she shivered for her more than nakedness. When she stuck her head out the window, there were the rhinestones of Sydney glittering on the neck of darkness. But it was a splendour she saw could only dissolve.

'You Austrahlian girls,' observed Tibby Szabo, 'ven you are not all gickle, you are all cry.'

'Yes,' she said. 'I know,' she said, 'it makes things difficult. To be Australian.'

And when he popped inside her mouth a kiss like Turkish delight in action, she was less than ever able to take herself in hand.

They drove around in Tibby's Jag. Because naturally Tibby Szabo had a Jag.

'Let us go to Manly,' she said. 'I have got to look at the Pacific Ocean.'

Tibby drove, sometimes in short, disgusted bursts, at others in long, lovely demonstrations of speed, or swooning swirls. His driving was so much the expression of Tibby Szabo himself. He was wearing the little cigar-coloured hat.

'Of course,' said Miss Slattery through her hair, 'I know you well enough to know that Manly is not Balaton.'

'Balaton?'

Tibby jumped a pedestrian crossing.

'Faht do you know about Balaton?'

'I went to school,' she said. 'I saw it on the map. You had to look at *some*thing. And there it was. A gap in the middle of Hungary.'

She never tired of watching his hands. As he drove, the soft, cajoling palms would whiten.

Afterwards when they were drawn up in comfort, inside the sounds of sea and pines, and had bought the paper-bagful of prawns, and the prawn-coloured people were squelching past, Tibby Szabo had to ask:

'Are you trying to spy on me viz all zese kvestions of Balaton?'

'All these questions? One bare mention!'

Prawn-shells tinkle as they hit the asphalt.

'I wouldn't open any drawer, not if I had the key. There's only one secret,' she said, 'I want to know the answer to.'

'But Balaton!'

'So blue. Bluer than anything we've got. So everything,' she said.

The sand-sprinkled people were going up and down. The soles of their feet were inured to it.

Tibby Szabo spat on the asphalt. It smoked.

'It isn't nice,' she said, 'to spit.'

The tips of her fingers tasted of the salt-sweet prawns. The glassy rollers, uncurling on the sand, might have raked a little farther and swallowed her down, if she had not been engulfed already in deeper, glassier caverns.

'Faht is zis secret?' Tibby asked.

'Oh!'

She had to laugh.

'It is us,' she said. 'What does it add up to?'

'Faht it edds up to? I give you a hellofa good time. I pay ze electricity end ze gess. I put you in ze vay of cut-price frocks. You hef arranged sings pretty nice.'

Suddenly too many prawn-shells were clinging to Miss Slattery's fingers.

'That is not what I mean,' she choked. 'When you love someone, I mean. I mean it's sort of difficult to put. When you could put your head in the gas-oven, and damn who's gunna pay the bill.'

Because she did not have the words, she got out her lipstick, and began to persecute her mouth.

Ladies were looking by now into the expensive car. Their glass eyes expressed surprise.

'Lof!' Tibby Szabo laughed. 'Lof is viz ze sahoul!' Then he grew very angry; he could have been throwing his hand away. 'Faht do zay know of lof?' he shouted. 'Here zere is only stike and bodies!'

Then they were looking into each other, each with an expression that suggested they might not arrive beyond a discovery just made.

Miss Slattery lobbed the paper-bag almost into the municipal bin.

'I am sursty,' Tibby complained.

Indeed, salt formed in the corners of his mouth. Could it be that he was going to risk drinking deeper of the dregs?

'This Pacific Ocean,' Miss Slattery said, or cried, 'is all on the same note. Drive us home, Tibby,' she said, 'and make love to me.'

As he released the brake, the prawn-coloured bodies on the asphalt continued to lumber up and down, regardless.

'Listen,' Miss Slattery said, 'a girl friend of Phyllis Wimble's called Apple is giving a party in Woolloomooloo. Saturday night, Phyllis says. It's going to be bohemian.'

Szabo Tibor drew his lower lip.

'Austrahlian-bohemian-proveenshul. Zere is nossing veuorse zan bohemian-proveeenshul.'

'Try it and see,' Miss Slattery advised, and bitterly added: 'A lot was discovered only by mistake.'

'And faht is zis Epple?'

'She is an oxywelder.'

'A vooman? Faht does she oxyveld?'

'I dunno. Objects and things. Apple is an artist.'

Apple was a big girl in built-up hair and pixie glasses. The night of the party most of her objects had been removed, all except what she said was her major work.

'This is *Hypotenuse of Angst*,' she explained. 'It is considered very powerful.'

And smiled.

'Will you have claret?' Apple asked. 'Or perhaps you prefer Scotch or gin. That will depend on whoever brings it along.'

Apple's party got under way. It was an old house, a large room running in many directions, walls full of Lovely Textures.

'Almost everybody here,' Phyllis Wimble confided, 'is doing something.'

'What have you brought, Phyl?' Miss Slattery asked.

'He is a grazier,' Phyllis said, 'that a nurse I know got tired of.'

'He is all body,' Miss Slattery said, now that she had learnt. 'What do you expect?'

Those who had them were tuning their guitars.

'Those are the Spanish guitarists,' Phyllis explained. 'And these are English teddies off a liner. They are only the atmosphere. It's Apple's friends who are doing things.'

'Looks a bit,' the grazier hinted.

Phyllis shushed him.

'You are hating it, Tib,' Miss Slattery said.

Tibby Szabo drew down his lip.

'I vill get dronk. On Epple's plonk.'

She saw that his teeth were ever so slightly decalcified. She saw that he was a little, fat black man, whom she had loved, and loved still. From habit. Like biting your nails.

I must get out of it, she said. But you didn't, not out of biting your nails, until you forgot; then it was over.

The dancing had begun, and soon the kissing. The twangling of guitars broke the light into splinters. The slurp of claret stained the jokes. The teddies danced. The grazier danced the Spanish dances. His elastic-sides were so authentic. Apple fell upon her bottom.

Not everyone, not yet, had discovered Tibby Szabo was a little, fat, black man, with serrated teeth like a shark's. There was a girl called Felicia who came and sat in Tibby's lap. Though he opened his knees and she shot through, it might not have bothered Miss Slattery if Felicia had stayed.

'They say,' Phyllis Wimble whispered, 'they are all madly queer.'

'Don't you know by now,' Miss Slattery said, 'that everyone is always queer?'

But Phyllis Wimble could turn narky.

'Everyone, we presume, but Tibby Szabo.'

Then Miss Slattery laughed and laughed.

'Tibby Szabo,' she laughed, 'is just about the queerest thing I've met.'

'Faht is zet?' Tibby asked.

'Nossing, darling,' Miss Slattery answered. 'I love you with all my body, and never my soul.'

It was all so *mouvementé*, said one of Apple's friends.

The grazier danced. He danced the Spanish dances. He danced bareheaded, and in his Lesbian hat. He danced in his shirt, and later, without.

'They say,' whispered Phyllis Wimble, 'there are two men locked in the lavatory together. One is a teddy, but they haven't worked out who the other can be.'

'Perhaps he is a social-realist,' Miss Slattery suggested.

She had a pain.

The brick-red grazier produced a stockwhip, too fresh from the shop, too stiff, but it smelled intoxicatingly of leather.

'Oh,' Miss Slattery cried, 'stockwhips are never *made*, they were there in the beginning.'

As the grazier uncoiled his brand-new whip, the lash fell glisteningly. It flicked a corner of her memory, unrolling a sheet of blazing blue, carpets of dust, cattle rubbing and straining past. She could not have kept it out even if she had wanted to. The electric sun beating on her head. The smell of old, sweaty leather had made her drunker than bulk claret.

'Oh, God, I'm gunna burn up!' Miss Slattery protested.

And took off her top.

She was alarmingly smooth, unscathed. Other skins, she knew, withered in the sun. She remembered the scabs on her dad's knuckles.

She had to get up then.

'Give, George!' she commanded. 'You're about the crummiest crack I ever listened to.'

Miss Slattery stood with the stockwhip. Her breasts snoozed. Or contemplated. She could have been awaiting inspiration. So Tibby Szabo noticed, leaning forward to follow to its source the faintest blue, of veins explored on previous expeditions.

Then, suddenly, Miss Slattery cracked, scattering the full room. She filled it with shrieks, disgust, and admiration. The horsehair gadfly stung the air. Miss Slattery cracked an abstract painting off the wall. She cracked a cork out of a bottle.

'Brafo, Petuska!' Tibby Szabo shouted. 'Vas you efer in a tseerkoos?'

He was sitting forward.

'Yeah,' she said, 'a Hungarian one!'

And let the horsehair curl round Tibby's thigh.
He was sitting forward. Tibby Szabo began to sing:

> 'Csak egy kislány
> van a világon,
> az is az én
> drága galambo-o-om!'

He was sitting forward with eyes half-closed, clapping and singing.

> 'Hooray for love,
> it rots you, . . .'

Miss Slattery sang.

She cracked a cigarette out of the grazier's lips.

> 'A jó Isten
> de nagyon szeret,'

sang Tibby Szabo,

> 'hogy nékem adta
> a legszebbik-e-e-et!'*

Then everybody was singing everything they had to sing, guitars disintegrating, for none could compete against the syrup from Tibby Szabo's compulsive violin.

While Miss Slattery cracked. Breasts jumping and frolicking. Her hair was so brittle. Lifted it once again, though, under the tawny sun, hawking dust, drunk on the smell of the tepid canvas water-bags.

*'Only one little girl
in the world,
and she is
my dear little dove!

The good God
must love me indeed
to have given me
the most beautiful one!'

Miss Slattery cracked once more, and brought down the sun from out of the sky.

It is not unlikely that the world will end in thunder. From the sound of it, somebody must have overturned *Hypotenuse of Angst*. Professional screamers had begun to scream. The darkness filled with hands.

'Come close, Petuska.'

It was Tibby Szabo.

'I vill screen you,' he promised, and caressed.

When a Large Person appeared with a candle. She was like a scone.

'These studios,' the Large Person announced, 'are let for purposes of creative arts, and the exchange of intellectual ideas. I am not accustomed to louts – and worse,' here she looked at Miss Slattery's upper half, 'wrecking the premises,' she said. 'As there has never been any suspicion that this is a Bad House, I must ask you all to leave.'

So everybody did, for there was the Large Person's husband behind her, looking though he might mean business. Everybody shoved and poured, there was a singing, a crumbling of music on the stairs. There was a hugging and kissing in the street. Somebody had lost his pants. It was raining finely.

Tibby Szabo drove off very quickly, in case a lift might be asked for.

'Put on your top, Petuska,' he advised. 'You vill ketch a colt.'

It sounded reasonable. She was bundling elaborately into armholes.

'Waddayaknow!' Miss Slattery said. 'We've come away with the grazier's whip!'

'Hef vee?' Tibby Szabo remarked.

So they drove in Tibby's Jag. They were on a spiral.

'I am so tired,' Miss Slattery admitted.

And again:

'I am awful tired.'

She was staring down at those white rugs in Tibby's flat. The soft, white, serious pile. She was propped on her elbows, Knees apart. Must be looking bloody awful.

'Petuska,' he was trying it out, 'vill you perhaps do vun more creck of ze whip?'

He could have been addressing a convalescent.

'Oh, but I am tired. I am done,' she said.

'Just vun little vun.'

Then Miss Slattery got real angry.

'You and this goddam lousy whip! I wish I'd never set eyes on either!'

Nor did she bother where she lashed.

'Ach! Oh! Aÿ-yaÿ-yaÿ! Petuska!'

Miss Slattery cracked.

'What are the people gunna say when they hear you holler like that?'

As she cracked, and slashed.

'Aÿ! It is none of ze people's business. *Pouff! Yaÿ-yaÿ-yaÿ-yaÿ!'* Tibby Szabo cried. 'Just vun little vun more!'

And when at last she toppled, he covered her very tenderly where she lay.

'Did anyone ever want you to put on boots?'

'What ever for?' asked Phyllis Wimble.

But Miss Slattery found she had fetched the wrong file.

'Ah, dear,' she said, resuming. 'It's time I thought about a change,' she said. 'I'm feeling sort of tired.'

'Hair looks dead,' said Phyllis Wimble. 'That is always the danger signal.'

'Try a new rinse.'

'A nice strawberry.'

Miss Slattery, whose habit had been to keep Thursday evening for Tibby Szabo, could not bear to any more. Saturdays she still went, but at night, for the nights were less spiteful than the days.

'Vair vas you, Petuska, Sursday evening?' Tibby Szabo had begun to ask.

'I sat at home and watched the telly.'

'Zen I vill install ze telly for here!'

'Ah,' she said, 'the telly is something that requires the maximum of concentration.'

'Are you changing, Petuska?' Tibby asked.

'Everything is changing,' Miss Slattery said. 'It is an axiom of nature.'

She laughed rather short.

'That,' she said, 'is something I think I learned at school.

Same time as Balaton.'

It was dreadful, really, for everyone concerned, for Tibby Szabo had begun to ring the Providential. With urgent communications for a friend. Would she envisage Tuesday, Vensday, Friday?

However impersonally she might handle the instrument, that old Huthnance would come in and catch her on the phone. Miss Slattery saw that Huthnance and she had almost reached the point of no return.

'No,' she replied. 'Not Thursday. Or any other day but what was agreed. Saturday, I said.'

She slammed it down.

So Miss Slattery would drag through the moist evenings. In which the scarlet hibiscus had furled. No more trumpets. Her hair hung dank, as she trailed through the acid, yellow light, towards the good address at which her lover lived.

'I am developing a muscle,' she caught herself saying, and looked round to see if anyone had heard.

It was the same night that Tibby Szabo cried out from the bottom of the pit:

'Vhy em I condemned to soffer?'

Stretched on mink, Miss Slattery lay, idly flicking at her varnished toes. Without looking at the view, she knew the rhinestones of Sydney had never glittered so heartlessly.

'Faht for do you *torture* me?'

'But that is what you wanted,' she said.

Flicking. Listless.

'Petuska, I vill gif you *any*sink!'

'Nossing,' she said. 'I am going,' she said.

'*Gowing*? Ven vee are so suited to each ozzer!'

Miss Slattery flicked.

'I am sick,' she said, 'I am sick of cutting a rug out of your fat Hungarian behind.'

The horsehair slithered and glistened between her toes.

'But faht vill you do visout me?'

'I am going to find myself a thin Australian.'

Tibby was on his knees again.

'I am gunna get married,' Miss Slattery said, 'and have a washing-machine.'

'*Yaÿ-yaÿ-yaÿ! Petuska!*'

Then Miss Slattery took a look at Tibby's eyes, and rediscovered a suppliant poodle, seen at the window of an empty house, at dusk. She had never been very doggy, though.

'Are you ze Defel perheps?' cried Tibby Szabo.

'We Australians are not all that unnatural,' she said.

And hated herself, just a little.

As for Tibby Szabo, he was licking the back of her hand.

'Vee vill make a finenshul arrangement. Pretty substenshul.'

'No go!' Miss Slattery said.

But that is precisely what she did. She got up and pitched the grazier's stockwhip out of the window, and when she had put on her clothes, and licked her lips once or twice, and shuffled her hair together – she went.

HAL PORTER
Party Forty-two and Mrs Brewer

I don't know Sydney very well. The daylight part of my fevered forays there are spent in an ague of traffic terror on a pedestrian-refuge I can't remember why I'm on, or soothing myself in the saloon bar of Aaron's Hotel. Otherwise, I inhabit taxi-cabs *en route* to yet another party . . . somewhere.

See me, then, about eightish on a Sunday summer evening so recent that I am surprised to be already de-alcoholized enough to control a pen, sliding out a taxi-cab . . . somewhere, some suburb *somewhere*. There were three other men with me, though they seemed more because of Da-vid's banjo. We were just late. We had been lost, long enough for it to be droll, and almost long enough for it not to be, in vertically lofty streets swanking it as avenues. The house was so new that I felt paint-splashed shoes still to be in the garage; there could have been no time for corks and string to overrun kitchen-drawers; the frangipanis each side of the front door were infantile.

As we entered, I perceived, nearly not in time, that it was not a gathering to enter rather vividly with a dilly-bag of witticisms: the room – the *lounge-room* – self-consciously contemporary (one stubbornly wall-papered wall), was chock full of men and women jumbled together like general-store kitchenware. There was an air of bathwater . . . sub-tepid . . . gurgling down the plug-hole. On the wallpaper I could see, Belshazzar-like, intimations of the near speech-riddled future: 'Ladies, and gents, and others! Now, let's have a little bit of shush . . .!'

Indicatively, the hostess, a doggedly brisk secretary when normal, was called Dot. She wore, of course, a pleated skirt that could not not swish and whip about. Her husband, an s.-p. bookmaker, was – it goes without saying – called Frank.

There would be, I also instantly knew, a belt of husbands called Frank – the sort of Franks whose wives buy their shirts and ties. Over Dot's newly-bingled hair I saw these Franks in the glimmering worsted trousers with an abundance of buttoned pockets by which Australian men can be picked in Trafalgar Square or Montmartre. It was as patent as massacre that something supremely dreadful had happened, early, so early, too early: there was a surfeit of out-of-tune gaiety. Men, and the unmarried women with fingernails lacquered pallidly, were laughing *Ha, ha, ha!* with their eyes fixed. The married women, with fingernails lacquered darkly, talked with earthy verve, and immodest decisiveness, of detergents. I am, I thought, going to shrivel with boredom. I deserved, of course (I also thought), no more.

You see, I had been being off-the-chain (hang the expense!) for six weeks, in *Sydney*! This was my forty-second (you get it?) and final party. The next day I would be returning to South Gippsland, behind Wilson's Promontory, to be a sobersides among the peat, the grass trees, the black cockatoos always flying north with rain at their tails, the surely false-eyelashed Jerseys, and the high-heeled Berkshire piglets.

In my visitor's guise of Simple Country Boy I had over-enjoyed the six weeks. I had, among other things, spent four hours in Darlinghurst lock-up, punched a drama critic, broken a rib, told-off an editor, conversed with a negro, four Communists and a lesbian, drunk half a bottle of South Australian whisky during a rococo performance of *Love's Labour's Lost*, and been turfed with skill and taste out of the Journalists' Club.

I was staying in Elizabeth Bay, downstairs from King's Cross, in a sort of underground palace coated with *Ficus stipulata*. It contained chandeliers from Murano, a bathroom bigger than a kitchen, a kitchen smaller than a bathroom, and seeming acres of entertainment-inducing parquet like a shot-silk chessboard. Sky-high camphor-laurels, which once edged the drive of Elizabeth Bay House, fastidiously dropped an odd leaf or two to impel perfectly circular ripples, *à la* Disney, on the surface of the swimming-pool. One of my forbearing hosts was a psychic ABC producer with the mien of an intellectual koala, a Whistleresque tongue, all the Belafonte recordings, a cat called Mrs Woffington, and a 24-carat heart. The other host was a well-heeled, middle-aged playboy called Da-vid who twangled his little banjo in the only room I've known subdue a television-set. Life-sized Goddesses of Mercy closed their golden eyes with repulsion on the top of vast carved, lacquered and gilded chests and tall-boys.

We three, *plus* Laurence, an actor awash with a Sunday of gin-and-milk, were all discreetly middle-aged, two bachelors and two *divorcés*, and as disenchanted and potentially sparkling as a quartet of Bemelmanses. We had been driven to this forty-second party by a Singapore Chinese university student, driven to wherever the party was . . . Cammeray, Collaroy . . . some fairly perpendicular suburb with a view of other vertical suburbs' electric lights, and their reflections in an area of liquid – a lake, or harbour, or something.

This Oriental taxi-driver, with whom I had been coincidentally lost for an hour the night before (the forty-first) on similar perpendicularities near Beauty Point, was called Peng Chin.

Until we entered the house, I considered Peng Chin a surefire entrance topic. This topic, burgeoning like a Jacobean tapestry as we climbed a million concrete steps to the house, died its sudden death in the open door. Half a visual sniff, and one thought – I repeat – I am going to shrivel with boredom.

However and however, one had not foreseen – how could one? – Mrs Brewer, the hired help.

Hi-Jinx's Melbourne Cup win a week over. Dot was doing the grand on Frank's rake-off. A buffet meal, eighty-guest-sized for the forty in the living-room was set out more heartrendingly and lavishly than in women's magazine illustrations. There was more than a touch of Mrs Beeton in the cairns of prawns and oysters, in the ham, the chickens, the turkey, and the subsidiary delicacies.

Mrs Brewer had been engaged, I later learned, to help prepare and arrange these succulences, to pass out plates and forks and, more brutally, to wash-up and clear away. She was *cachet.* After the cleaning-up she would put on a browbeaten hat of navy-blue felt and (surely) speed off on an old bicycle.

Not so.

By the time Peng, after consulting his map often on the brinks of precipices, had nosed out Dot and Frank's eyrie, Mrs Brewer had, as it were, dramatically rocketed from the sink to the height of Nazidom.

'God!' said Dot, wild-eyed parlourmaid at what she had considered her own door. 'Oh, God, thank God, you've got here! I'll kill her; I'll *kill* her!'

We imagined she spoke thus impatiently of some time-honoured murderee: a mother-in-law or a busybody aunt.

'That woman. My *char*. She's drunk as a wheelbarrow. She's *let* us have two – *two* – drinks each before we eat. And no more. She's taken charge of the bar. *We can't move her.*'

She seemed to feel her neck scorching. She raised her voice, and swished her pleats as though she still possessed rights.

'Here they are, Mrs Brewer. They're *terribly* sorry to be so late. Their taxi-man got lost.'

We had said not a word. Da-vid dropped his banjo and said, 'Witch!'

'Shut *up*,' hissed Dot. ''Fyou want a snort, for God's sake, charm, charm, charm.'

Then, 'Come on, boys,' she trilled with the most bogus jubilation, 'and meet our Mrs Brewer.'

She led us, like a cinema usherette, through and past the standing Franks, and the sitting wives and women, who gave us, long-entombed miners at sight of rescuers, glances of positive love.

We reached Mrs Brewer.

The long, Laminexed counter which cut off the kitchen from the living-room cut her off from the world of capricious mortals. Klytemnestra her very self, she was alone, fiercely imperious, sacrosanct. She and her domestic sanctuary were beyond rape of any kind.

In the manner of one sponsoring gormless serfs to a Celtic warrior-queen, Dot began a spirited, near-hysteric litany of introductions.

Mrs Brewer closed her eyes as against a silly willy-willy. I had a blood-curdling impression of inner eyelids moving horizontally across the eyeballs as the outer eyelids contemptuously descended.

Dot faltered.

Mrs Brewer spoke.

'One at a toime, love,' she said nasally, malcontentedly, but with eyeless power. 'One . . . at . . . a . . . toime. *Please.*' Oh, the perfect lady. She vouchsafed her eyes. 'Do you moind?'

The *Do you moind?*, despite its irrefutable Queensland accent, was delivered as offensively as the English deliver it, attended by a smile as false as her teeth. Mrs Brewer was drunk. Not wheelbarrow-drunk; but firmly drunk, at the *idée-fixe*, no shenanigans stage where life was real, life was earnest, and administration was all.

She, Mrs Brewer, was logic's king-pin, and alone could save.

She was short, stocky-short – nuggety – and swart. All this suggested the fortune-telling gipsy, but she really resembled nothing so much, particularly about the eyes, as a middle-aged cocker-spaniel with an obsession. It was easy to suspect her face of, at that moment, much unused mobility.

Without delving, I can remember seeing only two other women with her cast of unhaggling directness. One was an Italian matron in a little bar in Cremona where an American millionaire's alcoholic son and I, doing Italy in a Fiat 500, were drinking grappa and avoiding buying veesky-sodah for a German prostitute in a dress of a houndstooth pattern so large that it blinked blackly and whitely as one looked.

The matron, who was perhaps the owner's passing-by sister or sister-in-law, was feeding one of those Belgian milkcart dogs with ice-cream to amuse us into spending more *lire* on more grappa, when a brawl began between two nasty little Italian men.

Nasty little eyes appeared – four.

Nasty little knives appeared – two.

Everyone scattered, jabbering operatically, knocking over chairs unnecessarily, for effect. The prostitute screamed with Teutonic verisimilitude.

Handing me the ice-cream and, so to speak, the dog, the matron reached a Michael Angelo arm over the counter for a broom. With the *handle* she chopped, she hacked – *crack! crack! crack-crack-crack! (da capo)*: Punch killing Judy.

The two men knifeless, she picked up and chucked the

knives through the door, replaced the broom, and returned to dog and ice-cream with no more than a draughty brief smile which said, in effect, 'Thank you for looking after Toto while I was busy.'

The other woman, I remember, was called Bunny Something and, dressed in cheesecloth and beads as Cleopatra at an Artists' Ball in the St Kilda Town Hall, some summer in the 'thirties, lifted a helmet from a policeman's head, sauntered the length of the hall with it, and disappeared, and for ever.

The third was Mrs Brewer, to whose leery and alarming façade Laurence, the actor, was the first of us to be (the word is hand-picked) presented.

She absorbed Laurence's status, and him, with a damp and dampening gaze. He gave her, steadily, a famous look. The suspense was killing. No one would have been surprised if she had barked – or bitten.

After three years: 'Wotillut be, love?' she said, unsmiling, but mollified to melting-point.

'Gin-and-tonic. If I *may*. If you will be so kind. *Please*. My *dear*,' said Laurence, as on carnal knowledge bent, throbbing like a motor-launch, and unleashing a smile of some brilliance.

'May I beg a fairly *strong* one?'

He augmented the smile from sufficiently to quite brilliant.

'My ticker . . . a little dicky,' he improvised, setting his fingers (slender, sensitive, *et cetera*) on his dove-grey waistcoat, and releasing a light cough.

'Wotchew want, love, is a noice great big brandy,' said Mrs Brewer, her spaniel eyes having appraised and estimated. She had put her right hand on the Laminex, and was judicially tapping on this member's glazed and toad-back mottlings with stubby left-hand fingers, in the proper one of which was embedded a time-smoothed wedding-ring, vintage 1921.

'Brandy!' Laurence's voice sounded as if it wore a muzzle, and the pouches beneath his eyes momentarily sagged in dismay.

'Laurence, *honey*,' said Dot, toothily, showing strain and an inclination towards hysteria even though in a model lacy blouse and too much mascara. 'Do listen to Mrs Brewer. She *knows*. *Have* a brandy.'

For God's sake, let's get it over! was understood.

'Huh!' said Mrs Brewer instantly scuppering the idea of brandy. 'Huh! Women! Stuck-up! Ear-rings too toight. *And* nag, nag, nag.'

As abstractedly and confidently as a blindfold knife-thrower she whizzed a curare-dart glance, bull's-eye, at Dot, and reached for the gin-bottle, meantime tossing sidelong, 'You better get those ear-rings off, me girl.'

No one, but no one, had ever called Laurence anything except Laurence, yet: 'Oi seenya on the telly, Laurie, love,' said Mrs Brewer sloshing out three-quarters of a goblet of gin. 'Oi seenya. You're a gennulmun.'

She poured, negligently competent, about a teaspoon of lemonade on the surface of the gin.

'Drinkitup, love. It'll warm the cockles. But don't . . .' She began to act conspiratorially, leaning forward to give the impression of whispering, but declaiming loudly: '. . . don't give none to that thing in the green. Him all mockered-up in his corjaroy pants!'

The mild young man, with his green cumbering pullover and medievally-pointed shoes, simulated deafness but went paeony-pink under his organised fringe of bull's-wool, sipped in a poised way at his empty tumbler, and dropped a sophisticated *mot* into the grassy coiffure of the skittish widow perched like an imp on a Port Said pouffe.

'Corjaroy, but! A tonk, that's what. If me hubby was aloive . . .'

'Mrs Brewer,' said Dot, just able to keep to the social rails, and schismlessly gracious, 'please excuse. I'd like you to meet Mr Jack, of the ABC who . . .'

'Some people, Laurie,' said Mrs Brewer, sparing no more than an oblique though envenomed dart, 'some people are prolly so drunk that they don't know no better. Manners! Interrupting, but! *And* won't take advice about ear-rings and *im*flamed lobes and cancer. Drinkitup, Laurie, love.'

'Mrs Brewer,' said Laurence, perceiving his duty, and smiling back as far as wisdom-teeth. It was the best acting or, at least, the most magnetic I've seen him do. It approached the classic. A second before, he had started from his devil's nostrum of gin as from a bowl of hemlock. Now, his eyes were melting with ardour in the direction of Mrs Brewer's three-haired mole, and his voice was saccharine as a chocolate laxative: '*Dear* Mrs Brewer . . .'

'Reet,' said Mrs Brewer, licking a finger to wipe along one tousled eyebrow. 'Call me Reet. Rita Jessica's me full name. But friends call me Reet, but. You call me Reet, Laurie love. Me late mister useta call me Reet.'

She licked an opposite forefinger, and spittled the other and higher eyebrow.

'The old basket, me late,' she said ruminatively, with a tincture of dislike.

'Reet,' said Laurence in the tone of one deeply purring, *Dolor-es, my be-lov-ed*, 'Reet, *ducks*.'

Was he getting too far into character?

'My *friend* Mr Jack – of the ABC – is dying to meet you. Reet.' And he added, for better measure, 'But!'

Mrs Brewer emitted a clear and involuntary hiccough. It surprised her.

'Beg yours, love,' she said. 'Gherkins!'

Brandy, being gherkins, revealed her unfaltering grasp of the situation, and: 'Any friend of yours, love,' she said and turned her mole, her dog-eyed gipsy face and groomed eyebrows towards her waiting subject.

'Pleastameetcha,' she said. 'Oi lissen to "Green Paddocks" on the woireless. It's . . .'

She considered.

She admitted.

'. . . It's very true to loife. You're a gennulmun. Wotillut be, Jacko, love?'

It was in this manner that the four of us – Laurie (love), Jacko (love), Davie (boy) and Hal (-pal) – received each our ration of two terrifying drinks. As we got them down (mine was a quadruple whisky with an accidental addition of gin) we could not have fawned more on wicked duchesses than on Mrs Brewer.

The world awaited us and its buffet meal.

The women had dropped detergents for children drinking kerosene.

The men seemed to have got into a stalag-prisoners' huddle, perhaps planning a tunnel under the counter, perhaps lynching.

Dot had gone, with brave straight back and subdued skirt-pleats, to the lavatory, to forestall cancerous lobes, to cry, to restore cried-off mascara, and purge herself of filthy language.

'And don't, moind you,' we were warned, 'give nothing to that thing in the green. Or' – her eyes became small as sweet pea-seeds as they sighted another enemy – 'to that bit he's earbashing. Deliquids! Lairs!'

That Bit wore a quantity of black hair arranged like a busby from beneath which a diminished, floury pokerface confronted humanity with unmoving Japanese eyes.

'If me late hubby was aloive, he'd *do* him, but, the little tonk.'

'What,' I said (oh, brightly, subject-changing) 'was your husband's name, Mrs Br . . . Reet?'

I hoped for *Frank*, to prove something my second drink was making me think I thought.

She didn't quite turn on me.

'*Mis-ter* Brewer,' she said, non-committal, with sinister flatness. Her eyes performed some female insincerity, a side-glance mentally and visibly: she hadn't *liked* Mr Brewer.

'He's passed on. Old basket. Trouble with his tubes.'

Tubes?

We put our brows into furrows.

Jacko, love, told me later that he saw a very involved ants'-nest in section, I favoured the disembowelment of a dead horse I'd witnessed as a boy at Seaspray in Easter, 1930.

'Oh, nod t' worry, nod t' worry,' said Mrs Brewer as one saying, 'Hiroshima! A bagatelle!' and as though we looked, we and our furrows, as if we *were* unduly, unnecessarily and neurotically worrying.

The widow of the late *Mis-ter* Brewer stimulated herself: her inner clock had struck a serious hour.

'Drinkitup!' she said, addressing us each severally and with maternal severity. 'Drinkitup! Drinkitup! And you, too, bozo, drinkitup. Quick-smart! That woman's left it all to Reet. Cancer of the lobes, that's what the poor liddle thing'll finish up with.'

To our fascination she began to pound on the Laminex with a soda-siphon. The hubbub of factitious joy faded. Into this abatement she shouted, as from a far-off hilltop, 'Come and get it!'

They came to get it, shuffling rather, laughing somewhat

and somewhat showily and with much ease, and mingling in a sort of factory-canteen queue.

Mrs Brewer regarded this immoral pattern with deep distaste.

She bided her time.

She struck.

'Ladies first!' she cried. 'Think you're Russians, eh? Ladies first! Do you moind . . . *gennulmun*?'

The brutes, the roughnecks, the animals, the bronzed Anzacs who'd forgotten their courting-days, sidestepped, sincerely abashed though wishing not to show it; the women became unnecessarily elated and decidedly showed it.

Mrs Brewer took up a handful of forks, and then remembered that she was, after all, a general.

'Me heart,' she said, attempting faintness, and placing the handful of forks on her Roman matron bosom. 'Davie, boy . . . Jacko, love . . . Hal-pal . . . You come around here with me. You're gennulmen. The plates and forks. Me heart! Where's me brandy? A noice quiet liddle brandy'll set me to roights.'

She began, the ghost of Hamlet's father, to drift off. She sat on a low stool by the refrigerator, screening her goddessliness from the common gaze with an open cupboard-door. As we turned to our task of handing over plates and forks, there was the sound of fluid descending from bottle to tumbler, and the voice of the all-knowing and ever-watchful: 'One plate per person. One fork per person. Oyster-shells to go in the . . .' Brandy washed that one out of hearing.

While we handed over plates and forks, as it were from the altar, we and the guests exchanged many a merry quip. But how censored! How underlined with winkings and shruggings and smiles of a certain sort! How censored even these voiceless gestures!

Dot appeared again, bereft of tears and with cold-cream-shiny lobes, having learned of life, as her guests had, that no matter how closely they had electric-shaved, or how constricting their new girdles were, no matter how heedfully they walked on social eggs, they were, right there and then, no more than visitors in a world of runaway pantechnicons bull-dozing into the bird's-eye maple bedroom, a world of burning toast, enamel bedpans, hangnails, influenza, and unsuccessful permanent waves.

Mrs Brewer, heart or no heart, brandy or no brandy, was the objectification of this intrusive world, the bitch goddess, the schoolmistress with sour stomach, the rude salesgirl, the malicious mother-in-law, the tram-conductress handing on her headache, the one who hamstrung you when you were about to caper to *The Spring Song*. Even in her retirement Mrs Brewer was a force; gurglings and glassy clinkings from behind the cupboard-door testified to her reality.

She was, moreover, resurrectible.

Indeed, just as the young man in the green jumper was about to take his plate, Mrs Brewer slammed the cupboard-door shut, and revealed herself.

She was now immortally shicker.

She swayed like a more squat foxglove, sadder and swarthier.

She doubtless saw more of each of us than each was.

The young man, disposed too centrally, retracted the guilty leprous hand that had been about to tarnish the rim of a plate.

'You!' croaked Mrs Brewer.

Facing the Angel of Death the young man was courageously steady, but his pullover seemed suddenly bluer than green.

'You!' She appeared to wish to have the refrigerator-handle let go her hand. Tears suddenly flowed down her cheeks. She was understood to say, 'Shorry, love . . . shorry . . . Call me Reet. Odly a boy. Odly a chuvenile deliquid. Reetie's been rude. Oh, Oi been thinking . . . Laurie, love . . .' she said, uprooting herself to take, like a toddler, a few bowlegged steps towards Mr Jack, producer, ABC, and, laying hands upon his Harris-tweed sleeves, to implore: 'Laurie, love, givim a noice liddle brandy, the poor boy. Letum allhava noice . . . lid-dle . . .'

In a manner gymnastic and stylised, with some flexibility, no noise, a bottle clasped to her diaphragm, Mrs Brewer descended towards, sank to, the highly-coloured floor, and passed out.

As in a republic founded on the assassination of a despot, there were immediate and disgraceful confusions, there was undisciplined and pointless drama. There were cries, bumpings-into-others, orders and counter-orders, even some immediately-rebuked incivilities of gloating.

'Oh, poor old *dear!*' cried Dot and a number of women with chicken-greasy mouth-corners, and they entered the temple where the priestess lay, the brandy-bottle welded to her hands, curled up like a crayfish.

With conscious tenderness, and a clattering display of warm humanity, and a sense of burying and praising Caesar in one, she and the undetachable bottle were carried to the bedroom, laid on the candlewick quilt and, when her worn little bunion-moulded shoes were removed, concealed beneath an eiderdown. The bobble-edged bedside-lamp was turned out. The queen was dead. The war was over. The drought had broken.

The party now adopted shapelessness.

We four were thrown out of the kitchen.

Frank recaptured manliness, and poured drinks competently as though that were the thing.

Owners of orchid-coloured fingernails began asking for drinks that needed slices of things in them.

Owners of ox-blood fingernails washed plates or one-upped each other's tales of hepatitis, fibrositis, tonsilitis, appendicitis.

Dot, renewed into hostess, showed guests who lived in *old* houses how doors opened (and shut), how drawers slid out and slid back, how cupboards worked, and what shelves were for.

Presently, a young man who could have been Ern, for people called him so, a man young enough to wear a bandeau of blackheads on his inch-and-a-quarter of brow, professionally remotely exercised a concertina below his dreamy but disdainful grimace. One felt that, should the listeners' wariness have faltered, he would have executed, masterfully and brilliantly, *The Warsaw Concerto* and, to astounded and oceanic applause, torn off his lubricated wig and unsatisfactory Ern-mask.

The mood was, however, otherwise. Voices implored for sadder music. And sadder. The yearning melodies of thirty years before were wailed with much attention to melancholy. Loneliness, broken dreams and hearts and vows, depressed their spirits and discouraged drinking.

Two reckless creatures, man and wife, who had won a Charleston competition in 1927, shamelessly called for madder music. His bald head and glossy, huge, silver-grey behind, and her legs of sinew and bone spastically flailing, did nothing except recall *I Wonder Who's Kissing Her Now?* and *All Alone* and *Melancholy Baby.*

Everyone was well on the way to asking Ern for *Won't You Buy My Pretty Flowers?*, *The Letter Edged in Black*, and *It's Only a Beautiful Picture in a Beautiful Golden Frame.*

'All passion spent,' said Da-vid from a corner of his mouth.

'All dreaming done,' said Mr Jack from a corner of his.

'Let us telephone for a taxi-cab,' said Laurence, ventrilo-quistically not moving a muscle.

'Peng Chin!' I said. 'The ball is over. Let's get lost outside rather than here.'

I knew that, somewhere in the cigarette smoke and melodious dirges lurked the man with more eyebrows than hair who was aching to spring into prominence through the merest second's gap and . . .

He sprang.

Little Grey Home in the West had sadly guttered out; there was a pause; *there* was the tiny sandy man like a football-club secretary.

'Hey!' he roared. 'Hey, ladies and gents. And *others.*' No one did anything. 'Now, let's have a little bit of shush. I would like . . .'

We had our hands on the telephone.

'Aw, don't be auntie,' crowed a hoarse and heavenly voice. 'No bloody speeches, but. Do you moind?'

I seemed to hear *High School Cadets* being played, master-fully and brilliantly *and* loudly, by six angelic brass bands.

It was Madame Lazarus. It was dat ol' devil She. It was life. It was Mrs Brewer.

She blinked at the door. She surveyed disorganisation. Her geiger worked. She licked two forefingers and burnished her eyebrows.

'Gawd, you're a broight lot of so-and-so's,' she said.

Slowly, very slowly, she crossed her eyes and said, 'Poor Old Reet can't get her shoes on, but.'

It was royalty proclaiming, 'Our crown has shrunk. So sorry. Nevertheless, on with the *levée.*'

She uncrossed her eyes, cried out, 'Drinks on the house!' raised her skirts above the knees of her lady-harrier's legs with hairs flattened like scales beneath the nylon, and began a delirious witchdoctor's prancing while she shrilly sang 'Kneesup, Mother Brown! Kneesup, Mother Brown . . .!'

Her face, as it bounced, was radiant rubber with enough permutations and combinations of expression to outlast anyone anywhere. I'll swear her ears moved contrapuntally but wittily.

Da-vid grabbed his banjo.

Mrs Brewer's warped suspenders were more exhilarating than skiing.

We forgot telephones and Peng Chins.

At last, with a roar, the party began.

Ern dropped his disdain; his brow shot up an inch.

That Bit opened her eyes, which flashed like . . . like stars! She smiled! She had teeth! White!

The thing, the tonk, the mild young man in the green pullover, advanced at a canter towards Mrs Brewer.

'Knees Up, Mothah Brahoon!' he sang. 'Knees Up, Mothah Brahoon . . .!'

It was a gaudy, a lively, an orgy, a bawdy, a rort. It was far and away the best of forty-two.

I cannot clearly understand how Reet (bull) and Hal-pal (toreador) and Hal-pal (terrified spinster) and Reet (bottom-pinching Latin) managed to break three Noritake bread-and-butter plates by 4.16 a.m., when one would have been more than enough. Since I've had to buy six to replace the three, Dot and Frank are three plates, two hangovers and a successful party up.

That's only natural.

It was Mrs Brewer's party.

JOHN MORRISON
The Children

He was almost ready to go when I found him. He was, to be exact, engaged in putting the final lashings onto his big truck. Blackened and blistered, and loaded up with all his worldly possessions, it was backed right up to a dry old verandah littered with dead leaves and odds and ends of rubbish. He turned to me as I got near, his bloodshot eyes squinting at me with frank hostility.

'Another newshawk.'

'The *Weekly*, Mr Allen.'

His expression softened a little. 'I've got nothing against the *Weekly*.'

'We thought there might be something more to it,' I said gently. 'We know the dailies never tell a straight story.'

'They did this time,' he replied. 'I'm not making excuses.'

With the dexterity of a man who did it every day, he tied a sheepshank, ran the end of the rope through a ring under the decking, up through the eye of the knot, and back to the ring.

'I've got something to answer for all right,' he said with tight lips. 'But nobody need worry, I'll pay! I'll pay for it all the rest of my life. I'm that way now I can't bear the sight of my own kids.'

I kept silent for a moment. 'We understand that, Mr Allen. We just thought there might be something that hasn't come out yet.'

'No, I wouldn't say there's anything that hasn't come out. It's just that – well, people don't think enough, they don't think, that's all.'

He was facing me now, and looking very much, in his

immobility, a part of the great background of desolation. The marks of fire were all over him. Charred boots, burned patches on his clothes, singed eyebrows, blistered face and hands, little crusts all over his hat where sparks had fallen. Over his shoulder the sun was just rising between Hunter and Mabooda Hills, a monstrous ball of copper glowing and fading behind the waves of smoke still drifting up from the valley. Fifty yards away the dusty track marked the western limit of destruction. The ground on this side of it was the first brown earth I had seen since leaving Burt's Creek; Allen's house the first survivor after a tragic procession of stark chimney stacks and overturned water tanks.

'It must have been hell!' I said.

'That?' He made a gesture of indifference. 'That's nothing. It'll come good again. It's the children.'

'I know.'

The door of the house opened. I saw a woman with children at her skirts. She jumped as she caught sight of me, and in an instant the door banged, leaving me with an impression of whirling skirts and large frightened eyes.

'The wife's worse than me,' said Allen, 'she can't face anybody.'

He was looking away from me now, frowning and withdrawn, in the way of a man living something all over again, something he can't leave alone. I could think of nothing to say which wouldn't sound offensively platitudinous. It was the most unhappy assignment I had ever been given. I couldn't get out of my mind the hatred in the faces of some men down on the main road when I'd asked to be directed to the Allen home.

I took out my cigarettes, and was pleased when he accepted one. A man won't do that if he has decided not to talk to you.

'How did it come to be you?' I asked. 'Did Vince order you to go, or did you volunteer?' Vince was the foreman ranger in that part of the Dandenongs.

'I didn't ask him, if that's what you mean. I don't work for the Commission. The truck's my living, I'm a carrier. But everybody's in on a fire, and Vince is in charge.'

'Vince picked you . . .'

'He picked me because I had the truck with me. I'd been

down to the Gully to bring up more men, and it was parked on the break.'

'Then it isn't true . . .'

'That I looked for the job because of my own kids? No! That's a damned lie. I didn't even have cause to be worried about my own kids just then. I'm not trying to get out of it, but there's plenty to blame besides me: the Forestry Commission, the Education Department, and everybody in Burt's Creek and Yileena if it comes to that. Those children should never have been there to begin with. They should have been sent down to the Gully on Friday or kept in their homes. The fire was on this side of the reserve right up to noon.'

He wheeled, pointing towards the distant top of Wanga Hill. Through the drifting haze of smoke we could make out the little heap of ruins closely ringed by black and naked spars that had been trees. Here and there along the very crest, where the road ran, the sun glinted now and then on the windscreens of standing cars, morbid sightseers from the city.

'Just look at it!' he said vehemently. 'Timber right up to the fence-lines! A school in a half-acre paddock – in country like this!'

His arm fell. 'But what's the use of talking? I was told to go and get the kids out, and I didn't do it. I got my own. Nothing else matters now.'

'You thought there was time to pick up your own children first, and then go on to the school, Mr Allen?'

'That's about the size of it,' he assented gloomily.

I'd felt all along that he did want to talk to somebody about it. It came now with a rush.

'Nut it out for yourself,' he appealed. 'What your paper says isn't going to make anybody think any different now. But I'll tell you this: there isn't another bloke in the world would have done anything else. I should be shot – I wish to God they would shoot me! – but I'm still no worse than anybody else. I was the one it happened to, that's all. Them people who lost kids have got a perfect right to hate my guts, but supposing it had been one of them? Supposing it had been you . . . what would you have done?'

I just looked at him.

'You know, don't you? In your own heart you know?'

'Yes, I know.'

'The way it worked out you'd think somebody had laid a trap for me. Vince had got word that the fire had jumped the main road and was working up the far side of Wanga. And he told me to take the truck and make sure the kids had been got away from the school. All right – now follow me. I get started. I come along the low road there. I get the idea right away that I'll pick up my own wife and kids afterwards. But when I reach that bit of open country near Hagen's bridge when you can see Wanga, I look up. And, so help me God! there's smoke. Now that can mean only one thing: that the Burt's Creek leg of the fire has jumped the Government break and is heading this way. Think that one over. I can see the very roof of my house, and there's smoke showing at the back of it. I know there's scrub right up to the fences, and I've got a wife and kids there. The other way there's twenty kids, but there's no smoke showing yet. And the wind's in the north-east. And I'm in a good truck. And there's a fair track right through from my place to the school. What would you expect me to do?

He would see the answer in my face.

'There was the choice,' he said with dignified finality. 'One way, my own two kids. The other way, twenty kids that weren't mine. That's how everybody sees it, just as simple as that.'

'When did you first realise you were too late for the school?'

'As soon as I pulled up here. My wife had seen me coming and was outside with the kids and a couple of bundles. She ran up to the truck as I stopped, shouting and pointing behind me.' He closed his eyes and shivered. 'When I put my head out at the side and looked back I couldn't see the school. A bloke just above the creek had a lot of fern and blackberry cut, all ready for burning off. The fire had got into that and was right across the bottom of Wanga in the time it took me to get to my place from the road. The school never had a hope. Some of the kids got up as far as the road, but it's not very wide and there was heavy fern right out to the metal'.

I waited, while he closed his eyes and shook his head slowly from side to side.

'I'd have gone through, though, just the same, if it hadn't been for the wife. She'll tell you. We had a fight down there where the tracks branch. I had the truck flat out and headed for Wanga. I knew what it meant, but I'd have done it. I got it into my head there was nothing else to do but cremate the lot, truck and everything in it. But the wife grabbed the wheel. It's a wonder we didn't leave the road.'

'You turned back . . .'

'Yes, damn my soul! I turned back. There was fire everywhere. Look at the truck. The road was alight both sides all the way back to Hagen's. Just the same, it would have been better if we'd gone on.'

That, I felt, was the simple truth, his own two innocents notwithstanding. I had an impulse to ask him what happened when he reached Burt's Creek, but restrained myself. His shame was painful to witness.

A minute or two later I said goodbye. He was reluctant to take my hand.

'I kept trying to tell myself somebody else might have got the kids out,' he whispered. 'But nobody did. Word had got around somehow that the school had been evacuated. Only the teacher – they found her with a bunch of them half a mile down the road. And to top it all off my own place got missed! That bit of cultivation down there – you wouldn't read about it, would you?'

No, you wouldn't read about it.

In the afternoon, at the Gully, standing near the ruins of the hotel, I saw him passing. A big fire-scarred truck rolling slowly down the debris-littered road. Behind the dirty windscreen one could just discern the hunted faces of a man and woman. Two children peeped out of a torn side-curtain. Here and there people searching the ashes of their homes stood upright and watched with hard and bitter faces.

CHRISTINA STEAD
Street Idyll

Jenny was going to the hairdresser down the hill. Everything was in order, gloves, bag, key in purse, milk bottles to take down, fires out, time to go.

At the last, she held up the magnifying mirror to her face, checked in the bathroom mirror, wardrobe mirror for skirt, shoes. She knew she would see him somewhere on the hill.

She came neatly downstairs, not to fall on the old ragged matting in the smeary brown hall. Up the street, fresh and bright: rosebush, white patch on stone fence, don't stare at it, it resembles a face; curtains in basement opposite, sort of crochet grid; flagged yard, hello to red-haired cleaner, garage to let: and so to the corner where the big church is and the red pillarbox where she posted so many letters.

Beside it, a seat for old people for sunny days. Once, even she and Gill had sat there. A wedding for a neighbor's daughter; her tears dried, her throes past, the future assured. They were not invited, but they were glad; women, men, girls, craning like pigeons at the church gate, confetti like pigeon food.

Jenny and Gill liked to look at weddings; marriage was in their minds. They had nothing but good to say of marriage. It was the best state for men and women; there was calm and thrilling joy, there was forgiveness, solace, peace, certain home and country, without passport, rent book, marching, petitions.

Otherwise, Jenny would not have sat on a bench; she had a horror of it, as a proof of old age, impotence, neglect.

True, she thought, if some old person actually was sitting there, it is sad to have to creep out of a back room, unloved

233

by relatives, or a sole chamber, a bedsitter in one of the old buildings down this street.

It was, in a way, a very good place, in the air at the top of the hill, with traffic going 10 ways, the schoolchildren from the council high school and three private schools up and down, the respectable girls two by two for church, from that school; what? The Rasputin? The Razumovsky? Voronoff? Impossible. Some Russian name.

Name of Royal family?

The people saw children in the lunch hour heading for the wine shop at the corner, which also served as a tuck-shop, ice-cream, peanuts, chocbars; the women toiling home with shopping trolleys, dog people walking dogs, the greyhound, hairless dachs, longhair fox, ancient alsatian, small white peke, cherished mongrels.

Yes, old lonely people liked the noise, dust, oil; they liked the hundred children, 15 dogs – it reminded them of another earlier life perhaps. Loquacious, silent, self-muttering, frozen in bitterness, terribly ridged, valleyed with age; what were their relatives – loving, rude, sullen, venomous?

They were people who knew they did not count except when they showed up at the post office for their pensions or at the polling station.

Jenny softened her heart. Gill liked to sit on park benches and talk to people. He liked everyone. Once or twice she had met him there, in the park and he told what people said, or what the children had done, dangerous things or naughty things. 'The woman did not answer, she seemed offended; we had not been introduced, this is England.' Gill believed everyone was his equal and had a soul as sunny as his; he hoped others were like that.

Such ideas would flit through her head in an instant as she passed the bench by the letterbox. Now, she was round the horseshoe bend of the churchyard and she started downhill, searching in the far distance for Gill who might now be visible among the shopping crowds.

She stared carefully, not only to see him at the first moment possible, but to see him make the crossing, for it was a death spot, a traffic black spot down there, where three streets met, not to mention the station yard, hotel parking lot and parade. Gill was shortsighted.

Gill had beautiful eyes, hazel with a bluish rim, and, in fact, his father had dark blue eyes. Gill said blue in a peculiar manner, 'blew' to rhyme with dew, and she teased him, saying: 'And twitched his mantle blew.' He laughed and was hurt. Though perhaps, who knows, that was the way Milton said it?

When they played *Cymbelline* at Newcastle-upon-Tyne in 'the Doric', as they say up there, in Northumbrian; Cymbelline, Cloten, Guiderius, Arviragus, even Philario and Iachimo spoke Northumbrian – the program notes said that this was closer to the language in Shakespeare's ear than anything you will hear at the Old Vic or on the BBC.

Iachimo, Lachimo, yes. Was that where she got the name for one of the two large glossy photos of Gill she had, one sober, one glad, and which she called *Tristan Lachrimo* and *Baron Lachlaches*, which pleased Gill?

There was Gill, a short square peg in a quadrilateral situation, streets, footpaths, flagged courtyards, low block buildings, trudging along.

She could see him and knew that soon he would mark her out, coming down the hill with no one about. What is more, he knew her height and lope, which he called a stride. 'You think I stride?' 'You do stride.' She reined in her steps, but on the hill you had to take long steps, go fast. He was looking about now, crossing; he could not see her yet – 500 yards and more.

Just where would they meet? It was always exciting; her heart beat a little faster. Not too soon – spin it out! Now he was across, looking left and right and over.

He began to pass the real estate agent's, the little alley, the dress-shop, the bingo parlor, once a cinema where they had seen foreign films; now he was at the auctioneer's.

Now they were close, they did not look any more. She glanced to one side – the house converted to business premises, with neglected lawn and low bushes where someone threw away his or her gin bottles.

Now his big dark eyes were on her; she looked away. They met, their faces lighting up. Why were their eyes for a moment on the ground? So that passersby would not see the rapturous, intimate smiles which they felt irrepressibly forming behind their cheeks right up to their ears. They halted, fastened their eyes on each other.

This had all happened before. Sometimes, a passerby, a pillowy, hatless woman, in a print dress with parcels, a nice thinning elderly man in a hat, climbing the hill with his washing, had hesitated in surprise, almost as if they feared an incident.

This square-cut, dark man, and this tall fair woman who came to a stop suddenly, and, without greeting began, to murmur – they were not alike, they looked like strangers to each other; and they had never lost this look; reared in different countries, different traditions.

They stood there, not knowing what to say, for there is nothing to express the emotion that brought them together the first time and now brought them together.

She described arcs with the toes of her shoes – her best shoes, for she had known she was going to meet him; he looked around, filling in time, as a cat or bird does.

Then they looked at each other flatface, smiled and she said: 'I saw you when you were passing Sainsbury's.' 'I saw you too, way up the hill.' 'You know my look.' He corrected her: 'It was your walk, your Australian walk.' 'It's true, I saw an Australian in Tottenham Court Road the other day; it was his walk.'

There was a pause, because the last words were only to fill a pause. There was nothing to say, but they could not break the web which had already grown between them, a quick-weaving, thick-netting web, which occurred always, in speech, in silence; but was more embarrassing in silence, because so felt.

It tugged like the moon at waters, sucked like a drain, had already grown part of them like barnacles on rocks, difficult to get away from; nothing fatal in it. They stood quiet, embarrassed, unable to move away; their thoughts going 'Er-er-er-'.

'Well,' then a slight smile, a grin, too, 'All right – ' 'I won't be long.' 'Okay.' Each takes a step to pass, hesitates. The tissue is dissolving, but strands hang on; they take another step and turn, 'Goodbye.' 'Goodbye.'

They wave. They really hesitate to quit each other. It would be better to turn and go up the hill with him, than to go on to the hairdresser; it seems a pointless, vapid business; but to go up with Gill at this moment when he knows she is expected elsewhere would be impossible, an extraordinary weakness, and inconceivable swoon of personality. There is danger in such disorder.

Elle garde son secret, elle le garde.

'I'll be home by twelve,' says Jenny. 'I'll be waiting for you,' says Gill.

For the fact is, though this took place every time they met, this leaning forward to meet, this painless suffering of separation, Jenny and Gill were husband and wife and had spent nearly 40 years together.

Jenny and Gill are no longer there; someone has hacked to pieces the bench for the old people; there are small changes; but very often I now meet on the hill another couple, he short, handsome, with his fair hair bleached by age, she bleached too, but once very pretty; and they have one motion, in harmony, and predetermined, like figures on a town clock famous for its coloring and carving; and by the air they carry with them, and the look of gold, I know that is how they feel, also.

MICHAEL WILDING
The Words She Types

Advertised it looked an interesting job: Writer requires intelligent typist. It sounded more interesting than routine copy-typing; and the 'intelligent' held out the bait of some involvement. Amongst dreams had hung one of success as a great writer. Other dreams: but that one had hung there. So she answered.

The appointment required an old apartment block with heavy doors at the entrance, old, varnished wood, that swung to with a heavy oiled smoothness and closed off time at the street.

'What I expect is not difficult,' the writer said; 'accuracy, precision neatness. And if you succeed in them, perhaps a little more, a little discretion. The initiative to correct, without constant recourse to me, slight carelessnesses of spelling, grammatical solecisms. But let us go along stage by stage and see how we find each other.'

And within the heavy doors, the high-ceilinged still apartment, footfalls deadened on the soft carpet, walls sealed with wooden bookshelves carrying their store of the centuries, the windows double glazed against the sounds and temperatures of the street. And a small table for the tray of coffee or fruit juice or lemon tea to be placed, soundlessly. She missed only music, would have liked the room resonant to rich cadences against the deep polished wood and leather bindings.

She would come to her desk and at the right of the typewriter would be the sheets he had put for her. And as she retyped those sheets she would place them at the left of the typewriter and as soon as she had completed a piece she would collate the sheets and the carbons and leave them in

239

manila folders for him to collect from the drawers at the left of the desk.

The earliest days were easy, copying from typescript. No problems, no uncertainties, no ambiguities. Occasionally he had jammed the keys or jumped a space or missed off the closing quotation mark; but often he had pencilled in the corrections himself. Later, though, perhaps as he became more sure of her, he omitted to make the corrections. And his typing became less punctilious. Words were sometimes misspelt, whether through ignorance or the exigencies of typing it was not for her to ask. He would sometimes use abbreviations, not spelling out a character's name in full but giving only the initial letter. And when he began to give her manuscript sheets to type from the abbreviations increased, the effort of writing out the obvious in longhand too much for him, unnecessary.

And she always managed. It was her pride always to manage, to transliterate from his degenerating scrawl that day by day yearned towards the undifferentiated horizontal, to expand the abbreviations, to fill out the lacunae with their 'he said' or 'she replied'. Her intelligence at last being fulfilled she did not complain of the scrappier sheets that over time were presented to her. Her electric typewriter hummed quietly as ever, nothing retarded her rhythmic pressure on the keys.

He would write instructions in the margin of the drafts. Indications of where to fill out, where to add in, how to expand, interpret. And she would fulfil these instructions, incorporating them into the draft he had roughed out and presenting one whole and finished fabric. And when he offered sheets only of instruction, she knew his manner well enough to develop the sketched out plan as he required.

Was it a shock one morning to find blank sheets on the right of the typewriter? Yet her ready fingers took paper and carbons from their drawer and without hesitation touched the keys. Her eyes read over the characters as they appeared before her.

She read of a girl who saw advertised what looked an interesting job: Writer requires intelligent typist. It sounded more interesting than routine copy-typing: and the 'intelligent' held out the bait of some involvement. Amongst dreams had hung one of success as a great writer. Other dreams: but that one had hung there. So she answered.

Without prompting her fingers touch the keys and tell the story. The girl cannot tell, as she writes this story of herself, if it is indeed of herself. Always the words she has typed have been the words he has presented, suggested, required. But are the words she types now any different from other words she has typed? The girl cannot tell the truth of her situation, because for her to write is to give expression to his stories. Is this but another story she is typing for him, and the truth of her story irrecoverably lost? He has given her no notes from which to tell. And if it is not his story it is even more his story. For if she is telling the story of her story, it was he who established the story. The words she uses will be the words he has set up in setting up her story, even if they are coincidentally her own words.

She sees only what the keys stamp out on the blank paper before her. If it is her truth no one will know. He will collect the typescript in its manilla folder from the drawer on the left, and will publish it whether the words were the words he required or were her words. Readers will read and register amusement or boredom or fascination or disdain, and her truth, if it is her truth, read as fiction will never after be available as truth, whether or not it ever was.

ELIZABETH JOLLEY
A Gentleman's Agreement

In the home science lesson I had to unpick my darts as Mrs Kay said they were all wrong and then I scorched the collar of my dress because I had the iron too hot. And then the sewing machine needle broke and there wasn't a spare and Mrs Kay got really wild and Peril Page cut all the notches off her pattern by mistake and that finished everything.

'I'm not ever going back to that school,' I said to Mother in the evening. 'I'm finished with that place!' So that was my brother and me both leaving school before we should have and my brother kept leaving jobs too, one job after another, sometimes not even staying long enough in one place to wait for his pay.

But Mother was worrying about what to get for my brother's tea.

'What about a bit of lamb's fry and bacon,' I said. She brightened up then and, as she was leaving to go up the terrace for her shopping, she said, 'You come with me tomorrow then and we'll get through the work quicker.' She didn't seem to mind at all that I had left school.

Mother cleaned in a large block of luxury apartments. She had keys to the flats and she came and went as she pleased and as her work demanded. It was while she was working there that she had the idea of letting the people from down our street taste the pleasures rich people took for granted in their way of living. While these people were away to their offices or on business trips she let our poor neighbours in. We had wedding receptions and parties in the penthouse and the old folk came in to soak their feet and wash their clothes while Mother was doing the cleaning. As she said, she gave

243

a lot of pleasure to people without doing anybody any harm, though it was often a terrible rush for her. She could never refuse anybody anything and, because of this, always had more work than she could manage and more people to be kind to than her time really allowed.

Sometimes at the weekends I went with Mother to look at Grandpa's valley. It was quite a long bus ride. We had to get off at the twenty-nine mile peg, cross the Medulla brook and walk up a country road with scrub on either side till we came to some cleared acres of pasture which was the beginning of her father's land. She struggled through the wire fence hating the mud. She wept out loud because the old man hung on to his land and all his money was buried, as she put it, in the sodden meadows of cape weed and stuck fast in the outcrops of granite higher up where all the topsoil had washed away. She couldn't sell the land because Grandpa was still alive in a Home for the Aged, and he wanted to keep the farm though he couldn't do anything with it. Even sheep died there. They either starved or got drowned depending on the time of the year. It was either drought there or flood. The weatherboard house was so neglected it was falling apart, the tenants were feckless, and if a calf was born there it couldn't get up, that was the kind of place it was. When we went to see Grandpa he wanted to know about the farm and Mother tried to think of things to please him. She didn't say the fence posts were crumbling away and that the castor oil plants had taken over the yard so you couldn't get through to the barn.

There was an old apricot tree in the middle of the meadow, it was as big as a house and a terrible burden to us to get the fruit at just the right time. Mother liked to take some to the hospital so that Grandpa could keep up his pride and self-respect a bit.

In the full heat of the day I had to pick with an apron tied round me, it had deep pockets for the fruit. I grabbed at the green fruit when I thought Mother wasn't looking and pulled off whole branches so it wouldn't be there to be picked later.

'Don't take that branch!' Mother screamed from the ground. 'Them's not ready yet. We'll have to come back tomorrow for them.'

I lost my temper and pulled off the apron full of fruit and

hurled it down but it stuck on a branch and hung there quite out of reach either from up the tree where I was or from the ground.

'Wait! Just you wait till I get a holt of you!' Mother pranced round the tree and I didn't come down till we had missed our bus and it was getting dark and all the dogs in the little township barked as if they were insane, the way dogs do in the country, as we walked through trying to get a lift home.

One Sunday in the winter it was very cold but Mother thought we should go all the same. We passed some sheep huddled in a natural fold of furze and withered grass all frost sparkling in the morning.

'Quick!' Mother said. 'We'll grab a sheep and take a bit of wool back to Grandpa.'

'But they're not our sheep,' I said.

'Never mind!' And she was in among the sheep before I could stop her. The noise was terrible but she managed to grab a bit of wool.

'It's terrible dirty and shabby,' she complained, pulling at the shreds with her cold fingers. 'I don't think I've ever seen such miserable wool.'

All that evening she was busy with the wool, she did make me laugh.

'How will modom have her hair done?' She put the wool on the kichen table and kept walking all round it talking to it. She tried to wash it and comb it but it still looked awful so she put it round one of my curlers for the night.

'I'm really ashamed of the wool,' Mother said next morning.

'But it isn't ours,' I said.

'I know but I'm ashamed all the same,' she said. So when we were in the penthouse at South Heights she cut a tiny piece off the bathroom mat. It was so soft and silky. And later we went to visit Grandpa. He was sitting with his poor paralysed legs under his tartan rug.

'Here's a bit of the wool clip Dad,' Mother said, bending over to kiss him. His whole face lit up.

'That's nice of you to bring it, really nice.' His old fingers stroked the little piece of nylon carpet.

'It's very good, deep and soft,' he smiled at Mother.

'They do wonderful things with sheep these days Dad,' she said.

'They do indeed,' he said, and all the time he was feeling the bit of carpet.

'Are you pleased Dad?' Mother asked him anxiously. 'You are pleased aren't you?'

'Oh yes I am,' he assured her.

I thought I saw a moment of disappointment in his eyes, but the eyes of old people often look full of tears.

On the way home I tripped on the steps.

'Ugh! I felt your bones!' Really Mother was so thin it hurt to fall against her.

'Well what d'you expect me to be, a boneless wonder?'

Really Mother had such a hard life and we lived in such a cramped and squalid place. She longed for better things and she needed a good rest. I wished more than anything the old man would agree to selling his land. Because he wouldn't sell I found myself wishing he would die and whoever really wants to wish someone to die! It was only that it would sort things out a bit for us.

In the supermarket Mother thought and thought what she could get for my brother for his tea. In the end all she could come up with was fish fingers and a packet of jelly beans.

'You know I never eat fish! And I haven't eaten sweets in years.' My brother looked so tall in the kitchen. He lit a cigarette and slammed out and Mother was too tired and too upset to eat her own tea.

Grandpa was an old man and though his death was expected it was unexpected really and it was a shock to Mother to find she suddenly had eighty-seven acres to sell. And there was the house too. She had a terrible lot to do as she decided to sell the property herself and, at the same time, she did not want to let down the people at South Heights. There was a man interested to buy the land, Mother had kept him up her sleeve for years, ever since he had stopped once by the bottom paddock to ask if it was for sale. At the time Mother would have given her right arm to be able to sell it and she promised he should have first refusal if it ever came on the market.

We all three, Mother and myself and my brother, went out at the weekend to tidy things up. We lost my brother and then we suddenly saw him running and running and shouting, his voice lifting up in the wind as he raced up the slope of the valley.

'I do believe he's laughing! He's happy!' Mother just stared at him and she looked so happy too.

I don't think I ever saw the country look so lovely before.

The tenant was standing by the shed. The big tractor had crawled to the doorway like a sick animal and had stopped there, but in no time my brother had it going.

It seemed there was nothing my brother couldn't do. Suddenly after doing nothing in his life he was driving the tractor and making fire breaks, he started to paint the sheds and he told Mother what fencing posts and wire to order. All these things had to be done before the sale could go through. We all had a wonderful time in the country. I kept wishing we could live in the house, all at once it seemed lovely there at the top of the sunlit meadow. But I knew that however many acres you have they aren't any use unless you have money too. I think we were all thinking this but no one said anything though Mother kept looking at my brother and the change in him.

There was no problem about the price of the land, this man, he was a doctor, really wanted it and Mother really needed the money.

'You might as well come with me,' Mother said to me on the day of the sale. 'You can learn how business is done.' So we sat in this lawyer's comfortable room and he read out from various papers and the doctor signed things and Mother signed. Suddenly she said to them, 'You know my father really loved his farm but he only managed to have it late in life and then he was never able to live there because of his illness.' The two men looked at her.

'I'm sure you will understand,' she said to the doctor, 'with your own great love of the land, my father's love for his valley. I feel if I could live there just to plant one crop and stay while it matures, my father would rest easier in his grave.'

'Well I don't see why not.' The doctor was really a kind man. The lawyer began to protest, he seemed quite angry.

'It's not in the agreement,' he began to say. But the doctor silenced him, he got up and came round to Mother's side of the table.

'I think you should live there and plant your one crop and

stay while it matures,' he said to her. 'It's a gentleman's agreement,' he said.

'That's the best sort,' Mother smiled up at him and they shook hands.

'I wish your crop well,' the doctor said, still shaking her hand.

The doctor made the lawyer write out a special clause which they all signed. And then we left, everyone satisfied. Mother had never had so much money and the doctor had the valley at last but it was the gentleman's agreement which was the best part.

My brother was impatient to get on with improvements.

'There's no rush,' Mother said.

'Well one crop isn't very long,' he said.

'It's long enough,' she said.

So we moved out to the valley and the little weatherboard cottage seemed to come to life very quickly with the pretty things we chose for the rooms.

'It's nice whichever way you look out from these little windows,' Mother was saying and just then her crop arrived. The carter set down the boxes along the edge of the verandah and, when he had gone, my brother began to unfasten the hessian coverings. Inside were hundreds of seedlings in little plastic containers.

'What are they?' he asked.

'Our crop,' Mother said.

'Yes I know, but what is the crop? What are these?'

'Them,' said Mother, she seemed unconcerned, 'oh they're a jarrah forest,' she said.

'But that will take years and years to mature,' he said.

'I know,' Mother said. 'We'll start planting tomorrow. We'll pick the best places and clear and plant as we go along.'

'But what about the doctor?' I said, somehow I could picture him pale and patient by his car out on the lonely road which went through his valley. I seemed to see him looking with longing at his paddocks and his meadows and at his slopes of scrub and bush.

'Well he can come on his land whenever he wants to and have a look at us,' Mother said. 'There's nothing in the gentleman's agreement to say he can't.'

PETER CAREY
The Last Days of a Famous Mime

1

The Mime arrived on Alitalia with very little luggage: a brown paper parcel and what looked like a woman's handbag.

Asked the contents of the brown paper parcel he said, 'String.'

Asked what the string was for he replied: 'Tying up bigger parcels.'

It had not been intended as a joke, but the Mime was pleased when the reporters laughed. Inducing laughter was not his forte. He was famous for terror.

Although his state of despair was famous throughout Europe, few guessed at his hope for the future. 'The string,' he explained, 'is a prayer that I am always praying.'

Reluctantly he untied his parcel and showed them the string. It was blue and when extended measured exactly fifty-three metres.

The Mime and the string appeared on the front pages of the evening papers.

2

The first audiences panicked easily. They had not been prepared for his ability to mime terror. They fled their seats continually. Only to return again.

Like snorkel divers they appeared at the doors outside the concert hall with red faces and were puzzled to find the world as they had left it.

3

Books had been written about him. He was the subject of an award-winning film. But in his first morning in a provincial town he was distressed to find that his performance had not been liked by the one newspaper's one critic.

'I cannot see,' the critic wrote, 'the use of invoking terror in an audience.'

The Mime sat on his bed, pondering ways to make his performance more light-hearted.

4

As usual he attracted women who wished to still the raging storms of his heart.

They attended his bed like highly paid surgeons operating on a difficult case. They were both passionate and intelligent. They did not suffer defeat lightly.

5

Wrongly accused of merely miming love in his private life he was somewhat surprised to be confronted with hatred.

'Surely,' he said, 'if you now hate me, it was you who were imitating love, not I.'

'You always were a slimy bastard,' she said. 'What's in that parcel?'

'I told you before,' he said helplessly, 'string.'

'You're a liar,' she said.

But later when he untied the parcel he found that she had opened it to check on his story. Her understanding of the string had been perfect. She had cut it into small pieces like spaghetti in a lousy restaurant.

6

Against the advice of the tour organisers he devoted two concerts entirely to love and laughter. They were disasters. It was felt that love and laughter were not, in his case, as instructive as terror.

The next performance was quickly announced.

TWO HOURS OF REGRET.

Tickets sold quickly. He began with a brief interpretation of love using it merely as a prelude to regret which he elaborated on in a complex and moving performance which left the audience pale and shaken. In a final flourish he passed from regret to loneliness to terror. The audience devoured the terror like brave tourists eating the hottest curry in an Indian restaurant.

7

'What you are doing,' she said, 'is capitalising on your neuroses. Personally I find it disgusting, like someone exhibiting their club foot, or Turkish beggars with strange deformities.'

He said nothing. He was mildly annoyed at her presumption: that he had not thought this many, many times before.

With perfect misunderstanding she interpreted his passivity as disdain.

Wishing to hurt him, she slapped his face.

Wishing to hurt her, he smiled brilliantly.

8

The story of the blue string touched the public imagination. Small brown paper packages were sold at the doors of his concerts.

Standing on stage he could hear the packages being noisily unwrapped. He thought of American matrons buying Muslim prayer rugs.

9

Exhausted and weakened by the heavy schedule he fell prey to the doubts that had pricked at him insistently for years. He lost all sense of direction and spent many listless hours by himself, sitting in a motel room listening to the airconditioner.

He had lost confidence in the social uses of controlled terror. He no longer understood the audience's need to experience the very things he so desperately wished to escape from.

He emptied the ashtrays fastidiously.

He opened his brown paper parcel and threw the small pieces of string down the cistern. When the torrent of white water subsided they remained floating there like flotsam from a disaster at sea.

10

The Mime called a press conference to announce that there would be no more concerts. He seemed small and foreign and smelt of garlic. The press regarded him without enthusiasm. He watched their hovering pens anxiously, unsuccessfully willing them to write down his words.

Briefly he announced that he wished to throw his talent open to broader influences. His skills would be at the disposal of the people, who would be free to request his services for any purpose at any time.

His skin seemed sallow but his eyes seemed as bright as those on a nodding fur mascot on the back window ledge of an American car.

11

Asked to describe death he busied himself taking Polaroid photographs of his questioners.

12

Asked to describe marriage he handed out small cheap mirrors with MADE IN TUNISIA written on the back.

13

His popularity declined. It was felt that he had become obscure and beyond the understanding of ordinary people. In response he requested easier questions. He held back nothing of himself in his effort to please his audience.

14

Asked to describe an aeroplane he flew three times around the city, only injuring himself slightly on landing.

15

Asked to describe a river, he drowned himself.

16

It is unfortunate that this, his last and least typical performance, is the only one which has been recorded on film.

There is a small crowd by the river bank, no more than thirty people. A small, neat man dressed in a grey suit picks his way through some children who seem more interested in the large plastic toy dog they are playing with.

He steps into the river, which, at the bank, is already quite deep. His head is only visible above the water for a second or two. And then he is gone.

A policeman looks expectantly over the edge, as if waiting for him to reappear. Then the film stops.

Watching this last performance it is difficult to imagine how this man stirred such emotions in the hearts of those who saw him.

MORRIS LURIE
Pride and Joy

I never had the pleasure of meeting Mr Ernest Hemingway,
so all I know about him is what I've read, but the first time
I saw Ned Matthews, that's who I thought of. Hemingway.
Not that Matthews looked much like him. Hemingway wasn't
that short. Hemingway had more hair. Hemingway sported
a grizzly white beard, and all Matthews had was a moustache.
But his chest was Hemingway, a broad barrel, stretching his
shirt. And his walk. He walked as though he'd just shot a lion,
a mixture of offhand and proud. And then there were his
fingers. His fingers were definitely Hemingway. It was eight
o'clock in the morning, the first time I saw him, we were all
eating our breakfast, and the fingers of Ned Matthews' right
hand were wrapped around a large glass of frothy ice-cold
beer. You could see the bubbles rising in the glass and
popping out on top. You could practically hear them too, it
was suddenly that quiet.

Eight o'clock in the morning on an island on the Great
Barrier Reef. A Hemingway time for a glass of beer.

He came up the centre aisle of the dining room, making
for my table, at the far end of the room, furthest from the door,
me and sixty other holiday-makers staring at his glass of
frothy ice-cold beer, filled with the morning sun.

He wasn't alone. Right behind him came a boy who looked
about sixteen, tall, with curly blond hair and a cocky smile.
The smile was as much in his eyes as on his lips. He walked
with an exaggerated swagger. He had a glass of beer in his
hand too. And then came another man, taller than the boy,
a thin, sinewy man with colourless eyes and his hair all
shaved off at the sides and on top plastered down hard with

oil. He wore a dirty tee shirt, battered jeans, no shoes. There was a beer in his hand too. The three of them came towards me in proud procession, through the hushed dining room, though now there were a few whispers.

'This free?' said Matthews, pulling out a chair. 'Help yourself,' I said, but he already had. He sat down, not giving me a second look. 'Billy, you sit here,' he said to the boy. 'Stan, over there.' He had that kind of voice that likes giving orders and was used to having them obeyed. The three of them made a lot of noise with their chairs, sitting down, getting comfortable, more noise than they had to. None of them looked over at me.

'Well, boys,' said Matthews, raising his glass. 'Bon appétit!' He drained his glass in one gulp. The thin man did likewise. The boy, I noticed, had to take a breath halfway down, but he made it, then banged his empty glass down on the table, sat back in his chair, looked serious, and then let out a great burp. Then he smiled at Ned Matthews, who smiled back, pleased with the performance. 'Only way to start the day, son,' Ned Matthews said. 'Yeah,' said Billy. Then the three of them lit up cigarettes. They were like three ham actors playing at being tough. For us? I thought. For each other? But it was too early in the day for games for me, and I went back to my cornflakes.

So that's Ned Matthews, I thought. That's what everyone's been waiting for. Well, well.

A waitress came over to take their order. She was a young girl, about seventeen, very pretty, without sophistication, not yet completely sure of herself. She dropped three menus on the table and then stood waiting, hands on hips, looking vaguely bored. Matthews reached over and picked up a menu. So did the thin man. But the boy left his where it was, turned around in his chair to face the waitress, who was standing behind him, and a little to one side, looked up, and gave her a cocky smile, his cigarette bobbing between his lips.

'What's ya name, honey?' he said. 'Why?' said the girl. 'I always like to know the names of the girls I sleep with,' the boy said. The girl didn't bat an eyelid, but her face turned hard. She stared straight back at him. The boy let out a small laugh, and then, slowly, so that it wouldn't look as though she had stared him down, he turned back to face his father.

Very casually, he removed his cigarette from between his lips and gave him a big wink. Then he lolled back in his chair and took a slow, arrogant puff on his cigarette. 'Easy, son,' said Matthews, but his face was beaming with pride. I looked away.

But the performance wasn't over. Matthews had a loud voice, and I heard the rest. 'Girl,' he said to the waitress, 'let's have some eggs. Four eggs each. Fried. And some bacon. And some sausages. And a lot of toast. Hot.' 'Dad, I couldn't eat four eggs,' I heard the boy say. *'Four eggs each,'* Matthews repeated to the waitress. There was an edge of irritation to his voice. Not much, but it was there. 'And coffee,' he said. 'Black.'

The waitress went away. I turned a little in my chair, away from Matthews and his son and the other man, away from their games, and looked out of the window at the palm trees and the sea.

The sea was blue, the sky was another blue, the palm trees were green, and the buildings and huts scattered under them were white. It was a lovely place. It took an hour and forty minutes to walk around the island, an hour and five minutes to hike up to the top of the hill in the middle. The sea was warm, the bar was well stocked, the management put on barbecues and music at night, you could take a boat and hop around to other islands, if you wanted to. Or you could do nothing. Most people did nothing. It was a holiday place. I was there to sort out what I thought about a girl back home. Did I want her? Did I want her forever? I took a daily walk around the island, alone, just me and my thoughts, stopping off halfway for a swim. Captain Cook had been here before me and had left behind some goats, and their offspring watched me suspiciously as I sauntered past, an old man goat with a white beard and a dozen skitterish young ones. Sometimes I'd surprise them and they'd bound off through the long grass, making a hell of a noise. There were about eighty people on the island, sixty guests, twenty staff. And now there was Mr Ned Matthews and his son Billy and their hired man. It had been very peaceful up to now. And now?

Jim, a gardener and general handyman about the place, had told me about him. This was on my second day, when I had finished my walk around the island and was sitting under a palm tree, contemplating the flat sea, thinking about my girl. She was beautiful. She was magnificent. But. But what? 'Quiet, isn't it?' Jim said to me. 'Well, it is.' I said, 'but I like it.' 'Wait'll Ned Matthews gets here,' Jim said. 'Then things'll liven up a bit. This place is a morgue without him. Just you wait till he comes. Should be here any day.' He stared out to sea, as though expecting any moment something to appear. 'Who's Ned Matthews?' I said. 'Millionaire,' Jim said. 'Rich as blazes. Got himself a yacht, the *Southerly*. Beautiful.' 'What does he do?' I asked. 'Do? He don't do nothin'. He's a millionaire. He drinks, that's what he does. You'll see some real drinking when Ned gets here. I'll tell you what he does. He sails around from island to island, raising general hell. Should be here any day.' Again he scanned the horizon for some sign. 'I'll look out for him,' I said. 'Oh, you'll see him,' Jim said. 'You'd know he was here even if you was blind.'

Well, he was here, sitting at my table. I kept looking out of the window at the palm trees and the sea, waiting for the waitress to come with my coffee. I couldn't see the jetty, it was out of view. I took a sip of my pineapple juice. I heard Ned Matthews, in his loud voice, organising his labour for the day.

'That tide'll be out in about three hours,' he was saying. 'Stan, straight after breakfast, I want you to lash *Southerly* up tight. Get her high and dry. Billy, you can start stripping her underneath. I'll work on the pumps and the motor. I want to get her done in two days.'

'Okay, boss,' I heard Stan say. 'Yeah, Dad,' the boy drawled. The waitress brought my coffee and I took it outside to drink in the sun.

Now I could see the yacht. It really was a beautiful piece of work. It was dead white, with gleaming brass flashing in the sun. It looked small, riding in the blue water at the end of the jetty, a toy, a rich man's toy. I sipped my coffee and lit a cigarette and thought about a millionaire's life of sailing from island to island, greeted everywhere with open arms, raising hell. Beer before breakfast. And the boy? I thought. Is he grooming him for that kind of life? Well, the boy seems to like it. Hell, at his age I was still at school. I was thinking about that when I heard a door slam and Matthews and his son and the hired man strode across the lawn past me and went out onto the jetty. They got to work without preamble. Matthews crushed out the cigarette he was smoking and stripped off his shirt. The Hemingway chest expanded in the sun. I watched him for a while and then I stood up and took my coffee cup back inside and then I went to renew my acquaintance with Captain Cook's goats.

He was Hemingway at lunch too, striding in with his glass of beer, his son and the hired man with theirs, down the centre aisle, a repeat of their morning's performance. They hadn't washed or changed, and seemed to wear the grease on their faces and hands like badges to an exclusive club. Matthews, as before, ordered for all three, in his loud, commanding voice. Billy was cocky to the waitress, exchanging winks with his father. 'Keep at her, son,' Matthews told him, flashing his wide, even smile, and then they talked about the yacht.

He wasn't Hemingway at dinner, though. He was Clark Gable. He came in alone, wearing a dark blue yachting jacket and trim grey slacks. He smiled to left and right as he came down the aisle, his eyes merry and sincere. His son came in a few minutes later, and then the hired man. Matthews let them order their own dinner. He was polite to the waitress. He ordered a bottle of wine and sipped it slowly. He even smiled at me. 'Nice weather,' he said.

When I had finished my meal, I went outside to smoke and to look up at the stars and listen to the palm trees moving about in the breeze coming in from the sea. I took a walk along the front beach. The tide was way out, and I saw the *Southerly*, out of the water, tied up to the end of the jetty. She really was a beautiful boat. The moon shone on the polished brass. The sails were the colour of rich cream.

After a while, I went in to the bar. Matthews and his son and the hired man were there, down one end. Matthews was talking to a fat stockbroker who had taken too much sun and looked scalded, like a lobster. He looked a little hemmed in by Matthews, and kept saying, 'Is that so? Is that so?' to everything Matthews said. The stockbroker was wearing a lilac shirt and canary-yellow slacks and white shoes. He looked over-festive and a little uncomfortable. Matthews was describing the effects of certain drinks he had sampled in his time. 'Try this one,' he said to the stockbroker, and handed him something in a long-stemmed glass. The drink was bright green, with a white froth on top. Matthews handed one of the same to his son, and picked up a third. The hired man was drinking beer. 'Three of these and you'll roar like a bull,' Matthews said to the stockbroker. 'Cheers!' He drained his in one gulp. 'Cheers,' said the stockbroker, looking perplexed.

I bought myself a beer and sat down on a cane chair at the other end of the bar. 'Say goodbye to your hair,' I heard Matthews saying to the stockbroker, handing him another drink. This one was a vivid red. 'This little invention is guaranteed to take it out by the roots,' Matthews said. 'Is that so?' said the stockbroker. 'God's truth,' said Matthews' son, upending his own glass.

Matthews then ordered something that looked like milk, but came out of four bottles, then something pale blue, then he went back to the bright green. His son matched him drink for drink. 'I do believe I'm bringing up a little alcoholic here,' Matthews said, putting his arm around his son's shoulders. Billy seemed to swell with pride. Matthews laughed, and then broke away from his son and gave him a playful jab in the ribs. 'Watch it, old timer,' his son said. 'I can drink you under the table any day.' Matthews threw back his head and laughed, showing his white, even teeth. 'That'll be the day, son,' he roared, and then he turned to the bartender and shouted, 'Hey! How about getting off your fat behind and giving us a bit of service round here?' The bartender was standing not two feet away from him. 'Yeah, shake it up there,' Billy shouted. I felt I'd suddenly had enough of Matthews and his son, put down my beer glass, and went to my room to read.

Actually, I was tired. I was sharing a room with a retired Irishman and I wasn't getting much sleep. I had had the room to myself the first night, but the next day a new boatload of people had come and the Irishman was put in with me. He was an enormous man, weighed at least sixteen stone, moved slowly, as big men do, and was jovial, smoked cigars and told ribald stories. I liked him. He had been retired for four years, he told me, his two sons now managing his business, and he was on perpetual holiday, going where he fancied, doing a little oil painting to pass the time. He must have been over-tired that first night, because he went to bed straight after dinner, and he snored till five in the morning, louder than anyone I had ever heard in my life. He was like an engine. There were no pauses. At three in the morning I couldn't stand it any longer, and I sat up and shouted, 'For God's sake, stop that snoring!' But the snoring went on, and I felt a fool for shouting in the night, and the first thing I did after breakfast was to go to the office and demand another room. 'I'm exhausted,' I told the manager. 'I didn't sleep three minutes all night.' The manager was a small man with a face like a nut, crinkled and burnt with sun. He nodded sympathetically. 'I know,' he said. 'You get one every now and then. The thing is, can you put up with it one more night? I haven't got a spare room in the place. There'll be one coming up tomorrow. I'll move you in there. But please, just one more night. I'm sorry. Believe me. My first wife used to snore, I know how it is.' 'Okay,' I said, and that night before going to bed I drank three large brandies and then two tots of rum, but there wasn't a sound out of the Irishman all night. Not a squeak. 'Listen,' I told the manager in the morning, 'don't move me out of that room. He didn't snore at all last night, so I think I'll stay. You know how it is on an island. I don't want to create bad feelings. He must have been over-tired, that's all. He didn't utter a peep all night.' 'Sure,' said the manager, and that night the Irishman outdid himself, not only snoring but moaning, grunting, and giving whistles. He sounded like at least three men. The next night he snored again, then for two nights he didn't, and then he came back again, worse than ever. He was unpredictable, there was no pattern to it. Some nights he snored, some he didn't, and between the snores and the anticipation I was getting little sleep.

Just after midnight, the Irishman came in. He sat down very carefully on the end of his bed, lit a cigar, and then told me three or four ribald stories. When he had finished his cigar, he went into the bathroom, came out in his pyjamas, got into bed, and began to snore. I put on my shoes and went out to the bar.

A party was in progress, with much shouting and laughter. The cooks were there, the gardeners and handymen, and all the waitresses. There were three or four holiday-makers, including the stockbroker, who was redder in the face than ever and had spilt something on his canary-yellow slacks. Ned Matthews was in the middle of it, and next to him was his son. Billy had an arm around the waitress from our table, who was flushed with drink, but didn't look too happy. Everyone was drinking something purple. I bought myself a brandy. Jim the gardener pushed through to me. 'I told ya the place'd liven up,' he said. 'And we haven't started yet.' He downed his purple drink and waved the empty glass over his head. 'Tastes like paint stripper, but what the hell,' he said, giving me a wink. 'I'm not payin'. Listen, we're all moving down to the beach, in about an hour. It's all organised.' 'Not for me,' I said. 'I'm just having a couple of brandies and then I'm going to bed.' 'No crime to change your mind,' Jim said.

By half past one I'd had enough brandy to take the edge off the Irishman's snoring, but I could hear the party down at the beach. There was a lot of screaming and singing, and it seemed to go on all night. I slept two hours at most and woke up feeling hollow and haggard, not at all in the mood for Matthews and Billy and the hired man walking down the centre aisle at breakfast with their frothy ice-cold glasses of beer, but there they were, right on time, performing the ritual.

There was a lot of drinking that night too, and the next night, and the night after that, and each morning in they came, always in the same order, always with their glasses of beer.

The drink was showing on them. They were puffy about the eyes. Matthews appeared on the third day with a plaster across his forehead. The hired man had a bruised lip. But each ravagement, each wound, seemed to increase their pride. 'Bon appétit.' Matthews roared, and down went the beer. Then he ordered the breakfasts. Four eggs a-piece, sausages, bacon, toast, black coffee. I watched the boy. How long can he last? I thought. How long can he keep it up?

Five days after Matthews had appeared, a new boatload of people arrived. I watched them getting off the boat. They were the usual crowd, middle-aged, cluttered with luggage, bright and bold in holiday clothes. Except for one. She was twenty-two or three, with dark hair to her shoulders, and looked like a princess. She stepped neatly ashore, showing lovely long legs, and then turned, and helped a grey-haired woman step down. 'Thank you, dear,' said the woman. 'Come on, Mother,' said the princess, and together they walked along the jetty and under the palm trees across the lawn to reception.

The Irishman had added a fire engine to his nocturnal noises the night before, and I went off to have a sleep before lunch, on a quiet beach I had found on the other side of the island, away from everyone, just me and Captain Cook's goats.

At lunchtime, Matthews and Billy and the hired man downed their beers, lit their cigarettes, and waited for the waitress to come. 'When are we going to have some real drinking, Dad?' Billy asked his father. 'I thought you told me we was gonna have some real fun.' 'I want to get the boat out this afternoon,' Matthews said. 'Then I'll show you some drinking.' 'Careful, old man,' Billy said. 'I don't want to carry you to bed like I did last night.' 'That's enough of that,' Matthews snapped. I sneaked a look across at Billy, but his face was turned away and I couldn't see his expression. But for a second the table was tense. Don't tell me Billy is outdrinking him. I thought. His own son. His own pride and joy.

He was Clark Gable again that night, in his yachting jacket and grey slacks, and from the dining room windows you could see the *Southerly* afloat, about half a mile out. She looked beautiful. Matthews ordered a bottle of wine with his meal, and, when it was over, lit up a cigar.

After dinner, I took my usual walk along the front beach, the sea so flat and shining with moon it looked like mother-of-pearl. The palm trees stirred and rustled, and I wanted my girl. But forever? I lit a cigarette, and when it was finished went into the bar. Matthews wasn't there. It was quiet and pleasant. But the princess was there, with her mother. And Billy. Billy was talking to the girl. He looked very neat and polite. The girl was listening to what he was saying and nodding her head. She had wonderful eyes. Then Matthews came in, went over to them, and put his arm around his son's shoulders. I don't know what he said, but everyone smiled. He was a model of charm. Then he left them, went over to the bar, and came back with two of his green drinks. 'Compliments of the *Southerly*,' he said, and handed the first drink to the mother, and then the other one to the girl. And then, with a bow and a smile, he excused himself, and went down to the other end of the bar where his hired man was drinking beer. I bought myself a beer and took it to a cane chair in a corner. Billy and the girl were laughing together. He asked did she want a cigarette. Then the manager, in a dark suit, came in and announced that the steeplechase game had been set up in the dining room, and would we all care to move in there? We moved in, taking our drinks. The princess went in with her mother and Billy. Matthews went in with the hired man.

The steeplechase game went like this: there were four wooden horses and they moved down a ten-yard long course, according to a throw of dice. You could own a horse for a race by successfully bidding for it, or you could just bet.

Matthews paid forty dollars for a horse in the first race. Billy moved it for him. 'It's your money if you win,' Matthews said. The winner got whatever was paid for the other horses. It was about a hundred dollars. The race was neck and neck right to the end, and then Matthew's horse flashed over the line.

'Drinks are on me,' Matthews announced. 'So long as it's champagne.'

He paid sixty dollars for a horse in the second race, which his hired man moved for him, and he almost won that one too, except right at the end it stalled and a real-estate agent in a gay madras cotton jacket ran past him to win. Matthews was charming in defeat. He presented the winner with a bottle of champagne and a cigar.

He stayed out of the third race, and only bet in the fourth, where he won, but for the fifth, the last race, he staggered us all by shooting the bidding up to a hundred and fifty dollars. The money seemed to appear in his hand out of nowhere, crisp, new notes. He handed them nonchalantly to the manager, and then poured himself a glass of champagne.

And then, more Clark Gable than ever before, he approached the princess's mother, and with a bow asked, 'Would you allow your daughter to move my horse for me in this race?'

He was incredible. It was like watching a snake, each move so deadly and calculated, impossible to take your eyes away.

'Of course,' the mother said. 'Cynthia?'

'I'd love to,' the princess said.

Matthews put his arm around Billy's shoulders, gave him a playful punch, then a wink. They stood together like that all through the race, both beaming, father and son. Billy, I saw, was looking quite flushed. With excitement? With drink?

And of course Matthews' horse won. It romped home. The princess cried with delight. Champagne flowed.

I looked at the girl and suddenly I felt immensely sad. Everyone was shouting and laughing. I wanted my girl. 'Champagne for everyone!' Matthews cried. I pushed past him and went outside.

There was a full moon. Ned Matthews' yacht rode calmly at anchor, bobbing slightly, a millionaire touch to the night. I wanted to be a million miles away.

I sat down under a tree, my back to the trunk, lit a cigarette, closed my eyes. Everything was mixed up inside my head, my girl, Ned Matthews, the princess, Billy, and over it all a great sadness. And then I must have fallen asleep, because the next thing I knew I was lying on the grass and someone was shouting.

I sat up. I looked at my watch. It was nearly three. The shouting seemed to be coming from the bar. I stood up. My head felt too heavy to hold. I stood for a while, blinking and swaying. Then I heard someone yell 'Help!' and then, quickly after, the sound of breaking glass. A lot of glass. I started to run.

The bar was in chaos. The floor was strewn with bottles, half of them broken. A window was broken too, the jagged glass glinting with moon. The hired man was sitting on a cane chair, his mouth open, a glazed look on his face. A couple of handymen were at the bar, not looking too good either. Our waitress was at a table, fast asleep. The princess was near the door. She was crying. The front of her dress was torn, and she was holding it together with both hands. Her face ran with tears. And, in the centre of the room, in the chaos of broken bottles, Ned Matthews and his son faced each other, their fists balled, their faces bleary with drink.

'You're a pig!' Billy shouted. 'A dirty pig!'

His father swung and hit him in the nose. Blood gushed out at once. Billy yelled 'Jesus!' and kicked his father as hard as he could in the ankle. His father swore, almost fell, but came back and landed two punches in his son's ribs. Billy fell down.

'Oh, you pig, you pig, you pig,' he moaned, on the floor, and then he started to cry.

They came in for breakfast right on time, in the usual order, Matthews, Billy, then the hired man, each with his glass of beer. Eight o'clock in the morning. Right on the dot.

They looked terrible. Matthews' eyes were rimmed with red. He hadn't shaved. There was a cut on his right cheek. His son looked half asleep. The bridge of his nose was puffy and his face was unnaturally white. The hired man looked grey. The silence in the dining room, as they came down the centre aisle – Matthews at one point stumbling and almost falling – was electric.

They sat down. 'Well, boys,' said Matthews, raising his glass. 'Bon appétit!' Down went his beer. The hired man drained his quickly too, and then licked his lips, as though he could have done with another. Billy raised his glass, took one sip, and then put the glass down. 'You can finish mine,' he said to the hired man.

Ned Matthews looked astounded. 'Billy!' he snapped. 'Drink your beer!' 'Ah, I'm not in the mood,' Billy said. 'Billy!' Ned Matthews roared. Billy looked up at him, opened his mouth to speak, but then changed his mind. Something seemed to pass over his face. He looked away. His father stared at him. And then he laughed. He meant it to be, I'm sure, a good-natured, jokey laugh, but it wasn't. It wasn't like that at all.

Then the waitress came up to the table. 'Six eggs today!' Matthews snapped. 'Double sausages and bacon. And coffee. A lot of coffee. Hot and black!'

'Not for me,' said Billy, in a voice I had never heard him use before. A young boy's voice. 'Can I have,' he said, not looking up from the table in front of him, 'a cup of tea?'

It was very quiet, for what seemed to me forever, and then the waitress spoke.

'Sure,' she said. 'Sure. I'll bring it to you straight away.'

OLGA MASTERS
On the Train

The young woman not more than twenty-seven slammed the gate on herself and the two children both girls.

She did not move off at once but looked up and down the street as if deciding which way to go.

The older girl looked up at her through her hair which was whipped by the wind to read the decision the moment she made it.

Finally the woman took a hand of each child and turned in the direction of the railway station.

'Oh goody!' cried Sara who was nearly five.

'The sun's out,' the woman murmured lifting her face up for a second towards it.

Sara looked again into her mother's face noticing two or three of her teeth pinning down her bottom lip and the glint in her eyes perhaps from the sun? She felt inadequate that she seldom noticed such things as sun and wind, barely bothering about the rain as well, being quite content to stay out and play in it. The weather appeared to figure largely in the lives of adults. Sara hoped this would work out for her when she was older.

The mother bent forward as she hurried the younger child Lisa having difficulty keeping up. Her face Sara saw looked strained like the mother's. Sara hoped she wouldn't complain. The glint in the mother's eyes was like a spark that could ignite and involve them all.

She saw with relief the roof of the station jutting above the street but flashed her eyes away from the buildings still to be passed before they reached it.

The ticket office was protected by the jutting roof.

Sara was glad of the rest while her mother had her head inside the window and laid her cheek lightly against her rump clad in a blue denim skirt.

The business of buying tickets went on for a long time. Sara's eyes conveyed to Lisa her fear that the mother's top half had disappeared forever inside the window. She clutched her skirt to drag her out and opened her mouth to scream. Lisa saw and screamed for her.

The mother flung both arms down brushing a child off with each. They dared not touch her when she turned around and separated the tickets from change in her purse.

She snapped it shut and looked up and around in a distracted way as if to establish where she was.

It was Sara who went in front taking the narrow path squeezed between a high fence on one side and the station wall on the other. She swung her head around to see that her mother and Lisa were following her bouncy confident step.

On the platform waiting for the train the few other passengers looked at them.

Sara's dress was long and her hair was long and she was not dressed warmly enough.

The people especially a couple of elderly women noted Sara's light cotton dress with a deep flounce at the hem and Lisa's skimpy skirt and fawn tights. They looked at the mother's hands to see if there was a bag hanging from them with cardigans or jumpers in. But the mother carried nothing but a leather shoulder bag about as large as a large envelope and quite flat.

'She's warm enough herself,' one of the women murmured to her companion with a sniff.

They watched them board the train noticing the mother did not turn her head when she stepped onto the platform. It was Sara who grasped the hand of Lisa and saw her safely on.

'Tsk, tsk,' said the watching woman wishing she could meet the mother's eyes and glare her disapproval.

The mother took a single seat near the aisle and let Sara and Lisa find one together across from her.

Dear little soul, thought the passenger on the seat facing them seeing Sara's face suffused with pleasure at her small victory. Lisa had to wriggle her bony little rump with legs stuck out stiffly to get onto the seat.

Sara read the passenger's thoughts.

'She doesn't like you helping,' she said.

This was almost too much for the passenger whose glance leapt towards the mother to share with her this piece of childish wisdom.

But the mother had her profile raised and her eyes slanted away towards the window. The skin spread over her cheek-bones made the passenger think of pale honey spread on a slice of bread.

She's beautiful. The woman was surprised at herself for not having noticed it at once.

She returned her attention rather reluctantly to Sara and Lisa.

She searched their faces for some resemblance to the mother. Sara's was round with blue worried eyes under faint eyebrows. Lisa's was pale with a pinched look and blue veins at the edges of her eyebrows disappearing under a woollen cap with a ragged tassel that looked as if a kitten had wrestled with it.

The passenger thought they might look like their father putting him into a category unworthy of the handsome mother.

For the next twenty minutes the train alternated between a rocking tearing speed and dawdling within sight of one of the half dozen stations on the way to the city and the passenger alternated her attention between the girls and the mother although at times she indulged in a fancy that she was not their mother but someone minding them.

'I can move and your mummy sit here,' she said to Sara with sudden inspiration.

I'll find out for sure.

Sara put her head against the seat back, tipping her face and closing her eyes with pink coming into her cheeks.

The passenger looked to Lisa for an answer and Lisa turned her eyes towards her mother seeing only her profile and the long peaked collar of her blouse lying on her honey coloured sweater.

Lisa looked into the passenger's face and gave her head the smallest shake.

Poor little soul.

The passenger stared at the mother knowing in the end she would look back.

The mother did her eyes widening for a second under bluish lids with only a little of her brow visible under a thick bang of fair hair. There was nothing friendly in her face.

The passenger reddened and looked at the girls.

'Your mummy's so pretty,' she said.

Sara swung her head around to look at the mother and Lisa allowed herself a tiny smile as if it didn't need verification.

'Do you like having a pretty mummy?' the passenger asked.

The mother had turned her attention to the window again and her eyes had narrowed.

The passenger felt as if a door had been shut in her face.

'Are you going into the city for the day?' she said to the girls.

Sara pressed her lips together as if she shouldn't answer if she wanted to. Lisa's mouth opened losing its prettiness and turning into an uneven hole.

There's nothing attractive about either of them, thought the passenger deciding that Lisa might be slightly cross-eyed.

She sat with her handbag gripped on her knees and her red face flushed a deeper red and her brown eyes with flecks of red in the whites were flint-hard when they darted between the mother and the girls and vacant when they looked away.

After a moment the mother turned her head and stared into the passenger's face. The girls raised their eyes and looked too. The train swayed and rushed and all the eyes locked together. The mother's eyes although large and blue and without light were the snake's eyes mesmerising those of the passenger. Sara swung her eyes from the passenger to the mother as if trying to protect one from the other. Lisa's face grew tight and white and she opened her small hole of a mouth but no sound came out.

The mother keeping her eyes on the passenger got up suddenly and checked the location through the window. Sara and Lisa stumbled into the aisle holding out frantic fingers but afraid to touch her. Sara stood under her mother's rump as close as she dared her eyes turned back to see Lisa holding the seat end. The train swayed and clanged the last hundred yards slowing and sliding like a skier at the bottom of a snow peak stopping with a suddenness that flung Sara and Lisa together across the seat end.

This was fortunate.

The mother level with the passenger now leaned down and sparks from her eyes flew off the hard flat stones of the passenger's eyes.

'I'm going to kill them,' the mother said.

HELEN GARNER
The Dark, the Light

We heard he was back. We heard he was staying in a swanky
hotel. We heard she was American. We washed our hair. We
wore what we thought was appropriate. We waited for him
to declare himself. We waited for him to call.

No calls came. We discussed his probable whereabouts, the
meaning of his silence, the possibilities of his future.

We thought we saw him getting into a taxi outside the
Rialto, ouside the Windsor, outside the Regent, outside the
Wentworth, outside the Stock Exchange, outside the Dio-
rama. Was it him? What was he wearing? What did he have
on? A tweed jacket, black shoes. Even in summer? His idea
of this town is cold. He's been away. He's lost the feel of it.
He's been in Europe. He's been in America. He's been in the
tropics. He's left. He's gone. He doesn't live here any more.
He's only visiting. He's only passing through. Was his face
white? His shirt was white. His hair was longer. Did you see
her? She wasn't there. He was on his own.

We saw them in a club. We saw her. She was blond. They
were both blond. They were together. They were dressed in
white, in cream, in gold, in thousands of dollars' worth of linen
and leather. They sat at a table with their backs to the wall.
The wall was dark. They were light. Their hair and their
garments shone. They knew things we did not know, they
owned things we had never heard of. They were from
somewhere else. They were not from here. They were from
further north, from the sunny place, the blue and yellow
place, the sparkling place, the water place. They were from
the capital. More than one of us had to be led away weeping.
He's gone. He won't live here again. He has left us behind.

He has gone away and left us in the cold. The music stopped and they got up and left and the door closed. We stood in our dark club in our dark clothes.

Invitations came, but not many. Hardly any. Very few. Did you get one? Neither did I. Maybe the mail . . . a strike . . . a bottle-neck at the exchange . . . There were very few. Only three or four. Will you go? Of course not. It wouldn't be right. It would hurt, it would be wrong, I couldn't do it, I wouldn't be able to live with myself, I would lose friends, I wouldn't be seen dead, if you don't I won't either, it's a moral issue, I couldn't possibly.

What happened up there? Did you go? Did you hear? What was it like? Tell us what happened. It was summer, he was early, she was late, she made an entrance, the bells were ringing, the organ thundered, his hair lay in stiff sculpted curls, she was all in cream, her hair was up, she was choked with pearls, his family was there, the church was packed, he gave her his arm, they stood sides touching. The minister threw back his head and shouted *Come into their hearts Lord Jesus!* The guests were embarrassed, they fluffed their bobs, they brushed their shoulders, they read the brass plaques, it was religious, it was low church, it was not what we thought, we imagined something else, it was not his style, it was a bit much, it was over the top, it was a church after all and what did you expect, the guests were clever, they knew better, they were modern, they sat in the pews and sneered.

And afterwards? Outside? The trees were covered in leaves and threaded with coloured lights, it was night in the garden, the air was warm, the night was tender, French at least we thought, we thought French, we held out our glasses, the waiters twirled among us, the bottles were napkinned, it was local, we had hoped for better, we drank it anyway, we became more grateful, the families stood in line, they shook our hands, they welcomed us, we were ashamed of our ingratitude. We saw him standing alone for a moment under a tree, we stepped quickly towards him to show him we had come, we had come a very long way, we had come to show him we had come, to deliver the compliments, to bring the greetings of the other place, we stepped up, we reached out, our fingers touched his elbow and she came swooping all creamy with pearls, he spun on one heel, his hands opened, he showed us his palms, he smiled, he melted, he was no longer there, he was gone, the trees were covered in leaves, their branches were threaded with coloured lights, our clothes were stiff, our clothes were dark, our clothes came from the other place, and we too came from the other place, we put down our glasses, we turned away, we turned to go back to the other place, we turned and went back to the other place, we went without bitterness, humbly we went away.

BEVERLEY FARMER
Caffe Veneto

Her father is there already when Anne comes. She sees him first, smoking under a streetlamp outside the misted windows with their gilt scrawl: *Caffe Veneto*. The seedballs and fingered leaves of a plane tree are touching him with shadows.

'You found it, then,' she calls out. 'Sorry if I'm late. I was held up at rehearsal.' He is holding a bottle wrapped in brown paper. 'Is this a celebration?'

'A Cabernet Sauvignon. Good to see you!'

'Yes. It's been a while. Two months?'

'Or three. Since Easter.'

'That's right. Well. What a strange phone call!' This furtive smile of his is strange as well; and how much he has aged since then. In this light his skin seems to have faded and creased, settled more slackly in the hollows of bones. His eyes are smaller. Even his teeth seem smaller, patched and stained, exposed in his uneasy smiles. This austerity of age, in his of all faces, is at the same time intimidating and pitiable. She wonders if he has seen it himself in mirrors.

'Is this place fit for the Cabernet Sauvignon?' she says. 'We could look for somewhere fancier.'

'No, why? They've only changed the name. I have been here before, I remember now.'

'Student food.'

'I live on it. The spaghetti's good, come on.'

The glass door opens and a laughing group pushes out. The bead curtains rattle. Then two barefooted girls go inside; a warm gust, a smell of coffee and smoke, blow out as visibly as breath. He holds the beads aside for her, and the door open.

Lamps hang inside, round and red like upturned glasses of wine. In the blurred light they shed, Anne leads him past crowded stools at the counter to the only table free, a long bench against a wall of theatre posters. Its top is carved like a school desk. Her father sits at her side tracing initials on it with his finger while their order is taken and the table set. Only when he pours the wine does he give her his usual undaunted, boyish smile.

'This whole table to ourselves? Well, cheers.'

'Cheers. A 1975! Napa Valley. California? Oh, it's nice.' The wine, plummy and dark, stings and makes her shudder. 'So we *are* celebrating?'

'No.'

'No?'

He shakes his head, lighting another cigarette.

'Is Mum all right?'

'Fine. She's minding the children for your Aunt Sheila. She said to give you her love and talk you into coming back for a coffee.'

'Oh. I only signed out for ten-thirty, though.'

He checks his watch. 'How's College?'

'Great.'

'What was that about a rehearsal?'

'Oh yes. The Drama Club's putting on *The Seagull*. Chekhov? You have to come.'

'Of course. Are you Nina?'

'No, only Masha. Poor dreary Masha in black.'

'Well, we must come.' His voice falters. 'When's it on?'

'In two weeks. I'll look after the tickets. Now tell me,' she smiles and holds up her wine glass, 'what we're *not* celebrating.'

'What if we eat first, talk later.'

'No, now. Come on.'

'Well – my study leave's come through.'

'Well, good! I thought you'd decided to withdraw your application.'

'I had. But I'd have missed out altogether. It was now or never.'

' "It's now or never. My love won't wait." So you'll be going to America after all?'

'That was the idea. Funny you should say that.' He gives a short laugh. 'I've fallen in love.'

'Oh Daddy, again?' Her smile is stiff from the wine. 'Not that I can talk. I have, too.'

'*Have* you? What's his name?'

'I don't know him very well.'

'Don't know his name.'

'Not telling. Not yet. He's – he's married. Separated.'

'That's what they all say, they say.'

'Is it now? Anyway, she's moved to Sydney and he's here.'

'Well. What can I say? So long as you're happy.'

'It has its moments. You?'

'Yes. And no.'

'Do I know this one?'

'No.' He hesitates. 'She's one of my post-grad students. She's doing her thesis on Sylvia Plath. Oh, she's mature age,' he adds quickly. 'She's thirty-nine.'

'Married?'

'Divorced with one daughter. As a matter of fact, she's a student here: Microbiology, I think. The daughter. Jenny.'

She nods. 'You've met the daughter. What's the mother's name?'

'Sandra.' He gulps more wine and wipes his lips with a finger.

'So this is not a celebration because now you wish you weren't going to America.'

'In a way.' He fixes earnest eyes on her. 'You haven't seen your mother all this time, Annie, have you?'

'There's never a moment free. There are extra tutorials when you live in at College. And this play. And essays all –'

'I know.' He breathes out smoke. 'I just wondered. When you didn't come home at the end of first term.'

'Did she complain, did she? But she knew I was going camping!'

'No. All I'm saying really, darling, is that now your mother's going to need all your love and support. Please.'

'She doesn't *know*, does she?'

'No. She doesn't.'

'Well. Good.'

'I may have to tell her.' He bows his head and she sees that his grizzled curls, redder under this lamp, are thinning at the crown. 'This time it's the real thing. I may have to leave your mother.'

'For this – for Sandra?'

'When you meet her, you'll understand.'

'Hang on. Hang on.' Bowls of spaghetti thud into place under their noses. She watches her own hand pick up a fork and coil red hanks round and round it, too disconcerted by his lack of composure to take in what he is saying. 'Why *me*?'

'We've always been close.' He tries to smile. 'Trial run?'

'Oh, so it's all *settled*?'

'Darling, nothing's *settled* yet.'

'It sounds settled to me.'

'Not so.'

He stubs out his cigarette and lights another. Anne bends over her spaghetti. She should eat, being unused to wine. She gulps one hot mouthful, feeling her whole head swill with tears; tears of shock.

'Annie.'

'It's the spaghetti. Hot.'

'Damn,' mutters her father. Two people are seating themselves opposite them at the table, backs to the wall, a boy in a football guernsey and a woman in black suede. As alike as the Mother and Child in an ikon – though he must be eight or nine, Anne thinks – they look at each other with pleased black eyes set widely under round brows in their amber faces. Anne moves the wine glasses to make room and the woman smiles.

'It's the only table left.' Anne shrugs, pushing her plate away. She wipes her nose. 'I won't meet Sandra. How could you suggest it? You should know better.'

'I admit I was hoping, well, at least that you'd be more –'

'Amenable?'

'Just understanding.'

'Oh yes. I under*stand*.'

'Not how I feel. Do you?'

'Why not? I've understood the other times. I've kept your secrets. Commiserated when it was over. Haven't I? What I *don't* understand is why this time my mother would deserve to be left.'

'Darling, you don't leave people because they *deserve* it. Or stay with them, either.'

'If that's true, then no one's ever secure.'

'That's how it is. There's no security.'

'If people were *faithful* –'

'Yes, in an ideal world, people would all be faithful and all be secure. I agree. Or there'd be no love and so no insecurity.'

'They go together, do they?'

'I'd say so. Wouldn't you?'

'No!' At her tone the woman opposite glances up from her struggle to tuck the boy's napkin round his neck, while he digs into ravioli; full of mournful surprise, her eyes meet Anne's. She thinks we're lovers quarrelling, Anne thinks, and looks away, down at her hands. They have been tearing a hunk of bread into crumbs. She picks some up on a fingertip and eats them.

'When do you have until?' she whispers.

'Not long. America, you mean?'

'Yes. Mum must have been thrilled about that?'

'I haven't told her, Annie.'

'Why not?'

'I can't decide, don't you see?' His hand is crepe-skinned and the bones show, bent round the red glass. He sees her looking and looks too, holding his thick fingers outspread.

'I just can't take it in. When will you tell her?'

He winces. 'Oh, we'll more than likely call the whole thing off.'

'Call America off? Because of Sandra?' He stares at her. 'She – Sandra – must have known all along you were married.'

'Of course. Of course. Sorry. I thought you meant when would I tell your mother about Sandra.'

Maybe I did, Anne thinks. She gulps down the tart red wine, feeling dazed. 'How long have you known her?'

'About six months.'

'Six *months*.'

'Sssh. We've been lovers for two. Three.'

'Since Easter. You can't be sure, then. It's too soon.'

'That's what she says.'

'Well?'

'Just that it isn't true. I do love her. I'm only not a hundred-per-cent sure if she's worth the price. If anyone is, I mean. No, I am sure.'

'You mean, worth what *you* will have to pay.'

'Yes.'

'That's – don't you see that's selfish?'

'In a sense it's selfish, I suppose.'

This is what love does, she thinks. Puts us at the mercy of the other's selfishness. And of our own.

'If you believe in love,' he says, 'you pay the price.'

'Except that Mum will be paying the most. And she's always been faithful to you, in spite of your other women.'

'Doesn't that in itself say something about our marriage?'

'Maybe just about marriage.'

'When you get married –'

'I won't.'

'Let's keep our voices down. What's he like?' He smiles. 'This fellow you're in love with? Not that History tutor, is it? What's his name again?'

'I'm never getting married. Never.'

He shrugs. 'Up to you.'

Already he doesn't care, then. 'You know,' she says, 'if you leave her now she'll feel that her life has been wasted.'

'Her love, perhaps. Not her life. Most love is wasted.'

'Her whole *life*.'

'Past life. Okay. Which is it worse to waste. I wonder? The past or the future?'

'Mum, of course, would be concerned about *her* future.'

'She's still a very attractive woman, darling. She'll find someone else.'

'Will she, though? She hasn't had the practice you've had.' There is a grim silence. She stares at the peeling theatre posters: there is one for *The Seagull*. Her mouth is parched, her throat swollen and furred. 'Besides,' she whimpers, 'she loves *you*. Doesn't that count?'

'Annie,' he sighs, 'we have to be mature about this.'

'Are you being?'

'Do you think love is immature?'

'Not in itself.'

He rubs his greying head. The hair on his chest, she remembers from last summer, is greying too, above and about his nipples. He has a young man's belly. Like a tree in autumn he is withering from the top down. Not since the upheavals of puberty has she been so aware of men, the presence of the male, as now. Is it because she has a lover now? Maybe all women feel like this. And men? I still know next to nothing about love, she thinks: and I'll suffer for it.

'You always said to take love lightly,' she says.

He sighs, breathing smoke out. 'I can't be sure I can even go on hiding my feelings at home.'

'But that's not a reason to leave! That doesn't make sense!'

'Why doesn't it?'

'If you can't hide it, tell her. She probably knows.'

'No, I'd know if she did.'

'She always has before.' He stares at her. 'I never told her. Of course not. She never told me straight out that she knew. She just – hinted. "I think you're like me," she said last time. "I let lying dogs sleep," and we laughed. You didn't take it seriously, so . . . And that's what she's doing now.'

'Why didn't you ever . . .?' He shrugs.

'Tell you? You *know* why. I didn't tell Mum what you told me either, did I? You both trusted me. And I would never have dared, anyway. Why do you think I wanted to live in at College? Because I was out of my depth at home.'

She sees herself wading for the first time beside the huge white legs of her mother and father into cold green slabs of water that tilted high and hurled her off her feet. Screaming, she clutched a hand, a knee, clambered on a slippery thigh. They carried her back to the sandbank. Lapped in pale water, she sat there alone wailing while they waded back in without her, deeper and deeper, until they disappeared.

'Secrecy. Lies. Hints,' her father is saying. 'Why wouldn't she say, if she knew? I didn't want to hurt her, that's all.'

'Oh, *what* can I say? Can't you just wait a while? You can't spring a thing like this on her. At least, give her time.'

'Time! That's just it. I'm afraid Sandra won't wait.'

'Won't wait?'

'Won't wait, I mean, if I go off to America for months with your mother.'

'Why not?'

'It'd be asking too much of her credulity, she says.'

'But if she loves you?'

'It's faith that she lacks. Not love. Faith and hope.'

'It sounds like she's blackmailing you.' He is silent. This is what he sometimes suspects. Resentfully, in spite of himself, he pictures Sandra curled and smug on her bed reading at this moment, the lamplight around her in flounces of smoke like a mosquito net; while he fights his daughter for her sake. 'Blackmailing you,' Anne says. 'She'll wait, if you go alone.'

'You still don't understand.'

'*Tell* me.'

'I can't not take your mother, can I,' he mutters, 'if I'm living at home?'

'You can't mean that you want to take *Sandra* to *America*!'

'Annie, enough now. Please. This is dreadful.'

'You do! You do! How *could* you? You can't *mean* it.'

'Annie, for God's sake.'

'You're my father and I love you. You know that. Maybe more than Mummy. But if you leave her, I'll be on her side. I won't even see you again.' She wonders as she says this if it is true; and if he would care. 'I mean that.'

'*Well*!' He pushes his untouched plate away in turn. The boy opposite pauses to stare curiously from the cold tangles of spaghetti to their faces, and back. 'What shall we talk about now?'

'Nothing. I'll go.' But, as he half-expects, she makes no move to. He fills the glasses, drinks his down, and lights a cigarette.

'Big match tomorrow,' he tosses defiantly across the table.

'Yeah!' The boy grins back at him.

'How do you like your chances?'

'Gunna win!' The boy looks for approval at his mother, who gives him an imploring smile. She has finished her ravioli. 'Great ravioli, Mum,' the boy announces, clearly to please her; and she looks pleased.

'I *fear* for my mother!' Anne shouts. 'I fear for her! How will she bear it?'

'Darling!' Shock makes him spill his wine. With his napkin he stanches the dark puddle, wondering if she can be drunk. After all, she has eaten only the bread. He gapes at her in such evident mute dismay that again he strikes her as boyish, an elderly bad boy, and a spasm of laughter crosses her face. Yes, she is, he decides. Grinning with relief, he throws his arm around her shoulders to pull her to him for a moment and she smells suddenly the drenching sweetness in the armpits of men who smoke. But she draws back from him.

'Gunna win, no worries.'

'I don't know, though,' her father teases. 'You're up against the best team, just about.'

'We aren't, they are! And my dad's playing!'

'Your dad, is he? Go on!'

'He's the captain!'

'Is he now? What's his name?'

Again the boy refers to his mother, then leans forward and whispers it.

'He's your dad? Well, good God!' The woman nods, ruefully, it seems to Anne; the dark eyes glimmer and close. 'You going to be as good as your dad?'

'Better!'

'Going to see him play?'

'Too right!'

'Might see you there.'

'Finish, finish.' His mother nudges him: heads are turning in the red haze. He scoops up his last shreds of ravioli, while her father turns his jovial smile on the mother. 'His dad's a magnificent footballer. One of the greats. And you,' he tells the boy, 'must be very proud.' The boy nods gravely, wiping his chin.

The woman springs up. 'Yes, goodnight.' Her voice shakes and she opens her pale palms in a beseeching gesture. 'We going now.' She stoops to the boy's ear. 'Come on. We going.'

'Oh? Can't I have a gelato?'

'Yes, in a cornet. Please, the bill.' She tugs the waiter's sleeve. But the boy wants to hear more. She wavers, but bends her head, blotting her cheeks with her black lapels, and rushes alone to the counter.

Anne leans forward. 'You mother wants you.'

A black suede arm is beckoning.

'Yeah, I better go.'

'Well, nice meeting you.' Her father puts out his hand; the boy's tawny hand is lost in it. Confused, he stands smiling at them, glancing now and then towards his mother until at last he can detach himself and run to her.

'How about that?' Her father sits back. 'Nice kid. If he turns out half the man his dad is!'

'I think she was crying.'

He looks round, but they have gone. 'Sorry?'

'She was crying. That's why she rushed off.'

'Why should she be?'

'I think, because of you. All that about his father.'

'He's a great player. Why shouldn't his kid be proud of him?'

'He takes after her,' Anne says. 'Both honey-coloured.'

'So are we in this light.'

'Dark honey. Like a Byzantine Madonna and Child.'

'I thought they looked Indian.'

'Yes? Or Maori.'

'Maybe.' He considers. 'Or Indonesian.'

'The thing is, they were so happy. A dinner out at the Caffe Veneto. She should have been safe.'

'From?'

'She was hurt. Shamed.'

'Why, though?'

'Who knows? The boy's father may have *done her wrong.* Anything. It's none of our business, that's all.'

'Well, she's not his wife. I've met his wife.'

'My point.'

'Anne, all I did was pay tribute to a marvellous bloody footballer!'

'You overdid it.'

'*Did* I.'

'What right had you to make her cry?'

'How was I to know?'

'*I* knew.'

'Well, *I* didn't, I'm afraid. Sorry.' Stung, he makes a hurt face. 'I see nothing I do or say tonight is going to find favour. Poor me.' His lined eyes meet hers. 'Cast into outer darkness.'

'It's all of a piece, that's all.' She tips her head back to empty her glass, and her face glows under the lamp. 'You can choose not to know you're doing it, but still the damage is done. People suffer. Lives are ruined.'

'*You're* overdoing it.'

'You really don't care.' She gazes in disillusion as he sighs. The impetuosity which all her life she has loved in him is not, after all, boyish. In the light of this evening it is shown up as shallow and rash; even, perhaps, brutal. 'You ride rough-shod. You'll always get away with it.'

'All right. I'm a clumsy galoot. That boy's mother's life is ruined. *Mea culpa.*'

'In a small way it does go to show,' she says, and holds out her glass for more, 'that you can make strange errors of judgement. Admit that. May I have some more American wine?'

'Just what I was about to say of you.' He fills her glass. His suddenly amused lips look as if they are bleeding, black from the wine. He watches her turn her glass so that the glow of wine moves on the table. 'Can this be our practical Annie?'

'Why can't it?'

'Burning incense to the Madonna of the Caffe Veneto.'

'She thought we were lovers quarrelling.'

'Did she? She can't have heard much.' He glances round. 'I'll bet she was on your side.'

'Being practical,' she says, 'if that's what's expected, tell me: have your loves ever lasted? Has love ever made you happy for long?'

He takes her hands. 'What has happiness got to do with love? "To love is to suffer," didn't Goethe say? "One is compelled to love, one does not want to." ' She shakes her head and pulls free. 'Annie.' But she turns away, one hand folded to hide her face.

He foresees himself at the moment when she will stand on tiptoe to kiss him goodnight holding her by the shoulders and pressing with his closed lips a kiss of finality on her stained lips; holding her away, then, to look in her eyes and compel not only resignation. Consent, absolution, belief. When he sees that she can't move first, he holds the bottle up under the lamp and shakes it. 'All gone,' he pouts. He sniffs it: the dregs have a smell of olives. She looks at him. 'Like a coffee?'

'No, thanks.'

'Sure?'

'No, I'd better get back.'

He glances at his watch. 'Let's go? It's after ten.'

While he pays she droops at his side staring at her shoes on the bare planks, in an attitude of reproach, as he notes wryly. Whatever gave me the idea, he thinks, that I could convince her of the imperatives of love? My shy and scrupulous daughter, of all people! No, her mother's daughter now. He holds her coat open for her to grope into. 'Drive you back to College?'

'I think I'll walk.'

'Walk you back?'

'All right.'

It is clammily cold. They walk on a wide path past shadowy trees holding their few brown leaves still in the mist. A full moon glimmers. His daughter's shoulders are folded in; her hair hangs in two rusty skeins along the line of her nose. At eighteen she is no longer a girl. Prettier now, yes, but shedding her young freshness. She will be late, as fearful of hurt as she is, to come to ripeness. She has a shrouded look, he thinks; her eyes, when for a moment she glances up, seem full of sorrow and foreboding.

'Give my love to Mum,' she says once. 'Tell her I'll ring.'

'I will.'

'You'll come to the play?'

'Of course. You'll see to the tickets?'

'You have to go to America. Don't you?'

'Yes.'

'With Mum or with Sandra.'

'Yes.'

'What's she like?'

'Beautiful.'

'You were my household gods,' she says as if to herself. 'Warm and luminous. One each side of the fire.'

'Oh, Annie.'

'Oh, I grew out of it.'

She has her hands in her pockets and is staring down at heaps of leaves as she shuffles through them, not close enough for an arm round her shoulders to seem unforced. She is exhaused, of course; so is he, barely able to speak. He breathes long trails of smoke out, thinking of Sandra reading; and of Margaret, at home with his sister's children, waiting.

They come round the crescent and the brick hump of her college stands black on the glow of the sky. Under the trees it is deeply dark. She catches a plane leaf as it floats loose: brown on one side, pale with brown veins on the other, like an imploring hand.

'Have a wish?'

'You know.' She looks at him. 'Daddy, you won't do it. Will you?'

'No.' He turns his stubbornly pleading face to her, but she

is looking down again. 'No, I don't suppose I can.'

'You mustn't.'

'I won't. No.'

On the gravel at the entrance she turns abruptly and kisses him, her hands on his shoulders, and runs up the steps. Her mouth tastes of tears. I never asked about her love affair, he thinks. He starts back, his shoes crunching in the mist. But she is inside the blurred glass door, which is slowly closing. Her shape stoops, signing in. The light goes out, and the lock clicks.

FRANK MOORHOUSE
Francois and the Fishbone Incident

This is a cautionary tale and a test. The cautionary tale is for bon vivants and the test is for cadet journalists.

In the role of Francois Blase, bon vivant and celebrated author, I was celebrating the publication of my latest book and had gathered around me my closest friends, Rosemary Creswell, my agent, and Murray Sime, my taxation lawyer – a far-sighted combination, even if it does indicate a certain limitation in human relationships on my part. We were in a merry mood, the champagne flowing, they doing private calculations in their heads (they together own 20 per cent of my life), and I on my feet making a fine speech, when a snapper bone in my throat stopped me in mid-flourish.

At first this seemed very funny for my luncheon guests, who fell into indulgent, but hearty laughter.

They laughed while I, caught mid-word, champagne glass in hand, began to stagger backwards, choking.

After their laughter died down they began exuberant back-slapping and folk remedies such as swallowing bread (I was later to learn that bread sometimes breaks the fishbone off leaving a piece of bone embedded in the throat). I went on choking.

At last, their meal ticket dying before their eyes, my friends became serious. The restaurant kindly put the snapper back in the oven and, champagne glass in hand, tears in my eyes, Murray walked me across the road to Balmain Hospital. I remembered that the singer Mama Cass choked to death on a ham sandwich.

He signed me in and went back to finish his lunch with

Rosemary, my only consolation being that one of them had to pay.

The young doctor in Casualty well understood my problem, but said there was little that could be done 'manually'. However, he said cheerfully that he'd read my books and they were terrific.

Finding it difficult to talk I simply kissed his hands appreciatively.

As he wheeled me to the Ear, Nose and Throat specialist he talked about the books, but the more he talked the more it became obvious that the book he was talking about was not my book *The Americans, Baby*, but Craig McGregor's *Up Against the Wall, America*.

Being unable to correct him, I could only nod glumly, smile weakly, gesture impotently.

I thought: I am going to die a bizarre newsworthy death like Mama Cass, and Craig McGregor is going to get all the publicity.

The young doctor got onto jazz – evidently McGregor wrote about jazz – and then left, giving me a thumbs-up gesture and saying, 'You can give me a 12-string Gibson anytime you like.'

A 12-string Gibson???!!! a 12-string Gibson . . .???

I've drunk a Gibson, but I've never played a Gibson.

While I waited for the specialist I noticed that my name had been mis-spelled, but at least it wasn't down as McGregor. My name is so often mis-spelled I may as well change it to Francois Blase.

The specialist squirted anaesthetic into my throat, which made me feel even sicker, and then tried manually to locate the bone, but failed because my throat kept expelling him and his instruments.

He accused me of being tense.

He concluded that he would have to put me under a full anaesthetic and operate. As punishment for being tense.

He wrote my name down, mis-spelled it, asked me my date of birth and wrongly calculated that I was 32, which at first was all right by me, but then worried me because I feared that the dose of anaesthetic was calculated by age and that I would die from an overdose, or worse, I would receive an 'under dose' which would immobilise me, but not kill the pain. I would lie there, unable to move or speak, while they operated and I felt it all.

I was wheeled by a nurse to the Admissions Office where I was asked questions that I could not answer – not only was I having trouble vocally, but the questions, while technically quite simple, could not adequately snare the mess of my life.

She asked me for my next-of-kin and I hesitated because my parents were holidaying in the Pacific Islands so it would be useless to name them; but even if they were home they wouldn't know who Craig McGregor was when the police called with the bad news.

'What about wife?' she asked. Well, I was married very young and I have never bothered to get divorced, although we had lived apart for years and she is living in London. I couldn't explain this to her, but to say 'yes' to 'married' meant that I had to give my wife's address, which I didn't have. I shook my head in reply to the question which was technically a lie, but more the truth – if you know what I mean.

I began to give my father as next-of-kin, but she asked me for his address and telephone number, which I did not know, but had written in my address book, which I did not have. She looked at me severely and put down 'care of the police'.

She asked me what rent I paid, and I didn't know because I pay a year in advance. I wanted to say, 'Look I'm dying here, can we do the questions when I'm being discharged?'

She asked me which medical fund I belonged to and I couldn't remember.

She asked me my weekly wage and I couldn't answer because I don't have a weekly wage, but I was now so desperate to have an answer to something that I invented a figure. She seemed to disbelieve me anyhow.

She was by now suspicious of my identity and asked me in a pointed tone who Francois Blase was. Murray as some sort of joke had written Francois Blase in brackets or vice versa on the form *he* filled in.

I am drowning in saliva. I am slipping into shock, my heart is racing, my skin is cold.

I made an agonised face at her and spelled out silently 'J-O-K-E'. She sniffed.

She decided to let me into the hospital, however, despite my unsatisfactory mark in the Admission Exam.

While being wheeled back to the ward I pondered the technical question of 'who am I' and so forth – every piece of information in the hands of the hospital was now either wrong, dysfunctional, or to my disadvantage. Some was technically correct, but misleading; some technically wrong, but true.

I was next dressed in surgical gown, leggings and a surgical nappy and an identity bracelet placed on my wrist.

I was very glad to see the bracelet. It said my name was 'Moorehouse', my age was 36, and the address on the bracelet was not my home address, but the address of the Volunteer Restaurant where I had been having lunch.

I was rather desperate to clear up the age question because I had convinced myself that this was crucial in determining drug dosage.

But if I did die, my next-of-kin would not be at home, my body would be delivered to a restaurant, and Craig McGregor would get all the publicity.

The nursing aides who dressed me in the operating gown asked me if I was married. Were they trying to trick me into giving the 'correct' answer – were they in conspiracy with the admissions clerk?

If I wasn't married, why not?

Was this aimed to determine if I was homosexual – and what different sorts of treatment did homosexuals get? Better treatment or worse? What about AIDS? Would I be put in an airtight, isolated room and handled only by remote-control, bionic arms?

If I were 36, which I wasn't, and unmarried, was I therefore suspected of homosexuality and treated thus? I told them I was married. Would they like me to contact my wife? No. Why not?

I saw then, quite clearly, poetically, that the whole world, every one of us, is adrift in a sea of misinformation and misunderstanding.

A Resident came to my bed and asked me more questions. He asked me, for instance, when I was last in hospital, which I misanswered unintentionally because I had forgotten about an incident in the country thirteen years ago. I told him my correct age and he wrote it down, but what about all the other forms – would it be corrected on those as well? He looked at me oddly and wrote something on his sheet which I feared was against me.

I lied to him about the food I'd eaten that day because I couldn't bring myself to tell him I'd had a Big Mac and a beer for breakfast. Francois Blase is happy to tell the doctor about the Moet champagne and the kidneys in wine for lunch, but he can't bring himself to tell about the Big Mac. But it wasn't only snobbery. It would again be dangerously misleading to tell him about the beer and the Big Mac. I had never before in my life had a beer and a Big Mac for breakfast. He would assume that I had a bad diet and was an alcoholic. A train of medical assumptions would follow and I would be put on the wrong drip and given the wrong dosages of all sorts of things.

How I came to have a Big Mac and beer for breakfast would take a long time to explain. This was a case where the correct information could be dangerously misleading, so I lied about breakfast.

All the way to the operating theatre I believed that I had been mistaken for someone else – some other 'Moorhouse' or 'Moorshouse' or 'Moorehouse' who had gangrene and was to have his leg amputated. Or a certain 'Francois' who had AIDS.

I indicated over and over again to the wardsman, the nurse, the anaesthetist and the specialist that I had a bone in my throat and please not my leg, or whatever they amputate in cases of AIDS. I used emphatic gesticulation and mime – mimed a swimming fish with my hand, mimed eating with a knife and fork, I gave a great re-enactment of me giving a speech, pain in the throat, choking.

The operation found no fishbone, but they said they could see where it had been.

A few days later, when I visited the specialist for a check-up, he found that he had no card for me.

That did not surprise me.

But then he said, 'Oh this must be you,' looking at a card, 'it's the right complaint, but the wrong name.' How would he know that? I didn't ask if the name he had was Francois McGregor. I didn't care.

He told me that bon vivants should not order fish when they are in an excited or celebratory mood.

Now for the test for cadet journalists. How would you get the correct name, age, and address of the patient, given that the doctor in Casualty would have been genuinely helpful and told you I was Craig McGregor.

It would have been no good asking the patient when he had a fishbone stuck in his throat, was in philosophical confusion about his identity, saw himself as Francois Blase, bon vivant, and thought he was dying like Mama Cass.

TIM WINTON
Neighbours

When they first moved in, the young couple were wary of the neighbourhood. The street was full of European migrants. It made the newly-weds feel like sojourners in a foreign land. Next door on the left lived a Macedonian family. On the right, a widower from Poland.

The newly-weds' house was small, but its high ceilings and paned windows gave it the feel of an elegant cottage. From his study window, the young man could see out over the rooftops and used-car yards the Moreton Bay figs in the park where they walked their dog. The neighbours seemed cautious about the dog, a docile, moulting collie.

The young man and woman had lived all their lives in the expansive outer suburbs where good neighbours were seldom seen and never heard. The sounds of spitting and washing and daybreak watering came as a shock. The Macedonian family shouted, ranted, screamed. It took six months for the newcomers to comprehend the fact that their neighbours were not murdering each other, merely talking. The old Polish man spent most of his day hammering nails into wood only to pull them out again. His yard was stacked with salvaged lumber. He added to it, but he did not build with it.

Relations were uncomfortable for many months. The Macedonians raised eyebrows at the late hour at which the newcomers rose in the mornings. The young man sensed their disapproval at his staying home to write his thesis while his wife worked. He watched in disgust as the little boy next door urinated in the street. He once saw him spraying the cat from the back step. The child's head was shaved regularly, he assumed, in order to make his hair grow thick. The little boy stood at the fence with only his cobalt eyes showing; it made the young man nervous.

In the autumn, the young couple cleared rubbish from their back yard and turned and manured the soil under the open and measured gaze of the neighbours. They planted leeks, onions, cabbage, brussels sprouts and broad beans and this caused the neighbours to come to the fence and offer advice about spacing, hilling, mulching. The young man resented the interference, but he took careful note of what was said. His wife was bold enough to run a hand over the child's stubble and the big woman with black eyes and butcher's arms gave her a bagful of garlic cloves to plant.

Not long after, the young man and woman built a henhouse. The neighbours watched it fall down. The Polish widower slid through the fence uninvited and rebuilt it for them. They could not understand a word he said.

As autumn merged into winter and the vermilion sunsets were followed by sudden, dark dusks touched with the smell of woodsmoke and the sound of roosters crowing day's end, the young couple found themselves smiling back at the neighbours. They offered heads of cabbage and took gifts of grappa and firewood. The young man worked steadily at his thesis on the development of the twentieth century novel. He cooked dinners for his wife and listened to her stories of eccentric patients and hospital incompetence. In the street they no longer walked with their eyes lowered. They felt superior and proud when their parents came to visit and to cast shocked glances across the fence.

In the winter they kept ducks, big, silent muscovies that stood about in the rain growing fat. In the spring the Macedonian family showed them how to slaughter and to pluck and to dress. They all sat around on blocks and upturned buckets and told barely-understood stories – the men butchering, the women plucking, as was demanded. In the haze of down and steam and fractured dialogue, the young man and woman felt intoxicated. The cat toyed with severed heads. The child pulled the cat's tail. The newcomers found themselves shouting.

But they had not planned on a pregnancy. It stunned them to be made parents so early. Their friends did not have children until several years after being married – if at all. The young woman arranged for maternity leave. The young man ploughed on with his thesis on the twentieth century novel.

The Polish widower began to build. In the late spring dawns, he sank posts and poured cement and began to use his wood. The young couple turned in their bed, cursed him behind his back. The young husband, at times, suspected that the widower was deliberately antagonising them. The young wife threw up in the mornings. Hay fever began to wear him down.

Before long the young couple realised that the whole neighbourhood knew of the pregnancy. People smiled tirelessly at them. The man in the deli gave her small presents of chocolates and him packets of cigarettes that he stored at home, not being a smoker. In the summer, Italian women began to offer names. Greek women stopped the young woman in the street, pulled her skirt up and felt her belly, telling her it was bound to be a boy. By late summer the woman next door had knitted the baby a suit, complete with booties and beanie. The young woman felt flattered, claustrophobic, grateful, peeved.

By late summer, the Polish widower next door had almost finished his two-car garage. The young man could not believe that a man without a car would do such a thing, and one evening as he was considering making a complaint about the noise, the Polish man came over with barrowfuls of wood-scraps for their fire.

Labour came abruptly. The young man abandoned the twentieth century novel for the telephone. His wife began to black the stove. The midwife came and helped her finish the job while he ran about making statements that sounded like queries. His wife hoisted her belly about the house, supervising his movements. Going outside for more wood, he saw, in the last light of the day, the faces at each fence. He counted twelve faces. The Macedonian family waved and called out what sounded like their best wishes.

As the night deepened, the young woman dozed between contractions, sometimes walking, sometimes shouting. She had a hot bath and began to eat ice and demand liverwurst. Her belly rose, uterus flexing downward. Her sweat sparkled, the gossamer highlit by movement and firelight. The night grew older. The midwife crooned. The young man rubbed his wife's back, fed her ice and rubbed her lips with oil.

And then came the pushing. He caressed and stared and tried not to shout. The floor trembled as the young woman bore down in a squat. He felt the power of her, the sophistication of her. She strained. Her face mottled. She kept at it, push after push, assaulting some unseen barrier, until suddenly it was smashed and she was through. It took his wind away to see the look on the baby's face as it was suddenly passed up to the breast. It had one eye on him. It found the nipple. It trailed cord and vernix smears and its mother's own sweat. She gasped and covered the tiny buttocks with a hand. A boy, she said. For a second, the child lost the nipple and began to cry. The young man heard shouting outside. He went to the back door. On the Macedonian side of the fence, a small queue of bleary faces looked up, cheering, and the young man began to weep. The twentieth century novel had not prepared him for this.

JANETTE TURNER HOSPITAL
After Long Absence

For years it has branched extravagantly in dreams, but the
mango tree outside the kitchen window in Brisbane is even
greener than the jubilant greens of memory. I could almost
believe my mother has been out there with spit and polish,
buffing up each leaf for my visit. I suggest this to her and
she laughs, handing me a china plate.

Her hands are a bright slippery pink from the soap suds and
the fierce water, and when I take the plate it is as though I
have touched the livid element of a stove. In the nick of time,
I grunt something unintelligible in lieu of swearing. 'Oh heck,'
I mumble, cradling the plate and my seared fingers in the tea-
towel. 'I'd forgotten.' And we both laugh. It is one of those
family idiosyncrasies, an heirloom of sorts, passed down with
the plate itself which entered family history on my grand-
mother's wedding day. The women in my mother's family
have always believed that dishwashing water should be just
on the leeside of boiling, and somehow, through sheer
conviction that cleanliness is next to godliness, I suppose,
their hands can calmly swim in it.

I glance at the wall above the refrigerator, and yes, the
needlepoint text is still there, paler from another decade of
sun, but otherwise undiminished: *He shall try you in a refiner's
fire.*

'Do you still have your pieces?' my mother asks.

She means the cup, saucer, and plate from my grand-
mother's dinner set, which is of fine bone china, but Victorian,
out of fashion. The heavy band of black and pale orange and
gold leaf speaks of boundaries that cannot be questioned.

'I'd never part with it,' I say.

303

And I realise from the way in which she smiles and closes her eyes that she has been afraid it would be one more thing I would have jettisoned. I suppose it seems rather arbitrary to my parents, what I have rejected and what I have hung onto. My mother is suspended there, dishmop in hand, eyes closed, for several seconds. She is 'giving thanks'. I think with irritation: nothing has ever been secular in this house. Not even the tiniest thing.

'Leave this,' my mother says, before I am halfway through the sensation of annoyance. 'I'll finish. You sit outside and get some writing done.'

And I think helplessly: It's always been like this, a seesaw of frustration and tenderness. Whose childhood and adolescence could have been more stifled or more pampered?

'But I *like* doing this with you,' I assure her. 'I really do.' She smiles and 'gives thanks' again, a fleeting and exasperating and totally unconscious gesture. 'Honestly,' I add, precisely because it has suddenly become untrue, because my irritation has surged as quixotically as the Brisbane River in flood. 'It's one of . . .' but I decide not to add that it is one of the few things we can do in absolute harmony.

'You should enjoy the sun while you can,' she says. Meaning: before you go back to those unimaginable Canadian winters. 'Besides, you'll want to write your letters.' She pauses awkwardly, delicately avoiding the inexplicable fact that the others have not yet arrived. She cannot imagine a circumstance that would have taken her away, even temporarily, from her husband and children. All her instincts tell her that such action is negligent and immoral. But she will make no judgments, regardless of inner cost. 'And then,' she says valiantly, 'there's your book. You shouldn't be wasting time . . . You should get on with your book.' My book, which they fear will embarrass them again. My book, which will cause them such pride and bewilderment and sorrow. 'Off with you,' she says. 'Sun's waiting.'

I've been back less than twenty-four hours and already I'm dizzy – the same old roller-coaster of anger and love. I surrender the damp linen tea-towel which is stamped with the coats of arms of all the Australian states. I gather up notepad and pen, and head for the sun.

They are old comforters, the sun and the mango tree. I think I've always been pagan at heart, a sun worshipper, perhaps all Queensland children are. There was always far more solace in the upper branches of this tree than in the obligatory family Bible reading and prayers that followed dinner. I wrap my arms around the trunk, I press my cheek to the rough bark, remembering that wasteland of time, the fifth grade.

I can smell it again, sharp and bitter, see all the cruel young faces. The tree sap still stinks of it. My fingers touch scars in the trunk, the blisters of nail heads hammered in long years ago when we read somewhere that the iron improved the mangoes. The rust comes off now on my hands, a dark stain. I am falling down the endless concrete stairs, I feel the pushing again, the kicking, blood coming from somewhere, I can taste that old fear.

I reach for the branch where I hid; lower now, it seems – which disturbs me. Not as inaccessibly safe as I had thought.

Each night, the pale face of my brother would float from behind the glass of his isolation ward and rise through the mango leaves like a moon. I never asked, I was afraid to ask, 'Will he die?' And the next day at school, and the next, I remember, remember: all the eyes pressed up against my life, staring, mocking, hostile, menacing.

There was a mark on me.

I try now to imagine myself as one of the others. I suppose I would simply have seen what they saw: someone dipped in death, someone trailing a shadowy cloak of contamination, someone wilfully dangerous. Why should I blame them that they had to ward me off?

This had, in any case, been foretold.

I had known we were strange from my earliest weeks in the first grade. 'The nurse has arrived with your needles,' our teacher said, and everyone seemed to know what she was talking about. 'You'll go when your name is called. It doesn't hurt.'

'It does so,' called out Patrick Murphy, and was made to stand in the corner.

'With a name like that,' said the teacher, 'I'm not surprised.' She was busy unfurling and smoothing out the flutter of consent letters which we had all dutifully returned from home, some of us arriving with the letters safety-pinned to our pinafores. The teacher singled out one of the slips, her brow furrowed.

'I see we have our share of religious fanatics,' she said. She began to prowl between the desks, waving the white letter like a flag. 'Someone in our class,' she announced, 'is a killer.' She stopped beside my desk and I could smell her anger, musky and acrid and damp. It was something I recognised, having smelled it when our cat was playing with a bird, though I could not have said what part of the smell came from which creature. The teacher put her finger on my shoulder, a summons, and I followed to the front of the class. 'This person,' said the teacher, 'is our killer.'

And everyone, myself included, solemnly observed. I looked at my hands and feet, curious. A killer, I thought, tasting the double *l* with interest and terror, my tongue forward against the roof of my mouth.

'Irresponsible! Morally irresponsible!' The teacher's voice was like that of our own pastor when he climbed into the pulpit. She was red in the face. I waited for her, my first victim, to go up in smoke. 'Ignorant fanatics,' she said, 'you and your family. You're the kind who cause an epidemic.'

I always remembered the word, not knowing what it meant. I saw it as dark and cumulous, freighted with classroom awe, a bringer of lightning bolts. *Epidemic*. I sometimes credit that moment with the birth of my passionate interest in the pure sound of arrangements of syllables. *Epidemic*. And later, of course, in the fifth grade, *diphtheria*, a beautiful word, but deadly.

I know a lot about words, about their sensuous surfaces, the way the tongue licks at them. And about the depth charges they carry.

My mother brings tea and an Arnott's biscuit, though I have been out here scarcely an hour, and though I have not written a word. I have been sitting here crushing her ferns, my back against the mango tree, remembering Patrick Murphy: how no amount of standings-in-the-corner or of canings (I can hear the surf-like whisper of the switch against his bare calves) could put a dent in his exuberance or his self-destructive honesty.

Once, in the first grade, he retrieved my shoes from the railway tracks where Jimmy Simpson had placed them. In the fifth grade he was sometimes able to protect me, and word reached me that one of his black eyes was on my account. One day I brought him home, and my parents said later they had always believed that some Catholics would be saved, that some were among the Lord's Anointed in spite of rank superstition and the idols in their churches. But I was not seriously encouraged to hope that Patrick Murphy would be in the company of this elect. When my mother offered him homemade lemonade, he told her it beat the bejesus out of the stuff you could get at the shops. He also said that most of the kids at school were full of ratshit and that only one or two sheilas made the place any better than buggery.

One morning Patrick Murphy and I woke up and it was time for high school. We went to different ones, and lost touch, though I saw him one Friday night in the heart of Brisbane, on the corner of Adelaide and Albert Streets, outside the Commonwealth Bank. The Tivoli and the Wintergarden ('dens of iniquity', the pastor said) were emptying and he was part of that crowd, his brushback flopping into his eyes, a girl on his arm. The girl was stunning in a sleazy kind of way: close-fitting slacks and spike heels, a tight sweater, platinum blonde hair and crimson lips. My kind of sheila, I imagined Patrick Murphy grinning, and the thought of his mouth on hers disturbed me. I rather imagined that an extra dollop of original sin came with breasts like hers. I rather hoped so.

I was praying Patrick Murphy wouldn't see me.

From my very reluctant spot in the circle, I could see that his eyes were wholly on his girl's cleavage. I moved slightly, so that my back was to the footpath, but so that I could still see him from out of the corner of my eye. Our circle, which took up two parking spaces, was bisected by the curb outside the Commonwealth Bank. There were perhaps fifteen of us ranged around a woman who sat on a folding chair and hugged a piano accordion. We all had a certain *look*, which was as identifiable in its own way as the look of Patrick Murphy's sheila. My dress was . . . well, *ladylike*, I wore flat heels, I might as well have been branded. I hoped only that my face (unspoiled, as our pastor would have said, by the devil's paintbox) might blend indistinguishably with the colourless air.

At the moment of Patrick Murphy's appearance, my father had the megaphone in his hand and was offering the peace that passeth understanding to all the lost who rushed hither and thither before us, not knowing where they were going.

The theatregoers, their sense of direction thus set at nought, appeared to me incandescent with goodwill, the light of weekend in their eyes. I (for whom Friday night was the most dreaded night of a circumscribed week) watched them as a starving waif might peer through a restaurant window.

'I speak not of the pleasures of this world, which are fleeting,' my father said through the megaphone. 'Not as the world giveth, give I unto you . . .'

Patrick Murphy and his sheila had drawn level with the Commonwealth Bank. Dear God, I prayed, let the gutter swallow me up. Let the heavens open. Let not Patrick Murphy see me.

Patrick Murphy stopped dead in his tracks and a slow grin of recognition lit his face. I squirmed with mortal shame, I could feel the heat rash on my cheeks.

'Jesus,' laughed his sheila, snapping her gum. 'Will ya look at those Holy Rollers.'

'They got guts,' said Patrick Murphy. 'I always did go for guts,' and he gave me the thumbs-up sign with a wink and a grin.

At Wallace Bishop's Diamond Arcade, he turned back to blow me a kiss.

It was the last time I saw him before he hitched his motorcycle to the tailgate of a truck and got tossed under its sixteen double tyres. This happened on the Sandgate Road, near Nudgee College, and the piece in the *Courier-Mail* ran a comment by one of the priests. A bit foolhardy, perhaps, Father O'Shaughnessy said, a bit of a daredevil. Yet a brave lad, just the same, and a good one at heart. Father O'Shaughnessy could vouch for this, although he had not had the privilege, etcetera. But the lad was wearing a scapular around his neck.

Rest in peace, Patrick Murphy, I murmur, making a cross in the dust with a mango twig.

'What are you doing?' my mother asks, smelling liturgical errors.

'Doodling. Just doodling.' But certain statues in churches – the Saint Peters, the faulty impetuous saints – have always had Patrick Murphy's eyes.

A few minutes later, my mother is back. 'We've had a call from Miss Martin's niece in Melbourne. You remember Miss Martin? Her niece is worried. Miss Martin isn't answering her phone so we're going over.' They call out from the car: 'She still lives in Red Hill, we won't be long.'

Miss Martin was old when I was a child. She's ninety-eight now, part of the adopted family, a network of the elderly, the lonely, the infirm, the derelict. My parents collect them. It has always been like this, and I've lost count of how many there are: people they check in on, they visit, they sit with, they take meals to. My mother writes letters for ladies with crippled arthritic hands and mails them to distant relatives who never visit. She has a long inventory of birthdays to be celebrated, she takes little gifts and cakes with candles.

By mid-afternoon she calls. 'We're at the hospital. We got to her just in time. Do you mind getting your own dinner? I think we should stay with her, she'll be frightened when she regains consciousness.'

They keep vigil throughout the night.

At dawn the phone wakes me. 'She's gone,' my mother says. 'The Lord called her to be with Himself. Such a peaceful going home.'

The day after the funeral, my father and I drive out to the university.

'It's not easy,' he says, 'trying to get a BA at my age.'

But there is pride, just the same, in this mad scheme I have talked him into. I have always thought of him as an intellectual *manque* whose life was interfered with by the Depression and the Gospel – (His aunts in Adelaide never recovered from the distress. 'Oh your father,' they said to me sadly, shaking their heads. 'He was led astray.' By my mother's family, they meant. 'We do wish he hadn't been taken in by such a . . . We do wish he would come back to a *respectable* religion.') – and whose retirement is now interfered with by all the lives that must be succoured and sustained. 'It's hard to find time to study,' he confesses ruefully.

People will keep on dying, or otherwise needing him.

In the university library, he leafs through books like an acolyte who has at last – after a lifetime of longing – been permitted to touch the holy objects. He strokes them with work-knotted fingers. But we are simply passing through the library today, we are on our way to meet friends of mine for lunch at the staff club. I am privately apprehensive about this, though my father is delighted, curious, secretly flattered. He has never been in a staff club lounge.

At the table reserved for us the waiter is asking, 'red or white, sir?' and my heart sinks. The air is full of greeting and reminiscence, but I am waiting for my father's inevitable gesture, the equivalent of the megaphone outside the Commonwealth Bank. I am bracing myself to stay calm, knowing I will be as angered by the small patronising smiles of my old friends as by my father's compulsion to 'bear witness'. He will turn his wineglass upside down at the very least; possibly he will make some mild moral comment on drink; he may offer the peace that passeth understanding to the staff club at large.

He does none of these things.

To my astonishment, he permits the waiter to fill his glass with white wine. He is bemused, I decide, by his surroundings. And yet twice during the course of the meal, he takes polite sips from his glass.

The magnitude of this gesture overwhelms me. I have to excuse myself from the table for ten minutes.

For a week I have cunningly avoided being home with my parents for dinner, but the moment of reckoning has come. We are all here, brothers and sisters-in-law and nieces and nephews, an exuberantly affectionate bunch.

The table has been cleared now, and my father has reached for the Bible. A pause. I feel like a gladiator waiting for the lions, all the expectant faces turned towards me. It is time.

The visitor always chooses the Bible reading, the visitor reads; and then my father leads family prayer.

It should be a small thing. In anyone else's home I would endure it with docile politeness.

It cannot be a concession anywhere near as great as my father's two sips of wine – a costly self-damning act.

It should be a small thing for me to open the Bible and read. There is no moral principle at stake.

Yet I cannot do it.

'I am sorry,' I say quietly, hating myself.

Outside I hug the mango tree and weep for the kind of holy innocence that can inflict appalling damage; and because it is clear that they, the theologically rigid, are more forgiving than I am.

But I also move out of the shaft of light that falls from the house, knowing, with a rush of annoyance, that if they see me weeping they will discern the Holy Spirit who hovers always with his bright demanding wings.

I lean against the dark side of the mango tree and wait. A flying fox screeches in the banana clump. Gloating, the Holy Spirit whispers: *Behold the foxes, the little foxes, that spoil the vines.* One by one, the savaged bananas fall, thumping softly on the grass. From the window the sweet evening voices drift out in a hymn. The flying fox, above me, arches his black gargoyle wings.

MARION HALLIGAN
Belladonna Gardens

Il faut cultiver notre jardin

On the map it had the charm of a labyrinth. The streets curved round one another like the steps of a formal dance. On another scale it could have been a medieval herb garden. It was called a gardens, and he was going there to live. It's a dump, Sybil said. But even in half an hour at a party he'd picked up that as one of her phrases. Do you like living in Canberra? he'd asked her. It's a dump, she said. It's a slum. Whereas everyone knew that Canberra was a garden city, if anything too pretty, exotic with trees, and that even the suburbs circled round parks.

Garden. It was the most powerful word in his vocabulary. The syllables hung in his mind like a drop of water in sunshine, glittering yet soft. He could think of the Alhambra with its fountains, its minutiae of mosaics, of Versailles and its water games strictly formalised, of Capability Brown's careful wildness. He could do them all.

He seemed to have been in the taxi for quite a long time. The ticking of the meter began to hammer in his head: the cost the cost the cost. It was a long time since they'd left the railway station. He'd been busy with the views; hadn't cared for the brutalism of the Art Gallery or the High Court, had admired the classicism of the Library, been touched by the sober pewter beauty of the lake, even on this sky blue day.

Now they were on a motor-way running through grey-brown paddocks, and then, over to the left, in the middle of the dun, were building blocks in primary colours.

- Offices, said the taxi driver. Government offices. Called by the colours. Aqua, Green, all that.
- What is this place?
- Belconnen.

He hadn't realised that Melba was so far away. Sybil had given him a map, but only of the place where the flat was. Not really a flat, she said, sort of a little house, but joined on to others, here and there, sort of, and they spread up and down and round about, over the side of the hill. You can see the Brindabellas from some places. But I warn you, it's a dump.

Lovely names. They sang themselves. Belconnen. Brindabella. And the cluster of little houses was called Belladonna Gardens, and all the streets that curved in their labyrinthine fashion in and out of one another had flower names: Amaryllis Crescent, Hellebore Close, Paeony Place, Camellia Walk. He wondered if each would be planted with its name flower, so that you could stand at the bottom of the hill and see the whole area mapped out in bloom and leaf. And Nymphaea Grove would have water gardens.

He'd met Sybil at a party, in Sydney. In Juniper Hall, in a flat made up of several towering white rooms: white walls, white floors, white leather sofas. And paintings. There was the usual gallery crowd, and his beloved Adrian with Sylvio, voices soft and fingers touching. He'd been choked by the danger of looking at them. He turned away and saw Sybil sitting on the arm of a sofa. She was wearing a pale green kimono, and he went up to her.

- I saw your kimono, he said. I wanted to talk to you.

Sybil smiled, like a charming witch, a thin curving smile, sinister and full of promise under the smoky halo of her hair.

- It belonged to a lady of the Japanese court, she said. It's a hundred and thirty years old.

They looked at the ancient beautiful patterns. He put out his hand and traced them, where the fabric was pulled smooth across her leg. After that he found out that she came from Canberra, and she said, It's a dump.

- I've never been there, he said. His name was Frank and he was English. I'm curious to see it. It might be a good place for me to work.

– I've got a flat. Well, it's a sort of pokey house-thing. You can have it for a while, if you pay me some rent.

So he was in this taxi, ticking expensively through dun-coloured paddocks, taking him further and further from the briefly-glimpsed city. Finally it turned off among houses with struggling new gardens, went round several corners, and stopped near some brick walls.

– Belladonna Gardens, mate. Which bit was you wanting?

– Hellebore Close. I've got a map.

But when the taxi had turned into the labyrinth he couldn't make any sense of it. The streets curved and turned, there were brick walls and letterboxes, and a jumble of dwelling boxes that seemed to have stuck together higgledy-piggledy where they had been strewn across the slope. Not a sign of Amaryllis, or Paeony, or Cineraria or Aubretia or Delphinium, not the names and certainly not the objects. Just dry grass brittle in the wind, and rusty cars, and tricycles, and so many rubbish bins it was difficult to see why there should be so much littering the ground.

The taxi crawled, still ticking. A woman came running up the hill, her hair blowing in her face, calling something. He wound down the window.

– Cassandra! Cass! Cassie!

– Can you tell me where to find Hellebore Close? asked Frank.

– Down there. On the left. It's written on the footpath. Have you seen a little girl? Dark brown hair? Her hand showed the height.

Frank shook his head. No. Sorry. The woman began to run again, calling Cass! Cassie!

By the time the taxi had found the place, and he'd unloaded his luggage, and paid, and transferred the luggage to the front door step, and was shaking out the key, the woman was coming from the other direction. She must have made a circuit in the maze. She was holding a little girl by the hand, bending towards her, and every now and then she would shake her arm.

– You found her then, said Frank.

– Yeah. She had me scared to death and back. This place. Anything could happen.

Frank looked at the littered dying grass, at the weedy

gravel, at the metal mesh that made walkways, at the scattered vicious fragments of broken glass.

– Bit rough, is it?

– You can say that again. She stared at his luggage, the suitcases, the boxes. Moving in?

– For a bit.

– Sybil gone?

– I don't think so. Not for good. She's letting me have the place for a couple of weeks, while she's in Sydney.

– Living it up, eh?

– I expect so.

– Friend of hers, are you?

– I suppose you'd say so.

The flat was two rooms, with a bathroom and kitchen. The walls were painted beige, and there was hardly any furniture; a mattress on the floor, a table, some chairs, and a sofa that looked like the sort of stuff that a family would shed as it made its way up in the world. A poster had come unstuck from the wall. A potplant had died. The windows seemed to be in funny places, and looked out over derelict yards. The light fell crookedly through them. It's a dump, Sybil had said. It's a slum. He hadn't thought she'd meant it. Or at least only in the context of Juniper Hall.

– A gin-king's mansion. Did you know? he'd asked her. Some chap made a fortune in old colonial days, distilling gin – used the water from the cascade, near here – Cascade Street, in fact. Gin, thus Juniper, Juniper Hall, see?

Sybil looked at him with her witch's smile.

– You're being a tourist, she said.

Frank blushed.

– Well, his architect certainly knew how to create beautiful spaces. Not many rooms could stand this whiteness. He waved his arms, shaping the height of the ceiling, the simple curve of the fireplace, the slenderness of the windows. The proportions are perfect, he said.

He'd imagined her living in a small flat, but of equally elegant proportions, a clever new little flat in Hellebore Close, Belladonna Gardens. It hadn't occurred to him that the names might have something to hide.

And the mountains? None to be seen from the windows. He went outside, up the walkway to the street, but although the buildings were squat and the land sloped, he couldn't see the horizon.

The mother of the lost child was coming along the street with two more children, carrying schoolbags.

– Excuse me, he said. Can you tell me where I can find the Brindabellas?

– The Brindabellas.

– Mm.

– I dunno. They're miles from here. You'd need a car.

– No, I mean just to look at. What direction are they?

– Oh. Thataway. She pointed across the slope of the land. You can see 'em from the top of the street.

On the way up he was swooped by some helmetless kids riding round and round on motorbikes, revving and skidding. He gave himself a fright by thinking that he wouldn't find Sybil's house again, and went back to memorise the place. At the top of the street he turned round and there were the mountains, lying low on the horizon, grey blue and very quiet, demanding nothing.

After a week he knew how to live there. Could work the buses and shop. Had learnt to walk down Amaryllis through Nymphaea and along Hellebore like a cat in its own territory, remote but in control, ignoring everybody. Except Teresa, who'd finally decided that he was to be trusted with a cup of tea. She said that it was pretty lonely. Sybil was the only person she'd ever talked to. The other people were a pretty poor lot, by and large.

– The dregs of society. You've got to be to live here.

– Why is that?

– No luck. No jobs. Too sick, too many kids, too stupid, too spaced out, too stoned to work. We're all subsidised here. Pensioners of the government. Dear kind government.

– But what about Sybil?

– Supporting mother's pension. The baby.

He'd known Sybil had known he was gay. That was why she had let him follow the patterns of her kimono, with his fingers on her leg. But he hadn't known she had a baby.

– A baby. Where is it now?

– God knows. Perhaps she's dropped it on her mum.

– And what about you, Teresa?

There was a bravery about her little house. It was as dull

as Sybil's, but Teresa had infused it with some sort of spirit, was by some terrific effort of will making it a place to live in. Frank could see her will holding up, no, not holding up, creating, the whole frail edifice of her life and the life of her children, Jodie and Nathan at school, and Cassandra the small wandering girl endangered by the wilderness outside.

– Deserted mother, she said. She offered him the crudeness, the banality, of the category, defying him to accept it; then she softened, and explained.

– Joe had a decent job. We had a nice house. The three kids. We lived well. Plenty of debts. Big mortgage. Stacks of hire purchase and all that. Two cars. Parties. But we seemed to be able to afford it. Turned out it was the old Bankcard lurk.

– What's that?

– It's pretty common in Canberra. So I find out later. You need all these things, essentials, see? So you put them on Bankcard. Up to the limit. And you can't pay it off. But you still need all these things, essentials, right? So you get another Bankcard from a different bank. Do the same there. Keep doing it, till you run out of banks. You can get away with it for quite a while. Borrow money on one Bankcard to pay off the other. Vice versa. Backwards and forwards. And all the time the interest climbing sky high. You've got a good job, you've got a good credit limit, there's quite a lot of money. Then it catches up with you.

For a minute her will flagged, her face drooped. The light was more crooked in the small room. Of course, she said, I was the real dummy. I ought to have cottoned on how wrong things were. So many arguments. So much anger. I never knew why, but gee it was catching. And he hit me. That was a bit of a shock, for both of us. A man who wears a suit to work isn't supposed to hit his wife.

Cassie climbed on her lap and she hugged her.

– My Bankcard was okay. Joe made sure of that. By the time I found out what was going on . . . she shrugged. I still think we could have saved something. Ourselves, or something. But Joe panicked. Disappeared. Dunno where he is. And here I am.

Frank saw the little box closing round her. The grim beige room was almost defeating her. But then she straightened and her spirit flashed out again and the shabby walls fell back.

– And what about you? What do you do? Oh, sorry, that's a rude question in Belladonna Gardens.

– I'm a painter.

– Great, we sure could do with one of them around here.

– Well . . .

– Oh. You mean, not walls and houses and stuff?

– Not really. Though I do paint walls. I do *trompe l'oeil*.

– Come again?

– *Trompe l'oeil*. It's French. It means to trick the eye. Deceive. With illusions.

– Yeah?

– Imagine. Suppose you had a house, with a boring wall, no view. I could paint you one. A lake, or mountains, or a garden. I like gardens. And it'd seem real.

– Like mural wall paper.

– Well, not exactly. The point is, it's supposed to look as though it's really there; when you come into the room it's supposed to look as though you could actually walk out into it.

– That's weird.

– It's quite expensive.

– You after a job here?

– I've put advertisements in the paper, but nobody seems to want a *trompe l'oeil* painter.

– I'm thirty-three, said Teresa. He didn't know whether she said it with despair, or with pride. Whether she meant she was only thirty-three, though she looked older, or that she was *actually* thirty-three, and looked younger. He could fit her into either role. She was small, and lean, with wrinkling tanned skin, her hair was long and straight, her legs slender. Her heels were crackled black, and she always wore thongs.

– I tried going to Parents without Partners. I thought I could do with some moral support. But they're a funny lot. All the blokes want is to get into your knickers. Not my scene.

He came out of his front door. Teresa was standing on her walkway, which some violence had twisted and buckled out of shape.

– Watch out! she called.

He'd nearly put his foot in a small pile of shit on the top step.

– That's human, she said. Human animal.

She went into her flat and brought newspapers and a bucket of water thick with disinfectant.

– Scary, isn't it? You never see anyone. But you know they're there. Visiting cards all over the place.

When they'd cleaned it up Frank said, You know, this complex should be quite pleasant. It's quite well-designed. If there really were gardens – you'd think all these unemployed people might like to make gardens . . .

– Oh duckie. Did you come down in the last shower? I'll show you gardens.

She took him through the house and out the back. The clothesline hung diseased and the weeds were past their prime. You know not to leave clothes out, she said, but he wouldn't have trusted his clothes to the outside world anyway. She led him round like one pointing out beauties. There were beer cans and chip packets and plastic bags and faded wads of free advertising, and a number of condoms.

– You're out of luck. No syringes today. Na – wait a minute. I tell a lie.

Her foot pushed a tall tufted clump of dead weeds aside. There were two syringes, complete with needles.

– I clean mine up every now and then, but it doesn't do any good. You can't let the kids play outside. I take 'em down to the park.

– How's the tricky painting?

– No luck.

– I suppose all the rich people've already got views and gardens. Real ones. So've the poor, come to that. And going out of their minds trying to work out how to pay for them. That's what the social worker told me. All those comfortable pretty houses. Just a front. Riddled with debt. Like apples with the moth. Rotting away inside. I should know.

The banging on the door was loud enough to burst it in. He

was sucked from sleep like a body from a depressurising aeroplane. When he opened the door three big blue men in caps pushed in; he hadn't stopped for his glasses and couldn't see them properly.

– Momcilo Misevicius.

– Pardon? He wanted to say, I don't speak . . . but they were shaking him. They said the words again, and he understood.

– No. No. Not here. That's not me.

They didn't want to believe him.

– ID, they barked.

He brought his passport. They looked at it – a pom, eh – and at him, and walked around him looking from all angles. It took them a long time to decide he was himself.

– Sorry mate, they said. You know how it is.

After that he noticed how often he heard the sirens, and on an old newspaper in the kitchen he saw a small headline: *Belladonna Gardens Knife Murder Man Charged.*

Sybil wrote: How is life in the Gardens of the Lost? I am really living here and won't be back for at least a month. You're welcome to the dump till then.

He realised that disappointed him. He had no desire to go back to Sydney, to the same places, the same parties, and in all of them the risk of seeing Adrian in love with Sylvio. But he didn't like living in the Gardens, with no work. If she'd thrown him out he might have gone to Melbourne, where rich people lived in circumscribed city houses, and could need him to paint the views they lacked. But Canberra was very cheap for him because of not needing much of his money for rent.

He took a bottle of wine and went to visit Teresa.

– Geeze, she said. Real wine in a bottle. I'd just about forgotten what it tastes like.

She got out Vegemite glasses and polished them on a tea-towel, but then he had to go back to his place to fetch a corkscrew. Teresa held her glass up to the light, then smelt it.

– Joe liked wine. He used to go to Farmers', buy nice bottles – on Bankcard. People'd come for dinner and lap it up.

He told her about being able to stay in the flat.

– I'd get out if I was you. What is there here for you?

– It's cheap.

– I sometimes think of getting out. Teresa stared into the wine. You say to y'self, get a job, get out – I was quite a good typist, you know. Even did shorthand once. She sipped the wine as though it would bring her old skills back. It's not worth it but. Y'lose all y'perks – free doctors and chemists and cheap rent, and telephone, and buses. It's not worth it. It'd take all I earn and I wouldn't live as well as I do now. And who'd look after the kids? Still, I'd like to get out of the Gardens.

– Seems mad not to encourage people to work.

– I thought of getting a job cleaning houses, off the record, like. Not letting on. But the social security check up on you. You know? They hide, and watch, and they follow you, and catch you, earning honest money for honest work, and bam! you lose the lot.

When he opened the door to his flat the dreary dirty wall opposite lunged at him like a slap in the face. It was then that he had his idea.

He was well away when Teresa next saw him. He had his front door open wide and had taken all the curtains down so as to let in as much light as possible. He'd already painted the high coral-coloured gate, high as the ceiling, not quite as wide as the wall, its top bar curving into wings.

– There'll be gilt here, along the edge, he said.

Inside this frame, far away at the back, was a conical mountain draped with snow. Closer was a bridge, with wistaria flowers, and a stream with rocks and plants. All these were sketched in black and white.

– It's a Japanese garden, because of Sybil's kimono. With a bit of Monet – that's his bridge.

Several times a day Teresa would put her head in the door to see how it was going; often she'd stay and watch. Cassie liked to watch too, and Frank gave her a brush and some paint and newspapers so she could make a picture of her own. Towards the end he wouldn't let them see it. Teresa bought bread and cheese for him at the shops because he didn't want to stop. We'll have champagne when it's done, he said. He went to bed early and got up with the light.

The day came when he rushed in to fetch her and the children. He flung open the door, and there across the brief gap of the room, through a tall coral gate, was a magic sunlit garden, with steps down to a little pebbled path, and a stone lantern, and further off Monet's bridge, a darker coral than the gate, with wistaria in marvellous purple panicles; beyond that were small figures in fields, and far far off the mysterious icy majesty of Mount Fuji.

– You could cross the room and step into it, breathed Teresa. I could walk along that path and cross the bridge. I could even climb the mountain, except that I don't think I could walk that far. Oh Frank, it's beautiful.

– How do you do it? asked Jodie.

– It's the perspective. How close things are, how far away. There's rules. Get that right, you've got the lot.

Cassie patted the wall to feel its flatness. Nathan went to the very end of the walkway to get the long view. Frank gave them lemonade, and opened the champagne.

– I'll shout us all Chinese tonight. It's nearly right for a Japanese garden. He telephoned the takeaway, and for a taxi to go and collect it; he would hardly have been more extravagant had he been getting a good fee for the job.

They had a party, and the Japanese garden tempted them to walk into it. Teresa kept saying, Oh Frank, I didn't know you were such a good artist. The children would turn their backs to it, and then suddenly swing round to catch it unaware.

Frank was sorry it was finished. He packed up his paints and his brushes and charcoal and rags and his sketches and reference books – the pictures of gardens and bridges, plants, flowers, trees, Georgian houses and fountains and gazebos, all the things a client might choose to cancel out a boring wall.

– At least Sybil's picture's a good reference, he said to himself. Better than a photograph to show a client what I can do.

But there still weren't any clients.

He went to see Teresa.

– Would you like me to do you a *trompe l'oeil*? On the same wall?

– I'd love it. But Frank, I can't afford . . .

– Who's talking money? I know just what I'll do – if you

like it, that is. French windows, and a terrace, and then a garden like a maze, and in it all the flowers of Belladonna Gardens: amaryllis, and hellebore, and paeony, and camellia. Around a pool, with nymphaea – water-lilies, you know: Monet again. And away in the distance, the Brindabellas, which you ought to be able to see, and can't.

Every afternoon the children would rush in from school to see where it had got to. Nathan said, You can't walk in it yet, and Teresa replied, Give it time, give it time.

And then it was done, and Teresa's living room had French windows opening on to a paved terrace, with enamel-flowered camellias in tubs and a pond with nymphaea – I can see goldfish too, said Jodie – and the drooping delicate green heads of hellebore, the Christmas rose, the blue spikes of delphinium, and the lily trumpets of amaryllis, made patterns like the steps of a stately dance. The windows had small square panes with bevelled edges that caught the light, and on one of them an intricate blowfly crawled.

– It's a magic garden, all right, said Frank. There's no way you'd get all those blooming at once in nature. And look, hidden away, just here, just to propitiate her, like the wicked fairy at the christening, is Belladonna the lovely lady, the deadly nightshade. Don't touch her, she's poisonous, that's why we give her such a flattering name.

He caught Teresa giving him a look, as she had when he talked about Monet's garden and the nymphaea and the coral-coloured Japanese bridge. He puzzled over it, and decided it was indulgence. Just so she looked at Jodie and Nathan when she thought they were being clever.

Teresa had made lasagne to feast the new view. Nathan said it was like living in a picture book.

Frank went to the National Library to stock up on more ideas. He collected photographs of Canberra monuments, just in case a client wanted the water jet or the War Memorial on his wall. He thought of advertising an exhibition of his two paintings, but suspected he'd only get people on outings to amuse their children.

He was in the sitting room organising his files when he saw a man snooping round the house. A burglar. In broad daylight. He went to the window and stared out at him. The man stopped acting furtively and knocked at the door. Frank thought of armed robbery. But then he remembered that the man had been wearing a tie, so he opened the door.

– Inspector. Housing branch. He flicked a card out.

– You want to look at the flat?

– You're not wrong.

He put out his hand and without touching him pushed Frank out of the way.

– Oh dear me. Dearie dearie me. What's this? Defacing the wall? It's going to be one of those days, is it?

He opened a folder.

– Sybil Flanagan. Hm. He squinted at Frank, up and down. *You* Sybil Flanagan?

– Of course not. I'm . . .

– You're the *de facto*, I suppose. Dangerous, that. Could lose her the supporting mother's.

– No, no. I'm not living with her.

– Oh, I see. Should've guessed, I suppose. Though you never can tell these days.

The way the inspector's eyes slid all over Frank made him feel slimy. There were long pauses while he wrote things in the folder.

– Well, then. Subletting, is she? Oh dear me.

Frank tried to think of any more traps. No, he said, not at all. Sybil's an old friend of mine, of the family, I'm just here from England for a bit and I've come to visit her.

– I see. She in the other room, then?

– Well, she's not here just now. She . . . The baby . . .

– Mmm. Very irregular.

The man's slow sliding way of speaking, like a snake creeping towards his prey, might have been meant to mesmerise. Frank expected the forked tongue, the fang, the hiss.

It came.

– Well. Next time I come I expect to see Miss Sybil Flanagan in residence. In person. And make sure she gets that cleaned off, there's a good man. She should know the rules. No defacing the walls. No structural alterations. I expect to see it all nice and clean and back to normal. Quite soon.

– Did he tell you to get the walls cleaned up too? What sort
of a shit could look at a beautiful thing like that and tell you
to get rid of it? I ask you. What are you going to do, Frank?

– I was going to Melbourne, anyway. In the next couple
of days. There's no work here.

– Yeah. Well, that's all right for you. I have to live here.

– Look, I'd leave it. They're not going to make you do it.
Not when it comes to the crunch. Most likely they'll forget
all about it.

– You reckon?

– Typical bureaucracy. Nasty, but not very efficient. I'm
sure it'll be okay.

– I dunno. We're all losers here, you know. That's why we're
here. We don't win.

Teresa and Cassie waved him goodbye when the taxi came.
Teresa stood thin and brown, forlorn but with the strength,
and the grace, of the child on her hip. She would look good
in his pink silk shirt. Its pretty faintly fishy colour would suit
her. He'd been very disappointed to find that it made him
look green at parties; he hadn't given it away without a pang,
but he knew he would never wear it again. And it was right
for Teresa. The taxi ticked through the dun-green landscape,
past the primary-coloured office blocks where the bureaucracy played, ticked through the city to the bus station: the
cost the cost the cost. In Melbourne he might be able to stay
for a while with Jonathan who worked in an antique shop.
Perhaps he would know of some rich clients, who would want
to pay to have their eyes deceived.

DELIA FALCONER
Acqua Alta

I had been working on the Book of Despair for some months. In the course of my research I had travelled the world to interview somnambulists, insomniacs, lovers and failed heads of state. By the time I reached Venice I had filled the heavy paper of three large notebooks with their stories; all of which were, in different ways, about love.

The book had begun as an act of desperation with the recording of my own story. Having reached that point where depression buries or alters a person I had opted for decisive change. I had left the man who turned his body from me in sleep and cried each night for a relationship which he might have had when he was eighteen: having never failed, it was a perfect dream which turned our days into pale imitations. Riding on my own in trolley buses and car ferries, I had begun to take pride in my talent for fathoming the precise depth and tidal flux of other people's sorrow.

It began to dispel my own. I had transferred the heaviness of my heart into a weight in my suitcase which I felt now only as a pulling at the end of my arms. Each story I collected was another anchor by which I resisted the dangerous buoyancy of hope.

Often my subjects found me themselves. If I sat alone in a public square they would come to me, attracted like pigeons to my silence, hopping tenderly from side to side on the scaly feet of their miseries. Once, on a precipitous train between Carcassonne and Lourdes, a pilgrim stole the books from my case. I returned from the toilet to my seat to find him hiding them in the pressure bandage beneath his shirt. When I confiscated the books he refused to tell me his own story. He was jealous of the grief of others recorded there.

Mark Ivory did not look for me: he was too busy negotiating the waters of the Grand Canal. They had overflowed its edges into the market place and raised a floating carpet of cabbage leaves, crab claws and mandarins which bobbed around his knees. When I reached him, my own legs dry, he turned to me. He pointed to the capitals of fish which stared down from the tops of the columns supporting the roof of the market. 'When the sea reaches them,' he said, 'it will all be over.'

His is a peculiarly Venetian story. It has to do with the subsidence of the foundations of the heart; with watery dissolution; with an awareness that love often takes the form of theft. Venice is a reminder of the frailty of certainty. It is contagious. In my own dry home town the Rialto Building has just been built and already it is sinking.

It began, Mark Ivory told me, when he realised that he could love a place more than a person. He had come with his wife to Venice for their honeymoon. Their hotel was at the end of a blind alley which dropped away to a small canal. To reach their room they climbed three flights of stairs, disturbing cats which moved like liquid in the gloom. It was two weeks before Lent. From the window one twilight they saw maskers with impassive porcelain faces slipping through the darkness on their way to San Marco. Their bodies were couched in layers of blue satin and tulle which filled the gondola to its edges like water, conferring on it the same appearance of floating improbability as Venice. To his shame Mark Ivory realised that he was more interested in the outside of the room.

That night he dreamed he slept between the leaves of paper he had seen in dim shop windows, marbled with oily crimsons and greens. When he woke the next morning he longed to run his palms down banisters. In the afternoon he hungered for the taste of a cake he had eaten on his first day in Venice on the winding route from the railway station to his hotel – a lump of fruity sugared dough with the surprise of hot sweet custard at its centre – but he could not find the way again. The next day he left his wife alone to walk over cold bridges and sit on the smooth steps of churches. From under the well heads in empty squares he could feel the water of the lagoon rising into the walls of houses, revealing dappled layers of ancient pigments, staining with the unevenness of dissipated ink. If you broke a stone here, he thought, it would bleed salt water. He let his eyes sink deep into the archaeology of colour.

Flesh made him uncomfortable. He preferred to contemplate the fine glazeless whisper of porcelain masks which hid the expressions of their wearers, who posed in the dark arches of the Doges' palace. He removed the mattress from the bed and filled its dark cavity with carnival fabrics until it overflowed. He wrapped crimson cellophane around the lightbulbs to suggest the lamp glass of the Rialto. It was not enough. He spent a day on a ferry, seated outside, staring through iron water gates and up wet stairs into the secret interiors of houses.

Mark Ivory's wife realised that he had taken his heart from her and given it to the city. She left alone. From the steps of the train she cursed him: *Each step you take will be weighted with tears*. He stood and stared along the straight line of the train's departure. At the far point of his perspective, before Mestre, the wide flat water engulfed the shadow of the tracks. He turned and headed for the bright canal.

The theft of Mark Ivory's heart was not the first Venice had demanded. Once the wharves here were thick with the passage of stolen saints. Ships returned from Rhodes, Chios, Sidon and Cephalonia, with their bodies packed in crates of pork and oranges, or bobbing amid rigging in cocoons of sailcloth. Nuns made silk cushions to which the holy bones were pinned as carefully as butterflies. The dried skin of a flayed saint, which clung to the fingertips like gold leaf, was coaxed into its stone urn on a priest's breath.

It is possible to love a city so desperately that you will do anything for it – even destroy an empire for four bronze horses because they might improve the looks of a cathedral roof.

Mark Ivory realised this and felt himself drift from human company. He followed the signs on walls to San Marco which were also the markers of his betrayal. His sadness followed him in the damp tracks of his shoes. He passed outdoor sweet stalls in coloured tents and scarcely saw them through his tears. The hot sugared almonds in the mixers refused to dry while, in his wake, the nougats wept, disgorging blobs of red and green. He stopped at a church. In its urn a saint's skin grew moist, stretched and unfolded like a bat's wing.

When he reached San Marco the jade green water of the canal had spread across the square. It was as high as his thighs: in some parts higher. Outside Florian's the band played a disintegrating tune as its members followed sheets of music floating on the waves. Finding no pavement, pigeons landed on tables and hands, and perched among the band, their claws slipping on the brass lips of horns. Mark Ivory watched a gondola glide across the square and pass through the doorway of the Basilica.

This *acqua alta* continued for weeks. Mark Ivory noted the city's indifference to its encroachment with incredulity. Nobody walked slower, no one laid down wooden planks. One day he walked through a shoal of white wax candles washed across from the cemetery of San Michele. Once he thought he saw his heart and grabbed at it, but it bobbed through the hole in a wall and caught in the vines of a hidden garden. It is around this time that I found him at the markets, walking with long exaggerated strides. He had lost his way, feeling with his feet for invisible steps, holding his breath through underground passages.

I tried to help. I told Mark Ivory to place his fingers on the hem of my long jacket and feel that it was dry. I urged him to staunch his tears on the thick pages of my books. He turned from me to watch a muscular wave break the windows of a jeweller's shop. Before him, strings of glass beads as frail as the spines of saints unwound in their cases and bobbed on the surface of the water. They caught around mooring poles and clicked against the slick black sides of gondolas. High on their columns at the markets the fish felt the waters on their bellies. They opened stone gills and flexed their strong stone tails.

The space where Mark Ivory's heart had been was filled with welling sadness. He could feel its weight loosening his ribs. 'It is my fault,' he said, watching cracks appear in the roof of the market. He slipped away from me and broke into my room. The thieving city required the rest of him.

The stories in my trunk, which he had strapped to his back, dragged him swiftly to the bottom of the Grand Canal. As his lungs filled Mark Ivory opened his eyes. Around him he saw Napoleon's handkerchief as thin as light and belled out like a jellyfish; a hunk of uncut Istrian marble; a piece of the true cross; the ring of a Doge fallen from his finger in a moment of desire; a fifth bronze horse for the roof of Saint Mark's, dropped from the loading docks by drunken hands and forgotten in the face of the blue light of that dazzling lagoon. He regarded these objects with faint surprise and love. He could make no connections between them. He had given up on history.

Some time later my trunk was returned to me by an embarrassed boy who wore the tight pants and automatic weapon of a police officer. After three days Mark Ivory's body had unburdened itself of grief and floated to the surface. When my notebooks dried out I was able to continue my work. Only the pages containing Mark Ivory's despair are strangely supple to the touch and continue, stubbornly, to stick together with traces of salty water.

NOTES ON THE AUTHORS

William ASTLEY ('Price Warung') (1855-1911) was born at Liverpool, England, but was brought up and educated in Melbourne. A freelance journalist, he settled in Sydney in 1890 where he became the *Bulletin*'s most prolific contributor of short stories. He was a radical political activist and an enthusiastic student of early Australian history, which he used to good account in his many stories dealing with the effects of the convict system.

Marjorie BARNARD (1897-1988) was born in Sydney, graduating with First Class Honours from Sydney University in 1920. A prolific writer under her own name, she also collaborated with Flora Eldershaw on a number of articles, historical monographs and novels, the best known of which is *Tomorrow and Tomorrow and Tomorrow*. These were published under the pseudonym 'M. Barnard Eldershaw'. She was made AO for her services to literature in 1980 and received the Patrick White Award for Writers of Distinction in 1985.

John Arthur BARRY (1850-1911) emigrated to Australia when he was twenty to join the search for gold. He was a trained seaman and worked at sea and in various itinerant jobs inland until he joined the Sydney *Evening News* in 1896. His real passion was writing fiction. He published stories in both English and Australian magazines and brought out his first collection in 1893. Over the years he published another seven collections of stories, mostly solidly based on his own adventures on land and at sea.

Barbara BAYNTON (1857–1929) was born the daughter of a carpenter in Scone, NSW. She had three children by her first marriage to a selector whom she divorced in 1890 to marry a retired surgeon, Thomas Baynton, a deeply cultivated man who moved in Sydney's literary circles. A third marriage to the fifth Lord Headley, though shortlived, brought her wealth and social position both in Australia and England. Her literary output was small in terms of quantity, but the power and conviction of her writing, its depiction of the ugliness and harshness of bush life and, in particular, her clear-eyed portrayals of women's sufferings and victimisation in the outback, offer inescapable correctives to the once widely held view of Australian mateship and the bushman's ethical code.

Peter CAREY (1943–   ) was born at Bacchus Marsh, Victoria, and now lives in New York. A distinguished novelist and short story writer, he has won all the major Australian literary awards including the National Book Council Award (three times), NSW Premier's Award (twice), the *Age* Book of the Year and the Miles Franklin Award. In 1988 his novel *Oscar and Lucinda* won the coveted British Booker McConnell Prize for Fiction. He has been described as a fabulist and a surrealist but his work cannot be so simply categorised. He is an adventurous and prolific writer with great imaginative resources which, at this stage in his career, are unlikely to be exhausted. He also writes for film.

Marcus CLARKE (1846–81) was born in Kensington, London, and emigrated to Australia in 1863 when his hopes of inheriting a substantial fortune were dashed. He was a prolific and highly successful journalist, wrote plays, sketches and novels, the most famous of which is *His Natural Life*, a searing tale of murder, vengeance, dispossession and the horrors of convict life in the penal settlement of Van Diemen's Land. His business ventures as editor and publisher were unsuccessful forcing him twice into bankruptcy. The strain of his financial burdens caused his collapse and death at the age of thirty-five. He left behind a wife and six children, all destitute.

Jessie COUVREUR ('Tasma') (1848–97) came to Tasmania as a small child when her English family emigrated. For a time she lived with her first husband on his property near Kyneton, Victoria, but the marriage was not a success and she spent most of her time overseas, supporting herself by freelance journalism. In 1885 she married a Belgian politician, Auguste Couvreur, and began writing novels, the best known of which is *Uncle Piper of Piper's Hill*. She published five other novels and a collection of short stories, *A Sydney Sovereign and Other Tales*.

Arthur Hoey DAVIS ('Steele Rudd') (1868–1935) was born on Queensland's Darling Downs. He left school at fourteen and worked at various jobs while developing a reputation as a freelance contributor to various papers. His *Bulletin* pieces chronicled the fictional and often comical adventures of the Rudd family, especially the characters Dad and Dave Rudd, on their bush selection. In all he published ten collections of Dad and Dave adventures which enjoyed enormous popularity. Stage plays and films based on his stereotypes were highly successful as was a long-running radio serial called *Dad and Dave*.

Edward DYSON (1865–1931) was born at Morrison, Victoria. As a child and young man he travelled and worked at various goldfields, eventually becoming a journalist and prolific writer of novels, short stories and ballads, most of them humorous in intent. His story 'The Golden Shanty', included in this collection, is regarded as a classic goldfields tale. Much of his work was illustrated by his younger but equally successful brother, Will, an outstanding caricaturist.

Delia FALCONER (1966–   ) was born in Sydney and worked in a variety of occupations while she established her reputation as a writer and settled down to teach creative writing in Melbourne. She burst on the literary scene by winning the *Island* essay competition in 1994 with 'Columbus Blindness', a risky and imaginative piece which has been reprinted a number of times. An award-winning short story writer, her work is frequently anthologised though she has yet to bring out a collection. Her acclaimed novel, *The Service of Clouds*, was published in 1997.

Beverley FARMER (1941-   ) was born in Melbourne and educated at the University of Melbourne. She lived for some time in Greece, which provided the background for some of her writing. A novelist and short story writer, she won the Alan Marshall Award in 1981 and her collection *Milk* won the 1984 NSW Premier's Award for fiction.

Mary FORTUNE ('Waif Wanderer') (1833?-1910?). Little is known about this prolific writer who may have been the first woman in Australia to make her living by the pen. There is little doubt that she was the first woman in Australia and possibly in the world to write detective stories, a genre in its infancy at that time.

Helen GARNER (1942-   ) was born at Geelong and has worked at a variety of occupations including teaching, journalism and acting. She has won several major literary awards including the National Book Council Award in 1978 for her novel *Monkey Grip*, which was later made into a film. In 1986 she won both the NSW Premier's and South Australian Premier's Awards for fiction.

Marion HALLIGAN (1940-   ) was born and educated in Newcastle, NSW, but has lived most of her adult life in Canberra. She has worked as a part-time schoolteacher, a freelance journalist and a book reviewer. She has had more than fifty short stories published in magazines in Australia and overseas and has won several awards. She now works full time at her writing and has published several short story collections. Her first novel, *Self Possession*, was published in 1987 and her first short story collection,

The Living Hothouse (1988), won her the prestigious Steele Rudd Short Story Award.

Janette Turner HOSPITAL (1942–   ) was born in Melbourne but grew up in Brisbane. She has lived in Boston, Los Angeles, India and London and currently lives in Ontario, Canada, making frequent trips back to Australia where she is in demand as a Writer-in-Residence. She draws on her experiences of these varied backgrounds for her work and has won major literary awards both in Canada and Australia. She is married and has two children.

Elizabeth JOLLEY (1923–   ) was born in Birmingham, England, was educated at a Quaker boarding school, and trained as a nurse during World War 2. She emigrated to Australia with her husband and three children in 1959 and began publishing short fiction and novels in 1976. She served as President of the Australian Society of Authors 1985/6. Her literary awards include the NSW Premier's Award in 1985, the *Age* Book of the Year Award and the Miles Franklin Award. She lists her hobbies as 'a fruit farm and a flock of geese'.

John George LANG (1816–64) was born at Parramatta and is thought to have been Australia's first native-born novelist. He practised law briefly in Sydney before emigrating to India. He published nine novels, a travel book and a volume of short stories and was a frequent contributor to leading English journals and newspapers, including Charles Dickens' *Household Words*.

Henry LAWSON (1867–1922) was born on the goldfields at Grenfell, NSW, the son of a Norwegian seaman. His parents separated while he was very young and he moved with his mother and the other children to Sydney where his mother, Louisa, became an active campaigner for women's rights and started the magazine, *Dawn*. Lawson had little formal education and worked at a variety of badly paid jobs. He began contributing poems and stories to the *Bulletin* in 1887. His initial popularity was sparked by the democratic and republican sentiments expressed in his verse, sentiments strongly endorsed by the *Bulletin* at that time. Today he is acknowledged as a master of the short story, particularly as the clear-eyed chronicler of life in the bush and as the champion of the Australian code of mateship.

Morris LURIE (1938–   ) was born in Melbourne of Jewish parents from Poland. He has published more than twenty books, mainly novels, short story collections and children's fiction. He has also written plays, articles, features and what he calls 'prose pieces' and has been widely published in prestigious overseas magazines, newspapers and journals, including *Esquire*, the *Transatlantic Review*, the *New Yorker*, *Punch* and the London *Times*, to name just a few. He has won many awards including a National Book Council Award for his highly acclaimed autobiography, *Whole Life*.

Olga MASTERS (1919–86) was born in Pambula, NSW. Her first job at seventeen was as a journalist, an occupation she pursued part-time while her family of seven children was growing up. She began her more serious writing in her fifties, and between 1977 and 1981 won nine prizes for her short stories. Her first collection, *The Home Girls*, won a National Book Council Award in 1983. She then published three much-admired novels and was working on a second short story collection, *The Rose Fancier* (published posthumously), when she died after a brief illness.

Frank MOORHOUSE (1938–   ) was born at Nowra, NSW. He has worked as a journalist, editor, screen writer and union organiser. He has been a full-time writer for some years and has served as President of the Australian Society of Authors. He is widely regarded as a leading exponent of short fiction in Australia and as a radical and successful innovator in his use of a 'discontinuous narrative' method and his focus on a group of Balmain bohemians – writers, artists and intellectuals, depicted as politically, philosophically, socially and sexually adventurous. He has published many short story collections and, in 1989, was awarded the Australian Literature Society's coveted Gold Medal for his novel, *Forty Seventeen*, which also won the *Age* Book of the Year Award.

John MORRISON (1904–98) was born in Sunderland, England, and migrated to Australia when he was nineteen, earning his living as a bush worker before settling in Melbourne in 1928. He spent most of his working years as a gardener with a break of ten years as a wharf labourer. Both occupations provided backgrounds for his stories, which he began publishing when he was in his thirties. He has published two novels and a number of short story collections. His work has been translated into at least ten languages. He was awarded the Australian Literature Society's Gold Medal for *Twenty-Three* (1962) and the Patrick White Award for Writers of Distinction in 1986.

Hal PORTER (1911–84) was born in Melbourne but grew up in Bairnsdale, Victoria, where his family moved when he was six. He worked for many years as a schoolteacher, then at a variety of occupations until, at the age of fifty, he decided to become a full-time writer. He wrote novels, verse, plays, several general books and three volumes of autobiography (including the classic *The Watcher on the Cast-Iron Balcony*), but his most consistent successes were in the short story. His lush and extravagant style made a dazzling break from the plain realism favoured by writers and editors until the late 1950s when his stories began to appear regularly in the *Bulletin*. He won most of the major Australian literary awards (some of them more than once) and was made AM in 1982.

Katharine Susannah PRICHARD (1883–1969) was born in Fiji, but spent her childhood in Tasmania and Melbourne. She determined early to become a writer and won the colonial section of an English literary competition with her first novel,

The Pioneers (1915). She became a founding member of the Communist Party of Australia in 1920 and took an active role in the establishment of organisations concerned with women's rights and with anti-fascism. She wrote plays, verse, short stories and political pamphlets as well as novels and won a number of awards which are now defunct.

Ethel ROBERTSON ('Henry Handel Richardson') (1870–1946) was born in Melbourne and grew up in the various Victorian towns where her father practised as a doctor. Between the ages of thirteen and seventeen she boarded at Melbourne's Presbyterian Ladies College, drawing on this experience for her autobiographical novel *The Getting of Wisdom*. Most of 'Richardson's' work is solidly anchored in her personal experience, including her masterpiece, the trilogy *The Fortunes of Richard Mahony*, whose main character is based on her father.

Christina STEAD (1902–83) was born in Sydney, graduating from the Sydney Teachers' College in 1921. She left Australia in 1928 and lived abroad until she returned permanently in 1974. She wrote eleven novels, some novellas, many short stories, edited several anthologies and translated three French books into English. None of her books was published in Australia until 1965, with the result that her work was slow to achieve proper recognition in this country. Her autobiographical novel *The Man Who Loved Children* is an acknowledged masterpiece of twentieth-century fiction. In 1974 she received the Patrick White Award for Writers of Distinction.

Patrick WHITE (1912–90) was born in London of Australian parents and educated in Australia and England. He spent many years living abroad, returning to Australia permanently in 1948. He was awarded the Nobel Prize for Literature in 1973, the first Australian writer to be so honoured. With the prize money he established the Patrick White Award made annually to Australian writers of distinction. He won many Australian awards including the Gold Medal of the Australian Literature Society (twice) and the Miles Franklin Award (twice).

Michael WILDING (1942–   ) was born at Worcester, England, and came to Australia to take up a post as Lecturer in English at the University of Sydney. He has published widely in the fields of Australian and English Literature and has also achieved distinction in the varied roles of editor, publisher and critic. As a writer of fiction he has been a prolific producer of anti-realist novels and short stories, which are innovative in various ways and which offer unexpected challenges to the reader.

Tim WINTON (1960–   ) was born in Perth, WA. He has been writing full time since he was twenty-two. His first novel, *An Open Swimmer*, was joint winner of the 1981 *Australian*/Vogel Award. He has published a number of novels and short story collections. He won the Miles Franklin Award in 1984, the youngest writer to achieve this distinction.

PENGUIN – THE BEST AUSTRALIAN READING

The Penguin Book of 19th Century Australian Literature
Michael Ackland, editor

'There is a wealth of novel inspiration for the writers who will live Australia's life and utter her message,' wrote A. G. Stephens. Nineteenth-century authors were not slow to exploit this potential.

Initially their works were inspired by the new land itself, and later they had to grapple with issues raised by the convict past, changing gender roles, and upheavals caused by the undermining of Old World certainties. Their efforts produced a literature of astonishing breadth and interest, which has remained too long unknown, or at best only partly known, even in the land of its origin. This collection brings together familiar and recently rediscovered works, and provides contexts in which we can see them anew. The result is exciting and compelling reading.

'Australie', Barbara Baynton, Christopher Brennan, Ada Cambridge, Ellen Clacy, Marcus Clarke, Louisa Clifton, Albert Dorrington, Edward Dyson, G.E. Evans, Barron Field, Miles Franklin, Charles Harpur, 'Oline Keese', Henry Kendall, Henry Lawson, Louisa Lawson, Frank Macnamara, Catherine Martin, Ethel Mills, A.B. Paterson, Rosa Praed, Henry Savery, Frederick Sinnett, Catherine Helen Spence, A.G. Stephens, 'Tasma', James Tucker, Mary Therese Vidal, 'Waif Wander', 'Price Warung', William Woolls.

The Penguin Book of the City   Robert Drewe, editor

For an instant after takeoff, a kind of map spread itself underneath him, and then was gone. Yet . . . he seemed to have come to know the city intimately; it was like, on other of his trips, a woman who, encountered in a bar and paid at the end, turns ceremony inside out, and bestows herself without small talk.

John Updike, 'The City'

Symbol of humanity's energy, optimism, art and civilisation, the city is the fount of intellectual and sexual freedom – a continuing source of wonder and modernity. And yet, in uncaring mood, the city can be overbearing, anonymous, alienating, even savage – with the ability to chill the soul.

Urban life, with all its challenges, pleasures and angst, is the theme of this outstanding international collection of short stories selected by Robert Drewe. In their wonderful variety, they are as different – and impressive – as Paris and Los Angeles, London and Tokyo. Deeply moving, wryly cynical, blackly humorous, these twenty-nine stories by the world's most intriguing contemporary writers will leave you gasping. Set against the backdrop of some of our great cities, they reflect the extraordinary power and the mystery of the city itself.

Candida Baker, Donald Barthelme, Maeve Binchy, Peter Carey, Ron Carlson, John Cheever, Don DeLillo, Junot Díaz, Joan Didion, Robert Drewe, Beverley Farmer, Helen Garner, Barry Hannah, Neil Jordan, Evelyn Lau, Naguib Mahfouz, Gabriel García Márquez, Frank Moorhouse, Jess Mowry, Bharati Mukherjee, Joyce Carol Oates, Salman Rushdie, Will Self, Graham Swift, Rose Tremain, John Updike, Irvine Welsh, Tobias Wolff, Banana Yoshimoto.

PENGUIN – THE BEST AUSTRALIAN READING

The Penguin Book of Death

Gabrielle Carey & Rosemary Sorensen, editors

'In a world filled with risk and speculation, death remains one of the few things which can be relied upon.'

John Ralston Saul

Yet does that make it any easier to acknowledge? For some, the rituals surrounding death ease the pain of those left behind. For the grave digger, the funeral director and the seller of relics it's business – handled with discretion and sensitivity, of course. And for the sceptical, those same rituals are evidence of the spiritual frailty of modern society.

Some of these eighteen pieces are provocative and irreverent. Some are poised and philosophical. They all boldly confront the dark spectre that is our final taboo and obsession.

Phillip Adams, Gabrielle Carey, Inga Clendinnen, Anne Deveson, Richard Flanagan, Githa Hariharan, Kathryn Harrison, Christopher Hope, Nigel Krauth, Greg Lehman, Thomas Lynch, Mungo Mac-Callum, Jennifer Maiden, Jan Mayman, Cassandra Pybus, John Ralston Saul, Rosemary Sorensen.

Fellow Passengers   Elizabeth Jolley

'In trying to write, I seem to start from one little picture, a few words, an idea so slender it hardly matters and then, suddenly, I am exploring human feelings and reasons . . .'

Elizabeth Jolley

One of Australia's most loved authors, Elizabeth Jolley first found recognition as a writer of short stories distinguished by their individuality and insight. *Fellow Passengers* brings together the best of her short fiction in a remarkable collection that encapsulates the extraordinary breadth, warmth and originality of her work.

Drawing on previously unpublished stories, new offerings as well as some of her most lauded work, *Fellow Passengers* sheds light on the evolution of one of the most innovative writers of our time. Many of the short stories gathered here introduce characters and themes that have served as the basis for Jolley's highly acclaimed novels. All are underpinned by humanity and consideration, enlightened by her uniquely perceptive brand of irony and understanding.